MNEMOSYNE'S KISS

MNEMOSYNE'S KISS

Peter J Evans

VIRGIN WORLDS

First published in 1999 by
Virgin Worlds
an imprint of
Virgin Publishing Ltd
Thames Wharf Studios
Rainville Road
London W6 9HT

ISBN 0 7535 0380 8

Cover illustration by Mark Salwowski

Typeset by Galleon Typesetting, Ipswich
Printed and bound in Great Britain by
Mackays of Chatham PLC

GREEN

1
Lannigan

Two months after she died, Cassandra Lannigan woke up in a hospital bed in Nairobi.

The intervening time seemed very small, little more than a stumble, a flicker of pain. For a moment she thought she was still running, but the pounding rhythm was only the pulse in her head. It faded as she listened.

There was a nurse in the room, a young girl in a starched white uniform. She was standing by the window, her arms folded, face pensive in the harsh light. Her mahogany skin was the only contrast in the whole room: everything else was white, bleached into oneness by the hot Kenyan sun. Lannigan watched her for several minutes.

Suddenly, the nurse turned. 'You're awake.'

Lannigan didn't attempt a reply. She felt insubstantial, unreal, a scribble on the room's surface. If she spoke, she would blow away.

The nurse said, 'I'll fetch the doctor.'

Her contact had been a woman, a Pacifican with mournful eyes and mouse-brown hair down to her shoulders. Taller than she, and thin as a whip: that month's fashion in Tokyo and Seoul.

They had met in London, near St Paul's. Lannigan stood

against the black iron railings surrounding the churchyard, smoking nervously, checking over her shoulder every few seconds. Her hair was itchy because she'd just had it bleached, and the cigarettes – so clear now, in her mind's eye – were black Moonlight Silks with gold bands round the filters.

For all her glances, she didn't spot Kobayashi until the woman was right beside her.

They took the underground as far as Tottenham Court Road, then walked quickly past the Dominion Theatre to a small sushi bar. She smoked incessantly while Kobayashi ordered *ramen* and iced coffee, watching the cranes replace the Dominion's ancient roof with arcing polycarbon braces. 'Even in London, huh?'

Kobayashi took a precise sip of coffee. 'The dictates of safety. Several tourists were injured when a ceiling collapsed during a performance of *The Manchurian Candidate*. It was a featured story for several hours.' The woman gave her a look over the rim of her cup. 'You do not access newsfeeds?'

'Not if I can help it. Besides, the feeds are a little more insular in my neck of the woods.'

'Of course.' Kobayashi finished her noodles, set the bowl aside and dabbed at her mouth with a napkin. 'You have the list of requirements.'

It didn't sound like a question. She took the datapad from her bag and handed it to Kobayashi. 'Eighth file.'

The Pacifican nodded and began to scan the list. 'Everything here can be made ready within two days.' Kobayashi paused, tilting her head slightly. 'A question. Now that you have studied the technical specifications, how long do you suppose it will take to perform the test?'

'With the power up, half an hour max.'

'Ah.' The woman looked at her guardedly. 'And without?'

'Well, that puts a different spin on things.' She thought for a moment. 'Two hours?'

The Pacifican nodded. 'That is acceptable.'

'Great.' She stood up. 'One more thing. The advance payment I can handle as you suggested, but I'll need the completion fee in cash.'

'Cash?' Kobayashi used the word as if she wasn't quite sure what it meant.

'Yeah, US dollars or ICUs – your choice. I don't want anyone chasing me down a credit line.'

Kobayashi's mouth quirked up at the corner. 'Oh ye of little faith.'

'That's me all over.'

She was sitting up when the doctor came in. He smiled at her appraisingly. 'Not bad.'

The nurse had been away ten minutes, long enough for Lannigan to start hurting. Her throat was reintroducing itself to her in pulses of raw dryness. She didn't dare speak, but raised a shaky hand to mime drinking instead. Even breathing made her eyes water.

The doctor turned briefly to the nurse, said something Lannigan didn't catch. The girl nodded and walked briskly out of the room, heels tapping faintly on the carpet. 'Don't worry. I won't ask you any questions until we've got you something.'

She tried to smile, but her lips felt like sand.

The nurse came back, holding a plastic bulb, like those used by astros. She bent to slip the tube into Lannigan's mouth. What came out was sweet and mellow and very cold. Lannigan didn't know what it was, but the pain in her throat faded after the first swallow. She grabbed the bulb with both hands and yanked it out of the nurse's grip, squeezing hard, greedily.

The last drops made her cough a little, but even that felt good, as if using her lungs had been something denied her for a long time. 'Thanks,' she croaked.

'Well, your motor function seems yokay, but the medicom told us that much.' The doctor smiled, a warm sickle of teeth in his very dark face. 'If it isn't a silly question, just how do you feel?'

Lannigan considered this for a second. 'As though I've been stepped on,' she said finally.

The doctor nodded to the nurse, who took the bulb away. 'You've made a remarkable recovery, considering.'

'Considering what?' There had been something in the drink. Talking was easier all the time. 'What happened to me?'

The doctor smiled again. 'We'll go into that later. I wouldn't be surprised if there was some temporary amnesia, but it shouldn't last long.' He bent to a panel near the bed, began tapping at it with a fingertip. 'Can you recall anything?'

Lannigan closed her eyes, feeling the past running towards her, rain and broken glass. 'Yeah. Osaka . . .'

They had taken a room at the Nakashima Inn, overlooking the maglev station. Barges hooted and growled their way up the grimy, mud-choked river, weighed down with Chinese spices and stacked sheets of gas-giant composites for the arcologies at Nishi-Kujo. The dummy data was packed into the shell of a chipplayer she had bought the day before. She showed Kobayashi the unit, how to unclip the casing.

'The test rig downloads on to terabyte SRAM. I'll dump half an hour's jazz on first, just in case anyone checks.' Lannigan closed the unit again and slipped it into her bag. 'Any preferences?'

'Shinji Goda.'

'I might have guessed.' She resolved to get some Beiderbecke and throw the Pacifican a curve. 'Where do you want the backup?'

Kobayashi blinked at her. 'Backup? You are expecting something to go wrong?'

She gave the bag a tap. 'Expect, no. Guard against, yeah.'

'That is probably wise.' Kobayashi walked over to the window. 'Still, I would prefer that there were no copies.'

'Dangerous way of working, Kobayashi.' She tore open

a pack of Moonlight Silks and lit one up, the igniter sparking once as she flicked the end away. 'Anything can happen. If the data gets corrupted you'll end up with nothing.'

Kobayashi looked back at her, over her shoulder. 'As will you.'

'Oh right, I'm supposed to look on this as a kind of incentive.'

'You may look on it in any way you please. Get in, do the test, get out. I get the results; you get paid.' The Pacifican almost smiled. 'In my country, we call it business.'

'In your country you call raw fish food.' She mashed the cigarette in a crystal ashtray. 'Doesn't make it taste any better.'

A week after regaining consciousness, Lannigan was taken to the roof. It was her first time out of the room.

Walking was still a talent that eluded her. It was something she had done easily enough in the past, in the brief, almost meaningless, fragments of memory she had been able to regain, but somewhere along the line she had lost the trick of it. Her legs seemed intent on betraying her at every step. It was enough to worry the doctors, enough to necessitate the use of a wheelchair on her trip to the hospital roof.

The chair was a slender, skeletal thing, and Lannigan didn't like the look of it at all. 'What is this, chicken bones? I'll go right through it.'

'You put on a hundred kilos while I wasn't looking?' The nurse, whose name was N'Tele, grinned at her. 'With the food in here?'

They gave her a jacket to wear over her hospital robes. The clear skies over Kenya held little warmth, and once the sun was gone temperatures could drop sharply. As Lannigan emerged from the service lift she felt a coolness on her face and neck, the cloudless green-scented breeze rolling down from Aberdare and the mountains there. She sniffed warily and drew the jacket a little tighter.

The sky above her was almost completely black, a fading ribbon of purple haunting the western horizon. She looked up as the chair trundled her across the wide helipad, trying to see which of the stars was brighter than the rest, which of them was beginning to move.

N'Tele walked beside the chair. 'You won't see it for a few minutes yet.'

'I've got good eyes.' Lannigan squinted. 'I saw what you paid for them.'

Most of the hospital was up here with her, spread out across the pad in little whispering bunches. Any patient who was mobile had been wheeled out to see the fireworks, more, Lannigan suspected, as an excuse for the nurses to get a breath of air than due to any ideas of therapy. Still, it was good to see something other than white plastic and the facile inanities flicking across her infonet screen. Some secret part of her had been looking forward to the sight for days, ever since it had been predicted.

The chair pulled up a metre from the edge, swung round to face east. N'Tele crouched beside it. 'We'll get a good view. I heard some PANN people wanted to set up cameras here, but the docs vetoed.'

Lannigan found herself taking the sentence apart in her head. ' "Docs"? Where did you train?'

The girl looked at her sideways, then back to the eastern dark. 'Mombasa, first. Then Chicago.' She smiled self-consciously. 'Good way of picking up an accent.'

Lannigan's voice was pure American, with vowels as flat and wide as the Midwest. She wondered briefly if she was speaking with the inflections of home or with some polyglot accent accumulated from a life of travel. She remembered Osaka and London – where else had she spent time?

She could feel N'Tele's eyes on her. The nurse said, 'I suppose you haven't –'

'There it is,' Lannigan whispered.

One of the stars was moving too fast.

Nairobi was to the south, a sprawl of glare on Lannigan's right. What she had thought was some especially bright advertising holo or shanty fire at the easternmost edge had detached itself from the horizon and was clawing its way into the indigo sky. She heard a gasp ripple through the assembled watchers, felt a stab of contempt until she realised that she, too, had drawn in an involuntary throatful of cold air at the sight.

Within half a minute the dot had grown enough to have colour: from a speck of brilliance to a distant smear of liquid orange. As it rose it described a shallow curve to the south. Lannigan flicked her head to the right, almost able to see the star's path, a scratch of imaginary fire, before it had moved a finger's width in her vision.

She had thought the meteor might make some sound as it ripped its way through the air. Maybe if she were closer she would hear the thunder of it, but from this far there was only the sigh of the wind across grass, the distant song of the city and the excited whispers of the other patients. Even N'Tele was speaking under her breath, words that Lannigan could neither catch nor understand, a mantra of wonder.

Lannigan couldn't have spoken even if she had wanted to. The sight had caught her throat.

The meteor was a shape now: elongated and shuddering. It looked like a comet, and Lannigan realised that it wasn't just curving across the sky: it was heading *downward*. The ceaseless hammer of atmosphere in its path was battering it back, robbing it of velocity and height. Speed turned to fiery heat as she watched.

'It's not gonna make it,' she muttered, as if the western horizon was a finish line, a sanctuary. She felt N'Tele's hand on her arm.

'You don't think it's going to hit the city?'

'No. Too far north. If any of it makes ground it'll hit

over there somewhere.' She waved vaguely into darkness beyond the edge of the pad, never taking her eyes from the growing speck. 'I think it's a little high for –'

'*It's breaking up*!'

A man with his arm in a complex-looking sling was bouncing excitedly. Lannigan noticed that in his free hand he had a pair of binoculars, the kind with an image recogniser that tells you where to look. She watched him put the binocs to his face then swing his head abruptly upward, as the sensors hunted down the image held in memory.

But she could see it herself now. The meteor was moving faster, perspective giving it a faux acceleration as it drew close. And now it had a companion – a smaller point of light was moving away, curving downward. Lannigan watched it flare and die.

With her eyes on the fragment, she missed the explosion.

When she next looked at the meteor it was a cluster of tumbling stars, a firework, spreading outward in a sky-filling cloud of brilliant fragments. The structure had broken down under heat and atmospheric stress, shattering explosively into unnumbered tiny meteorites. Lannigan watched the pieces whirling over the city, fading and dying, embers in a cooling fire. Within a dozen heartbeats, it was gone.

For a while, no one said anything. Then the people nearest the service lift began to turn and head back inside, into the light. Lannigan stayed where she was, unwilling to move just yet. The death of the meteor had tugged something inside her, something that made her feel old and lost.

N'Tele was leaning against the safety rail. 'Do you think it's true? What they said on *Pan-Africa*?'

'About it being a spaceship?' Lannigan tugged the jacket a little closer. 'Maybe. Yeah, I think it probably was. Something about the way it broke up . . .' She sighed, gazing out over the city, watching the tiny sparks of traffic. Thought about the people on board the ship, dead or waiting to die, and wondered if she should feel something other than vaguely curious.

'Nice sendoff,' she said quietly. 'Next time somebody kills me, I want one like that.'

She had been in Uhuru Park, Nairobi, when she saw the assassin.

It was a warm night. The sun had dipped out of view an hour before, and the slight drop in temperature had turned the punishing evening humidity into a fat, lazy shower. Raindrops the size of her thumb bounced and spattered, drumming against her umbrella, hanging like grubby gems at the tips of the frame.

The umbrella was black, smoothly expensive, matching the briefcase she held in her left hand. Memory-wire spines arced low over her head like a personal geodesic. Round her slim wrist, a Swiss chrono chirped the passing of another hour, humming against her skin. She nodded imperceptibly, her eyes flicking across the faces beneath the covered walkway as she turned to the gate. In that fraction of a second, she saw him.

And could not move.

It was something indefinable that froze her there: a fleeting change in his expression, perhaps; a surety of movement that was there and then gone. Nothing that she could name about his plain grey suit or smooth features, but the knowledge went through her just the same, and nailed her to the air. In that instant she knew that he was here for her and that she would die on this warm, rain-washed Kenyan night.

She stood in the rain, gazing at him with an odd curiosity.

Thunder rippled across the horizon, hot and slow. Her paralysis fractured at the sound and she began to move, walking briskly towards the west gate. Her mind had already surrendered to the inevitable: even as her body hurled itself forward in a blind and hopeless attempt to escape, some iron calmness in her soul was calculating how best to use death to her advantage.

Her eyes were grey now, like old steel.

'That was his idea,' said N'Tele. Lannigan was looking at the mirror again, in the bathroom. The nurse had helped her in. 'Doctor Lippincott. He's the worst lecher in the profession, but you've got to admit he has impeccable taste in eyes.'

Lannigan blinked. She was looking at a stranger, a rather sharp-faced woman of thirty or so, her hair a kind of pale auburn, her lips too thin, her nose too prominent. She looked as though she had been built for scowls, not smiles. 'He made this?'

N'Tele looked at the floor. 'Yes. Look, I'm not supposed to –'

'Quit worrying about my mental state, will you? My God, I think I've got a reasonable idea how bad things were.' She glanced at the nurse. 'Was there anything left?'

'Not too much. They didn't have a reference . . . He more or less put it together from scratch.'

'Talented.' She looked back to the mirror, trying to imprint the image on her memory. Cold, she thought. It's a cold face.

I can live with that.

Nairobi had been a live thing, a predator, that night. It stalked her, breathing hot behind a neon grin, snagging at her heels. She could feel the size of it, could hear its silent laughter.

It nearly had her a hundred times: crossings that flipped from green to red as soon as she approached, letting him get a little closer while she waited; automatic doors that stalled in their function; an AI longhauler that jumped a red light to sweep her briefcase away beneath its broad wheels. And each time she slipped its hot and rain-bright grasp she wondered if blind luck was keeping her alive or whether the city was letting her live a little longer for pleasure's sake, toying with her.

She headed for home. The chase was wearing her down, and she knew that it would only be so long before she felt the predator's talons on her skin. She couldn't run for ever. Back at the hotel room there was a gun, a snub-nosed Honda 2mm recoilless, taped under the toilet seat. Hardly an arsenal, but it gave her a straw at which to clutch.

There was a breath behind her, his breath. He was far closer than she had realised.

Later, in the plastic darkness of the hospital room, she would remember that moment with total incomprehension. It was as though her mind had turned itself round in her head, closed like a fist around the cold and certain knowledge of how to act. At the end of Milimani Road she whipped about and launched herself at the assassin.

He saw her at the last second, the heat in his eyes flying into the shadows, becoming something else, and then she was on him. He tried to step back. She threw the umbrella at him. His hands came up to ward it off and the hard and pointed toe of her expensive Ginza shoe slammed into his groin.

The man staggered. His eyes bulged, still watching the umbrella as it tumbled away. She kicked him again, twice, expert with a sharp and sudden skill, and then, as he toppled forward, drew back her foot and lashed it into his face as hard as she possibly could.

Something gave. The man made a peculiar coughing sound, and stopped moving. She stood above him, breathing hard, watching blood begin to collect under his nose, threading over the wet pavement.

She knew exactly, to the last second, how long it would take him to die.

The hospital was large, a U-shaped cluster of buildings hugging some dark and unpronounceable hill. As she regained the effective use of her body, Lannigan took the chance to explore a little, walking slowly and barefoot along the warm corridors, holding on to the ever present handrails for support, enjoying the freedom and the feeling of smooth carpet under her toes. She collapsed only twice.

N'Tele walked with her, some of the time. The hospital had a policy of assigning personal nurses to patients, building a supportive bond. Lannigan didn't feel especially supported, but she began to discover that, the longer N'Tele spent around her, the easier it was to use the young woman as an access to restricted information.

She had started slowly, practising with nuggets of gossip, details of home life and history. Within four weeks of waking, Lannigan had reached a point with N'Tele where she could regularly induce her to reveal facts that blatantly contravened hospital confidentiality guidelines. The details of her own treatment, for example.

'Doctor Lippincott wants you in for another week,' the nurse told her, as they stood in the observation lounge watching ripples of wind skate across open grassland. 'I heard him and Ross talking about it yesterday.'

Lannigan nodded, holding the handrail tightly. 'And Ross is . . .?'

'Resident nanotechnician.'

'Ah.' She knew that, but confirming past data seemed to be part of the process. It made the rest easier.

Lannigan counted five heartbeats, watching clouds gather over the plains. Far in the distance, tiny sparks began to flick from sky to ground. Storms in Africa. 'Well, that's nice to know. I've got no real love of surprises . . .' She left it hanging, and N'Tele grabbed hold, right on cue.

'I'll save you one. The cops are coming in tomorrow. They want to talk to you about what happened.'

'I thought they might.' A fat droplet spattered against the window close to her nose, making her flinch. She blinked, and saw a second, a dozen, a great sheet of stormfront rolling across the plain towards her. 'Wow. More rain.'

'Regulated nanotechnology, digesting sand into soil. It changed everything.' N'Tele turned to her, surprised her with a sudden tap on the side of her head.

'Just like in here.'

She never got as far as the gun.

There had been a presence in the room. She felt it before the lift doors had opened, but by that time there was nothing she could do about it. She spun round and a hand just came out of nowhere and grabbed her.

She tried to tug away, but the grip was tight as a handcuff and just as unbreakable. It pulled, dragging her into the apartment. She got a blurred glimpse of chaos as she flew across the room: they had been here all along, waiting for the decoy to drive her into their arms. They must have been amusing themselves by trashing her equipment. Her shoe caught a torn edge of carpet and she went over, face first into the glass table.

There was an explosion of pain as she struck, as she crashed through the pane and the black ash frame to strike the carpet in a welter of blood and broken glass. She tried to get up, and a boot slammed into her side, knocking the wind out of her. She gagged, choking out teeth and vomit.

Pieces of her face were hanging free. Somebody said, 'Now look what you've done.'

'Are you talking to me, or to her?' That was a woman's voice. The first had been male.

'You. She's all busted up now.'

'So?'

'So, I was going to have some fun with her first.'

'Ha. Now you can't. What a fraggin' tragedy.'

The man made a disgusted sound. 'Killjoy,' he muttered. He sounded bored, as though somebody had burnt a meal that he didn't particularly want.

She tried to get up again, pushing her bloodied, lacerated hands down into blades of cold glass. A foot hit her in the back and shoved down. As she tasted carpet again, a metal coldness pushed into the back of her neck. The man said, 'There?'

'Up a bit.'

'Oh, right.' The coldness moved. 'So what she do, anyway?'

'Ah, just do it, willya? I got a date.'

'Yeah, sure.'

He did it.

Knowing when the police were due to arrive was a benefit. Lannigan shut down the infonet screen five minutes beforehand and adjusted the bed just so, letting herself sink back into the pillows in the best imitation of a weak and faded cripple that she could manage. In truth, that part required little in the way of fabrication. According to N'Tele, her rate of improvement had dropped off sharply in the past week and the nanotechnician, Ross, was beginning to give up hope. Lannigan could well believe it: her right leg was still rubbery and unresponsive, prone to sudden pains and numbnesses, and she was terribly tired. It looked like she might be bedridden for a while yet.

She turned her head to the side, looking out of the window at the green plain and the crystal glitter of Nairobi beyond. According to *Pan-Africa* – least annoying of a thousand or more newsfeeds serving the African infonet – enough material had been retrieved over the past three weeks to prove that the meteor had indeed been a space vessel on fatal re-entry. Popular speculation said the ship was probably *Tucker's Net*, a plex-owned salver lost some months earlier, but no one was really sure. There was just too much traffic in low orbit these days, and if the ship was run by a plex – an independent microcorporation – it would have little in the way of backup.

Lannigan was wondering how anyone could be so stupid as to actually lose track of something as big as a spaceship when the police walked in.

There were two of them, both male, both clad in loose, dark suits. One looked Indian, a Sikh or one of the neo-Sikh splinters, his head wrapped in a black turban. The other was Bantu like N'Tele, but his hair was shaved back in a style that was, according to Lannigan's incessant net-hopping, medium to hot in Embu this week.

Lippincott came in with them. She gave him a nod, a faint smile. 'Doctor.'

'Hello, Cassandra.' He stood close to the bed and started tapping at the readout panel. It was a reflex. 'These gentlemen are from the police, Inspector Rahisi and Sergeant . . .' He paused, glancing at the Indian.

'Ghali.' The man's voice was very soft. Lannigan noticed the black thread of a comms mike curving down along his jawline from the turban.

'Sergeant Ghali.' Lippincott nodded. 'They want to talk to you about what happened. Do you feel strong enough?'

She waited, just long enough, then said, 'Yeah, I'm fine.'

N'Tele came in holding a couple of folding chairs. She set them down next to the bed, gave Lannigan a raised-eyebrow look of encouragement, and left again. Lippincott stood next to the window while Rahisi and Ghali sat on the chairs.

Rahisi was closest. 'I've been told you remember nothing about what happened to you.'

'Yes,' she lied. 'That's right.' She glanced over at Lippincott, a sick patient hungry for support. 'My head . . .'

'Ms Lannigan, have you been made aware that you had been under police surveillance for nearly three days when you were attacked?'

That was news. 'No. What kind of surveillance?'

'You had been observed purchasing certain equipment.' Rahisi looked over his shoulder at Ghali. 'Namely . . .'

'A portable DNA sequencer with level-two AI support,' said the Indian. Lannigan noticed the glaze of his eyes, wondered if he was reciting from memory or had some kind of datafeed into an optic nerve. 'A microcentrifuge. Seven multimode mixing tanks. A bioreactor. Separators, six of. A molecular scope, tunnelling, with pattern-recognition software. Four structant queens, in stasis. Assorted biomedical glassware.'

Rahisi looked back at her. 'You were buying out every medical-supply house in Nairobi,' he said. 'What were you planning to do, set up your own bioweapons factory?'

Lannigan sat up and stared at him, all pretence at weakness gone. 'What the hell are you talking about?'

'Because, if you were, a room in the Milimani Hotel wasn't exactly the brightest place to do it.'

'You were being watched by the drugs squad,' said Ghali.

Lannigan sat back, remembering a fleeting image of wrecked technology, just before the table had come up and carved her face open. Was that what they were talking about? She watched Rahisi take a slab of black plastic from his pocket and flip it open in front of her.

A flatscreen lit up. 'Remember this man?'

She glared at the picture, saw a black man with vivid hair. The image was grainy, taken from a peculiar angle. 'I only know my own name because somebody told me what it was. How many brainscans do you need to see before you'll grasp that concept?'

'What about this one?' White, untidy shock of brown hair over dark glasses. The quality of this one was even worse.

'Of course not!'

Rahisi blinked at her. 'Very well. Perhaps if we show you the whole segment –'

Lippincott had stepped forward. 'I really think that's a bad idea –'

'Ms Lannigan here had enough equipment in that room to bring back ebola,' snapped Rahisi. 'I think that justifies going through the footage.'

Something hard and cold was growing under Lannigan's ribs. 'What footage?'

'Let me know if you remember anything.' Rahisi touched a control.

The picture changed.

She was looking at a hotel room, trashed equipment and broken glass made strange by the false sharpness of computer enhancement. Most of the room was obscured, since the footage had been shot through a window. Surveillance, she thought. They'd been filming her from across the street.

Her face began to ache, deep behind her nose.

The door opened. A woman fell through, blonde hair in sodden tangles to her shoulders. A hand caught her wrist, dragging her through and over. She stumbled, face first into the coffee table.

Lannigan moaned softly, feeling the coldness of glass knifing through skin. She watched the woman on the screen try to get up. The man with the bright hair put his foot on her back and shoved her into the carpet.

He walked round her, a small silver brightness gleaming in one hand. His hair was chromomorphic, changing colour slowly from brown through gold and green. His lips moved, but Lannigan couldn't hear what he was saying. She could remember well enough, that part.

There was a woman there too, a nondescript white girl in jacket and jeans. There was a brief argument between her and the man, after which he put the gun to the back of the prone woman's head. There was a small flash, and the woman's face burst.

Lannigan put a hand to her nose. The bullet had come through there, ripping out everything from the teeth upward. Face gone, eyes gone . . . 'Keep watching, Ms Lannigan. I don't want you to miss this part.'

The woman was still, sprawled in a puddle of crimson stew. The girl was clutching her own shoulder, staggering back as the man fired repeatedly at the door, the tiny gun sparking like a cigarette lighter. He ducked towards the window a moment before something struck it and crazed the glass to an instant, chaotic whiteness.

'I'm afraid that's all,' said Rahisi.

By the time Lannigan could get her hands away from her face both policemen had gone. Only Lippincott remained in the room with her, sitting on one of the chairs, his arm round her shoulders. 'I'm sorry. I tried to warn them, but –'

'They'll come back.' Her voice was calm again, now. She sniffed back tears she hadn't realised were there. 'They always do.'

Lippincott nodded. 'They have more questions.'

'What the hell about? I've told them all I remember.'

'They want to know about the Caucasian. Apparently he was shooting at the assassins when the window broke – I think Rahisi might be looking to place him as your accomplice.' The doctor looked momentarily uncomfortable. 'And of course there was the Chinese woman they found with you . . .'

'Another woman?' The girl in the footage wasn't oriental. Lannigan frowned at Lippincott until he took his arm away. 'What does she say?'

He shook his head. 'She was DOA. There was a stab pack on her, just like you, but the A and E team couldn't save her.'

She watched him stand up and move back to the window. 'Stab pack?'

'Stabilisation pack. Paramedics use them. They keep the heart beating, inject antishock compounds, tissue-scavengers.' Lippincott put a hand to the glass, gazed out over the plain. 'You were wearing one when they brought you in. That's why you were alive.'

'Alive . . .' No, she thought. That eyeless, opened thing on the hotel carpet wasn't alive. The stab pack might have kept its heart running, but it was just cold meat twitching on the hook. 'The police carry them too, then.'

'Ah, no.' Lippincott seemed almost embarrassed. 'Too expensive.'

She looked up at him, finally dropped her hands. 'So they didn't . . .'

'It was on you when they arrived.'

On her last day at the hospital, Lannigan sat in the foyer, waiting for a taxi to take her into town. She had spent some time that morning in the licensed shopping mall in the west wing, buying new clothes, shoes, an extensible walking cane.

Outside the foyer's big glass door, raw afternoon heat rippled up from the compacrete roadway, folding the air. Lannigan's seat was in front of the aircon. She closed her eyes, luxuriating in the cold blast. Her things were stuffed into a cylindrical carryall, her hair neatly trimmed to a style she felt comfortable with: short enough to stay out of the way; long enough to hide the scars at the base of her skull.

Lannigan had been in the hospital for three months, comatose for eight weeks of that. After the episode with Rahisi and his horrible film she had discharged herself, fighting off the weakness with pills she had convinced N'Tele to steal. Lippincott and Ross had argued with her, begging another week's observation, a chance for the medical nanoengines still working along her central nervous system to complete their tasks and dissolve. Lannigan wanted none of it: watching somebody blast her skull open had made her eager to be away.

Most of her possessions had gone. In the hotel room the police had found nothing in the way of identification; Cassandra Lannigan was the name she had used to buy the medical equipment. She had no idea if it was real or not, but it hadn't mattered to any of the supply houses. She had made all her purchases in cash.

Forty thousand international currency units had been found in the room with her, locked in a sealed case and hidden above a ceiling panel. The police couldn't prove that it wasn't hers; nor could they charge her for any crime. Buying meditech and getting shot was suspicious, but not illegal. Lannigan had transferred the money to the hospital, paying off her stay and treatment in a lump sum and leaving just under four thousand in loose change. That was in the carryall, with the rest of her life.

Mosquitoes battered the glass, stunning themselves against the ultrasonics that kept the interior of the hospital insect-free. Lannigan listened to their tiny impacts, waiting for the taxi. She couldn't remember what it felt like to ride in one.

The assassin had fired a single 4mm bullet into the back of her head from a recoilless handgun. Lannigan, in a fit of morbid curiosity, had demanded to see the medical reports: the bullet had entered just below the lambdoid suture, erupted through her brain at a shallow angle, exiting through her nasal bone and seeding her cerebellum with bone fragments as it passed. The damage had been truly horrific. On that hot and rainy Nairobi night, the woman who was now Cassandra Lannigan had died instantly.

Events during the eight weeks following that were naturally sketchy. The police had called paramedics to the hotel room. The paramedics had taken her to hospital, and the surgeons there had effected emergency repairs. No one had expected her to survive.

Later, more surgery, by skilled humans and equally skilled machines. Damaged tissues had been cut away, replaced with cloned cells. Artificial subsystems had been installed: Lannigan had computers in her brain to tell her what to feel from the waist down.

She opened her eyes to watch a battered metal egg trundle on to the forecourt on three fat tyres. Over eighty per cent of her memories had been sliced away during those eight lifeless weeks. If she had family, she didn't remember. Her smoking habit had gone, along with her signature and her last birthday. She couldn't recall her sexuality.

The egg opened at the side. Lannigan got up, fumbling for the cane, heard the whicker of compressed air as it unfolded. She grabbed the carryall in her free hand and wondered if she should miss all those erased memories. The nanotech was still working inside her, tiny machines scooting up and down her CNS, eating blood sugar and building nerves. Maybe she would feel something other than empty when they had finished.

The glass doors parted for her, and the heat hit her like a wall.

The egg was full of music. It rocked and swung down the road like a drunken bumblebee, bouncing in counterpoint to the grinding Somali jive thumping from the sound system. Lannigan clutched at handholds, feeling herself being swamped in culture shock. 'Is this an old record?'

The driver's name was Jamboree. He had dreadlocks to his waist and teeth inlaid with gold, which he showed a lot. 'No, ma'am.' He grinned, tossing his head to a sudden and stormy riff. 'New chip, just over from Bardera studio this week.' He pattered his hands over the taxi's joystick and throttle bar, fingertips echoing the drumbeat. 'You like it?'

'I'll let you know.' She turned her head, watching the scenery leap by. The window was scratched and grimy, and marked with yellow paint along the frame where Jamboree had slipped with the brush a couple of times. Lannigan could remember little except Milimani Road and fear and the antiseptic perfection of the hospital, and found the randomness of it fascinating.

Kenya had always been agricultural; now it was a green explosion, fertility gone mad. Gene-tailored bacteria and amoeba-sized nanoengines had been introduced to dry soil, turning the parched land into rich loam veined with countless irrigation channels. Structants – a wholly artificial species of African termite modified down to the molecular level – were being used to alter the entire shape of the land. The increase in plant life had affected the air, the weather, drawn in the excess of rain caused by polar shrinkage. New crops thrived. There hadn't been famine in Africa for decades.

Nairobi was springing up around the taxi like accelerated forest.

The road was made of rutted dirt, the buildings formed from gas-planet plastic, painted in brilliant patterns. Corporate towers glittered in the distance like vast spikes of mirror. Children dressed in shorts and advertising T-shirts ran alongside the taxi, laughing, clutching toys and tubes of soda. With Africa's economic boom had come a vast new market for consumer goods: big companies regularly air-dropped advert-shirts in their thousands. Good for business. Lannigan saw a little girl in a blue Übergen shirt, and a sliver of ice ran down her back. She leant back in the seat, away from the window.

Jamboree flipped his locks at her, grinning wildly. Lannigan noticed that he was very good-looking, and wondered why that fact went nowhere inside her head at all, no more so than the colour of the taxi. Nanotech. He was asking her if she had decided where to go yet.

'I have to get to Mombasa. The shuttleport.'

'Ah, you want the maglev.' He tugged the stick, swinging the taxi down a side road. 'Sure you don't wanna hotel? Bar?'

Seeing the Übergen shirt had altered her mood, filled her head with rain and broken glass. That steel-blue logo gleamed down the barrel of her walking cane, had topped most of the treatment files N'Tele had accessed for her. Übergen Aktien-Gesellschaft had the basic patent on medical nanotechnology.

'Just the station,' she whispered.

'I know some good places.' Jamboree swung the taxi right, tooling it along a narrow street where amusement arcades nestled close to coffeehauses and surgical boutiques. The road was full of electric vehicles, darting and hooting and spilling music from open windows. 'Nairobi centre at night: get some good beer, a little ganja. Just the trick after a stay in the House of Pain.'

Lannigan blinked at him, suddenly feeling sad and cold, listening to the music and the sunny, smoky hum of Nairobi gearing up for night-time. It was quite a different place now it had stopped trying to kill her, but still the emptiness inside her swelled, billowing up huge and dark. She shook her head, gripped the cane tighter. 'I'm sorry.'

He shrugged, tugging back on the throttle bar. The taxi began to slow. 'No problem. But lissen', you gotta feel good if you wanna feel well.' He flashed her the grin again, ivory and new gold. 'God's truth, sister.'

'I'll try and remember that.'

The maglev was new, built alongside the railway line that stretched for 500 kilometres through Konza and Kibwezi and Tsavo National Park. It glittered in the sun, curving like a scalpel cut through the green plains, a child of new-materials technology and African prosperity. Teams from Germany and Japan had modelled their own maglevs after the Kenyan Line.

Jamboree dropped Lannigan at the terminal entrance. She paid him double, politely refused his offer of some Embu hash for the journey, and waved the little yellow egg goodbye as it bobbed away. When it was quite out of sight, she realised that she missed it.

Then she remembered that she hadn't said goodbye to N'Tele, and realised that she missed her, too.

The forecourt of the maglev terminal was plain compacrete, but the steps leading up to the doors were long slabs of something that looked like bluish marble but was as nonslip as tarmac. New materials were everywhere, changing the world: not just making their mark, like some electronic gadget or yet another translated fragment of genome, but utterly transforming it. Gas-planet plastics grew like mould in the right conditions, and were light, rigid, and tough. Structant colonies could chew the stuff up and repolymerise it in any form you wanted, from raw sheet to buildings. Cheap polycarbons and molecular laminates made everything stronger, smaller. The techniques designed to terraform Mars had turned the deserts of Earth into gardens. The world hadn't been this green since the dinosaurs.

Lannigan climbed the blue steps, leaning heavily on the cane. Her right leg still felt weak, not entirely her own. She hoped that would get better as the chips in her head forged their new connections, rerouted around the missing or damaged parts of her brain. She didn't like walking with a stick, but it beat falling over.

There was a row of ticket machines just inside the doors. Lannigan stood in front of one, wary of being obviously unable to use it and looking conspicuous, but the machine was fitted with AI. It asked her questions in a soothing voice, prompted her for money, then disgorged a plastic ticket in a neat paper envelope. First class, nonsmoking.

A maglev left the terminal every hour, which gave Lannigan just over twenty minutes to kill. To be honest, she was glad of the time. The journey had tired her and, although the terminal's concourse was airy and thermally controlled, she felt hot and thirsty.

N'Tele's pills must have been wearing off.

Somehow, she had expected the terminal to be gothic, archaic, a vertical stone nightmare. Maybe because Jamboree had called it a station. It was actually a long, shallow curve, half a kilometre from end to end, arched up and over the raised maglev track in the middle, a lazy sprawl of grey pseudomarble and gold chrome and glass. Or something that looked like glass: Lannigan found she couldn't be sure, because when she touched a pane of the stuff it felt smoother and stronger than glass did, not as harshly cold.

There was music on the concourse, bright classical complexities chiming out from hidden speakers, accompanying the images on vast suspended flatscreens: news items, balletic moments from televised sport, brilliant curlicues of cloud and pressure as seen from a geostationary weather satellite. Lannigan walked stiffly up a ramp, remembering someone telling her that the music was called baroque, not remembering who. There was a coffeehaus at the top of the ramp, over to the left. Right was the balcony: she glanced over the edge, at the floor. Stalls ranged along the curving walls bulged with merchandise: local pottery, fetishes, datacards. A troupe of mimes worked their routine in time with the Handel.

Lannigan went into the coffeehaus, ordered cappuccino with lots of sugar, two cups. The music was wonderful. It felt like crystal, every facet cut to perfection, polished notes filling the air. It rang in her head. She could almost see it, the mathematical whirl of it, could almost feel the notes move aside as she walked from the black marble counter to a nearby table, holding her cups in a plastic tray. There were no more than a dozen people in the place, and none of them were looking at her.

The coffee was hot and sweet, and the froth tickled her nose as she drank. She dabbed at her face with a napkin, glancing about, trying to imbed the coffeehaus on her memory. She had lost so much past, so much self: maybe it was time to start building again.

Most of the people in the coffeehaus were African. A pair of Korean tourists were eating ice cream at a corner table, spooning it from a communal bowl. Occasionally, one would feed the other. They seemed very young, and smiled a lot. Lannigan watched them over the rim of her coffee cup, wondering if they were married. Wondering what it felt like to be happy that way.

She finished both cups, then checked the nearest clock. Ten minutes until the maglev pulled out. Lannigan picked up her bag and saw someone duck out of sight behind a sushi stall.

A man, Ugandan by the cast of his face, nondescript but for the slow colour change of his hair. Green and gold and brown. Lannigan felt her heart jump inside her. The Milimani all over again, and she couldn't even run.

Idly, she picked up her carryall and set off, limping towards the sushi stall as though she had seen nothing. The smell of *ramen* and clear *miso* soup stung her as she drew close, setting her mouth to watering. She smiled, proud of herself, noting how the man went back into the shadows as she passed. He fell in behind her as she walked slowly across the grey pseudomarble floor, her cane tapping heavily at the smooth surface. Perhaps, as she changed direction, he realised that he had been waiting for her within moments of her only real sanctuary. Perhaps not.

Lannigan pushed open the door to the ladies' restroom and stepped inside, never altering pace until the door swung closed behind her. Then she faltered, stopped, sank back against the door. All the breath went out of her, for a second. Then she heard him curse, something in Swahili. She thought of a knife going through the door, and moved again.

The restroom was small, and quiet, comforting golden light from ceiling panels illuminating a short row of cubicles down one side, sinks and mirrors down the other. Lannigan frowned, scanned the room for another exit. There was something at the far end that looked like an access panel – if she squeezed, she might be able to get through. She started towards it and promptly tripped over.

She yelped in surprise, snatching at the nearest sink to avoid falling, losing the cane. A panicky glance down showed what had come so close to flooring her: a leg, clad in grubby denim and terminated in an oversized Nike trainer. Lannigan blinked at it, peered round the corner of the cubicle.

There was a girl inside, slumped on the floor with her back against the toilet bowl. The leg against which Lannigan had almost come to grief lay stretched before her; the other was drawn up; the girl's head tipped disconsolately against her knee, stringy black hair spilling down over the denim. As Lannigan watched, the girl drew in a long, snuffling breath, and let out something that might have been a sob.

Lannigan threw a glance back at the door, but it hadn't opened. Its software wouldn't unlock for a man, but he could come in with his female accomplice, if she was here.

But he wasn't sure. Her face had been different when he had blown it all over the carpet.

Lannigan crouched awkwardly, supporting herself against the cubicle wall while she grabbed for the cane. As she did so, she noticed something that lay in the girl's hand. Something small and glassy, with a long needle.

The girl was pressing the needle against her own thigh. Lannigan heard her gasp as the point slipped through the denim.

She reached out, grabbed the syringe and wrenched it away. 'Jesus!'

The girl's head came up. Tight little Hispanic face under a grubby mat of hair; three purple tattooed stripes on each cheek, like whiskers on a cartoon cat, and another across the bridge of her nose. Huge eyes, brown, huge jacket, black plax. Dirty and tired and thoroughly miserable. 'Leave me alone, man.'

Lannigan used the cane to push herself upright, leaning over on to the handgrip. She held the syringe up to the light and squinted at it. 'Skyhigh,' she said, automatically. Now how did she know that? 'There's enough in here to stiff a rhino. What are you trying to do, go out in a blaze of glory?'

The girl looked down, mumbling into her jacket. 'Something like that.'

Lannigan smiled at her. It didn't feel right, but she did it anyway. 'Well, honey, today's your lucky day.'

They bowled out of the door together, Lannigan slightly in the lead and hurling herself along as fast as her rubbery legs would take her. With each step the cane punched hard into the floor, its complicated internals cushioning some of the impact but still transmitting enough through her wrist and into her forearm to hurt like hell. She wondered how long she could keep this up.

The girl was right behind her, making worried little hurrying noises. 'Come *on*,' she moaned, bunching her fists in frustration. 'We only got four minutes!'

'We'll make it.'

'Can't you go no faster?'

'We'll *make* it!'

Abruptly the girl grabbed Lannigan's sleeve, nearly tugging her over. 'Hey *señora*, this way! The stairs.'

'I can't –' She never got a chance to finish, because the girl was off, dragging her along. Lannigan was shocked at the strength in those thin arms: maybe the kid wasn't so far down the Skyhigh slope after all. They careered down the steps, Lannigan's shoes and cane thumping over the not-marble. She just about stayed upright.

The girl glanced back. 'Skinny guy, chromo hair?'

'That's him.'

'He's on us.'

The boarding platform was on ground level, the maglev track sunk into a vast compacrete scar. Lannigan saw the ticket gates and cursed. 'They won't let you through!'

'A hundred ICUs will get anyone through, *señora*!' The girl let go of her arm and darted forward. Lannigan nearly fell. Her head was pounding, her legs singing their own songs. She staggered, watching the girl slap the money she had given her down on to the counter and begin yelling at the man behind the glass. She was nearly at the gate herself when a hand came down on her shoulder, hard.

She swung round. There was a gun in his other hand no bigger than a deck of cards. It would fire a tiny explosive dart capable of blowing Lannigan's insides to ribbons and leaving only a pinprick on her skin. He squeezed the trigger. A thin, plax-covered forearm whacked into his head and the dart blasted a fist-sized chunk out of the ticket barrier.

The assassin snarled, grabbed at the girl and shoved her away. She tripped over her Nikes and sprawled across the floor as Lannigan dived at the man, caught his gun arm and held on.

He hit her across the side of the head, snapping her teeth together, making her shout. The second blow slewed her clear round. The cane spun out from under her and she went down in a heap.

A long moment passed. Lannigan sat up and looked at the assassin. He was just standing there, not moving, the tiny gun centred unerringly on her forehead. His mouth was open. He was staring at the syringe buried needle deep in his right forearm.

'Ah,' he said.

The plunger was all the way down.

The man's legs gave out. He sank forward on to his knees, the gun dropping from his fingers. For a moment his face was level with Lannigan's; she watched as his eyes crossed, until he seemed to be studying a point about ten centimetres in front of his face. Then his head went back to leave him staring at the ceiling.

He looked like he was praying.

Lannigan felt a thin hand under her arm, pulling her up. The girl was speaking to her, shouting, but the assassin's blows were still ringing through her skull. She shook her head uncomprehendingly, and at that the world tipped violently about her. Everything became a sickening whirl of sensation, and Lannigan whirled with it, dragged in an eddy of nausea and exhaustion until the darkness came to take her away.

2
Rayanne

Hunting through the zipped and buttoned pockets of her jacket, Rayanne Gatita found the following items:

Half a permagraph pencil.

A Durex 'Glowboy' bioluminescent condom, out of its box but still in the yellow foil wrapper.

A single stick of cinnamon chewing gum.

Two photographs: one of a pleasant-looking middle-aged woman who Rayanne had always imagined to be her mother; the other ripped across the left side but showing a house with a blue-tiled roof.

A twin hygiene sachet from the Nairobi Meridian hotel: one side originally held toothpaste; one shampoo. Both were squeezed totally dry.

An empty packet of Crazy Eights cigarettes.

One segment of a Hershey bar, bundled messily in the rest of the wrapper.

A digital chrono, working, but with a broken strap.

As she located the objects, she removed them with elaborate care, dusting each free of the lint and fluff which accumulated inevitably in the linings of her jacket pockets, and set them down on the table in front of her. Within a few minutes – before the maglev had even finished accelerating, in fact – she had a small pile of seemingly random packets and mementoes.

She shifted them around on the tabletop, arranging them by size, by colour, by age. Trying to imbue them with some kind of meaning, as if they were something that she could read like yarrow stalks or a hand of cards. If the collection hadn't been all she owned it would just have been garbage, but its rarity gave it value. The objects were the dots and commas that punctuated the sentence of her life, and, looking at them, she realised that the exact order didn't matter, as long as she placed herself at the end. Rayanne Gatita: nineteen years old, flat broke, homeless, frightened, and sitting across the table from a woman who had just murdered somebody.

The *lisiada* was still out, slumped messily over the opposite seat. Rayanne had dumped the carryall and jacket on the seat next to their owner, and put the cane on the table where she could watch it change shape.

The thing must have been expensive: it was already reconfiguring itself, strengthening its handgrip, extending curves of polycarbon to hug the wearer's forearm and provide greater support. When Rayanne had first seen the thing it was just a walking stick. Now it looked like the top section of a complete surgical crutch.

Rayanne was fascinated. She rarely got to see expensive things.

She had entertained the notion – more than once, while hauling the unconscious cripple and her baggage on to the maglev – of just keeping the cane and the carryall and haring off. A ride on the Kenyan Line, however, was a great way of skipping Nairobi, and out of Nairobi was exactly what Rayanne wanted. Especially since there was a dead man on platform two with a syringe stuck in his arm, covered in bio-traces of Rayanne Gatita.

Plus there was Zenebe and the Embu Crew, but she couldn't let herself think about that now. Anyway, the woman had promised her a lot of money if they made it on to the maglev yokay.

Rayanne unwrapped the stick of gum, popped it into

her mouth and began chewing angrily. Yokay, maybe trying to delete herself had been a stupid thing to do, but she could blame that on crash haze. Maybe the *lisiada* had done her some kind of favour by taking the Skyhigh away. But that didn't mitigate the fact that the hobbling bitch had told her there was somebody outside who she'd 'rather not talk to', and hadn't mentioned a damn thing about the possibility of Rayanne getting an explosive flechette through her guts.

Rayanne knew a bit about weapons. She knew what the dart would have done if it had hit her. The thought made her cold and shivery, and she found herself wishing that not all of her Skyhigh had gone into the Ugandan.

She settled herself into the corner between the seat and the carriage wall, folding her arms tight, fists high up in her armpits. The jacket bunched up around her, creaking, smelling old and comfortable and warm. She pulled her feet up, jamming the soles of her Nikes against the table edge, until she was curled and braced into a plax-covered ball, world-proof. She let her head droop forward.

The maglev didn't rock or chatter like a railtrain, but there was a subtle swaying to it that Rayanne liked. She closed her eyes and relaxed. Slowly, the world fell away from her, piece by piece, a slow succession of random boxes and foil packets spinning away into the past, leaving her safe and alone.

She slept.

Rayanne couldn't remember exactly where her parents had gone, or how she ended up in the Home, or the trailer park, or any of the correctional centres. A small pharmacy's worth of memory crushers and sundry other recreational chemicals had, over the years, fulfilled all their promises and blotted her past into a kind of fog through which only the tangled edges of her pain could penetrate. As for her family, all she could really recollect was the memory of crying in the dark, for a long time, and as a result of that Rayanne had never been all that fond of the dark, except for the creaking gloom inside her jacket collar when she squashed herself up to sleep.

Sometimes, though, when the crushers had worked their magic on her synapses and the world had softened enough around the corners, she would dream about the woman in the photograph. It always began with the woman's smile and, minor variations apart, continued thus:

There was money. There was a man; not a boyfriend, because at the time in question Rayanne was no more than five years old, but a tall, kindly man with the kind of face she always thought a father should have. So she called him Papa. And Mom was there too, and sometimes there was a dog, but its existence tended to depend on whether Rayanne was taking Red Velvet straight or cutting with Pandorphin.

And there was the infonet screen, which played CGI cartoons and puppet shows and pictures of the city. The house with the blue-tiled roof was near the city by ground module, but a long way away when you were walking. Mom called the city Camaguey, and Papa just called it The City and said Turn it off, honey. It's depressing.

But Mom just kept on watching, as the men in combat fatigues and red felt hats talked about independence and imperialism, and the soldiers in their big jackets moved from building to building, fat multibarrelled SMGs held down low and laser projectors flicking bright threads of crimson through the smoke. Sometimes there were tanks, too: big six-legged tanks that Rayanne didn't like the look of, because they walked like the roaches out in the yard, only slower.

There must have been other things too – things like school, and friends, and bathtime and talking on the comm – but none of this made it out through the fog. Not until God knocked the house down.

Mom and Papa weren't indoors that day. They had gone off somewhere, to the mall, or maybe the airport. Papa had been talking about leaving. Either way, Rayanne had settled herself in front of the infonet and the babysitter was outside. If Rayanne was on Pandorphin then the sitter was playing with the dog, but Red Velvet had her standing in the driveway looking at a battered Mitsubishi monocycle and the boy on it was saying Come on, baby, let's go for a ride. The kid won't snitch. And then the sun came out.

Rayanne was watching the screen when it happened, so she was never quite sure whether it was actually the sun or something else that cast such brilliant and perfectly defined shafts of light through all the windows at once. Later she decided that the source of the light was probably God, since in the next instant the Good Lord picked up Rayanne's house with her inside, shook it until it came to pieces, and then dropped it.

Everything stopped working then. After a while Rayanne managed to get out from under the piece of wall that had fallen on her and tried to get the lights on, but they didn't work either. The house had sort of folded up on itself, making a kind of tent shape with ends made of blue-tiled roof and furniture. It was very dark. Nobody answered her when she called them, not Mom nor Papa nor the babysitter nor the boy on the monocycle, even though she kept trying for a week. The only thing she could hear was rain coming down and something scratching at the walls outside. The rain would drip through the holes where the roof had been, so she had something to drink, but it was black and warm and it tasted funny. As for what was scratching outside, she was never entirely sure, but after a while Rayanne stopped taking Pandorphin altogether, because if she did the dog would scratch its way back into the house on the eighth day, burnt through to the bone all along its left side and screaming and screaming until the soldiers came in after it and blew its skull open.

She often wondered if that was how it all actually happened.

Rayanne woke with her eyelids glued together and a taste like tinfoil in her mouth. The inside of her collar was wet where she'd dribbled down it, and her wad of gum was jammed up beside a back tooth, as warm and spongy as an abscess. Unchewed for some minutes, it had ceased exuding flavour, and Rayanne was grateful for that. With her stomach sacs full she felt sick enough without waking up to a mouthful of cinnamon.

She snuffled and raised her head to wipe her mouth with one sleeve. Her eyes came open with an effort, leaving a gritty residue at the corners which felt like sand. She had to scrape it away with a fingernail, then get the stuff off her finger by scrubbing the nail back and forth across the seat arm. She blinked a few times. Scratched her head. Yawned.

Looked around.

The *lisiada* was awake and staring right at her.

Rayanne gave a squeak of surprise and unfolded, way too fast. Her left shin smacked painfully into the table edge as her foot slid under; her right leg had gone numb through lack of circulation and failed to provide any support whatsoever, pitching her sideways into the blue-carpet wall of the carriage. Her head clipped the window frame. '*Mierda*! Ow!'

The woman gave a little sigh, thin eyebrows climbing a fraction under her fringe. 'Well. I guess you're awake.'

She had an irritating voice: flat and high, with a Midwestern whine.

'No shit.' Rayanne got herself straight and rubbed the side of her head. She hadn't hit too hard. 'How long have you . . . You know . . .'

'Not long.' Now the woman wasn't even looking at her, just peering around the interior of the carriage with her cold grey eyes. She spoke like she was throwing the words away, like Rayanne didn't matter at all. When she half got up and muttered, 'Slowing down,' she was talking entirely to herself.

Rayanne's stuff was still all over the table. She began gathering it up, glancing at the chrono display as she did so. 'Just Konza, man,' she said. 'Ages to go yet.'

'Not for you.'

'Huh?' She looked up. The woman was rummaging around in her carryall. After a few seconds she pulled out a fistful of ICU notes and tossed them across the table at Rayanne.

They were hundreds. Rayanne swallowed hard, looked briskly right and left, then scooped the money up and stuffed it into her inside pocket, with the photos and the condom. 'Thanks.'

'You earned it.' The side of the woman's mouth quirked up in what she probably thought was a smile. 'If you must spend it all on chem, don't take it all in one go, hm?'

Rayanne found herself nodding, and stopped. 'You want I should get off?'

'Safer for both of us.' The woman was getting up, slipping her right hand through the cane's new grips. The thing extended with a smooth, complicated noise, and she leant over on to it with a look of what could have been relief. 'If you still want to go to Mombasa, take the next one. If anyone asks about me, tell them everything you know.' She extracted herself from behind the table, edging awkwardly into the aisle. 'Which is nothing.'

'Yokay.' The maglev was shedding velocity, the light-spattered darkness beyond the windows growing in definition, in colour. Rayanne saw a digital signpost flicker by, its frame-rate matched exactly to the maglev's speed. WELCOME TO KONZA. FOUR MINUTES.

She looked back down the aisle. The woman was heading for the far hatch, jacket draped round her shoulders, carryall hooked over her arm and her free hand grabbing at the seat backs as she passed them.

Leaning heavily over on to the cane. From behind, she looked thin and small and older than she actually was. 'Hey,' called Rayanne. '*Señora*.'

The woman halted, turned her head sideways.

'Hope . . . You know, it's all yokay.'

There was a pause. And then the woman pivoted right round to look at her, and there was something in those grey shark eyes that made Rayanne go cold, made her think of darkness and warm rain and a horrible, persistent scratching. It was the look of someone who was seeing something brand new, something wholly unknown and frightening. As if no one had ever wished a kindness on the woman in her whole life, and she didn't know what it meant.

Rayanne got up and ran, shaking. Couldn't get off the maglev fast enough.

The transit lounge was a big, shallow dome, ringed with shops and stalls, dominated by an illuminated fountain that kicked water twenty metres up through a hole in the roof and back down in glittering, sculpted twists. There were seats round it, some of them unoccupied, and Rayanne dropped gratefully into the nearest, glad to be as far away from the maglev as she could get without actually leaving the station.

It was cool there, with the water jumping and crashing at her back and the dome's aircon at full blast. Rayanne sat back, eyes closed, gradually getting herself under control, shrugging the shiver from her shoulders and back. Letting the sweat dry off. Outside the station Konza would be hot, a steamy, smoky African evening sliding towards night-time, buzzing with bugs and neon. Rayanne didn't like the heat much. Six months in Africa hadn't made her like it any better.

Everywhere Zenebe made her go seemed to be hot: if it wasn't Mombasa or Nairobi it was Florida. Rayanne swallowed hard at that thought. Florida was where she went full, her stomach sacs bulging with whatever nameless drug Zenebe had programmed her system to produce this week. Florida was where she made contact with this black clinic or that biomedical plex, and got a tube stuck down her throat.

Rayanne had spent six months shuttling around, either feeling sick or feeling raw and violated. Six months hustling and scamming and trying, without much luck, to make some kind of a life. It's hard to find your feet when you've got somebody kicking them from under you, and harder still to quit using when the chem provides you with the only real enjoyment you can find.

And now Zenebe was dead, the top of his head sliced clean off by a thin, cold loop of memory wire.

Zenebe had always fancied himself the hustler, but he had picked the wrong people to hustle when he got involved with the quasi-religious Kenyan syndicate that called themselves the Embu Crew. A month ago Rayanne had never heard of them, and then suddenly Zenebe owed them so badly they were all he talked about. Eventually he had dealt Rayanne into their schemes, setting her off to meet them with a double dose of memory crushers in her gut. No middlemen, no profit margin. Just a single, straight deal to get the Crew off his back for good.

If she had turned up on time, it might have worked.

The Crew were more patient than most. They gave her an extra day to show, but after that they caught up with Zenebe and expressed their displeasure.

The wire took an hour or so to cut right through. They called it the Angola Bowler.

The thought was a fist in Rayanne's guts. She got up and made her way through the crowds of passengers and shoppers to the edge of the dome, then started walking round clockwise. The window of a consumer-electronics showroom caught her eye, and she spent a few minutes with her nose against the glass, checking out the latest in interface terminals and chipplayers, fresh in from Taiwan and the automated factories at Spandau. Next on from that was a bookstore, which didn't interest her overmuch, and then a bioware shop which grossed her out totally. They had structant colonies for sale, display setups in the window. She hurried past and tried not to look, but caught a glimpse of pyramids and little staircases glued together from polymerised sand and bug spit, hard as pseudocrete. Rayanne thought about the blind, squirming *sabandijas* with their brains so messed up they thought that building staircases was a really cool idea, and her skin crawled.

Her stomach was starting to cramp. She couldn't eat anything, hadn't eaten for days. Her sacs were still full of the Crew's memory crushers, all except the one that had started leaking in Mombasa. Rayanne had woken up after spending three days wandering downtown Nairobi in an amnesiac stupor, three days gone completely from what was left of her memory. She had been massively lucky not to have been killed, run down by traffic or snatched off the street by some psycho.

Zenebe, of course, hadn't been so lucky.

She ducked into a touristy gift place and spent a few minutes trying on pairs of sunglasses, peering at herself in the mirror on top of the plastic stand, poking her hair out of the way and wondering if she should go into a washroom and put her head in the sink. She found a pair she really liked, with little round green lenses and gold frames and self-moulding pads that snuggled against her nose. She was just getting ready to put them in her jacket and run when she realised there was a shopgirl standing behind her.

So much for that plan. She went into backup mode on automatic – ask the price, look disappointed, put the goods down and wander off. 'Ah, hi. How much are these?'

The girl grinned, a false plastic grin that said, Thieving bitch, I can spot you with my eyes closed. 'Thirteen fifty, miz.'

'Thirteen fifty, right.' Rayanne nodded, turning away, and as she did so the wad of money in her jacket bumped insistently against her ribs. She had totally forgotten about it.

'Er, how much is that in ICUs?'

The girl blinked. 'Thirty ICUs, miz.' The grin had gone now, faded, turned a little less certain. Seeing it, something inside Rayanne soared. 'Just thirty?' she asked, cool, like it was the kind of question she asked every day, and when the girl nodded she hauled a note out of her pocket and said, 'I'll take two.'

Outside, she realised she had been stupid. The *lisiada* had given her 800 and now she had 740 and two pairs of shades. And it was dark. Still, the look on the shopgirl's face had been worth every unit.

Konza was smaller than Nairobi, but it was noisier, too: there was a lot of traffic, and a lot of people, and behind all the motor-whining and yelling and chatter was the bone-deep thump of music, very loud, not too far away. Rayanne decided to head for the beat and took a left from the station entranceway, turned down a wide road lit with chromomorphic streetlamps that rainbowed as she walked under them, threading through the nighttime crowd. And away from the station. Tomorrow, maybe, she would go back, put some of that heavy wad of ICUs down on the counter and pick up her very own ticket to Mombasa, fast and air-conditioned all the way. Kick her Nikes up on the table and drink cold beer and watch the world go by. *Tomorrow*. Right now there were plenty of things to do with the maglev that she didn't even want to think about.

Memories. Her old enemies, poking their sharp little edges out through the fog, sniping at her in whiny Midwestern voices. If she didn't do something soon, every man on the street would have Zenebe's face, every woman a cane. She pushed them back in her head and turned right, waiting at the kerb until the walk light came on, then trotting across the zebra stripes, staying bunched up in the crowds.

Ahead of her, the road opened out on either side, forking and curving away around the edges of a public park. Rayanne could see low walls and railings, a tall entranceway shaped like a church's arched window; past that, trees and lawns, brilliant splashes of colour and light from rows of open foodstalls, the motile glare of a holographic lightshow. The music was coming from there, thumping out from some hidden and powerful source, and most of the people around Rayanne seemed to be heading straight for it.

She shrugged to herself, and went on in.

The park was big, even bigger than Uhuru Park back in Nairobi. Rayanne wandered along the central pathway, keeping to the bright areas, trying to blend. She even managed to pause in front of a couple of the foodstalls, checking out fried prawns and banana crisps while her mouth watered and her stomach cramped from the smell. It was all for show. If she tried to eat, it wouldn't stay down, and then her disguise would fold up and she'd be just another junkie puking into the bushes.

She bought a can of Jolt Cola instead, and downed it as she moved on. She knew the kind of place she had to look for, knew it by a sort of reflex, a buried memory. The dark places – the corners of burnt-out buildings, the shadowy areas between the support pillars of overways – were where the real losers shot up, slumping and dying among a litter of tab wrappers and old needles. Likewise, anywhere too close to the bright lights would be under police surveillance, or at least likely to draw the attention of some public-minded citizen who might just tip off the local heat for something to do. No, Rayanne needed somewhere in between.

There was a raised area in the centre of the park, a circular concourse stacked up on ten-metre compacrete pillars, edged with pretty railings and spotlamps and beds of flowers. It had a hole in the middle where a ground-level fountain jetted right up through. Two long, curved ramps led from the middle of the park up to the concourse, but there were stairways too, leading backward towards the road. Rayanne went up the right-hand ramp, skirted past the hole, and leant over the railing to check out the stairways. See if there was a face she recognised.

Dealers often shuttled up and down the Kenya Line, hitching lifts or saving enough to ride the railtrain. Never staying in one place too long, varying the customer base. Rayanne knew a few names from Nairobi who had dropped this way recently. One in particular wasn't too hard to find.

Doogie Baxter, white and thin as a bone, hands stuffed deep down into his coat pockets and his back against the stairway handrail. Rayanne glanced reflexively left and right, then headed down towards him. 'Hey, Doogie!'

He looked up, one hand coming out and reaching inside his coat, then he realised who had shouted and relaxed. 'Hey,' he said.

Rayanne had bought from Doogie exactly twice in Nairobi, but his stuff was good, reasonably pure, and he didn't try to hit on her every time they did business, not like some of them. He was English, a lanky white-faced Londoner who looked far younger than he actually was. Since Rayanne had last seen him he had shaved off his hair, leaving just a faint orange fuzz on his round head, but he was still wearing his brown cowhide jacket and Hawaiian shirt.

Rayanne didn't know how he'd managed to end up selling dope in Kenya, and didn't much care. 'Doogie. What you do to your head, man?'

He smiled, his teeth white and even. 'I'm in disguise. Rayanne something, innit?'

She nodded, laughed. 'Yeah, man. Rayanne something.' She came up beside him and leant over the railing. 'So how long you been in Konza, man? You like it here?'

'Weather's yokay, but the food's crap.' He looked at her. 'What you wearing sunglasses for, Rayanne? It's dark.'

'Yeah, but with these on it's dark and *green*.'

He chuckled, then his face went serious. 'Heard about Zenebe.'

'Yeah, who didn't.' Zenebe's face had been all over the infonet when Rayanne had gotten her brains back – an enhanced digital pic taken from a security camera somewhere. 'Still got the stuff, man.'

Doogie sucked his teeth. 'You'll be leaving the country, then.'

'Reckon I need to?'

He shrugged. 'Embu Crew, they're not the Yakuza. Not like they're gonna hunt you all over the world for half a litre of brain-drain. Still, wouldn't hang about here too long, yeah?'

She hadn't expected any different. Out of Africa was safe, and that was fine with her. She'd hole up until tomorrow, then haul ass. 'Don't worry, man. I got plans.'

It felt good to talk about Zenebe to somebody, but it felt strange, too. When they had been together Rayanne had found out to her cost that she couldn't talk about him to anyone, because he always used to end up hearing about it. And then life could get uncomfortable, quickly. It wasn't that he used to hit her a lot – he'd only beaten up on her twice, and neither time seriously – but he had ways of making Rayanne remember how much she relied on him. Which she hated. On balance, she decided that she'd rather be hit than owned.

So one day soon, when she'd loosened up a bit inside, she'd go into a bar somewhere and find somebody with a listening ear and pour it all out, every rotten detail of it. But not right now. Now she wanted to forget everything, get safe and raise the fog again. She moved in a little closer to Doogie's narrow shoulder. 'How much you holding today?'

'Not so much.' He twisted to look quickly over his shoulder. 'If you're looking for a big order I'll have to go hunting, give you a call tomor–'

'No, *now*, man!' Her voice went up, loud, and Doogie shrank back. She put up her hands in apology, dropped down to a whisper.

'I'm not after much, Dee. Just a hit for tonight, yokay?'

Doogie looked uncomfortable. 'Well, I dunno . . .'

'Hey, I can pay you. I got enough now.'

He frowned. 'How much?'

She reached inside her jacket and showed him some of the money. 'Enough, yeah?'

'Shit! Who'd you have to shag to get that?'

'Don't you gimme none of that static! I ain't no whore.' She looked around again, then leant in close. 'Hey, Doogie. You got some time later on, we go somewhere, yeah? Get some coffee – I'll tell you some stories, man. Weird *mierda*.'

Doogie looked interested. 'How weird?'

'Not like that, man. You letch. I mean strange . . .' She bugged her eyes out and waved her hands in front of his face.

He grinned. 'Yeah, yokay. Been a slow night, anyway.' He shot a glance up and down the stairway, pausing while a couple wandered down towards the road, arm in arm. 'So what do you need?'

'Watcha got?'

'Got some Tumboni, some Leb. Pandorphin . . .'

Rayanne made a face. 'Not that shit, man. Gives me nightmares. Any Velvet?'

He shook his head. 'No market, not since those cough sweets came out.'

'What's this?'

'You didn't hear?' She shook her head, and he made a disgusted face. 'Ah, some stupid drugs company brought out a brand of cough sweet with the stuff in 'em.' His thin hands made a shape in the air. 'Little triangular buggers. Blue. Anyway, some bloke in Glasgow works out how to distil the Velvet out of them with a kettle and an icebox. Puts it out on infonet.'

Rayanne giggled. 'Oh, man.'

'So now you can't get the bloody things at all, but for a while there were some really nasty coughs going around.' He spread his hands. 'Anyhow, the price went south and no one's holding. Hey, I've got some Wire? Skoot?'

Rayanne nodded vigorously. 'Yeah, man. Gimme some Skoot. Four, no, six tabs. And a tab of Wire.'

Doogie raised his eyebrows. 'You aren't gonna go barbing that stuff, are you? Turn your brains to mush, that will.'

'So what are you, my mama?' She snapped her fingers at him until he shrugged and rooted the stuff out from inside his jacket. 'Anyhow, what do you care?'

'Well, if you're dead, you're not gonna buy any more, are you? Hundred.'

'Shit.' The price was high, but Rayanne didn't feel like waiting around to haggle. She paid up, and had stuffed the pills into a pocket before Doogie had finished checking the note. 'Later, man.'

'What, you off already? What about my story?'

'Aw, c'mon, Dee.' She bunched her fists helplessly. 'Look, I'm gonna be around, yokay? I'll come find you.'

He looked at her for a long time, then gave her a funny kind of smile. 'Yeah, go on. But look, you take care, all right? That Zenebe might have been a bastard, but at least he was there.'

'I'll take care, Dee. *Gracias*, man.' And then she left, off down the stairs as fast as she could go without stumbling. She thought she could feel his eyes on her all the way down, but, when she reached the bottom and looked back up, he wasn't there.

Must have been somebody else.

Rayanne found a cheap hotel, a stack of structant-built cubes one stage up from a capsule rack and one down from an honest-to-God flophouse. The sign on the door had a long list of things the room wouldn't have – no infonet, no running water, no bar, no heat – but all Rayanne really needed was a bed and a can of beer.

She'd bought the beer from a vending machine on the way in.

The guy on the desk had exchanged one of Rayanne's hundreds for sixty in change and a door token: a grubby disc of translucent green plastic, a silver sticky label on one side with her room number printed on it. Probably some circuitry in the foil, too, because the door recognised the token when she dropped it into the slot: it showed 23:59 on the display and unlocked with a complicated metal noise. Rayanne pushed her way inside, wondering how she would get back in if she went out again and the door locked behind her.

The lights were off in the room, which gave her a few seconds of panic as she tried to find the light switch without opening her eyes and seeing how dark it was. Eventually she found the pad and hit it, kick-starting a fluorescent panel in the ceiling. Squinting, Rayanne saw a bed, a small table with a cardboard key on it (*that's* how you got back in!) and a framed print on the wall of a big-eyed Mexican kid, crying. Rayanne looked at the picture with a special kind of horror, then stepped into the room and let the door shut behind her.

There was no window. The room was in the centre of the block.

At least it was clean. The walls had been sprayed with chromomorphic paint – slow colour shift from pastel green to pastel blue and back. The furniture was white laminate, the bedclothes a cheap white synthetic that felt yokay. Better than most of the places Rayanne could remember sleeping. She pulled the table over to the side of the bed and sat down next to it, putting the can of beer on the tabletop.

Harley Davidson Heavy, in a black can with a gold Harley logo embossed on the side. Rayanne cracked the tag and gulped down a precise half-can in a few quick swallows, getting some on her chin and down her neck. Then she put the can back down on the table, took off her jacket and spread it on her lap.

The inside lining was a black spider-tangle of writing, most of it Rayanne's, all of it in black permagraph pencil. Permagraph sold well to blankers, because it didn't come off, even if you sweated all over it, and a blanker needed somewhere to write down everything she didn't want to forget.

The jacket was Rayanne's memory, the only one she could rely on. She took out the pencil, found a free space near Doogie's infonet address, then wrote in her slow, careful hand 'No Velvet. Cough sweets'. Crushers tended to snip away the connections to a memory, not the memory itself, leaving little tags and frayed edges that could be latched on to later. That was good in a way, because a lost memory needed only a few words of mnemonic to bring it back out. The downside was dreams, when a random stimulus could bring hidden things crawling out of the woodwork. That's what happened to blankers, eventually. One unwanted memory would spark off two more, like particles in a nuclear reaction, and some day there would be one too many connections and they'd find you curled up in a corner screaming and you'd be like that for the rest of your life.

Thinking about that made her feel cold, so she shrugged the jacket back on, took out three of the Skoots and laid them out in a line, then put the Wire on the tabletop and looked for something to bash it with. Of course, she realised, if she'd been thinking she would have used the can before she'd opened it, flattened the pill and then pulled the tag. *Atontada*. Luckily the tab was fairly crumbly anyway, and she managed to powder it with her fingers.

Wire was an upper, a cheap analogue of amphetamine and cocaine that could be put together in any half-decent lab, given the right ingredients and a tech who knew what she was doing. It wasn't stable, though: added to alcohol the molecules started to break down and reform, and if ingested at the right moment it took a narcotic like Skoot and turned it into a whole new ball game. Users called it Barbed Wire. Unfortunately, Doogie had been right about the dangers: leave it to cook too long and it turned sour, started breaking down glial cells.

She tipped the powdered Wire into the Harley, watched it fizz for a count of ten, then looked up in horror as the door unlocked itself and swung open.

Busted again, she thought.

Everything froze, a split-second tableau of startling, adrenaline-rush clarity. Rayanne, sitting on the bed with a half-can of Harley bubbling in her fist and eighty ICUs' worth of illegal narcotics lined up on the table in front of her. The big plain-clothes cop, stubby little gun pointed at the ceiling, badge in his other hand, the long coat draped over his shoulders, filling the doorway like the cloak on a cheap netshow villain. The beat-pounder behind him, pale-blue uniform shirt and neat black tie. Holding an electronic pass-key.

The cop with the coat said, 'Rayanne Hernandez?'

Rayanne threw the can of beer at his face, as hard as she could. He stepped back, gun arm coming up to ward off the foaming missile, and she was past him, under a flap of coat and out of the door. The uniform yelled and grabbed her jacket collar, but Rayanne twisted and shrugged out of it in a fluid, practised motion, left the cop with the jacket in his hand, spilling ICUs over the carpet.

The hotel wasn't large – Rayanne rounded a corner within a few metres, putting some wall between her and the cops' guns, just in case they decided to get trigger-happy. Konza wasn't New York, but she wouldn't put it past the local heat to try to slow her down with a gyrojet taser or toxin dart, neither of which would make her day any better. The next right took her into the stairwell, and she clattered down the spiral of steps so fast that she tripped over halfway down and didn't actually fall until she was in the foyer.

She cursed, scrambled up, hearing the cops behind

her shouting in Swahili and Spanish, barrelled past the registration desk and the beer machine, out through the glass doors and into the night.

There was a police module parked outside the hotel entrance, a flattened polycarbon egg in glossy blue and white, rotary lamps scanning shadows around the alley. Rayanne didn't look inside to see if there was another cop waiting – even if she'd wanted to hang around, the module's windows were transparent from the inside only – but a door began to clamshell open as she got close.

She hared past it, the night air suddenly cool on her bare arms. The hotel fronted on to the back of another building, a Japanese-style multilevel vehicle park. This far back from the main streets, the spaces between buildings were narrow and dimly lit. Rayanne felt like she had a target painted on her back as she ran, unable to find a turning or a hiding place, just blank compacrete walls rearing up on either side. Arms outstretched, she could have touched both at once.

There was a doorway on her right, into the vehicle park. It was painted the same nondescript cream as the walls themselves, and if it hadn't had a fluorescent safety lamp above the frame Rayanne would have missed it and gone straight past. She skated to a halt and grabbed the locking bar, hauling it up to get the door open. As she ducked inside something the size of a pencil stub slapped into the frame next to her head.

There was a heavy snapping noise, like plastic breaking, and the safety light exploded in a shower of powdered glass. Rayanne yelped, getting a stinging jolt of residual voltage as she let go of the door, realising that she'd been right about the tasers. 'Son of a bitch!'

She had been lucky. The door was a fire exit, outward-opening and perpetually unlocked. It led straight into the lower floor of the park, and Rayanne found herself running between neat ranks of ground modules, each locked into a secure meshwork recess. The huge robot grab that shifted the modules around was moving a level or two above her head. She glanced upward through a towering forest of gantry, and saw it swing a compact six-wheeler round and down into a recess with quick, mechanical precision, opening huge padded vice-jaws with a hiss and whine of hydraulics.

Behind her, the door bashed open.

She couldn't hide here. The only way for a human to get to the upper levels of the park was by ladder, and the cops were too close behind her for that. She ran on, scampering now, keeping low and quiet while the noise of the grab settling back into its lair covered her footsteps. The modules would come into the park at the front, sliding through secure doors on a short conveyer belt before the grab would drop down and cart them off to a vacant recess. Automation or no, there had to be some kind of exit that way.

The light inside the park was dim, a greyish spill from bioluminescents placed haphazardly around the walls. Rayanne was close to the entrance doors before she saw them – a big, sawtoothed pair of metal gates, wide enough for a truck, stencilled with warning notices and grimed with hydraulic fluid and residual carbon – and the smaller fire door alongside. She was going for the door when the gates unlatched and began to grind apart.

The noise of the motors was almost deafening, bouncing around the walls and gantries and making Rayanne wince. She stepped back, watching the little groundbug slide forward on its juddering conveyer, then raced towards it, a foot on the front bumper and over the hood, sprawling across the roof.

The grab was emerging from the darkness behind her, scanning the module with fans of ruby laser, extending narrow silicon eyes and waving thin, needle-like probes. Rayanne slid down the back of the vehicle, her Nikes leaving grubby trails down the clean paintwork, and jumped, landing awkwardly on the conveyer. A few more steps had her at the front entranceway, past a couple of startled attendants in orange coveralls, and back on to the street.

The cop module was parked right in front of her.

Rayanne stared, turned, and a gyrojet taser sizzled out of the night and slammed into her shoulder with a ferocious impact, emptying its capacitors into her central nervous system and pitching her face down on to the oily floor.

3
Reflections

The Latina was out of sight by the time the maglev had pulled in at Konza station.

Odd, to see her scrambling away like that. Lannigan would never have thought of herself as frightening, especially to a street-hardened teenager with a fifteen-centimetre height advantage. But the girl had looked into her eyes, gaped, and bolted like a rabbit.

Lannigan gazed after her for a while, as the maglev shed the last of its velocity and slid to an imperceptible halt, then she shrugged and turned away. You could never tell with drug users – she remembered the articles she'd seen on *Pan-Africa*, the animated posters in the hospital waiting room. Something about a drug fashion spreading from Europe and the US: memory-crushing chemicals developed for use in psychiatric treatments being sold on the open market. People addicted to amnesia.

The Latina had exhibited many of the telltale signs (the stare, the words murmured as she slept, the jacket scrawled with random data), and if she was gradually wiping out her own past there was no telling what paranoiac nightmares were filling the gaps. In that light, her reaction was probably quite subdued.

Lannigan scowled. The idea that somebody could

throw their memories away by choice made her teeth itch.

She began heading between the seats, towards the back of the maglev. Between each of the train's long compartments was a restroom, a good enough place to hide until they got moving again. Lannigan still felt horribly weak, and the Ugandan's blows were echoing through her skull in thick, muddy waves of nausea and disorientation. She didn't like being exposed in a state like this. Too many people must have seen the Latina drag her on to the maglev.

The cane felt a lot more comfortable now. She was just looking down at it when somebody got up from one of the seats to block her path.

She stopped, swaying. He was small, just a fraction taller than her, a slender Caucasian with a rough mop of brown hair and a long, thin nose that made him look vaguely like a cartoon bird. He wore a faded leather raincoat over his shoulders, and he was smiling. 'Ms Lannigan?'

'I'm afraid not,' she replied, trying to keep the shiver from her voice. As she did so, she felt a sudden presence behind her. A second man had risen to his feet, very close to her back. She could smell a faint trace of cologne, something sweet.

'Ms Cassandra Lannigan,' whispered the second man, his voice smooth and dark and unhurried. 'I'm afraid I'm going to have to ask you to come with us.'

Lannigan turned her head, just enough to glimpse the man standing at her back. He was somewhat taller than her, but not as big as she had imagined. He wore shades. 'Who the hell's "us"?'

'Forgive me.' He took a small card from within his dark leather jacket and showed it to her. 'Detective Inspector Byron. This is my associate, Mr Swann.'

Lannigan looked back at the small man. He was grinning, bouncing up on his toes. 'Charmed,' he said.

'Likewise.' She kept her voice calm, but there was cold

metal in her guts, growing there. 'But I still don't –'

'We really don't want to go into too much detail on a public maglev,' said the African. He had an odd inflection to his voice, as though he were dictating instructions to a machine. 'If I say that we want to ask you about a certain gentleman you left on the Nairobi terminal platform . . .' He held out his hand for Lannigan's carryall.

'Ah,' she said. And nodded.

As she followed Swann off the maglev she remembered that 'Ah' was the last thing the Ugandan had said before he started to worship the terminal roof. The thought gave her little comfort.

The station was very different from that at Nairobi. Instead of the graceful, bone-thin curve of the larger terminal, Konza was a kind of architectural joke, three primary geometric forms half-buried in a facia of smooth pseudomarble: half a cube enclosing the platforms, a shallow cone for the administrative and processing sections, a wide dome for the transit lounge.

They walked her out through the rear of the cube to the vehicle park, a minimalist black square surrounded by a low wall. Lannigan noticed the design of the wall as she went through the gates; saw how, from the air, it would look like a giant picture frame. Somebody had spent time on the place, she realised. Tried to make it fun.

Under different circumstances, Lannigan might have appreciated the joke. As it was she stumbled between the ranked ground modules in a daze of rage and sullen, gnawing fear. Skipping hospital and shuttling out of Africa hadn't really been much of a plan, but it was all the plan she had. The arrival of this mismatched pair had brought it all crashing down around her.

And behind that notion was another thought: that something about this whole situation was horribly, terrifyingly wrong.

Swann stopped beside a grey four-seater, the kind Lannigan had seen in magazine adverts for rental companies. She watched him unlock the vehicle with a little remote-action key and then pull the door up. 'After you.' He smiled.

'A rental?' She stared at him, then at the module. 'What the hell's this?'

In the door window, his image, reflected . . .

Lannigan turned, whirling about on the cane, tried to scramble past the African but he had her with lightning speed, an impossible grip. She screamed, once, and then she was in the back of the module, the carryall hitting her in the legs, Byron shoving her down hard. The door whined downward and locked.

Swann got into the front as Byron took the cane away from her. She watched it snap closed, wondering with a kind of terrified clarity whether she would ever get the chance to lean on it again.

'She remembers you,' Byron said.

Swann turned round in the front seat, frowning at her as though he was looking for something. 'No,' he said. 'She doesn't. Not properly.'

He reached out to her and she shrank away, cringing back into the padding. Swann was the second image on Rahisi's datapad, the one the police computers had lifted just before the window had crazed. He had been in the Milimani, with the Ugandan and the girl, his face reflected in a fragment of glass beside her ruined head. He had been in the room where she'd died.

His eyes on her, small and dark, searching . . .

'No,' he said again, and turned back to the controls. He reached up and pulled his door closed, sliding a rental-agreement card into a slot in the dashboard. The readout panel lit up, greens and blues, a curving strip of yellow expanding as Swann pushed the throttle bar forward and eased the module out of its giant picture frame and into the street.

The African still had his shades on, glossy teardrops of

black plastic, fitted snug round his smooth skull. Lannigan wondered what lay behind them. 'Where are we going?'

Byron turned to her, a puzzled expression on what she could see of his face, as if he had just observed a minor malfunction in a recent purchase. 'Be quiet,' he said. 'Don't speak again.'

His indifference stung. 'If you're going to kill me why don't you just go ahead and do it?' she snapped.

He hit her then, a lazy backhanded slap that slammed her into the far window, sent her head crashing into the plastic. She shouted, involuntarily, as a sheet of pain enveloped her skull, sent sparks into her vision. She felt like he'd almost taken her head off.

'That was for Angel,' he whispered, and turned from her. Lannigan felt tears of pain welling up in her eyes and throat, felt the warm trickle from where the blow had connected. She slumped away from him, clutching her face and head. Her heart hammered at the shock of it.

The man was unbelievably strong. If he had put any effort into the blow at all he would have killed her in an instant, shattered her skull and her spine.

Someone had sent an E-human after her.

She had snatches of memory: brief mentions in magazines and infonet, rumours. Modified operatives stalking each other through the jungles of Central America and the Congo, their reactions increased to superhuman levels through myelic boosters, toxin filters protecting their bodies from poisons and the effects of ecosystem implosion. Fluorocarbon blood, bones of foamed titanium and carbon weave. Electronically enhanced senses. She thought about making a grab for the door, and realised that he wouldn't even kill her in reaction. He'd just hurt her, very badly, and still leave her capable of speech.

The module slewed over, hard. Swann had yanked the throttle back to STOP. He swung round in the driver's seat, his face a mask of pallid fury. 'For chrissakes, Byron,' he spat. 'What the hell do you think you're doing?'

The African raised his eyebrows a fraction. 'She spoke to me. I told her not to.'

'Yeah, right. And I'm fragging speaking to you right now, yokay? You do *not* touch her again.'

There was a pause. Then: 'Is that an order?'

'Yes, it's a goddamn order! Jesus!' Swann turned back. 'Just lay off the rough stuff.'

Byron cocked his head to one side. 'I think you're overreacting.'

'Yeah? You think *I'm* overreacting?' Swann leant round the seat with a gun in his fist, a little slab of black plastic. He pointed it at Lannigan. 'How does this grab you?'

Lannigan stared at the tiny weapon and said, 'Don't.'

Swann just shook his head. 'Sorry, honey.'

He shot her.

Events, for a while, became strange.

After the initial impact of the needles – fifteen, maybe twenty, splinters of frozen narcotic peppering the skin of her chin and throat – there was little more than darkness, a great swoop of icy shadow that flowed up from behind her eyes and enveloped her before she could react. Vaguely, as if from a great distance, she felt her body slump in the seat, as unresponsive as wax. Her senses fled.

For a time, there was nothing more. Until the heat began.

She became aware of a prickling warmth around the line of her jaw, where Byron had slapped her. Subtle heat began to spread across her shoulders, down her back, under her ribs. Her face began to burn.

Within minutes, she was alight from the inside. If she hadn't been completely paralysed she would have screamed aloud.

Sounds began to impinge on her tortured senses, thin,

waspish buzzings, flicker-fast and barely audible: the dreams of insects. Speckles of light danced in her vision. A thread of blood in her mouth made itself known to her slackened tongue in a riot of copper. And still the heat rose, turning her blood to fire. She could feel the perspiration bloom on the palms of her hands, her forehead.

The sounds in her ears were lowering in pitch, and she realised with a start that she was hearing voices. Byron and Swann were still arguing, but at a vastly accelerated rate. The sparks she saw through her closed eyelids were streetlamps blurring past the module's windows.

Something was seriously wrong.

Swann had blasted her with a needle gun, an effective, if extreme, way of keeping her quiet. The dose should have held her completely unconscious for a number of hours but, after what could not have been more than a few minutes, her faculties were starting to return. Albeit in a highly unusual way. Something Swann had given her was playing merry hell with her perceptions.

The voices were almost within reach now, and the heat, while still wildly uncomfortable, had lessened, the fires beneath her skin fading to a mere smoulder. The sweat was pouring off her in gobbets. She could feel herself soaked with it.

Lannigan remembered horror stories she'd heard at the hospital, apocryphal rumours of people who reacted badly to anaesthetic and remained conscious throughout arduous operations, feeling every cut and stitch of the surgeon's art and being unable even to cry out. For a while she wondered if this was occurring here, until she thought of all the time she had spent under the knife and been none the wiser.

The thought of surgery gave her a clue, however.

'Is she breathing yokay?' whined Swann, sounding like an insane cartoon character.

'She's sweating a lot.'

'Mm.' Swann sounded unconcerned. 'Well, she's still the right colour. As long as she doesn't go into anaphylactic shock or apnoea she'll be yokay.'

There was her answer. She still wasn't free of the medical nanoengines that had resewn so much of her neural structure at the hospital. The warmth she was feeling was generated by the tiny machines as they worked to metabolise the unknown toxin from her bloodstream, and they were initiating the sweat reaction in order to eject the stuff through her pores.

And Swann didn't know it. He and his enhanced goon thought she was still dead to the world.

Something inside Lannigan soared. Maybe, if she kept up the illusion, this could work to her advantage. She began working at her muscles, trying to move her tongue, her fingers and toes.

'How much further?'

That was Byron. Lannigan heard little blipping noises, probably Swann using some kind of map. 'According to this, an hour or so.'

There was silence for another few minutes. Lannigan started to get shooting pains down her right leg, and for the first time welcomed them. Moments after that her toes made their first feeble efforts at flexing under her command.

The module slowed down with a sideways motion that felt like Swann had changed lanes, and Lannigan froze. Had Swann heard her?

'I don't like it,' he said. 'There's something real screwy going on here.'

Byron made a rumbling sound in his throat. 'This situation has been "screwy" ever since Artemis,' he murmured. 'Keep driving.'

Fireworks went off inside Lannigan's head. She clamped her jaws shut over a cry of bewildered surprise while Swann made angry rustling noises. 'I'm heading back.'

'You're wasting time, Swann. Unless we get her back to Kitsumi we'll never find out what the deal is.'

'That girl's got something to do with this.'

'Forget the girl.'

The module moved to the side again, braked. There was the sound of Swann turning in his seat. 'They've got to be in it together. I want to know how far.' The blipping noises sounded again for a moment. 'I mean, Lannigan and that trailer trash? No way, not without a damn good reason.'

'Hardly her type, I'll give you that.'

'We could pick her up, no trouble. Pull a Cairo.'

'You lost an eye in Cairo.'

Swann chuckled. 'Yeah, well. Call it a learning experience. Look, there's a comms booth. Get on to Konza PD and tip them she's in town. We could run Facehunter to get a name and be back inside a quarter-hour.'

Byron gave a long, deep sigh, the only sound of emotion that Lannigan had heard from him. Then he moved away from her. The door swung up, letting in warm air, traffic noise. 'I'll be two minutes.'

Lannigan waited, exercising furiously, not daring to open her eyes but listening to Swann's tuneless whistling, wishing she could hear what Byron was saying. Her muscles ached as though she had run kilometres, and the ugly smell of her own sweat teased her nostrils. Her heart was beginning to pound, pulses jumping at her wrists and throat. She wondered if Swann would notice them.

Byron got back into the module. 'Done,' he said.

'Cool.' Swann started up the drives and swung the vehicle around. 'How long, d'you reckon?'

Byron paused, maybe checking a chrono again. 'I'd say not longer than thirty minutes. She's distinctive enough to trigger any eye she walks past.'

'Log on in forty. They should have her by then.'

Time passed without any particular event: Lannigan lay where she was, alternating between fake unconsciousness and real sleep. Neither provided her with any comfort. Dozing masked the fear and made keeping still easier, but she found it increasingly difficult to suppress a reaction upon waking, to stop herself twitching, opening her eyes, screaming aloud as she remembered where she was. After a while she withdrew into a kind of private hell, skewed over in the seat with her muscles aching and her skin greasy with sweat, hovering between terrified cogency and drifting oblivion.

But in the back of her mind there was a light, a quicksilver flash of unconnected memory that sparked and flared and wouldn't go away. 'Artemis', Byron had said, and the word had set Lannigan's brain ablaze.

She couldn't think why. Her reaction to the word had been painfully intense, as if something vast and terrible had ignited in her mind, sending sparks whining and glowing about the cave of her skull. If her brain had been undamaged she would undoubtedly have experienced some nightmarish memory, but too many nerve cells had been ruptured by the assassin's bullet, too much grey matter replaced by cold electronics and the fractal restructuring of nanoengines. Byron's word had let off a rocket of memory in her, but there was nowhere for it to go.

Still, she had been given back a snippet of her past. Nothing pleasant, she was sure, but to have replaced any fragment of what was stolen was inspiring. That, more than anything, drove her to begin planning escape.

Byron logged on to the police information net after an interval that was probably as close to forty minutes as made no odds. Lannigan wondered what he was using to crack the data, and guessed at some kind of portable terminal, one with enough muscle to gouge through infonet's public-access sectors and down into the dark and hidden places beneath. Expensive, then. Illegal.

It didn't take long for him to find what he needed. The E-human was obviously practised at data-trawling. Whatever Facehunter was it informed him that the girl's name was Rayanne Hernandez, and that she had been apprehended in a vehicle park about four kilometres away. A handful of keytaps more gave him the location of the police station where she was being held and the name of the investigating officer.

After a short diversion Swann parked the module and the pair got out, readying their weapons. Lannigan listened to their footsteps recede until she couldn't hear them any more, then opened her eyes and tried to move.

After so long in the same position her muscles cracked audibly, and hotspots of pain appeared in her limbs that she knew would stay with her for days. The meagre light beat at her eyes.

She sat up, peering groggily around the inside of the module. The first thing she noticed was her cane, which still lay discarded by her feet next to the carryall. It felt warm and comfortable in her fist, the slim polycarbon braces tightening reflexively about her forearm as if to provide emotional support as well as physical. She smiled as she held it, then noticed what Swann had left on the dashboard.

The needle gun, a moulded block of black plastic so small that even her hand almost enveloped it when she picked it up. There was a little indicator thread along the top of the thing, part red, part black. The magazine was half-empty.

She sat there, staring at it. He couldn't have been stupid enough to just forget it, could he? Perhaps this was part of some cruel ploy, an excuse for them to kill her and call it self-defence. Maybe the gun had been sabotaged.

No. Lannigan shook herself and stuffed the thing into her pocket, putting her faith in Occam's razor. The simplest explanation was carelessness on Swann's part, something she didn't find impossible to believe. Still, fool or not, the man could run. If she tried to escape on foot he or the E-human would have her in minutes. And Swann had not been obliging enough to forget the car's rental key as well as his gun.

She hauled herself out of the vehicle, her cane stabbing at the wet ground. The module was parked in some narrow backstreet, high walls on both sides, the far end receding into darkness. Pallid light from a bioluminescent strip created more shadows than illumination.

A nice enough spot for an ambush.

Lannigan found herself a place to wait, leaning against the wall with the gun bunched in her free hand. She would need to shoot Byron first, and hard: if he was as enhanced as she believed, his internal defences would absorb all but the biggest dose of narcotic she could deliver. Somehow the thought made her smile.

With luck, and a few needles over for Swann, she might even survive.

4
Wake-Up Call

The cop had a datapad, a flat sheet of clear plastic with a thin black frame, small enough to fit neatly into a coat pocket. Rayanne knew, with a kind of fuzzy hangover logic, that she must have seen dozens of the things before, but trying to actually remember any specific one just set her head aching. She gave up and tried to fix her gaze on the pad held in front of her now.

There was a picture on it, projected neatly on to the plastic: a film loop of a man's head, rotating slowly as though he were sitting in a swivel chair. Rayanne guessed that the rotation was actually computer-modelled from a set of front and sides: a CGI routine in the pad's circuitry was filling in the missing frames. She watched the guy's head go round four times before she spoke.

'Huh?' she said.

The cop – whose name was Motai – sighed and sat back. He had a neat, pointed beard and an educated accent. Large hands. Rayanne noticed a wedding band on his left hand, some kind of signet ring on his right. His long coat was draped over the back of his chair.

'Come on, Rayanne,' he said. 'Don't try and tell me you don't know this guy.'

'I . . .' Rayanne swallowed and shook her head. 'No, man. I don't know him.'

'VSA says you're lying, Rayanne.' Motai tapped the pad with a finger, where the output from an integral voice-stress analyser was blinking red. 'See?'

Rayanne shook her head again. 'No way, bro. That jolt you gave me, I'm all screwed up. I can't . . . you know . . .' She blinked, squinting. 'What you say his name was?'

'Joey Kotebe.'

'Yeah?' Rayanne peered at the picture again. Last time she had seen this guy he was kneeling on a maglev platform in Nairobi, enjoying the benefits of her entire Skyhigh stash. 'What does he say? He say he knows me? 'Cause he's lying, man, I ain't never seen him. *Jamás*.'

Motai put the pad down on the desk. 'He's not saying anything right now, Rayanne. He's in the hospital, having 200 milligrams of Skyhigh flushed out of his system.' He leant towards her, dropping his voice conspiratorially. 'And the syringe that put it there has got your bio traces all over it. Blood match, tissue-type, DNA, the works.'

'Yeah, well. Like that explains it, man.' Rayanne nodded, prodding the desk with her finger. 'Somebody stole my stuff, like ripped it right off.' Which was true, in a way. 'When I was in the jane. Can I go now?'

She had been in the interview room for a while: twenty minutes on her own, waiting, and another twenty with Motai and a uniform cop in there with her. Before that she'd been in the police station's medicom, getting checked out to make sure the taser hadn't done her any lasting damage. She wasn't sure how long that had taken, but at the end of it a policewoman had brought back her jacket. Minus most of the contents, of course.

The conversation with Motai had been mind numbing, a tedious cycle of lies and evasions that she knew wouldn't get her anywhere, since they had her on resisting, possession, and a list of minor offences that included everything from vagrancy to the wilful and malicious damage of a taser dart. Namely, allowing it to discharge itself into her shoulder. But she just sat there, playing ignorant, fidgeting in the grey plastic chair and prodding the grey plastic desk and staring about at the grey carpeted walls and floor.

Chances were, Rayanne was going to end up in a correctional facility again, and be there for quite a while. Still, at least the Ugandan hadn't died.

'Did Kotebe give you the money, Rayanne?' Motai was leaning right back in his chair, making it creak. 'Was he trying to buy something from you? Drugs? Sex?'

'Money's mine, man. I sold some stuff.' Rayanne realised that she could have made things easier on herself by just telling the truth, giving up the cripple woman and pleading diminished responsibility on the rest. But proximity to cops made her lie on reflex. It was a habit.

'What kind of stuff?'

'Ah, old chipplayer. Screen. Some jewellery, you know. Stuff.'

'Stuff,' repeated Motai, sounding tired, and then looked down as the datapad made a thin, blipping noise.

He touched a control in the frame. 'Interview suspended at 11.36 p.m.' Then he touched a different control and said, 'Yes?'

'Got a guy out here, detective,' replied the pad, tinnily. 'Says he wants to see a Rayanne Hernandez.'

Motai sniffed. 'I'm afraid we're a little busy right now, Ed.'

'Ah, he says it's kind of urgent?'

'Yokay.' Motai paused and looked up at Rayanne for a moment. She raised her eyebrows at him until he turned his attention back to the pad. 'I'll be right out.'

He got up. Rayanne frowned, wondering if maybe Doogie had come to try bailing her out. No one else could have known where she was.

As Motai reached the door there was a noise outside, a flat, muffled slapping sound. Hernandez, thought Rayanne suddenly. He asked for Hernandez.

She hadn't used that name in as long as she could remember.

She twisted round as Motai opened the door and said, 'Hey.' He turned to look at her, and there was an incredible noise and the side of his head splashed open in a wet crimson spray. Rayanne screamed as he fell, the whole right side of his head burst open and spilling thick red blood over his shoulder. The expression on his face was that of mild disappointment. He collapsed on to his knees and then sprawled sideways over the grey carpet.

The uniform was across the room, trying to haul his gun out of its holster. A man came in through the door, a little silver stub of metal in his fist, his arm stretched right out ahead of him. There was that noise again, horribly loud, like two big bits of wood being slapped together, and the uniform crashed backward against the wall. Rayanne gaped at him as he slid down, clutching himself. Something like a palm-sized cross of black wire tumbled from between his fingers.

The man looked sideways at Rayanne, then swung the stub round to point right at her. 'Get up.'

Rayanne stared at it, at the tiny hole in the smooth metal above the trigger guard. The whole thing was small enough to hide in the guy's hand, but the memory slugs it fired would unroll in the air into a wire cross and slap her harder than a baseball bat.

Or unroll inside her, if she was too close. Like it had unrolled inside Motai.

She got up, quickly, the chair falling over behind her, eyes locked on the gun. The guy – a tallish African in a leather jacket and slightly out-of-date wraparound shades – inclined his head a fraction towards the door and said, 'Swann?'

Another man darted into the room, smaller, white-skinned. He had a battered leather raincoat draped over his shoulders and a thin, hooked beak of a nose. Rayanne saw him out of the corner of her eye because she was still looking at the gun.

'Coreframe's scrambled,' said the small man, whose name must have been Swann. 'But I just heard an alarm.' Then he looked at Motai and said, 'Aw shit, Byron.'

The African gestured at Rayanne with the gun. 'Stand over there, by the wall,' he said. 'We're going to have to go through the window, Swann.'

'Way ahead of you.' As Rayanne ducked back against the wall she saw that Swann had taken something out of his pocket, a small aerosol can with a short, thin nozzle. He held the end to the wall, a hand's width away from the mesh-covered window, and pressed the trigger. Thick, brownish foam jetted out, swelling and solidifying and hardening. He drew the can right around the window, making a rough frame of bubbly brown gook. It took him about ten seconds. 'Byron? Better get behind the door, her too. I dunno how tough this wall is.'

'Right.' The African grabbed Rayanne by the arm and pulled her back past the doorway, opening the door right out to form a shield between him and the window. Rayanne saw Swann pushing something small and black into the foam and said, 'Oh shit.'

Swann stepped away and turned his back. Rayanne almost had time to close her eyes before the foamed explosive detonated with a surprisingly dead noise and blew the window out into the street in a hail of glass and concrete. The shockwave slammed into her like a fist, filling the room with powdered wall.

There were voices outside the door, yells. Swann was already scrambling through the hole where the window had been, his long coat catching on the spikes of reinforcing steel that poked through the rough concrete edge. Byron grabbed Rayanne's arm again and shoved her forward. 'After him.'

She followed, coughing from the dust, and hopped up into the hole just as Swann hit the street outside. She heard Byron fire the gun twice more, two flat, whip-crack sounds as the tiny bullets hammered kiss marks into somebody's sternum. There was a scream. As she scrambled through she saw that the foam had blasted clear through two layers of concrete wall and the insulation between.

'Move it, for chrissakes,' snarled Swann, reaching up to hook a skinny hand round her arm and haul her down. She hit the street awkwardly, and almost fell. Swann steadied her by shoving her against the wall.

Byron landed next to her, like a cat, then straightened and looked about, the gun centring unerringly on Rayanne's forehead. 'I hear sirens,' he said, very calm.

Rayanne didn't hear anything, but that might have been because of the explosion. 'Hey, look, mister?'

'Shut up,' he muttered. 'If you speak again I'll hurt you.' He said it like he really wanted to, like he'd already worked out what he was going to do and how he would do it, and was just waiting for the opportunity. Rayanne nodded.

Swann was already off, scuttling round a corner. Byron shoved her after him and she followed, stumbling. Her legs felt too shaky to support her, as though someone had scooped all the flesh and bones out from under the skin and replaced it with cold water. She would have fallen, if it weren't for the knowledge that Byron would get his excuse to hurt her if she did.

There was a narrow space round the corner, between the police station and the next building along, grubby and dark. Swann had stopped next to a small grey groundbug parked among the trashcans. He was looking open-mouthed at it. 'Shit!' he screamed.

Byron stopped next to him and glanced at the side window. 'Where is she?'

'She was right there, man, I swear to God. Shit!'

'You didn't dose her enough.'

'No way, man! I gave her the full whack. No way she walked.' Swann stepped back and began looking wildly around, walking behind Rayanne. 'Somebody found her.'

Rayanne saw that Byron wasn't holding the gun on her any more. She wondered if they might start arguing, really going for it, and if she might make a break for it if they did.

And then a memory, unbidden and unwanted, popped into her forebrain through all the drugs and the fear: a toy she had once owned as a child, a plastic whistle. It was yellow and shrill and cheap, and when Rayanne was very young she had broken the thing, probably through loving it too much. The part that made the note had come away, leaving only the pea and a rattling, hissing sound when she blew it.

There was that same sound again, no louder but maybe a little thinner, out from the darkness. And Byron was snapping round with his face contorted and his hands clawing at the cactus forest of tiny spikes that had appeared in his face and neck. He collapsed.

Someone had hosed him with a needle gun, emptying a clip of toxin or narcotic splinters into his skin at close range. Rayanne turned round and slammed the heel of her hand into Swann's face, just under his sharp nose. As he fell she drew back her foot and kicked him as hard as she possibly could between the legs.

Then she did it again. On the second kick something gave, and on the third she broke both his hands, because that's where they were.

He rolled over beside the car and lay still, as curled and unmoving as Byron. Rayanne thought about kicking him again, but there was a footfall and a click behind her, and she knew who it was before even turning round.

They stole the grey module.

Rayanne drove. She had taken the rental licence from inside Swann's coat, since the module wouldn't start without it and she didn't want to hang around trying to hotwire the thing. She could have done it, but Byron was already beginning to stir despite all the tranq in his system.

'I think he's enhanced,' said the cripple, rummaging through her carryall to make sure the goons hadn't taken anything from it. 'Let's just hope they didn't leave some kind of tracer here, or they'll be down on us like flies.'

'On *you* like flies, man.' Rayanne wrinkled her nose. 'When was the last time you took a shower?'

The woman glared at her. She was in a pretty disgusting condition. She was dripping with perspiration, her clothes soaked with it, hair matted to her head and face. 'Shut up,' she snapped.

'Screw it, I'm gonna open a window.'

'I'm dosed up with medical nanoengines.' The woman wiped a hand over her face, doing no good at all. 'When those two spiked me the nanites must have mistaken the narcotic for an infection. Sweated it right out.'

Rayanne grimaced. 'That's disgusting.'

'Don't knock it. If I hadn't woken up early they'd still have us. Turn left here.'

'Why?'

'Just do it! Jesus!'

'*Olorosa lisiada puta,*' muttered Rayanne, but she took the turning. They drove in silence for a few minutes, through the centre of Konza.

After a while Rayanne said, 'So, you gotta name or what?'

'Hm?'

'Your *name*.' She gestured towards herself. 'Rayanne Hernan– ah, Gatita. Yeah, Rayanne Gatita.'

The woman nodded. 'Kitten,' she said. 'Explains the whiskers.'

'You speak Spanish?' Rayanne shrunk down in her seat, wondering how much of the insult the *lisiada* had understood. *Mierda,* she thought.

'I guess.' The woman shrugged. 'Some. I don't know.'

The town was beginning to thin out, the buildings becoming smaller, the lights less bright. Rayanne said, 'So?'

'What? Oh, Lannigan. Cassandra Lannigan. Start looking for a place to stop, like a motel or something.'

Rayanne nodded. 'Look, *señora* –'

'Lannigan.'

'Er, yeah. Right. Look, we gotta work out what's going on here. I mean, who were those guys? They know that Kotebe dude, the one you spiked in Nairobi?'

Lannigan looked at her sharply. 'How do you know his name?'

'Cops told me.'

'Oh.' The woman stared at her for a second or two, then slumped back. 'I don't know, Rayanne. Right now I'm too tired to think. If we can just get a room, maybe a shower. Things might look clearer tomorrow.'

'Right.' Rayanne hated to admit it, but now the adrenaline rush had faded the exhaustion and shock-hangover were creeping back up on her, making her feel like someone had moulded her out of old clay. 'Ah, Lannigan?'

'Hm?'

'Cops took all my dough . . .'

Lannigan sighed, then pointed to a flickering holographic sign that said JOY NIGHT MOTEL in rotating green light. 'Try over there.'

They left the module two streets away, unlocked and with the rental licence lying on the seat. The only thing in it worth taking was the needle gun, and Lannigan had stolen that already.

The room was small, but it had a bed and a shower. Rayanne locked the door carefully, still burning from the desk clerk's lascivious grin as they had booked a single, and when she turned towards the bed Lannigan was already on it. 'Hey.'

The woman tossed her the needle gun. 'You're on first watch,' she said, wincing as she hauled her unresponsive right leg on to the bed. 'Ow. I'll wake up and take over later.'

Rayanne looked at the gun, turning it over in her hands. The magazine counter read almost empty. 'How come I gotta wait up first?'

There wasn't an answer. She scowled at Lannigan, who was either already asleep or faking it real well, then slumped unhappily into a small plastic chair by the window. 'Those assholes come in here, they can have you, man, I swear to God.'

The lights were turned down low, but still glimmering, which was about as dark as Rayanne really felt comfortable with. Especially since, despite the smoothly faced and painted interior walls, she knew for a fact that the place had been built by structants.

That didn't bother her as much as it used to. When she had first learnt about structant buildings she had been totally grossed out and refused to go into any of them. Once, she had seen a bughouse actually going up, a half-finished structure under an inflatable plastic dome. Most of the covers contractors used were opaque, but this one was quite clear, either for display purposes or a sick joke. Rayanne hadn't known what was going on and had stopped for a good look inside. She had watched the half-building for a good few seconds before she realised that the surface of it was moving.

It was horrible. Millions of structants were squirming over the walls and support beams, each building its own little kind of material, blindly chewing up the sand and metal that had been left for them and breaking it down, spitting it back out again as rapidly hardening polymer. Some made girders, some smooth floors, some walls and window frames. They couldn't make glass or complicated things like electrics or plumbing but they could have the entire structure of a normal-sized house up inside a month.

Maybe people could do it faster, but structant-building didn't require any effort. They would breed on their own until there were enough, build whatever they were programmed for, then commit mass suicide when they were done. The whole process was marvellously easy and cost-effective, now all the molecular biology and genetics work had been done. It made Rayanne feel sick. When she had realised what was going on inside the dome she had got into a screaming fit, right there in the street. Later the guy she had been seeing had thought it was funny to tell her that bughouses always had a few thousand resident structants holed up in the wall cavities, to make repairs. It wasn't true, but it kept Rayanne out of any building that had rounded corners and rippled walls, for a period of years.

At least the owners of the Joy Night had made some effort to cover the fact. Rayanne could relate to that.

Outside, green light from the motel sign spilt across the courtyard, creating ripples of reflection on the swimming pool, among patches of darkness where bits of palm leaves had fallen into the oily water. Lights were on in a couple of the opposite rooms. Somebody was playing music, a steel guitar piece, lazy and mournful and slow. Rayanne listened to it for a while, trying not to let her head drop forward, trying to stay awake, knowing how important it was not to sleep.

She was snoring inside three minutes.

She woke up on the bed, fully clothed, curled up with her jacket collar tugged up around her face and her fists jammed into her armpits. Edges of watery, dusty sunlight had made it past the leather, and there was a coppery taste in her mouth. Her gums often bled while she was asleep.

There was something prodding her in the ribs.

It was the end of Lannigan's cane. Rayanne slapped at it, groggy and uncoordinated. 'Get offa me, man!'

'Will you get up?' That thin, Midwestern voice, whiny and insistent and instantly annoying. 'And what the hell happened last night?'

Rayanne turned over, waving the woman away. She screwed her eyes shut and put her hands over her ears.

'You were supposed to be on watch,' Lannigan snapped. Rayanne listened to her hobbling round to the other side of the bed. 'I woke up at three and you were spark out! What if those guys had come in here?'

Rayanne sat up. 'Lady, if those guys had come in here they would have deleted us whether we were awake or not.' She rubbed her eyes with her fists, yawned, and then looked over at Lannigan.

The woman must have spent some time tidying herself up while Rayanne had been asleep. She had showered all the sweat and dust from her skin, brushed her hair down straight, and changed into a flimsy grey business suit which would have looked quite good on her, if it hadn't been pushed out of shape by the way she was skewed over on to the cane.

Apart from that, and a few minor bruises, she looked almost normal.

Looking at Lannigan all prettied up made Rayanne feel scummy. She swung her legs off the bed and stood up, putting a hand against the wall to keep herself upright until the dancing lights in her vision went away. 'How long have I got?'

Lannigan checked the wall clock. 'I want to be out of here in half an hour.'

'No way, man. Gimme an hour.' Rayanne walked past her, towards the bathroom. Lannigan eased herself on to the vacated bed, then let the cane contract and stood it on the nightstand.

'Forty-five minutes. Any longer and I'm coming in after you.'

Rayanne shrugged. 'Guy at the desk was right about you, man.' She closed the door fast and locked it, shutting out Lannigan's indignant reply.

She couldn't remember the last time she had showered, or worn anything other than the clothes she had on. The face that looked out at her from the mirror above the sink was so streaked with ingrained dirt that she wasn't entirely sure what it should have looked like, and only God knew for sure what was living in her hair.

Her jacket went on to a hook by the door, and the rest of her clothes in the bathtub. When she turned on the taps the water just bounced off the fabric until she opened up some soap sachets and threw them in as well. That began to cut through the grease a little, and the process was cumulative. Rayanne spent a fascinated few minutes just watching the water change colours: she must have been carrying half of Kenya around with her.

She showered, washed her hair, then took her clothes out of the bath and hung them over the heat unit. While they dried she got back into the shower again, and kept on scrubbing until there weren't any sachets left, not of anything. That done, she dried off, dressed, and raked her hair through with the complimentary plastic hairbrush.

Somebody totally different looked out of the mirror this time. She still wasn't going to win any beauty contests: her hair was raggy and her face was too pointy and her jeans had oilstains on the knees. Her clothes felt damp. Her skin was unaccustomed to the scrubbing and itched fiercely. If she tried to walk into a fancy hotel, she would still get thrown out. But at least they wouldn't beat her up first.

When she opened the door Lannigan glanced up at her with the expression of someone who has waited a long time for a particular insect to emerge from its cocoon, only to find that it came out looking very much as it did before. 'Oh,' she said.

Rayanne glared at her. 'What?'

'Nothing.' Lannigan retrieved the cane, heaved herself up, and headed for the door. When she got there she pointed vaguely to where her carryall lay on the floor. 'You wanna get that?'

'Yeah, I'll get it.' She waited until Lannigan was outside, so she'd have a warning if anyone was waiting, then went and picked the carryall up. Just in case she needed anything heavy to hit the *lisiada* with.

* * *

It was early, the morning air still cold and misty. The room they had rented was on the second floor of the motel complex, which was a long, U-shaped double stack of cubes formed around the courtyard and pool. Rayanne followed Lannigan along the balcony and down the short flight of stairs to ground level, scanning the area for skinny white guys with leather coats or Africans in shades. All she saw was trash rolling around the court in complicated, windblown dances.

Lannigan took a while getting down the stairs. Rayanne stuck close behind her, going down a step at a time, feeling exposed and impatient. '*Señora*? You wanna tell me something?'

'Like what?'

'Like why the frag I'm following you around and holding your damn bag?'

Lannigan stepped off the last stair, stopped, and swung herself round. 'If you want to go, go.' She held out her free hand for the carryall.

Rayanne blinked. 'What?'

'Go on. I'm sure you've got other fish to fry.'

'Fish? *Mierda*!' Rayanne scowled and stalked past her. 'I hate it when you talk like that, lady!' She stopped a few yards on, making Lannigan turn again to face her. 'Anyway, those dudes are after me too, remember? They came all the way into a damn police station to drag me out, splashed some poor cop all over the wall, Christ knows what else!' Her voice went up, into a kind of thin yell. 'I *hate* this, man! I shoulda stayed in Nairobi!'

Lannigan just stood there, her lips pursed, her head turned slightly away as though she were waiting for a ranting child to exhaust itself and calm down. Rayanne felt like throwing the carryall at her, but she just dropped it instead. 'Don't you get it, I almost got offed last night! If you hadn't had all that nano-shit inside of you I'd . . . I . . .' She faltered, a tiny voice in the back of her head telling her, Shut up, Rayanne, shut up. 'I mean, we'd both be . . . er . . .'

'You know,' interrupted Lannigan, walking slowly up to her, 'if you always answered your own questions like that you could probably save us both a lot of time.' She reached down and grabbed the carryall, then continued past Rayanne. Left her just standing there, in the courtyard, feeling cold and stupid and frightened, with her hair still wet and yesterday's newszines blowing around her Nikes.

Lannigan stopped at the desk office, but Rayanne didn't want to go in. 'Let's just dump the key and split.'

'No, I want to ask him something.' Lannigan cocked her head to one side. 'What's your aversion, anyway?'

Rayanne shuffled uncomfortably. 'I dunno, man. Way he looked at us last night. Like he thought we were, you know, together? And now we're all showered up –'

'Oh, *please*.' Lannigan screwed up her face, then sighed and shrugged. 'Yokay, stay out here. I won't be long.'

'You crazy?' Rayanne hugged herself and glanced nervously around. 'Cold out here, man. And what if those guys come back?'

Lannigan appeared to consider this for a moment or two, her thin eyebrows up a little and her lips pressed together. 'Well,' she said, shrugging, 'I guess they'd grab you first, and I'd hear you screaming, and that might give me a little time to get away.' She brightened. 'You know, that sounds like a plan.'

'Screw you, man. I ain't stayin' out here.' Rayanne pushed past her, and the glass doors slid open to let her in. The clerk wasn't behind his desk, so she headed for the free-vend coffee machine in the corner and ordered a paper cup of extra strong. Multiple sugar.

Lannigan limped in and leant against the desk. 'Excuse me? Sir, are you there?'

The coffee was rather horrible, but Rayanne was thirsty. She gulped some down, throwing it to the back of her throat so she wouldn't have to taste it. It didn't work. 'Eww.'

She looked up. The *lisiada* was watching her, skewed round with that weird twisting motion of hers, as if her back swivelled more easily than her neck. 'What?'

'Oh, nothing. Just something one of those guys said. I wouldn't worry about it.'

Rayanne opened her mouth, then snapped it shut as the desk clerk wandered into view, rubbing his eyes. When he saw them, his lumpy round face broke into a predatory leer. 'Ah, ladies! I trust you spent a *comfortable* night?'

Lannigan smiled right back and started asking about bus stations. Rayanne went outside.

By the time the *lisiada* limped out the sun was starting to burn the mist away and kick the temperature up. Rayanne was sitting on a low wall outside the motel entrance, with her back against the holosign projector so she couldn't be seen by anyone driving past. She grinned wanly as Lannigan screwed up her face and turned her head away from the light. 'Hey, *señora*. You wanna get yourself a pair of these.'

Lannigan looked at Rayanne's shades, eased herself on to the wall next to her. 'I'd rather blind myself with a spoon.'

There was a period of silence. A ground module whined past, stirring the dust, music thumping from an open window. Rayanne listened to it fade, then said, 'Those two, Swann and . . .'

'Byron?'

'Yeah. Look, I never seen them before, *señora*. I don't know them.'

Lannigan put her head on one side. 'Neither do I,' she said, her voice as flat and dusty as the road. 'But they know us, don't they? Now isn't that strange?'

Rayanne turned away. She couldn't look into those pale eyes for long without feeling as if she was at the wrong end of a microscope. Or a scalpel. 'I've done some stuff around here before. Work, you know?

Maybe it was business,' she said.

The woman blinked. 'Now I'm only guessing,' she murmured, voice low, lips quirked into a sort of conspiratorial smile, 'but would I be right in thinking that some of your "work" might not have been completely within the law? Hm?'

Rayanne shrugged, and then a horrible thought struck her. 'Hey, they didn't mention Embu, did they?'

'Embu? Where the hash comes from?'

Rayanne began gnawing on a fingernail. The drugs still inside her were worth some considerable amount to the Embu Crew, but they were organic, unstable. If somebody fragged her the stuff would begin to break down in pretty short order, and the Crew Papas wouldn't want that. It would make sense for them to get her kidnapped rather than order a simple hit. They would dice her after extraction, make it public and painful and messy, just like with Zenebe. Only worse, because she was a girl.

Maybe Lannigan had crossed the Embu Crew as well. 'We gotta get out of the country, man. Over the border and out.'

'Good plan. The hard part is, we've got to do it without showing up on infonet.' Lannigan rolled her head round and rubbed at the back of her neck. She winced. 'That's how they tracked you down.'

'Oh, man. They got access that far?'

'I couldn't get too much sense out of the desk clerk.' The woman fished around in her jacket pocket and took out a tiny black notebook with a pencil on the side. She flipped it open. 'But, between the propositions and the veiled speculations as to our sexuality, the guy actually came up with a few possibles. One of whom is his brother-in-law, so I think we can safely ditch that.' The pencil made a scratching sound against the paper as she scrubbed out the entry.

Rayanne looked at it. 'That's a permagraph, huh?'

'A couple of clicks that way –' Lannigan waved the

pencil at the north end of the street '– is a bus depot that isn't online. Cash only, so your guess as to the quality of his operation is as good as mine. Unfortunately they don't run weekdays.'

'I got one of those, too. But I kinda bit the end offa mine.'

'Back that way looks better. There's a vehicle dealership, ex-rentals and second-hand bugs. We could get ourselves something small, volt up while we're there. But that's four clicks away.'

Rayanne looked at the pencil, at the notebook, at the little Anglo sitting next to her on the wall with her cane folded up and her bad leg stretched right out. She felt something shift in her head, the connection from one memory tag to another and another . . . 'I got an idea.'

'Don't even think about it.'

'Think about what?'

'Stealing a module.'

Rayanne blinked. 'Who said anything about stealing? Look.' She struggled out of her jacket, ignoring Lannigan's grimace of distaste, then spread it out and began to hunt around in the lining. 'There!'

' "Cough sweets?" '

'No, *there*. Doogie's number.'

Lannigan tilted her head just slightly to look at her. 'And Doogie is . . .?'

Rayanne hesitated. 'A friend,' she said. 'He's in town. I saw him yesterday. He knows people.'

'Do you trust him?'

'I –' Rayanne stopped, her mouth abruptly dry. Lannigan was looking at her, those eyes right on her, as cold and grey as comet ice. There was something alien in that stare, something horrible and analytical and razor-edged. It pinned Rayanne like a butterfly to a board, made her want to turn away, to bolt, just like on the maglev. It stole the breath from her.

'No,' she gasped finally. 'No, I don't.'

'I see.' Lannigan nodded, turned away.

'Lady?' Free at last from that terrible gaze, Rayanne sagged, then sucked in a long breath. 'Doogie's yokay. I don't trust him, but he won't give us up.'

Lannigan gestured down the road. 'There's a diner close by. You can call him from there.' She stood up, leaning hard on the cane.

Rayanne didn't move. '*Señora*? If I'd said yeah . . .'

'Then you would have been wrong.' Lannigan began walking away from her. Rayanne watched her for a moment, then got up to follow, tugging the jacket back on over her thin arms.

Even with the collar up and the black plax soaking up the sun, she found herself shivering.

5
Duty Men

Lannigan had spotted the diner as they drove past the night before. What she had seen flickering in the darkness had made her view the prospect of actually entering the place with little enthusiasm, but daylight was somewhat kinder.

It was a small building, brightly painted, a vague semicircle with its flat side facing the road. There were kitchens up on the second floor, under a collapsible roof that could fold away for parties and open-air barbecues, according to a poster in the doorway. Lannigan blinked at it and wondered what a barbecue was.

Rayanne went to the back and found a booth with a good view of the door. Around the bar, township jive hammered out from concealed speakers, mixing with the smoke and the steam from the coffee machines. Lannigan counted a dozen or so customers, a roughly equal division between those who were up early and those who plainly hadn't been to bed yet.

She folded herself into the booth, let the cane close and put it on the table in front of her. The music, she realised, was ridiculously loud. 'This is a little punishing.'

Rayanne leant closer. 'What?'

'Hold on.' She hunted for a moment, then found a silence slot in the booth wall and stuffed a coin into it. A phased pulse of antisound surrounded the music and muffled it into a distant murmur, built a soft wall of quiet between her and the world. She'd seen someone do that on infonet.

Which made her think about just how much of what she knew came straight from the idiot screen. She scowled at Rayanne. 'Are you hungry?'

The girl shook her head. 'Nah.'

'You look hungry. You should eat something.' She took a cardboard menu from its slot, ran her finger down the list of drinks and dishes. Most of the names were in Swahili, and none meant much to her. She flipped the thing round and shoved it at Rayanne, pointing. 'That, there. What is that?'

'Get offa me, man!' The girl waved her away, a sick look on her face. She began scrambling out of the booth, muttering about calling Doogie. Lannigan watched her back as she retreated. She was ready to call out, to tell her to order something and not look so damned obvious, but Rayanne was already out of the silence field. Lannigan saw her get to the comms booth and lean heavily against the wall with her hand to her head, and then a waitress was blocking her view.

A tall girl with silver wire in her hair, the waitress moved towards Lannigan in eerie underwater silence until she passed through the pulse and let in the jangle of her jewellery and the clicking of boot heels. Lannigan put on a smile and ordered a random handful of items, plus four coffees and an unfeasibly large helping of real sugar. The nanotech still punting about in her bloodstream seemed to be as hungry as she was, giving her a fierce craving for sweet things. She wondered how many of the items she had just bought were desserts, and whether she should worry about putting on weight.

By the time Rayanne got back the food was starting to arrive. Lannigan wolfed her way through a massive sandwich, tasting pickles and meat and a relish that hacked the back of her throat like acid. 'You took your time.'

'Ah, Doogie, you know? Guy kept putting on this fake Chinese accent, saying he was some eatery in Canton.'

Lannigan nodded. 'Professional paranoia, I can live with that.' She started spooning sugar into her first coffee, but stopped when she noticed Rayanne staring. 'What?'

'You want coffee with that?'

'Give me a break, Rayanne. I told you, I've got nanotech.' She gulped the stuff down, then started filling the second with white grains. 'You're sure you don't want any of this food?'

'Nah, but gimme that over there.' Rayanne slid one of Lannigan's cups across the plastic and took a sip. Her face crumpled up. 'Oh man. How'd you get so full of that stuff?'

Lannigan was eating noodles, disappointed at their blandness, relishing the smell of the soup and the way globes of orange oil drifted between slices of spring onion and soya block. 'Shot through the brain.' She flicked the fingers of one hand, miming an explosion. 'Stone dead.'

'Yokay, man, if you don't wanna tell me, fine.' Rayanne folded her arms and sat back, glaring. 'Fine. 'Cause I don't even care, yokay? Jesus.'

Ice cream, biting at her teeth after the hot soup. 'So. Doogie. Did you get him to make any sense at all?'

'Ah, I got the tape off yokay. He's coming over, says he knows this guy who can help us out. Maybe.'

Lannigan didn't know what Rayanne meant by getting 'the tape off', but wasn't about to ask. She scraped up the last dregs of ice cream with her spoon. 'Thank you,' she said, very quietly.

The words sounded odd, but judging by the sudden and bewildered smile they caused on Rayanne's face they must have been highly efficient.

After Lannigan had finished her last two dishes (a pie filled with quite startling curry, and a sad-looking prawn cocktail), her stomach was starting to get warm. She resolved to be a bit more careful with what she ate in future. Her time on hospital food might have been an exercise in culinary boredom, but she had little doubt that only the presence of nanotech in her system was protecting her from a royal case of indigestion.

Useful stuff. She would miss it when it was gone.

Rayanne suggested moving to a table nearer the door, so they would see Doogie arrive. Lannigan didn't wholly understand the necessity of that, but her whispered thanks to the girl had had such a positive effect that she was loath to risk an argument, and so complied. Following her through the smoke and the music, she decided that Rayanne probably hadn't been thanked all that often until now. Well, if the girl could be turned by a little politeness, all the better. It was a small enough price to pay for control.

She had decided to keep Rayanne Hernandez around for a while, hence her lie about Swann. Letting her know that she had been kidnapped simply because the little man thought she was Lannigan's accomplice would have been a sure way of sending her scurrying for cover, but Rayanne seemed easy enough to manipulate. It hadn't taken any more than a basic massaging of the facts, something that Lannigan was getting rather good at.

Her satisfaction evaporated when she followed Rayanne's gaze out of the window, and saw what was pulling up on the diner's forecourt.

'Oh no,' she muttered.

One of the other customers started laughing.

Rayanne was already out of the door. Lannigan fished her carryall from under the table and used the cane to push herself up from the seat. By the time she got on to the forecourt, a man that must have been Doogie Baxter was helping the Latina up into the back of his vehicle.

It was a Desert Rover. Lannigan had seen one advertised, somewhere, and had decided even then that it was quite the ugliest piece of machinery she had ever witnessed. With its ridiculously large and upright windscreen and its four fat tyres sticking out from the sides on articulated axles, it was probably well suited to scrambling around the most unreconstructed terrain Africa had to offer, but that didn't stop the thing looking like a brick.

In terms of condition, the Rover had seen better days. Lannigan wondered how many.

Baxter was leaning against the open door, watching her. 'Awright?' he said.

He was very white, very thin. He wore foil shades hooked over ears that protruded like cup handles. His shirt was horrible. Lannigan felt to make sure she still had the needle gun in the pocket of her suit jacket.

'Mr Baxter.' She limped closer, looking at the head-sized dents along the machine's flank. 'This is . . . extraordinary.'

'Beauty, ain't she?' He slapped the roof affectionately. Dust rose.

'You own this?'

'Nah. Belongs to a mate of mine. He might be able to help you out, see?'

'Mm.'

Rayanne stuck her head out. 'Hey, *señora*! You gonna admire this thing all day or what?'

Lannigan took a long, deep breath, handed Baxter the carryall and climbed awkwardly into the front passenger seat. She jumped as the door slammed closed next to her. 'Rayanne –'

'Don't start on me, man.'

Baxter dropped into the other front seat. 'Stashed your stuff in the back, yokay?' He watched Lannigan wedge the retracted cane between the dashboard and the windscreen. 'Nice.'

'I beg your pardon?'

He gestured. 'Übergen. Pricey.'

'Yes, it was.'

'What happened to your leg, then?'

'Nothing at all,' she said levelly. Which, in its way, was completely true.

Baxter shrugged and started the engine. Lannigan sat back and closed her eyes, feeling quite satisfied again. There were occasions, she had discovered, when it was perfectly acceptable to tell people the truth. As long as they had no chance of believing it.

The Rover was rugged, but it wasn't fast. It didn't have many of the things Lannigan would have expected from a normal ground module, like aircon, or infonet, or GPS. It didn't even have rearcams; in their place were two rectangles of mirrored plastic emerging from the vehicle on stalks. They were simple and effective, and Lannigan rather liked them. She twisted slightly to get a reflection in view, and saw Konza receding from her, a bright cluster of forms behind a dust-grey triangle of road.

Another twist showed her Rayanne: eyes closed, mouth open, hands in her armpits. 'Hey, Rayanne?'

'She's asleep.'

Lannigan glanced at Baxter. 'Just checking.'

'She won't be eating, see. Drugs.'

'Mm.' Lannigan thought she understood. Many addicts lost the ability to digest food, once they got too far down the slope. The thought that Rayanne might have damaged herself to that extent disturbed her, for some reason.

Baxter swung the Rover on to a connecting road, his head weaving left and right on the end of his thin neck. Lannigan waited until he had settled before she said, 'You've known her a long time?'

'Rayanne? Nah, not really.'

'So what's your stake?'

There was a long pause. Baxter made faces and rocked his head about, as though he were wrestling with some internal dilemma. 'Bit complicated. The guy we're going to see, Marcus?'

'Go on.'

'Well, he owes me a favour. Big one.'

'So he asked you to –' She broke off. Baxter was shaking his head.

'He doesn't know about you yet. Thing is, Marcus doesn't like owing favours. Much prefers it the other way round. And I don't like to make the man edgy.'

'Ah.' Lannigan nodded, smiling to herself. 'You're setting him up to pay you back, get things balanced again.'

'Anything for a quiet life,' said Baxter, and hauled the Rover violently off the road.

Lannigan yelped and grabbed the dashboard as the vehicle bounced through a line of bushes. She heard Rayanne's head connect solidly with the window, followed by an explosive curse, and then the bushes were gone and there was nothing in front of her but a vertical drop.

She shut her eyes.

The Rover tipped horribly. The grumble of the hub-drives rose to a whine, then a kind of bouncing snarl. Lannigan felt the vehicle shudder, grind sideways for several metres, then lurch forward. She looked up on reflex and saw grass whipping at the windscreen, a tree trunk scrape past the tyres on her side.

The Rover was skating down a wide escarpment, a vividly angled slope dotted with acacias and vicious-looking rocks. The road was off to Lannigan's right, rising on a series of concrete pillars to cross what looked like a small river valley. It didn't feel all that small – the first part of the slope had been almost vertical, and even now Baxter was only just keeping the Rover under control. The vehicle was convulsing under him.

There was water at the valley floor: a flick of reflection at first, then a rock-strewn torrent. Before Lannigan could speak, the Rover was careering along with its tyres half-submerged in foam.

'Oops,' said Baxter, rather breathlessly. 'Should have turned off a tad earlier.'

Lannigan stared at him. 'A *tad*?'

Rayanne was moaning something in Spanish, holding her head. Lannigan realised she still had both hands clamped over the dashboard. She let go. It took some effort.

The cane had bounced clear into the back seat.

'Oh man,' muttered Rayanne, rubbing the side of her skull. 'Oh, man. Where did that spring from?'

'Wasn't here until about twenty years back. When the weather patterns shunted over.'

Lannigan gave him a look. 'That's not what she meant.' She glanced back over her shoulder. 'You yokay?'

The girl nodded, wincing. 'Until he drives us off another cliff.'

Baxter was grinning. He shot a glance at Lannigan, his foil shades giving her half of his face, half of her own, putting an expression beneath her eyes that had no business being there. 'Anyone wanna do that again?'

Lannigan glared at him, her heart hammering, trying to get her breathing back under control. She was uncomfortably aware that she was too frightened to be as angry as she wanted. 'I hope you did that because Marcus lives down here.'

'Marcus lives all over. But he's sort of visiting.' Baxter steered the Rover out of the stream and on to the bank, the fat tyres bouncing over slabs of wet rock. 'See those trees?'

Lannigan saw a gouge in the valley wall a hundred metres across, a ragged scoop of rock strewn with rubble and trees. Blue gums formed a barrier of waving green and shadow. 'In there?'

'Kind of.' The Rover trundled up to the tree line and stopped, the hubdrives idling down until Lannigan could barely hear them. She squinted through the windscreen. There was something about the patch of forest ahead of her that was odd, but it took her a few seconds to work it out.

Some of the shadows ahead of her were moving in the wrong direction.

It was almost noon. White sunlight carved down through the canopy, through the branches and leaves of the trees, sent fractals of light and shade chasing each other across the bright grass. A few metres in, those same patterns still skated over the leafy ground, but not all of them moved as they should. Lannigan felt she was looking at some kind of illusion, a twisting of perspective. The more she concentrated, the more her eyes began to ache.

'What *is* that?'

'Mimetic camo,' said Rayanne, leaning between the two front seats. 'Something past those trees ain't trees. Doogie?'

'Hold on.' Baxter was fiddling with his wrist chrono, rolling the tiny trackball with the tip of his index finger. Lannigan noticed a sliver of magic tape covering the unit's video pickup, and wondered whether that was what Rayanne had meant about getting 'the tape off.' The stuff would blur the pickup's image, preserving Baxter's anonymity until he chose to strip it away.

Within a few seconds there was a chirrup from the device, and the screen lit up. 'Doogie.'

A man's voice, crisp and quick, with an edge that even the chrono's tinny sounder couldn't disguise. Baxter nodded. 'I borrowed the Rover.'

'Rented. All right, bring it in.'

And the forest grew a door.

She stood aside as Baxter and Rayanne hid the Rover under a wide sheet of camouflage netting, watching as the stuff began to move with a twisted approximation of light through trees. As she waited, the patterns grew more realistic, as if the fabric were regaining an art it had forgotten. Within a minute, the illusion was good enough to send her gaze skating away from the Rover's bulk whenever she tried to focus on it.

The door was screened by more of the same fabric. Baxter held it open and she limped through into pale fluorescent light. Rayanne followed her and when Baxter closed the door she realised that it was *big*, a thick slab of armoured plastic that locked itself hard when it met the frame. She could hear the magnetic bolts firing home.

'Command post,' Baxter said, walking past her. 'Korean, from the war.'

Lannigan didn't know which war, but she wasn't about to display her ignorance. She peered around the chamber, at the grey plastic walls, the mesh floor, the luminescent ceiling panels. If the rest of the post was anything like this, the Koreans must have had a very dull war indeed.

The chamber was big enough to put a couple of Rovers in.

There was one other door. Baxter keyed it open and motioned Lannigan through. She stepped back to let Rayanne walk in. If the girl wanted to be trusting, so be it. There was every possibility that they were walking into a spider's web, and it made sense to throw in a bug and see if anything unpleasant came scuttling down the line. Baxter was close enough, and the needle gun was still in her pocket.

From beyond the door, Rayanne said, 'Hey. Wow.'

Lannigan tilted her head at Baxter. 'After you.'

He grinned and took off his shades, making his face look open, naked. The shades rolled up into a silvery tube the size of a cigarette. He put the tube into the pocket of his awful shirt and stepped through the doorway. 'Mind the step.'

She waited two heartbeats, then followed.

The next chamber was larger, the ceiling higher. Aluminium-framed folding worktops had been arranged along one wall, stacked with an array of screens, keyboards, CPU blocks. Half a dozen more flatscreens had been epoxied to the wall above the worktops, trailing a nest of cables on to the floor. There were a few seats: camping stools, foldouts, a plastic deckchair.

The place looked thrown together. Lannigan sniffed. 'The Koreans lost, I take it?'

'It isn't much, but I call it home.'

It was the voice from Baxter's chrono, but spared electronic reproduction it was as rich and dark as polished mahogany. Lannigan turned.

A man had emerged from a nearby hatchway. He was tall, as tall as Baxter, and his skin was so black it was almost blue. Neat braids of hair hung down to the collar of a suit as white and crisp as origami, worn over a black silk shirt and tie. He gave Lannigan a smile, a theatrical little bow.

'Marcus Gray, at your service.' He straightened, but kept his eyes on hers. They were very dark. 'Doogie, what have I told you about bringing your dates home? We haven't even been introduced.'

Baxter scratched his head nervously. 'Er, yeah, hi, Marcus. Look –'

Gray strode abruptly over to Rayanne, snatched up her hand and kissed the back. Quick and fluid, like a dancer. Watching him made Lannigan feel small and awkward and broken.

'And you are?' he asked, his voice honey.

'This is Rayanne, Rayanne Gatita.' Baxter glanced quickly at Rayanne, who was staring at Gray in amazement. 'And this –'

'Cassandra Lannigan, sir.' Lannigan stepped forward. She saw Gray's eyes flick down to the cane, then back up, almost imperceptibly.

'Charmed, I'm sure.'

'That's a very interesting accent, sir. Where is that? England, somewhere?'

'Dear lady –' Gray smiled '– I don't have an accent. Everyone else has an accent.' And then he whipped round to face Baxter, his smile gone, his face a mask of barely suppressed fury. 'What are they doing here?'

'It's business.' Baxter stuffed his hands into his pockets. 'Kinda.'

'Really.' Gray turned to Lannigan and gave her the smile again. He could switch it on and off like a bulb. 'Ladies, if you would excuse us. Doogie!'

The last word was snapped out, edged. Gray whirled as he said it and marched out of the door, with Doogie following. The Londoner gave Lannigan a hopeless glance, and then they were gone.

'Oh, man,' Rayanne whispered. 'What the hell did we just walk into?'

Lannigan listened hard, hearing muffled argument from behind the door. 'Extra-legal transportation of some kind or another. What do you think, gunrunning?' she said.

'Could have a lab out back.' Rayanne stuffed her hands into her pockets. 'I've heard about this Gray dude, once or twice. People say he's into a bit of everything, yeah? Like a fixer. Never knew Doogie was tight with him. Hey . . .' The girl was peering at the flatscreens on the wall. 'This is where we came in. Musta been watching us the whole time.'

'Doogie must be hoping the guy can pack us in alongside his usual cargo. I wonder . . .' Lannigan glanced about and spotted a third door, opposite the screens. It was partially open. 'Wait here a second.'

'Hey, where are you –' Rayanne cut off as Lannigan gestured at her, but bunched her fists helplessly and started bouncing on her Nikes, mouthing. Lannigan waved her away, then limped over to the door and pushed it open.

A short corridor, with hatches on either side. There was a larger door at the end, also showing a few centimetres between edge and frame. In the gap, blue light snapped and flickered.

She threw a look over her shoulder, saw only Rayanne's histrionics, and crept forward, putting the cane down slowly with each step to muffle its clicking. The floor mesh was soft under her feet, some kind of foamy plastic, presumably to deaden the sound of Korean army boots.

If anyone emerged from one of the hatches, she would ask them where the restroom was.

She reached the door at the end of the corridor and put her eye to the gap. Beyond was a chamber the size of the diner, or bigger. There was oil on the floor, the stink of ozone and burnt insulation in the air. And packaging, the clean plastic smell of new goods.

Under the light, ziggurats of crates hugged the walls, their steps and edges softened by draped tarpaulins. Two ground-effect trucks hunched in front of a massive corrugated hatchway, flat black paintwork sucking at the light, flatbeds piled with interlocked crates. Men and women in white coveralls were readying the things, lashing down the loads with polymer webbing. There was the spit and spark of heavy-gauge volt hydrants, ill-maintained.

Little chance of hitching a ride on one of the trucks, Lannigan observed. The vehicles looked compact and utterly efficient, their windowless cockpits just large enough for a single pilot, who would no doubt view an infrared world through virtual-reality headsets and satellite guidance. Smooth slabs of equipment mounted above the aprons looked a lot like weapons packs.

All the techs seemed occupied. She slipped through the door, wishing she was more agile, and ducked behind the nearest mountain of crates. Gray's cargo was too big for drugs. Lannigan lifted a flap of tarpaulin to peer at the boxes beneath. She saw coloured cardboard packaging, a diagram of features, the sudden vertigo of a hologram logo.

'Looking in the wrong places,' said Gray, very close behind her, 'can be a good way of losing your eyes.'

Lannigan straightened and raised her eyebrows at him. 'A music system?' She looked around, trying to multiply the value of a single high-end chipplayer by the number of crates ranged against the walls and already packed on to the trucks. 'Quite an operation for shifting stolen consumer tech.'

He was studying her, coldly, his arms folded. 'Just what *are* you doing here, Ms Lannigan?'

'Exactly the same as you, Mr Gray. Attempting to transport certain items without too many people noticing.'

'Interesting analogy.'

She glanced over at the trucks. 'I guess this is why you're here, hmm? Overseeing tonight's little trip. I take it there's no chance of a couple of extra boxes –'

'Sorry. I don't do people. It's too risky – if this lot gets picked up by PATCo I've lost some merchandise, but nothing that can't be covered. Quite a different matter to be found transporting wanted felons.'

Lannigan blinked, slightly puzzled. 'They'd trace the theft back, surely?'

'Theft is such an ugly word. Besides, all this is perfectly legitimate, as long as it stays in Kenya.' Gray put an arm round her shoulders and led her gently away. 'My dear, you really don't have much notion of how this country works, do you?'

'I've been away.'

He glanced down at her cane. 'I'm surprised you aren't better informed. Now, if you wouldn't mind running along, I really have quite a lot of work to do.' He gave her a gentle shove in the direction of the door, then moved away, striding over towards the trucks.

Lannigan stood where she was, wondering. PATCo was the Pan-African Tariff Corporation: a private company that imposed trade restrictions between Africa's multiplicity of independent states. Set tariffs, collected duty . . . It had featured on her newsfeeds in relation to a minor bribery scandal. Not that such matters were exactly rare in Africa, but for some reason the incident had stayed in her memory.

Why did Gray keep looking at her cane?

The fixer was talking to one of his techs, a rapid exchange in Swahili and English and what sounded like German. Lannigan was just trying to make sense out of the polyglot when a spindly figure scrambled into the bay, dancing spasmodically over the trailing cables. It was Baxter, and he wasn't happy.

'Marcus? Got company.'

Marcus Gray at a stroll was faster than Lannigan could go. At a sprint, he was gone before she could speak.

She caught up with him in front of the screens, with Rayanne on one side of him and Baxter on the other. The three of them were watching the security output Rayanne had pointed out earlier. Gray was pointing, tapping at the plastic. 'You're sure.'

Rayanne nodded. 'Ain't gonna forget them in a hurry.'

Lannigan squeezed into the line, shunting the Latina out of the way. 'What?' She stared at the screen.

There was a grey rental ground module parked just outside the tree line. Two men stood next to it: Byron with his jacket slung over one shoulder, Swann sweating with his shirtsleeves rolled up. The smaller man was fiddling with a wrist chrono. His hands were bandaged.

Lannigan felt cold and sick. She looked hopelessly at Gray. 'How much did they pay you?'

He raised a finger at her. 'Don't,' he snapped, 'be stupid.' He shifted his attention back to the screen. 'There's no visual pickup this end, but I would advise you not to speak while he's on the line.'

She nodded, and Swann's angular face appeared on the adjacent screen. 'Gray? Gotta talk to you, man.'

'*Caveat emptor*, my friend.'

'Huh?' Swann's face turned off-screen, presumably so Byron could explain the Latin to him. Lannigan was amazed at how clear and steady the picture was. The chrono's video pickup must have been tracking his image, keeping it centralised. 'Oh, right. Look, it's something else, yokay? Important.' A hand came up and wiped across the forehead. 'C'mon, Marcus, it's steaming out here.'

'All right. Bring it in.' Gray killed the connection with a keypress: Swann's face disappeared. 'Doogie, go out and help them cover that little bug of theirs. And you two –' He turned to Lannigan and Rayanne. 'You two go through that door, close it, and wait. Don't move. Don't speak. And don't touch anything, or I might forget the fact that you aren't here. Understand?'

The internal doors weren't soundproof. Lannigan crouched next to Rayanne in the chamber, their heads close, each with an ear pressed to the plastic.

Their noses were almost touching, but Lannigan chose to ignore that.

She realised that she was gripping the cane like a sword. The expansion mechanism was very strong – if things turned ugly it could make an effective weapon. Not that, if Gray decided to give them up, having such a weapon would make very much difference at all.

Still, he hadn't yet. So far, he had offered Byron and Swann a cup of tea.

Swann had started to ask for a beer instead, but Byron had cut him off. 'We don't have time for refreshments, Gray.'

'So it seems. Well, I'm afraid I can't supply you with that second Tigercat. I moved out of that side of the business a few months ago.'

So Gray *had* been a gunrunner, then. Lannigan allowed herself a brief smile, then wondered how she knew what a Tigercat was.

Swann said, 'We're not buying anything, Marcus. We're looking for somebody.'

'Some*body*?'

'Yeah, couple of friends of ours. They went AWOL yesterday, and we know they're trying to get under the wire. Thought they might have come to you.'

'Really?' Gray's voice moved away. Lannigan strained to listen, imagining the man wandering around. 'I'm rather flattered. Pity I can't help you.'

'Can't or won't?' That was Byron. He sounded as though he was trying to get angry, trying to force some vestige of emotion out through the implants and the surgery. Or maybe he already was angry, but the rage couldn't claw its way out. Either way, Lannigan found herself pleased that she was on the opposite side of a door to the E-human, even if it was only a centimetre of impact plastic.

'You haven't seen them?' Swann again. 'You sure?'

'Positive. Sorry. I don't get many visitors, not if I can help it. But just in case anyone does turn up, who should I be looking for?'

'Two women,' said Byron.

'Scraggy Latina kid, stripy face, about one-eighty tall. I'd guess, what, sixteen or so? Calls herself Rayanne Gatita, but her name's Hernandez.'

Lannigan flicked a glance at Rayanne. The girl looked angry and hurt. 'Sixteen,' she mouthed.

'Sounds quite charming,' said Gray. 'And the other?'

'Ah, name's Lannigan. One-sixty or so, red hair, maybe thirty-five. Bad leg, face like an axe edge.'

Rayanne brightened. Lannigan scowled and turned her attention back to the door. Beyond the plastic, Byron was telling Gray just how bad her leg was, what kind of cane she used.

The cane. Lannigan turned the thing over in her hands, running her fingertips along the barrel, the edges of the wings, the logo. Gray had some interest there, of that she was sure. But was it the cane itself that had his fancy, or something else?

Maybe the man had a disability fetish. Stranger things existed.

It was raining by the time Byron and Swann left the command post; Lannigan could hear the drops slamming against the roof, on to the trees and the camo netting. The sound was a whisper, almost inaudible, but must have been a howling torrent to have registered at all through the thick plastic.

Rayanne heard it too. 'Hope he don't send us out in

that,' she muttered, straightening up.

Lannigan put the cane to the floor and used it to push herself upright. It seemed a long way up – she had been crouching there for a quarter-hour or more, and her right leg was practically numb. She leant against the door, breathing hard. 'That was as close to those two as I ever want to be again.'

There was a rapping at the door. Lannigan moved away as it opened to admit Doogie Baxter's round head. 'You're all clear.'

Lannigan stepped back and waved Rayanne through. Rayanne gave her a look, as though she knew exactly how Lannigan's mind was working. ' "Axe edge". Yeah, I can see that,' said the girl.

'Yes. Well, it's nice to see they got your mental age spot on.' She followed the girl out, went straight for the deckchair and dropped into it. Watched Gray's eyes as she retracted the cane.

The man was perched on one of his folding tables. Lannigan saw his eyes on the cane, then he saw her studying him and looked away. Almost fast enough. 'Mr Gray, what's your connection with Übergen Aktien-Gesellschaft?'

He sighed. 'Am I so transparent?'

'Either that or you have an unhealthy interest in top-quality meditech.'

Gray looked momentarily surprised. 'My, you are the happy customer, aren't you?'

Lannigan thought about telling him she was swarming with the company's nanotech, but decided against it. 'They've supported me so far.'

Gray grinned, wide and full of teeth. 'You and me both. Ever heard of Vivadyne?'

'Only on that box I saw.'

'Vivadyne and Übergen get on like nitro and glycerine. Been trying to drive each other out of the market for years. Übergen pays PATCo to impose massively unfair tariffs on Vivadyne goods, wrecking their profits. Ditto Fushigina

Systems, Collapsar, PLN . . . You know, I'm really rather honoured to have a fellow beneficiary walking about under my roof.'

Lannigan felt stunned. Marcus Gray, with his crisp French suit and Oxbridge accent and trucks full of consumer tech, was running under the front line of an African corporate war.

She looked down at the cane. Übergen had put her head back together. Their shares in the human genome had facilitated the cloned implants pulsing between her ears; their nanotech was reknitting her nervous system. She owed the corporation her life. 'What about those two?'

'Who, the Odd Couple? Why, I'm sure they have no connection to Übergen whatsoever.'

'I didn't mean that.'

'Yeah,' snapped Rayanne. 'You seem pretty chummy with those assholes.'

Gray shrugged. 'I sold them a Tigercat missile eight months ago. Oh, and a launch tube, but no guidance system. You just can't get the parts, you know.'

'And since?'

'Oh, they called up once or twice, trying to get hold of a second missile and such. After a time they stopped calling, and, as I said, I've moved out of that side of the business.' He smiled disarmingly. 'They're really quite harmless.'

'Harmless enough to need missiles. Harmless enough to send one of their goons after me with a flechette gun.' Lannigan forced herself up. '*Harmless*? Jesus!' Gray revolted her, suddenly. She spun on her heel and began stamping away.

'You know who they work for?' asked Rayanne.

'Anyone. They're part of a data-haulage plex. Based in Mexico, I believe, but then they do have this habit of moving around.' He made an extravagant gesture. 'Multiple offices, who knows?'

'Mexico?' Rayanne sounded shocked. 'They came right down here from Mexico? *Hostia Puta* . . .'

Baxter was snapping his fingers. 'Living something . . .'

'Living Glass MLC. My dear boy, your memory is appalling.'

Lannigan blinked. 'What kind of a name is that?'

'A plex name. Something to do with the properties of active silicon, I would assume.'

So Byron and Swann were part of a micro-limited company, sitting in Mexico and hauling data around for anyone who would pay. Kotebe too, most likely, probably as muscle, and the dark-haired girl in the Milimani. An oriental woman lying dead alongside her when the police arrived: Byron had mentioned Angel, and Kitsumi. A plex could run quite nicely with six members. Small meant fast when it came to microcorps, and speed was what plexes relied on to stay in business. Big companies like Übergen and Vivadyne and Fushigina Systems were dinosaurs, carnosaurs, huge and powerful and sharp of tooth. Plexes darted between their feet like rodents, getting fat on scraps.

Lannigan smiled. She knew it wasn't a nice smile, but she did it anyway. 'Living Glass,' she whispered. 'Rayanne? Can you run an infonet search?'

The girl started. 'What? Yeah, I guess . . .'

'If we're talking about a plex, they'd have to be registered, wouldn't they?'

'The plex registry.' Rayanne was on her feet. 'Hey, you think we could . . .?'

Lannigan felt something surge inside. She had been running blind for so long she had forgotten what it was like to open her eyes, but now she had a name, a connection. A way in.

It wasn't much, but she had her fingers around it now. If she squeezed hard enough, maybe she could make it bleed.

6
Rat Run

Marcus had a watch; not a chrono, but a real, honest-to-God pocket watch with a silver case and a fob chain. Rayanne could hear it ticking from across the room, especially when the lid was open.

It was open now. 'Nineteen minutes.'

Lannigan prodded Rayanne in the shoulder. 'Quit dawdling. This is costing me money.'

'I ain't dawdling.' Rayanne glared at the screen, at the search-engine display coming up empty for the third time. 'I'm going as fast as I can. There just ain't nothing here.'

'Try the services board again.'

'What did you get?' That was Doogie, coming in through the back hatchway with a four-pack of Tusker in his hands. He cracked one of the beers and passed it to Rayanne: she grabbed it without looking away from the screen and took a good, long swallow. Tusker wasn't her usual brand, but it was deliciously cold. '*Nada,*' she muttered.

Marcus was at the far end of the worktop, monitoring Rayanne's progress through infonet on a small and highly illegal piece of surveillance hardware. With its heavy, olive, drab casing and crude display, the device looked suspiciously army surplus, as though it had come with the command post as a fixture. Rayanne's screen was a standard Fushigina commercial setup; it was a couple of years old, and a little clunky, but that suited her. She hadn't surfed like this for a while anyway.

The Fushigina could drive a small army of output devices – remote-action VR headsets, retinal laser projectors, holograms – but like most people Rayanne preferred the flatscreen. She didn't trust the idea of a gizmo firing lasers into her eyes, and VR made her queasy.

Doogie sat down in the seat next to her, on the other side from Lannigan. 'You try the plex registry?'

'All of 'em. Started with Mexico and took it right up to the international net. Even tried cislunar. Checked out the services board, widebanded a callout on public access – nothing.'

'That's crazy.'

'Tell me about it.' Rayanne threw up her hands and sat back. 'If they don't show, how the hell do you find them? It's stupid, man. Real bad for business.'

'Maybe it's more obscure,' muttered Lannigan. 'Go through two or three unrelated addresses, something like that.'

'Too complicated,' snapped Marcus. 'It would lose them customers. Nineteen and a half.'

Rayanne gave him the sour eye, but his attention was fixed on his screen, watching the shifting interplay of graphics that would warn him should any interested party get too close to the command post's uplink. He kept his free hand very close to a heavy-looking knife switch bolted to the worktop. Rayanne wasn't sure exactly how much of the system that switch would cut, but she found herself wishing she had brought a flashlight.

'Screw it. I'm jacking out.' She killed the connection and sat back. Marcus checked his watch a final time, then snapped the lid closed and slipped it back into his top pocket. He looked across at Lannigan and smiled. 'Shall we call it a round hundred?'

The *lisiada* glared at him with utter venom. 'I'm going to the bathroom. Do I need to rent that, too?' She got up and hobbled out of the door.

Marcus raised his eyebrows at Rayanne. 'What a charming person. Tell me, wherever did you find her?'

'Nairobi. Marcus, you sure about that name?'

He looked wounded. 'My dear, I never forget a customer.'

'Pity you didn't get a forwarding address, huh.'

Marcus shrugged elegantly. 'I don't like to pry. Not unless I have a very good reason to do so. Living Glass wanted to be secretive, even down to insisting on cash, and so I complied.'

Rayanne looked at the floor. 'Yeah, but –'

'My dear, it's a business thing.' He leant close. 'Ask too many questions and people start to get edgy. I don't like to make my customers edgy. Besides, if people want something they come to me, not the other way around. I travel too light to go keeping dossiers.' He flicked a glance at Doogie. 'Unlike some.'

Doogie had cracked another Tusker and was downing it enthusiastically, his Adam's apple bouncing as he swallowed. He wiped the back of his hand across his mouth. 'Am I the only one who finds all this a bit iffy?'

Rayanne had been thinking about that herself. So far, none of the node AIs she could access would admit to ever hearing of Living Glass MLC. That in itself was odd – the ID wasn't the most imaginative ever devised, and there were a lot of plexes out there. Almost any handful of hopefuls could register as a microcorporation, so long as one of them was willing to sign on as CEO and take any legal heat. Rayanne was expecting to find a hundred Living Glasses on the list and end up having to cross-reference with the names Lannigan had given her.

Wrong answer. It was as if the ID was off limits.

Rayanne slipped the headset off and got up, taking her beer with her. Her stomach was beginning to hurt again, and the implications of the failed search made her edgy. If Marcus wasn't just jerking her around about this Living Glass setup, somebody had travelled all the way from Mexico to East Africa to get their hands on her. That was scary enough, but now it looked as though those same people had effected some sort of selective wipe through infonet, erasing their own name from any place she could get to.

If that was true, if she was being hunted by someone with the ability to dive right under the surface of the global comms network and hide, then she was in more trouble than she could really grasp. In that light, the Embu Crew suddenly seemed warm and rather fatherly.

She shivered, picked her jacket off the floor and shrugged into it, passing the beer from one hand to another as she did so. Something pricked at her memory when she did that, but she ignored it, unwilling to be distracted. It was getting hard to stay on track, to think about what she was doing instead of the drugs in her stomach or the last time she ate.

A clicking made her glance up. Lannigan was wandering back in, looking as sour as ever. 'I take it we're still dead in the water?'

Rayanne nodded. She finished her beer and squeezed the can until it folded. 'Name ain't worth shit, man. We're screwed.'

Lannigan sniffed at her. 'Mr Baxter,' she said. 'Any thoughts?'

Doogie shook his head. 'Sorry.'

'So am I. Mr Gray?'

'Yes,' said Marcus, getting up. 'You have my condolences. Now, if you will excuse me, I really must be getting on.' He went for the door, brushing past Lannigan on the way.

The woman twisted to glower at him. 'Better get those wagons rolling, hm?'

'No rest for the wicked.' The door closed after him, the whisper of plastic against sealant.

Lannigan dropped back into her chair. 'That's it then. Welcome back to square one.'

Rayanne's memory was still itching. She gave in and tried to figure out what it was she should be doing, but the clues skidded away from her. 'Wait up, man –'

'Maybe they got themselves bumped right off the register, broke some protocol . . .' Lannigan had her elbows on the worktop, chin cupped in her small hands. 'Maybe all the sysops got together and pretended they never existed.'

'What about the other missile?' asked Rayanne quietly.

Lannigan raised an eyebrow at her. 'Hm?'

'Well, Marcus went past that bit kinda quick, but he said they wanted a second missile and stuff, or something like that. I was just wondering, if they couldn't get it from him, maybe they'd go someplace else.'

Doogie frowned and scratched his ear thoughtfully. 'Could be. Marcus ain't the only fixer in Kenya.'

'Are you going to tell him, or shall I?' sniffed Lannigan.

Rayanne scrambled out of her jacket, spread it out on the worktop and began poring over the inner lining. 'There's gotta be something like that in here. Zenebe was always into that shit, like how he was the big mover and shaker . . . Who's Gabby Sparrow?'

Doogie drew a long white forefinger swiftly across his throat. 'Bought the farm about six months ago. Tried supplying the male-rights people in Congo, and the Amazon League strung him up by his –' He broke off, seeing the way Lannigan and Rayanne were looking at him. 'Well, they did him in.'

'Scratch one fixer,' said Lannigan. 'Any others?'

Rayanne chewed her lip. 'Broca? Does that mean anything?'

Doogie made a kind of sucking, whistling noise. 'Don't say that name too loud around here, yeah? Marcus and Broca are not the best of buddies, if you catch my meaning.'

'No, Doogie, I don't,' said Rayanne.

'Look, you know that old saying, the sky's only got room for one sun? Well Broca and Marcus both think the sun shines out of their respective seat cushions. They've been trying to edge each other out for ages.'

Lannigan's eyebrows went up. 'No wonder he skipped over Swann's shopping list. Ten to one Broca got the better end of the deal.' She looked across at Rayanne. 'Looks like our next step.'

'Ay? Are you crazy?' Doogie stared at her, horrified. 'Marcus'll kick my arse if you get Broca into this!'

'Yeah, well. Marcus is busy.' Rayanne went back to the screen and sat down, snugging the headset back on with the mike positioned at lip level. She grinned. 'So step aside and let the girl go through.'

She laced her fingers, stretched until her knuckles cracked, then yelped as a big brown hand came down hard on her shoulder.

'Well. Isn't this the little party?' Marcus was right next to her, his face stormy. 'Didn't Mummy ever tell you not to play with other people's toys?'

Rayanne's fingers were still knotted together. She tugged them free. 'We gotta talk to Broca, man. It's important.'

'I don't doubt. Doogie?' Marcus straightened. 'What have you been telling them?'

Doogie spread his hands helplessly. 'They were just asking about Broca, that's all. Wondering if we could get to Living Glass through her.'

'Not through my uplink, you don't.' He folded his arms and glared at Rayanne. 'I've had enough trouble with that delightful lady in the past. You want to go calling her up, I suggest you find a public comm – that uplink stays dead until you and your acidic friend are *very* far from here.'

The Rover was hot inside, almost suffocating, and it smelt musty. Rayanne sat in the driver's seat, smoking a Crazy Eights and watching rain course down the windscreen.

She had sat in some nice vehicles in her time, and could even remember a few of them. She had once spent some time in New York – a summer, maybe two – where local resistance to the environmental-control laws had meant that not all the internal-combustion vehicles had been replaced by electric drives or hub motors. They had cars there: not buggy little ground modules but actual cars, long and wide and sexy, with throaty fuel-burning engines and wide, hot exhaust pipes to blow smoke all over the guy behind you.

Rayanne could see the attraction; after all, New York was a long way from any ecosystem implosions, and distant problems often seem smaller. The people she knew there hadn't cared much about a bit of smog, as long as you could go outside without a mask on most days.

She had some good, if hazy, recollections about New York, and especially some of the guys she had dated there. But things must have turned bad after a while because, when she tried to remember how or when she had moved on, she came up against a familiar wall of chemical fog, a comfortable amnesia that smelt of drugs. It didn't bother her. If she had crushed the memory it must have been worth crushing, and she was obviously better off without it.

Most of the cities she had stayed in had bowed to environmental pressure years before she had been born, and given up their gas-driven gridlocks in favour of cleaner and cheaper modes of transport. Some, like Rio, had banned private transport altogether, but even in the more liberal conurbations the human love affair with cars had waned somewhat. Not due to the eco-disasters they had caused, but because it was hard to be proud of your module when it looked like a little polycarbon egg on legs. Affordable motors weren't all that great at hauling a lot of weight around, so compact two-seaters were the norm. And they all, barring colour, looked the same.

The Rover was at least different. She could forgive it a lot for that.

The door to the command post banged open. Rayanne watched Lannigan emerge: she was limping quickly across the sodden, bouncing ground, her suit jacket off and held over her head like a miniature tent. The fabric seemed to repel water as well as keep Lannigan cool in the sun: when the *lisiada* hauled open the door and got in beside her she gave the jacket a shake and all the rainwater just skated right off on to the floor.

Rayanne sniffed. 'Marcus gonna charge me for sitting in his Rover?'

'*My* Rover,' said Lannigan. She sounded angry and tired.

'You bought this? How much?'

'Too much. It helped calm him down. He isn't going to throw us out into the mud, at least for a while.' She stretched, rolling her head round. 'Besides, if all else fails I thought maybe we could drive this to Mombasa.'

Rayanne nodded miserably and stubbed the cigarette out on the window frame. Lannigan gave her a look, but she ignored it. 'What about this Broca thing?' Rayanne asked.

'Well, we might have something going there after all. I can't say for sure, but I think Mr Gray might have more reason to dislike Broca than he's willing to admit.'

'Yeah?' That was interesting. Rayanne looked at Lannigan and remembered how she'd felt back at the Joy Night, that icy gaze carving into her like a blade. Judging by the expression on the Anglo's face, Marcus might have felt the cold touch of that particular knife, too. 'What you talk him into?'

'Rayanne, I'm surprised at you.' A smile quirked at the corner of Lannigan's mouth. 'As if.'

'I don't know where Broca runs her operation from,' said Marcus, stalking unhappily through the command post.

'Any more than she knows the same about me. We're all rather careful about that kind of thing.'

'I can rhyme with that.' Rayanne was right behind him, staying close, with Doogie next to her. Lannigan was puffing away in the background, trying vainly to keep up. 'Gotta protect your interests, yeah?'

'Hm. However, I have located one of her storage depots, just a small one. You won't find anything of great value there. It's just a lockup for goods of dubious parentage, shall we say.' He stopped at a hatch. Rayanne peeked past him and saw that the door was heavily armoured with thick slabs of polymer, the surface bulging at equidistant points round the edge. Magnetic bolt housings, she guessed, and a keypad lock. Whatever this hatch had been originally designed to protect, it must have been important.

Marcus saw her looking. 'Active shielding with a phased magnetic pulse,' he explained. 'In case of EMP drops.'

Rayanne nodded sagely, as though she had some idea of what the man was talking about. She watched him key in a long code, then step back as the door shuddered in its frame. Behind her, Lannigan caught up and sagged against the wall, gasping. 'Do we really have to move everywhere at a sprint, Mr Gray?'

The hatch swung inward. Rayanne saw how thick it was. 'Woah. So what did those two assholes get from Broca anyway?'

'I haven't the faintest idea.' Marcus reached into the compartment and came out with a small aluminium briefcase. 'But I do know that they were trying to track down a Facehunter on easy terms.'

Doogie whistled. 'Blimey,' he said. 'No wonder you didn't keep their records.'

Rayanne shot Lannigan a puzzled glance, but the *lisiada* looked like she had other things to think about. She turned to Doogie instead. 'Face what-er?'

'Facehunter.' Marcus touched a control and the

armoured hatch swung back to seal the compartment. The latches punching home sounded like distant gunfire. 'Class-A prohibited software. Even being in possession of one can land you in some very unpleasant places.'

'Only the cops are supposed to have it,' said Doogie. 'It's the part of lawnet that checks all the security feeds in a given area and screams blue murder if it sees your face. Track you down like a bloodhound, that will.'

'They've got one,' Lannigan muttered absently, staring off into space. 'I heard them talking about it in Konza. That's what they used to find Rayanne . . .'

There was a long silence. Then Marcus let out a breath. 'Well,' he said. 'I suppose that rather gives the lie to the idea of Living Glass just moving data for their keep, doesn't it?'

The more Rayanne found out about Living Glass MLC, the more unhappy she got. By the sound of things, they were so tooled up with weapons-grade software that they made the Embu Crew look like a bunch of high-school net pranksters. If Byron and Swann had access to something like this Facehunter package, it wasn't hard to imagine them wiping their name from the plex registry to hide from her. That was just small beer – with a Facehunter they could find her anywhere, hack into a security-camera feed to get a shot of her and then send a billion copies of it crawling out through infonet, tireless little spiders of data hunting for nothing except a face that matched her own.

She wondered where they had gotten their original image from. Probably Nairobi station, she decided, but it didn't really matter. They had her now, and there wasn't anywhere she could run to where they couldn't see her.

The thought was terrifying. She took a big swallow of Tusker to steady her nerves, then nodded at Marcus. 'Yokay, man. I'll do it.'

The four of them had returned to the operations chamber, the one with the worktops and the screens.

Marcus had opened the briefcase and was unpacking the contents. 'Attagirl.' He smiled. 'Once you're inside, you'll need this.'

He handed her a flat slab of silvery material, featureless but for a tiny optical port on one edge. It was small, no bigger than two cigarette packets side by side, but it was heavy. 'What is it?'

'It's called a Line Rat. Broca will keep some kind of terminal in that lockup of hers, for stock control if nothing else. This will run past any encryption and slave her coreframe to the terminal. Then you can look at whatever you want.'

'And mess up anything with your name on it, right?' Rayanne peered into the optical port. 'Why you call it a rat?'

'Because it's got a rat's brain inside. Be careful!' He snatched it out of the air as she dropped it. 'This is worth more than you are!'

Rayanne's skin crawled. 'Rat's brains? What the frag?'

'Two grams of cerebral tissue cloned up from lab rats, grown on to a superconducting lattice.' Marcus gave the Line Rat back to her, placing it firmly in her hands. 'It just makes the computer inside more efficient, that's all. Better at solving labyrinths.'

Doogie was looking at the slab with a wary expression on his face. 'Efficient ain't the word.'

'Yeah,' Rayanne muttered, feeling vaguely sick. 'I think "ecch" is the word, man.'

'Sod that. Biocomps were banned by the UN treaty. Plus the fact that what you've got there is just a tad more illegal than Facehunter . . .' said Doogie.

'Yes, well, that's between you, me, and the AI board.' Marcus gave Doogie an evil grin. 'Besides, in an hour or so it will be Broca's problem, won't it?'

Driving the Rover was more difficult on the road than it was cross-country. Rayanne found herself keeping the speed lower than she would have liked, just to accommodate the wide spacing of the wheels. 'Steering's kinda mushy.'

'The fluid suspension leaks,' said Lannigan sourly. 'Take a left up here.'

Rayanne angled the joystick, steering the Rover across three lanes of unlit road and on to the junction. They had waited until nightfall before making the trip, and now the darkness seemed absolute, the moon hidden behind heavy clouds, the cones of her headlamps illuminating vast clouds of whining bugs.

Marcus had assured them that there would be no one around the lockup at this hour. Despite this, Doogie had taken Rayanne to one side while Marcus wasn't looking, and pressed a tatty Swiss army knife into her hand. 'All I could find at short notice,' he had whispered. 'Not much, but if you twist it . . .'

The knife was in her pocket, alongside the cold and uncomfortable weight of the Line Rat.

The access road swung drunkenly between a series of low hills. As she rounded the base of one Rayanne saw a metallic gleam in the darkness to her right: a long chainlink fence angled out of nowhere, hugging the roadside for as far as her lights would penetrate and beyond. 'Hey, is this it?'

'I guess. Slow down a little, see if we can find a gate or something.'

Behind the chainlink were rows of low, angular shapes. Some huddled in little pools of arclight but most were dark – black cutouts in the gloom. Rayanne eased back on the throttle bar.

There were no other vehicles on the road.

'Over there.' Lannigan was pointing. Rayanne followed her finger and saw a big double gate in the fence, steel-framed and topped with coils of razorwire. Arclamps on either side were surrounded by fleets of orbiting moths and mosquitoes.

Rayanne pulled up, wrenched open the door and hopped out.

The air still smelt of rain, backed with ozone and plains grass. She could hear the lights humming, the thin whine of the insects. A bird chattered out in the darkness, and there was the cool, slow sigh of wind through trees.

Lannigan hobbled up beside her. 'Is it locked?'

'Mm.' Rayanne walked over to the centre of the gate, where the two halves met. A short length of black chain was wrapped twice round the frames, secured with a padlock the size of both her hands together. She lifted the lock up, turned it over and spotted the logo stamped into the backplate. She grinned.

'A Yumruk. They used to have these back home. Hold on a second.'

The lock was a Turkish copy of a Chinese clone, and about as secure as a wad of chewing gum to someone who knew anything about them at all. Rayanne fished out the knife and unfolded its largest blade, jamming it deftly behind the backplate, right at the point where the rivets were faked.

'They screwed up on the design. The bits inside were too big, so this part here is real –' there was a metallic snapping sound '– thin!'

'I'm impressed.' Lannigan took the knife as Rayanne lifted the open lock away from its chain. 'Evidence of your misspent youth, I suppose?'

Rayanne pushed the gate, just enough to squeeze through. 'You coming in, or staying out here?'

'I can keep a better lookout from here.' Lannigan glanced around. 'Remember what Gray said – it's right next to twelve, yokay? There's no thirteen.'

'Yeah, I got it. Don't you go nowhere.' She darted off, keeping low and close to the fence, wondering which superstitious asshole had put these warehouses up in the first place. Didn't they realise that just missing out thirteen meant that fourteen was thirteen anyway? Probably jinxed the whole row, too.

No African would have done that. Rayanne looked up

at the unit next to her, at the number above the door. That was twelve, a paper storage depot, so she stopped, edging round the corner to peer at the next one along.

It had a sign bolted up above the door: FAST AND FOREMOST – TRANSPORT AND DISTRIBUTION. Rayanne grinned to herself, then nipped round the corner, staying as close to twelve as she could. If Broca was any kind of fence at all she would have some serious security on her place, probably a couple of wandering goons, too. Whatever Marcus had tried to tell her.

She checked out the structure with a practised eye. The lockup was small, standard, identical to countless others all over the world, bolted together from corrugated sheet metal and plastic. Probably a polyceramic liner, paper-thin but highly insulating and practically bullet proof. There were motion sensors and chipcams at the corners, positioned to eliminate blind spots, and no easy way to get on to the roof even if she could have made it to the wall.

All of which was negated by the fact that warehouse fourteen had been built a mere two metres from its neighbours. Rayanne skirted around to the rear of number twelve, where a late delivery had left enough bales of recycled paper to give her an easy climb, even though nearly a week on nothing but fluids had made her legs worryingly unpredictable.

She paused on the roof for a moment, near the edge where the metal wouldn't distort and make a noise. Then she crouched, aimed herself at a point between two of Broca's motion sensors, and jumped.

It almost went wrong, then.

She had jumped hard, as hard as she could, but somehow she ended up half a metre short. She slammed painfully into the side of the warehouse, the edge of the roof catching her in the midriff. Her fingers scrabbled frantically at the metal, Nikes sliding and squeaking at the wall, until she felt something loose, a cable, and grabbed at it with both hands.

Rayanne hung there for a long moment, breathing hard, listening for alarms. The warehouses were only a single storey high, so if anything went off she could drop to the ground from here without too much risk of injury. After a minute or so of silence she pulled herself up. Her flailing Nikes must have been too close to trip the sensors.

There were four skylights on the roof and two aircon vents. Rayanne edged next to one of the skylights and peered inside, down into a grime-hazed pattern of shadows and weak safety lighting. The translucent plastic was sealed with epoxy, and when Rayanne looked more closely she could see silvery threads of metal around the edges: brittle foil wiring, patched into the alarm system. If the epoxy cracked, shit would hit fan very quickly indeed.

Rayanne chewed her lip for a moment, then remembered the cable that had saved her ankle bones on the jump over. It was a fat bundle of fibre optics leading from the motion sensors and cameras, held to the roof with silver tape – an obviously amateur job. Rayanne traced it back, mainly by touch, until it disappeared into the metal.

'Yes!' Broca had cut her own access panel in the roof, a hole half a metre across, and boarded it with what felt like laminate sheet.

The sheet came up after a few tugs, trailing nails and fibre optic. Broca was probably relying on her surveillance gear preventing anyone from getting this far, but it was still a poor performance. The number of people who invested thousands in motion detectors and then forgot to lock their front door was a constant source of amazement to Rayanne.

Not to mention occasional profit. Rayanne had been warehouse shopping more times than she could remember, quite literally, and in tougher spots than this. She eased herself down on to a layer of palette racking, counted twenty heartbeats, and then, hearing nothing that sounded like trouble, clambered down on to the concrete floor.

After the darkness outside, the bioluminescent lights seemed very bright.

Most of the racking in the warehouse was empty, rows of cobwebbed wooden palettes stretching away into the gloom. Damp stung Rayanne's nostrils: old wood, rotting away under bulging cardboard boxes, and the cool damp of the floor beneath her Nikes. She moved from rack to rack, keeping as silent as she knew how, squinting in the grey murk and wishing she'd had enough sense to bring a flashlight.

From what she could see, Broca seemed to specialise in cheap commercial electronics, furniture and module parts. There was an entire ground module over to her left, an old Honda with the wheels and hubdrives stripped away and the interior turned to a white nightmare of spiderweb. A stack of plastic seats next to that, school chairs with integral desks, still wreathed in bubble wrap. Rayanne grimaced and moved on, edges of bad memory prodding at her from the darkness. That kind of seat was hard on girls who grew too tall and too fast.

She fumbled past a worktop loaded high with bottles of New Formula Coke and almost panicked when it groaned and moved, the bottles chiming a carillon of warning. Next to that a shelf was piled with military K-rations and plastic drums of Glen Rio whiskey.

One end of the shelf was bolted to the wall of an office cubicle, a cramped little box bolted together from cheap laminate. Clear plastic sheeting had been taped over the windows, and the door looked like it had come from somewhere else entirely. Looking at the office, Rayanne got a good idea of exactly how important this place was to Broca's setup. She probably didn't even know it still existed.

This is the kind of place Zenebe would have ended up running, had he actually known Broca at all. Which he hadn't. Chances were, even the address he had written into her jacket was bullshit, just something to impress her when they were first starting out.

She shook herself, pushing the thoughts away, and tugged carefully at the office door. It stuck a little, making the walls shake and the plastic sheet rattle, then opened soundlessly. She checked quickly for spiderwebs and ducked inside.

There was a table against the wall. No chair.

The table supported a desk terminal that was at least ten years past its sell-by. Rayanne lifted the screen open and felt a start of cold horror when nothing happened. Then she saw that the machine had a switch that you had to press to turn it on, no motion detectors or sleep mode or anything. She shook her head and hit the stud, offering a quick prayer that the thing would be fast enough to handle Broca's coreframe without exploding.

The screen blipped on, and the start menu came up. Rayanne let out a long sigh and took the Line Rat from her pocket.

She placed the slab in front of the terminal, where the optical ports of both machines could see each other. In the dim light of the warehouse the Line Rat's port looked unpleasantly like a rodent's red eye, and Rayanne wondered if the cloned brain slice was thinking at all, sealed inside its support system and its superconducting lattice. She hoped it wasn't.

She was just wondering what to do next when the Line Rat took over.

The screen began to fizz and strobe, its coruscations worryingly bright. Rayanne could see shadows flicking over the palettes, something stirring restlessly inside the Honda. Then the terminal appeared to settle down. A new menu scrolled into view, one with a lot more options than before.

Clever little rat. She was in.

Rayanne blew dust from the terminal's keys and then tapped up a search engine, set it racing through the gigabytes in search of Living Glass MLC. She hopped impatiently from foot to foot as the blue bar filled with red, left to right – she wouldn't have too much time before Broca's defences overwhelmed whatever the Line Rat had to offer. Already the optical ports were fluttering crazily.

An entire page on Living Glass MLC page popped up on to the display.

There was quite a lot there. Broca was a conscientious person. No wonder Marcus was worried.

Rayanne started to scan down, quickly, until she stopped short at a name she recognised. The context, for a moment, stunned her.

Kitsumi.

Boy, was Lannigan wrong about her.

She reached for the download key, ready to send the whole file into the Line Rat's backup, and then the screen went blank. The optical ports faded down to dark. For a moment Rayanne just stood there, convinced that she had done something wrong, that the system had glitched and it was all her fault, but then the display changed to show a single line of text. Rayanne read it and said, 'Oh shit.'

The core memory was clear. The Line Rat had eaten everything in Broca's mainframe.

It must have set up some kind of killer tapeworm when the systems had first linked. Gray had given her a core fragger, not a slaving system. He'd lied.

And somebody, out among the shelves and the spiders, breathed.

Rayanne froze, her own breath stopped like a bone in her throat. She saw the flick of a penlight beam, blue-white in the dimness, and became suddenly aware that the terminal's open screen was throwing its own pale glow right into her face. Very slowly, very quietly, she flipped the lid closed and sank to her haunches, below the level of the window.

Footsteps, careful ones, close to the Honda. Rayanne

waited, her back to the wall. Her heart was hammering behind her ribs, in her ears, making it hard to listen. Her calf muscles ached from crouching.

The footsteps were moving away. Rayanne let a breath out, then realised that the Line Rat was still in plain view on the table. She reached up, blind, and grabbed it on the first try.

The casing was scaldingly hot.

Rayanne jerked back, clamping down on a cry, flailing her hand wildly to cool her fingers. The laminate wall moved, shaking the window sheets, the shelf. The New Coke bottles rattled horribly. She stared up and saw one turn lazily, tap its neighbour, and overbalance. It toppled and shattered messily on the concrete floor.

Rayanne barrelled out of the door, and scrambled to a halt with the flashlight beam right in her eyes. Someone said, 'Naughty.'

The voice was male, young. Rayanne whipped her hand to the shelf and grabbed a bottle, hurling it past the light. It connected with a solid, meaty sound, and the penlight dropped to spin crazily on the floor, flipping away as Rayanne kicked it on her way past. Behind her, the Line Rat exploded in a hissing spray of fire, flash-melting the plastic windows, setting the laminate ablaze. The heat of it stung her back.

She headed towards the front of the warehouse, found the service door alongside the main access and banged down hard on the latch bar, stumbling out into the night. For a moment her bearings were gone – she was in darkness now, and facing the wrong way – but a panicky scramble between the lockup and its neighbour had her back at the chainlink in seconds.

Looking at an empty road. The Rover wasn't there.

Rayanne sighed, and turned to meet the figures running out of the darkness towards her. She would have raised her hands, but somehow she just didn't have the strength.

* * *

The contour couch was perversely comfortable.

When Rayanne had first seen it, when the men had bundled her into the big aluminium trailer and she had seen the couches and what hung between them, she had struggled and started screaming. The guy she had beaned with the New Coke bottle was still distracted by the shards of glass in his face, and she had managed to break an arm free and get an elbow into his jaw, sending him back into a row of medical scanners. That was when the other man had hit her, and after the lights had finished dancing around in her vision she found herself strapped firmly into the left-hand couch.

The trailer had been parked out of sight behind the warehouses. They must have been waiting for her all along.

She hadn't been able to see much of the thing's exterior on the way in. It was long, maybe nine or ten metres, with bright metal flanks and a cluster of bulges past the front linkage that suggested the bubble canopy of a hydrogen-cell longhauler rig. The tyres were fat and heavily studded.

She could feel them now, the vibration of tyre against road coming up through the floor and into the couch. They had been moving for almost twenty minutes, during which time the couch had moulded itself cosily around Rayanne's thin body, and Parsons – the tall, scarred American who had hit her – had put an infonet call through to the Embu Crew.

The plex who had her called themselves Medichus Procedures. He had mentioned that while he was telling the Crew to come and pick her up.

She hadn't heard of them before, but from the amount of biomedical technology hugging the trailer walls it was pretty obvious they were some kind of mobile freelance surgery. There were plenty of reasons people might want to go under the knife without too many questions being asked – face-changing, for example. Or the patching of wounds received during dubious activities. Or drug extraction.

Rayanne glanced up at the gleaming construction hunched above her head, and shuddered.

There was a control board at the very back of the trailer. It was the only part that Rayanne could see from where she lay, but she could hear two Kikuyu girls doing chemical work at the front end, and Parsons helping the injured man about midway along. She tugged at the straps holding her arms down, but they were heavy-gauge nylon webbing, fixed to a metal bar bolted to the frame. No handy fastenings just within reach, like on the netshows. No cuts in the fabric. They had her pinned down like a rat on a dissecting table, and after Medichus had syringed the drugs from her belly the Embu Crew were going to walk in and cut off the top of her head.

She saw Parsons walk past and sit down at the control board. 'Hey, *señor*.'

'Shut up.' He didn't turn round.

'You really think the Crew are gonna let you take the stuff? They gonna dice you up right along with me.'

He turned round, viewing her without malice. 'You might as well save your breath, honey. Letting you go would get me diced up even worse, yeah?' He swivelled his chair back to the board and started tapping at the keypads. 'Besides, they just said they wanted their runner back. Can't say for certain they're gonna do you harm. Those sacs don't come cheap.'

She thought about telling Parsons that she didn't belong to the Crew, never had, but there really wasn't any point. She felt horribly tired. 'Hey, look. When you get the stuff out . . .'

'Mm?'

'Can you give me something? What they're gonna do to me, they'll make it hurt real bad.'

He paused for a long moment. 'I think I can do that, yeah,' he said.

Rayanne felt the trailer swing over and stop. Parsons looked over his shoulder, up the trailer. 'Chen, get the uplink going. I should be done in about ten.' He gave Rayanne an encouraging look, like he actually felt sorry for her. 'I'll try and make this short, yokay?'

She nodded, and the thing hanging between the couches hinged over towards her, unfolding its glittering arms wide. Two of the limbs reached down to force her jaws apart, her head back, and when they locked tight a fat tentacle of articulated steel slid between her teeth and began worming its awful way down her throat.

Parsons was out on his estimation by a few minutes. The extraction took a quarter of an hour, after which one of the Kikuyu girls came back to tell him the Crew were on their way.

'Chen picked up a vehicle, heading towards us fast.' She flicked her locks at Rayanne. 'Whatever you are going to do for her, do it now.'

She went forward again. Rayanne lay on the couch, gasping like a fish on a rock. She felt raw, empty, as though someone had scraped out all her insides with something rusted. The half-litre of pale, slightly bloody fluid that Parsons had pumped out of her was winding its way through a series of chemical filters on the other side of the trailer.

She turned her heavy head to look at Parsons. He had a pressure syringe in his hand, and was slotting in a cylinder of bright metal. She heard the hiss of compressed gas as it loaded.

'Pandorphin,' he said. 'I'll give you the full dose, so it'll last a good while.' He put the tip of the syringe to her neck.

She closed her eyes, and heard Chen's voice rise in sudden, horrified disbelief: 'Oh *shit*!'

There was a sudden, ferocious impact, a whiplash shriek of overstressed metal, as the entire trailer was shunted sideways. Rayanne screamed, the side of her head whanging against the wall, her whole body slammed aside with agonising force. She saw Parsons fly across the trailer and into the end of her couch, folding up around it. The syringe skittered from his grasp.

The trailer tilted violently, then rolled back on its tyres, sending Parsons on to his back and shelves of medical supplies spinning and bouncing over the couches, the floor. Rayanne struggled, feeling the couch turn to liquid under her: the reactive gel that filled it had been shocked into fluidity by the impact. She twisted, thrashed, and found her arm free.

The lights in the trailer were flickering. Parsons was groaning on the floor, the Kikuyu girls yelling at each other, Chen screaming at everyone to calm down, find a weapon. As he said that the vehicle was struck again, not as hard this time, but with a horrible, grinding, sheering noise that told Rayanne that they were being shoved clear across the road. She wormed her way out from under the straps before the gel had a chance to restructure itself, and jumped down on to the floor. Her stomach flip-flopped, her legs almost gave way beneath her, but there was no way she was going to waste a chance like this by letting weakness get the better of her. She scrambled away, over the twisted floor. When Chen got in her way she just hit him.

If the Crew thought they could rub her out just by ram-raiding the Medichus trailer, they would have to think again.

Whatever had struck the trailer had folded it clear down the middle, the two ends now at an angle of thirty degrees or more. The door had ruptured in the impact, popped right open, and Rayanne dived out of it, hit the ground rolling and forced herself up, whipping round to locate the Crew's vehicle.

The sight of what was pummelling the trailer made her laugh out loud.

She bolted towards the Desert Rover, yanked the passenger-side door open and flung herself in. Lannigan was yanking frantically at the controls. 'How the hell do you get this thing to go backward?' she screamed.

'Pull the fragging bar back!'

'I *am* pulling it back!' Lannigan looked to be nearly in tears, frantic, hauling away on the throttle bar as though she wanted to drag it from its moorings. Rayanne tried to grab it, leaning across.

'No, *right* back! There's a stop . . . Ah, screw it! Lemme in there!' She clambered over Lannigan, drawing yelps of indignation.

They swapped places in a messy scramble, and Rayanne swung the Rover back and round, tooled it past the trailer and launched off down the road with the hubdrives squealing. 'Nice driving, man!'

'You call that driving?' Lannigan sagged back into her seat. 'I couldn't get the damned thing to go any way but forward –'

'No, you did yokay. I mean it.' Rayanne eased back on the throttle a little, cutting the speed down to a point that wouldn't tag any police satellites. She grinned. 'Hey, you really came after me.'

Lannigan gave her a cold stare. 'Don't flatter yourself. I was after the data.'

There was a long pause. Then: 'You did get it, didn't you?'

Rayanne grimaced, clamped a hand to her stomach. She had been through extraction enough times to recognise the beginning of a day of cramps and nausea. 'That freakin' Rat was a setup. It wiped the files. Then it caught fire or something, I dunno.'

'Gray.' Lannigan sounded disgusted. 'Son of a bitch must have planned the whole thing to clear Broca's database, whatever she had on him. Called up that trailer to clear the witnesses. And we walked right into it.'

'*I* walked into it, lady! You drove off and left me!'

A police module howled past in the other direction, sirens whooping, lights fluttering red and blue. 'I saw the bad guys roll up. Decided on a tactical withdrawal.'

Rayanne nodded. She didn't like that, but she could

understand it. She would have done the same herself. 'What, and then you followed me?'

Lannigan looked momentarily uncomfortable. 'In a manner of speaking, yes.'

Which meant the *lisiada* probably started off in the wrong direction and spent the next half-hour desperately trying to get the Rover to go straight. 'Lannigan?'

The woman pursed her lips. 'You didn't get the data, did you.'

'I told you, man. It caught fire.' She glanced across, saw Lannigan's expression and decided not to say any more. The woman looked thoroughly distraught.

Rayanne smiled to herself. Later, a few more kilometres down the highway, when her insides had settled and she felt a bit more like talking, she would tell Lannigan what she had learnt about Kitsumi. Or rather *Kitsumi Maru*, the ship, Living Glass MLC's base of operations, tethered on the polluted coast of Veracruz.

For the moment, however, the thought that she had something Lannigan wanted, a piece of information that the woman didn't have, *couldn't* have had without her, took some of the edges off the pain and the fear and the memory of looking through the chainlink to see only empty road. It was a feeling she wanted to keep, if only for a little while.

After all, it was a long way to Mombasa.

RED

7
Veracruz

There came a time, two days out of Africa, when Lannigan knew the nanotech had left her.

It was a nagging feeling, proved by the smallest of clues. The delays at Mexico City the previous day had set her to chewing her nails, a loathsome habit that she had probably picked up from Rayanne. When she had realised what she was doing she had torn the hand from her mouth, in the process yanking a minute but painful strip of skin from the edge of her left thumbnail.

And now, wedged into a hard seat on a landbus jumping and jolting its way down the east coast of Mexico, she turned her hand and studied a tiny bead of scab that the nanotech should have healed within an hour.

The realisation hit her a lot harder than she had been expecting. She had assumed the legion of mechanisms within her would remain active until the damage to her nervous system had been healed, but her right leg was still weak, intermittently numb and aching. A touch to the back of her neck confirmed that the scars there were unchanged as well. Lannigan felt a cold sinking in the pit of her stomach, an icy crawl across her shoulders that defied the stifling, sodden heat inside the bus.

Quite suddenly, she realised that she didn't want to be alone here.

The thought made her curse her own weakness, but there it was: she was utterly on her own in this strange, damaged country. Her nanotech had abandoned her and Rayanne Gatita, with her sulky, stripy face and her maddening accent, was gone, too, flown halfway across the world in a subsonic Kenyan Airlines lifting body. Lannigan was more unprotected than at any time since hospital. Exposed as an open wound.

She turned to gaze hollowly at the trees jerking past her window. The vegetation had a stunted quality here, a diseased look. According to the map she had bought at the airport, the city of Veracruz Llave was almost 600 kilometres from the Yucatan coast, but it was quite possible that a strong wind could carry pathogens from that blighted place and deposit them here. With her nanotech gone, Lannigan knew she would have to be much more careful in regard to infection and injury.

As if to emphasise that thought, the landbus rocked abruptly, almost sending her into the window. The wheels on Lannigan's side had found another pothole: she steadied herself, grabbing at the battered chrome bar topping the seat in front, holding on until the tyres cleared and the vehicle righted itself with an even more violent sway.

Lannigan resisted the urge to growl, and sat back, forcing herself more firmly into the seat. The road from Papantla had been rife with such incidents; it was a pockmarked, corrugated nightmare which had her wishing for the smooth highways of Kenya within minutes of leaving the terminus. Four hours of such jarring – plus another nine of heat and roadblocks and hairpin bends on the way from Mexico City – had left her feeling more beaten than she could remember.

She risked a glance around, but few of her fellow occupants seemed to have even noticed the jolt. They all looked local, to her untutored eye: all had the resigned air of people used to an infrastructure that was alive only because it hadn't died yet. Lannigan wondered how many were refugees from the Yucatan.

The bus rocked again, hard, shuddering from end to end. Lannigan gritted her teeth and held on, expecting the rusting vehicle to right itself and keep moving. Instead a sudden deceleration jerked her forward, then back into the hard seat. She gasped, the breath knocked out of her for an instant, and as she did so she heard the drives winding down.

There was no stop scheduled here.

'What the hell now?' She half stood, leaning on the seat bar. Through the windscreen, past the seats in front of her and the portly, sweating figure of the driver, she saw someone moving quickly towards the bus. Beyond that was the squat bulk of an electric jeep.

Lannigan muffled a curse, and sat down again, sliding lower in the seat. The jeep had been placed efficiently, close enough to a corner to be out of sight, far enough to avoid being rammed. The angle of it blocked the track quite neatly.

There was a rapping on the bus door, metal on muddy plexiglass. Lannigan hunched and began fishing around under the seat for her cane, wishing she'd been able to bring the needle gun through flight security. She couldn't believe Living Glass had found her again so soon. Then again, she had underestimated them before, to her cost. Byron's monitoring equipment could easily have spotted her flight to Mexico City. The infonet account she had opened there was under a false name, but some part of it must have given her away, maybe the voiceprint. She should have been more careful.

The door opened with a pneumatic sigh, and Lannigan looked up. A man she didn't recognise was talking to the driver.

He looked very young, his eyes dark above the bandanna that masked the lower part of his face, almost afraid. He wore combat fatigues, ragged and grubby, and the gun in his fist was the biggest Lannigan had ever seen. It was almost the size of her whole hand.

The other passengers were muttering, a litany of sullen anger and resignation. Some of them were already getting up. Lannigan sat where she was and listened – she remembered a little of the language, although she couldn't think where from. Among the swearing she caught '*amboscadores*', which was 'ambushers', and no great surprise. Then someone said 'Liberación Huasteca.'

'Oh, perfect.' Lannigan sagged, unsure of how to react. Liberación Huasteca had nothing to do with Living Glass, but they could be dangerous enough in their own right: there had been warning posters about them at the landbus terminus. An activist group with pretensions to revolution, for the most part they did nothing but complain on public-access infonet about the rights of the indigenous Huastec people. However, as Mexico's situation continued to deteriorate, groups like LH were starting to take things further. There were rumours of more militant splinter groups, attacks on foreign businesses, bombings. Corporate installations in the area had started to fortify themselves in response. The Fushigina launch facility at Poza Rica had employed an armed security plex.

That the non-Spanish-speaking Huastec liberationists had chosen a Spanish name for their organisation, said, Lannigan had decided, everything about them that she needed to know.

The passengers were leaving. Lannigan watched men and women file slowly between the seats, as if taking part in some practised drill. Of the fourteen she counted, nine already had their money out. She wondered if this kind of thing happened a lot.

'*Andale*!' The man was waving his gun at her, motioning her up. '*Pelirroja, andale*!'

She sighed and pulled the carryall from under the seat. The cane was resting on top of it, along with the floppy white hat she had bought in Mexico city. The stifling climate of Veracruz had demanded something lighter than the business suit that had served her so well in Africa, and, loath as she was to spend her dwindling resources on anything not completely necessary, she had stopped at a bargain clothes chain and kitted herself out with more suitable garments. Now she wore a loose-fitting shirt and trousers in pale polysilk, the draw-strings at the wrists and ankles drawn tight. Exposing too much pale skin was not a good idea in the lowlands, and not just because of ozone depletion.

Selling the Desert Rover in Mombasa had made enough just to cover the purchases and Rayanne's flight. Lannigan wasn't on her uppers just yet, but losing her remaining money to a gang of amateur Zapatistas would be a major disaster. She jammed the hat down on to her head, got herself on her feet and began edging down the aisle, the carryall bumping at her legs.

His eyes were on her all the way to the front; she could feel them, the glare. Outside, two more *amboscadores* were lining up the other passengers with their backs to the hot metal side of the bus.

Lannigan found herself shoved into the line, a slight stumble on the rough ground bringing the back of her head into sharp contact with a window. A curse snapped out of her before she could stop it: little more than a grunt of frustration, but enough to bring one of the activists to her nonetheless.

This one was older, his skin dark and shiny in the heat. Lannigan saw the gun slung over his shoulder, something written in red paint along the peeling leather strap.

His breath smelt of lemon. '*Pelirrojita.*'

She kept her silence, glaring up at him from under the hatbrim. She knew that she should act deferential and lower her gaze, avoid eye contact. But she couldn't. It was all she could do to avoid sneering.

He spoke, a rapid stream of Spanish and Huastec, too fast to follow. Lannigan looked at him blankly.

'*Mande*?' she ventured. 'Excuse me?'

His hands came up and he pushed her, hard. She went

backward and hit the side of the bus again, with enough force to set her head ringing. She staggered, hearing him shout, felt the heat of his spittle on her neck and then he had her again, dragging her away. In a few furious steps he had her round the front of the bus and against the other side, out of sight of the other passengers.

Past his tirade, she could hear the gunmen laughing.

She backed off as far as she could, trying to make sense of the man's snarling words, unable to decide whether he was berating her for being foreign, a woman, or both. '*L–lo siento mucho*,' she stammered. '*Haga el favor de hablar más despacio*.'

It was a poor effort, phrasebook Spanish for 'I'm very sorry. Please speak more slowly', but it seemed to have some effect. The gunman paused, then barked out another few sentences, this time without so much obvious rage. Lannigan shook her head hopelessly. '*No entiendo*.'

He nodded, then gestured towards her carryall.

Lannigan hesitated, weighing up the situation. The gunman could shoot her down with impunity, if he wished: she was a long way from anyone who would care. Even the other passengers seemed to have more in common with the Huastecs than with her. After all, many of Mexico's current problems could be traced back, however indirectly, to foreign intervention, and one pale-skinned corpse lying in the forest would probably invoke more satisfaction than investigation.

She could stay alive and be robbed, or be killed and then robbed anyway. Lannigan reached over and placed the carryall at the man's feet.

He dropped to his haunches and began rifling through her meagre belongings with a practised ease. The money wasn't hidden: he found it within a few seconds and transferred it to the top pocket of his fatigue shirt. The rest of her things ended up in the mud, the carryall overturned, emptied, and then kicked away.

Lannigan clamped her teeth together. She hoped he

wouldn't take a liking to her cane. Without clothes or money she might get by, but she couldn't walk without support. Besides, she had grown attached to the device in a manner that she could not wholly describe. The loss of both her nanotech and Rayanne was distressing enough, but being robbed of the cane as well would be too much to bear.

He looked her over again, then snapped out a hand and grabbed her wrist.

Her left wrist. He wasn't after the cane: he wanted her chrono.

By the time they had reached Mombasa airport Rayanne had wanted nothing more than escape, to leave both her drugs-related woes and whatever Lannigan was involved with far behind. Although strangely heartened by this sudden burst of independence, Lannigan was unwilling to leave the girl stranded. She had made Rayanne wait while she bought an infonet chrono and opened an account, and had personally written the address code on the inside of the girl's jacket.

Rayanne couldn't reach her if Lannigan didn't have access to her account. She snatched her hand away. '*Déjeme*!'

The Huastec snarled. He grabbed at the chrono again, slamming Lannigan against the bus when she resisted. She tried to turn away from him, to put herself between him and the device, but he was too strong. He wrenched her left arm out and began fumbling with the strap.

Behind him, out in the forest, something blew up.

Lannigan felt the shock of it through the ground, heard the whooping roar and the strange whipping of shrapnel through trees. The *amboscadore* spun round to watch a great puffball of flame rolling into the air, and then Lannigan lashed the cane up and around in a humming arc that terminated solidly on the side of his skull, hurling him over on to the ground.

She stood for a moment, breathing hard, then limped over to where the man lay squirming in the mud with his hands over his head. There was blood in his hair, a livid purple welt from temple to chin. Half his facial bones were probably broken.

There was a certain satisfaction in that. She prodded him roughly with the cane. 'Welcome to the wonderful world of Übergen AG, asshole.'

More explosions were sounding in the forest, and the distant, flat popping of gunfire. Lannigan crouched next to the moaning Huastec and began to empty his pockets. Her money went back into the carryall, along with a few thousand pesos she found in a belt pouch and a small bankroll from his left boot. She took his cigars, his lighter, and his knife, a ten-centimetre foldout with a pale bone handle and a blade honed down to scalpel sharpness. After that she got up and retrieved the carryall's original contents from the ground, packing them in mud and all.

She had moved fast. The whole incident had taken less than a minute.

Still, the other Huastecs would want to be away. Lannigan turned the activist over and found the gun, still dangling from its leather strap. She pulled it up and untangled it from the man's limp shoulder. He had stopped moving now.

The gun felt heavy in her hand. She flipped it over, loathing the feel of it, the potential. A tiny red LED glowed alongside the barrel. Lannigan took that to mean that the thing was primed. If she was wrong about that she was going to be in serious trouble, but she didn't have time to give herself a crash course in modern firearms. One of the other Huastecs was already walking around in front of the bus.

It was the youngest, the one who had ordered her off. Lannigan stepped in front of him, the carryall strap hooked round her cane arm, the gun in her left hand with the stubby muzzle centred directly on his forehead. He saw the gun before he realised who was holding it – Lannigan saw the outline of a smile half form beneath the bandanna, then his eyes met hers and he froze. He suddenly looked very young indeed.

Lannigan's vacation Spanish wasn't up to this situation. She gestured with the gun, and as he began to back away she followed him, keeping the muzzle no more than a metre from the smooth, sweat-pricked skin of his forehead, until they were both around the bus and within sight of the line of passengers.

The third Huastec was busy counting his money, perched on a rock with his own gun lying across his lap. He looked up lazily, no doubt expecting to see his comrades returning after their fun with the *norteamericana*. When he saw what was actually occurring he dropped his cash into the mud and snatched up the weapon. Lannigan yelped, took a step forward and squeezed the trigger.

The gun went off with a hellish noise and leapt in her hand, almost sending her over backward. The third Huastec's left knee bloomed into scarlet ruin.

Lannigan swore and dropped the gun, stumbling backward. The muzzle flash had left a green flare in her vision and her left hand was singing with the recoil. She shook her head violently, trying to shake the whining from her ears.

Both Huastecs were on the ground. The youngest man was sprawled in front of her, utterly still, his eyes closed and blood threading from his ear. His head had been right next to the gun when it had gone off: Lannigan guessed he would be lucky to escape with only a ruptured eardrum. His companion was rolling, shrieking, his hands wrapped round his knee and crimson soaking from between his fingers.

Stolen money lay around him in the mud, like an offering.

Passengers were starting to emerge from under the bus. Lannigan hadn't even seen them move. She found herself envying their reactions, then pitying a country that made them necessary. She raised her hand in a conciliatory gesture, but the passengers weren't even looking at her. All their attention was fixed on the downed Huastecs. Even the distant gunfire from the forest didn't draw them.

Lannigan looked at the landbus for a moment, and realised that she had no real desire to set foot on it again. She glanced around, to where the electric jeep was still blocking the road. If the controls were anything like those of the Desert Rover it could provide her with transport into the city, perhaps a means of searching for the *Kitsumi Maru* while she was there. She set off towards it.

A whimper from the shot Huastec made her look back.

The passengers had formed a circle, surrounding him. His cries had quietened, but as Lannigan watched a young woman walked warily up to the wounded man, drew back her foot and kicked him sharply, drawing fresh howls.

Then the bus driver walked forward and did the same.

Lannigan had no stomach for such play. Abruptly queasy, she climbed into the jeep and began looking for the start key.

Driving the Desert Rover had been a terrifying experience. While Lannigan's ruined memory had retained some talents – her small knowledge of Spanish, for example, a degree of medical lore – driving had not been one of them. Combining the use of the steering joystick and the throttle bar in any useful way had been quite beyond her, despite Baxter's hurried instructions. It was all she could do to keep the vehicle moving in a straight line while thanking whatever deities might be listening for empty night-time roads.

The electric jeep was worse.

It was as unspectacular to look at as the Rover had been ugly. Roughly a faceted metal egg with one side an open frame, it was held a metre above the road on four wheeled legs; higher than normal, Lannigan surmised, to lessen the damage from landmines. However, one of the hubdrives wasn't working. The offside rear wheel alternately dragged or spun free, causing the jeep to swoop and veer down the track as though piloted by a drunkard. If that wasn't enough, the damaged wheel was connected in some way to the leg's suspension. Within ten minutes of bobbing and weaving towards Veracruz Llave, Lannigan was feeling decidedly queasy.

She tugged the throttle back to its stop, leaving the jeep tilted but stationary. The bus hadn't caught her up, for which she was grateful: she would prefer not to encounter its passengers again, not after the sullen delight they had taken in punishing the wounded Huastecs. The crowd hadn't looked murderous, and so Lannigan clung to the hope that the three gunmen would survive their mistake, whatever their crimes. Wounding in self-defence was something she had few qualms about, but she had no desire at all to be a contributing factor in someone's death.

Still, she had no real idea of what the situation here was. She would be the first to admit that. What little she had been able to glean from public newsfeeds gave her almost no indication of what was going on at ground level, and even the grosser political situation was confused and hazy. Mexico had always been a clash of cultures, ever since Cortés and his fatal encounter with the Aztecs. But after decades of economic decline, foreign corporate exploitation and ecological damage, diversity had turned into fracture. The result was Liberación Huasteca and their kind. Mexico had broken up, and everyone wanted a piece.

The gunfire had faded, but a twist of smoke still showed above the canopy. Whatever had exploded out in the forest was still burning. Lannigan stood up in the jeep and looked around, but saw nothing except trees and a sun worryingly close to setting. The road stretched ahead of her. A rusted signpost pointed to Veracruz

Llave, but the distance figure was corroded away.

Lannigan dropped back into the seat and eased the jeep forward. The state of Veracruz had proved treacherous enough by day. Night in the forest held few attractions.

As Lannigan had planned, the jeep got her into the city of Veracruz Llave.

For a kilometre or two the mud track had opened out into a real road, a taste of what would have cut through the forest alongside the old Mexico 180 had the state's economy stayed on track. Tired-looking suburbs had appeared, small roadside shops and single-storey houses, lean-tos and shacks built from corrugated plastic and packing crates. Lannigan saw her first two-storey building within a minute of the city outskirts, and promptly collided with it.

The jeep had been driveable with a damaged hub-drive, but too much of its steering and suspension mechanisms relied on the same power as the wheels. Lannigan had been speeding a little, aware that the vehicle's batteries were running low and trying, against all logic, to get as far into town as possible before they ran flat. When she saw sparks and smoke erupt from the front right wheel she tried to slow down, but her reactions weren't nearly fast enough.

The drive seized. There was an awful sound from the wheel, a shriek of polymer tyre and grinding ceramic, and then the jeep slewed out from under her, tilting and pivoting and slamming with a bone-jarring impact against the stucco wall of a tourist hostel.

Something fizzed ominously from the jeep's innards. Lannigan groaned, feeling fragmented plaster sprinkling into her hair, smelling the unmistakable sweet-sour reek of burning insulation. She clambered over the side and pulled her carryall and cane from the stowage area, dragging them away. The ground seemed to be moving beneath her feet. She slumped against the wall, rough stucco scraping her skin through the thin shirt and her stomach lurching, emptying itself in a single, agonising heave over the ground. She staggered back, coughing. Spat the taste from her mouth.

The jeep was smouldering.

Lannigan leant back against the wall as her heartbeat slowed and her inner ears became accustomed to stillness. Her stomach threatened to rebel again but she forced the bile down, sucking in long breaths of the sticky, tainted air. She looked around.

There was no one in sight. None of the buildings around her were showing lights.

Either the crash had passed by unnoticed, or this part of the city was effectively deserted. When Lannigan looked more closely she could see that none of the streetlamps were functioning either, despite the rapidly failing light. Barring a few bioluminescent signboards, the area would be in complete darkness within an hour or so.

There was a distant sound, a susurration so faint and faded that for a moment Lannigan couldn't be sure if she was hearing the wind or the crashing of waves. Only when she moved away from the electric jeep and its dying sighs did she realise that the sound was people.

A lot of people. Lannigan didn't think they sounded pleased.

The situation in Veracruz seemed to be deteriorating fast. Lannigan found the door of the hostel, climbed the dusty steps and rapped on the plastic. 'Hello? *Ola*?'

There was no reply, so she pushed at the door. It swung aside on gritty hinges, presenting her with a rectangle of almost impenetrable darkness. She peered inside and saw vague, shadowy forms that might have been furniture, a lightswitch on the wall by her head that had no effect whatsoever. The power was definitely out.

She turned and hobbled back down the steps to the nearest signboard. It was an advertisement, some minor brand of cigarettes crudely holographed on to flat plastic, surrounded by a tube of glowing green bioluminescent. Lannigan supported herself on the wall, jammed her cane behind the lowest end of the tube and twisted sharply. A hand's length of plastic piping bent and cracked; a few more twists by hand gave her an unwieldy but usable source of light, as long as she didn't let too much of the fluid spill out. At the top of the steps she glanced back to see a trail of glowing spots on the pavement behind her.

A useful guide, perhaps, if she found herself truly lost. She stepped into a short corridor lined with framed holographic saints and instruction lists in four languages. Had she been planning to stay in the hostel, Lannigan noted, she would have needed to provide her own towels, bedding and bathplug.

It didn't take her many minutes to confirm that the building had been deserted for some days. Lannigan toyed briefly with the idea of barricading herself into a room and staying until morning, but she had a feeling that things might start to get ugly in Veracruz long before that. Besides, little in the way of creature comforts had been left her by the previous occupants; sharing a floor with roaches was no way to spend a night. She made her way to the upper floor, forced open one of the shuttered windows and looked warily out towards the city.

There were lights showing there, a kilometre away or less. If she moved fast, Lannigan decided, she could make it that far before the day failed completely. Once among the neon, she could relax a while and plan her next move.

She set off down the stairs, the broken tube of biolume held in front like a talisman.

Sunset brought no respite from the day's heat. The evening temperature and humidity were punishing, and after half an hour of walking Lannigan felt on the verge of collapse. She stopped, against her better judgement, at the first source of electric light she found.

It showed dirty yellow at the end of an alley between two anonymous buildings: a triangular sliver of window where the black plastic sheeting had torn free at one corner. Lannigan stared at it, wondering how many other such places she had limped straight past, how many sanctuaries had rendered themselves invisible to her by the simplest of measures. Suddenly, she felt rather stupid.

She approached the light cautiously. There was a door close by, the biolume sign above it painted out with rough strokes of tarry black. Lannigan listened, heard the murmur of voices, and pushed the door open.

The voices stilled, momentarily. Lannigan swallowed, and stepped inside.

The room was marginally more steamy than the street, but at least it was lit. There were tables, and a bar. Lannigan saw bottles and patched barstools and realised that she had found, by luck alone, some kind of tavern. If they would serve her here, she might have found a temporary sanctuary.

There was a scattering of people at the tables, men and women, and each one of them watched her as she limped towards the bar.

'Your camouflage is coming down, sir.' She sat down and nodded towards the window. 'I could see lights.'

The barman stared at her, chewing his lip. He was small and thin, not much larger than her, his long hair slicked back straight above a wide forehead. Lannigan was just about to attempt the sentence in Spanish when he turned and spoke quickly to someone behind her. She heard a chair go back, footsteps.

'*Gracias, señora*. Cannot be too careful tonight, yes?'

'Mm.' Lannigan decided to remain noncommittal for now. 'Ah, can I get a beer, or something?'

He gave a kind of shrug. 'The beer is not good . . .'

'Is it cold?'

'*Sí.*'

'Then I'll risk it.' She took out some money while he

operated an electric pump, some of the pesos she had taken from the Huastec. 'Is this enough?'

He smiled and swept the money away. 'Try the beer, then ask again.' There were litre glasses on the bar, a row of them, rims down. The barman began to place them carefully into an ultrasound washer. 'You *norte-americana*, yes? American?'

Lannigan took a sip of beer. It was foul, but as cold as promised. 'Yes, sir, I am.'

'Press?'

'No.' She paused, frowning. 'Should I be?'

The man shrugged, put the last glass into the washer and closed the lid. A thin, rattling whine rose from within. 'Lot of press in Veracruz. Come to see the big mess.' He made a dismissive gesture with his head. 'You get wounded, a big cut; you get flies, yes? Veracruz is wounded; we get newsfeeders.'

'I see.' A thought occurred to her. 'Has it been getting worse, then? Lately?'

'For weeks. Between Liberación and the corporates, between the refugees and the police . . . Now there is a curfew, and sometimes the power fails.' He sniffed. 'The world, they like to watch this on their screens. Better us than them, yes?'

Lannigan finished the last of her beer, wincing at the taste. 'There was a place just north of here. Everyone was gone.'

'*Sí.* Liberación let loose a bioweapon there, or so the Fushigina people say.'

She gaped. 'A bioweapon?'

'Liberación say it was the corporates. I say no one let anything loose, save for the rumour. But that is weapon enough these days, hmm? Another beer?'

Lannigan stared at him, then shook herself. 'Ah, no. I'd better be leaving.'

'It is past curfew.'

'Guess I'll have to risk it.' She eased down off the stool and let the cane extend. 'Thanks for the beer.'

When she was at the door, the barman called out to her. '*Señora*. Try the *zócalo*, Plaza de Armas. There are places to stay there.'

She nodded her thanks, and stepped out into the night.

Streetlamps still shone in the centre of Veracruz, clearly visible to Lannigan now, beacons. She made her way towards them more carefully than before, keeping to the shadows where she could, avoiding any signs of life she heard. Anyone she met in these dark and humid streets would either be breaking the curfew or enforcing it. Lannigan had no wish to explain herself to either group.

Her route was not without its dangers. At one point a man stepped sharply from the shadows in front of her, a sharp metal glitter in his hand, a colder gleam in his eyes. Maybe Lannigan had already endured too much that day, but the thought of fear never even occurred to her. She simply retracted the cane as she brought it up, then let it extend into his chest. The splayed end caught him just under the sternum. All the breath went out of him in a sudden, choking exhalation, and he just folded up on to the street. She left him there, listening to the small sounds he made as he tried to recall how to breathe.

Moments later she saw a newsfeed crew: a man wearing a portable net uplink, a woman with a shouldercam and a rack of airborne drones. She didn't recognise their feed logos, but they looked Pacifican. They were hurrying along on the opposite side of the street. Lannigan hugged the wall and let them past: if Byron was any kind of operator he would have image-recognition software agents scurrying through infonet as a matter of course, looking for her face. If she was so much as glimpsed by a feed pickup he could have her.

She had no idea whether Living Glass had followed her as far as Mexico or not, but for safety's sake she would act as if they were on her heels.

By the time she reached the open expanse of the *zócalo* the sea-swell rushing of distant crowds had defined itself, hardened and grown and separated into voices raised in anger. Lannigan paused near the entrance to the square, on the forecourt of a vehicle-recharge station on the corner of Lerdo and Landero Y Cos, and watched bulbous police modules circling slowly among the crowd.

There must have been a hundred or more people in the square, all moving, bunching and swarming in complex patterns like a vast shoal of fish. The ground beneath their feet was littered with debris. Lannigan saw the glitter of broken glass everywhere, and smelt the reek of burning and raw alcohol. As she stood, a young man in a white T-shirt ran past her, towards the police modules; she saw a flare of yellow fire arcing from his hand and striking the ground in front of the nearest vehicle, splashing into a wide puddle of guttering flame and scattering the crowd for metres on either side. A tube on the module's roof puffed in reply, and the man, turning, shrieked and fell squirming to the pavement.

Lannigan ducked back, understanding why the tavern owner had chosen to black out his windows and advert board. None of the sources she had accessed before coming to Veracruz had mentioned this level of civil unrest – either she had been dropped deliberately into something that was swiftly coming to resemble a war-zone, or else the local situation had gone downhill faster than anyone had anticipated.

She remembered an explosion in the forest, the pop and snap of distant gunfire. It was looking increasingly as though she had seen the flashpoint of this entire sorry business.

Out in the plaza, some of the shouts were turning to screams. Lannigan turned on her heel and limped away as fast as she could.

She walked until the sound of the riot had faded, then followed the tourist signs until she found a guesthouse.

The place was blacked out, but Lannigan knew better now. She pounded at the door until a light came on.

'*Ola*? Hello? I need a room.' She put her face to the slit window and waved. '*Ola*?'

'Piss off.'

Lannigan blinked. The voice was a woman's, gruff and sour with an accent that sounded Australian, maybe Kiwi. 'I beg your pardon?'

'I said piss off, you bloody hack. Go to Riccardo's, he'll put you up.'

'Erm, excuse me, ma'am, but I'm nothing to do with the press. I just need a room while the ruckus dies down a little.'

There was a long pause. Lannigan heard an electric lock snap open, and the door swung inward a fraction. A strip of face regarded her above a stout locking chain. 'You're not feed? No bullshit?'

'No, ma'am.' Lannigan tried to look innocent. 'I just got here at the wrong time, is all.'

'You're not kidding.' The door closed almost completely, then opened, minus the chain. A stocky woman with a wiry puffball of black hair reached across the threshold and tugged Lannigan in.

With the door locked behind her, Lannigan found herself in a short hallway, the light from fluorescent ceiling panels making her squint after the darkness of the street. The walls were refreshingly free of religious iconography; they were white plaster that looked old, but clean. 'How much?'

'Sixty ICUs a night, cash in advance.' The woman had the broad features and dark skin of a Native Australian, and a dressing gown with all the subtlety and taste of one of Doogie Baxter's shirts. 'I'll take pesos, but I won't like it.'

'I've got ICUs.' Lannigan fished some money from the carryall and handed it over. She nodded back towards the street. 'Is it always this bad?'

The woman shrugged and began to make her way up

the stairs, Lannigan following. 'Ah, comes and goes. It's been worse lately, what with that disease and LH kicking up a stink.'

'Disease?'

'*El plaga*. Here you go.'

The woman held open a door. Lannigan saw a small, box-shaped room, a single bed, a washstand. Her eyebrows went up. 'Sixty?'

'Bathroom's across the hall.' And with that the Aborigine was off, ambling her broad-hipped way down the stairs.

Lannigan went in and put her carryall on to the bed, then closed the door and locked it. There was a plastic chair next to the washstand which went against the door with the back jammed hard under the handle. The bed, when she sat on it, made squeaking sounds.

Outside, in the distance, a siren began howling mournfully.

At the end of the bed was a small table, supporting what looked like some kind of infonet feed. It was a solid-looking box almost half a metre across, with a screen of curved grey glass and a row of fat metal keystuds below a filigree pickup grill. Lannigan studied it warily, noting where a flat strip of optical fibre had been sealed into the back with epoxy and silver tape.

As a piece of retro design the device was certainly impressive. Lannigan hoped it had as much capacity as its size promised. 'Screen on. Give me a newsfeed access, something in English.'

There was a long silence. The glass screen stayed resolutely grey. 'On. Screen on, for chrissakes. *Poner*.'

Nothing. Lannigan scowled, hunched forward and began prodding at the keystuds. As she pushed at one it jolted inward with a snapping noise. The box fizzed, then gave vent to a soft whine. The screen flickered.

Lannigan gaped. The picture was a construct of clearly visible horizontal scan lines, the colours washed and muted, the sound tinny, crackling. She realised that she was sitting in front of an antique, something that was firing electron beams at a phosphorescent panel. There were high voltages back there, lethal ones, all manner of radiation pouring out into the room. The sound issuing from the grill had a background whistle that made her teeth ache.

She edged away, then used the end of her cane to push each of the keystuds in turn. There were six of them on the panel, and that was all the infonet access she had. The owners of the hostel had somehow patched the local netfeed into this buzzing contraption, with a single address link to each switch.

Lannigan thought about using her wrist chrono instead, but the account she had opened in Mombasa gave only thirty minutes of free access before she would have to start paying the service provider. Better to take what the box had to offer, and leave the chrono for necessities.

Much of what the box showed her was utterly without use or merit. An obvious tourist advertisement displayed long pans of lush forest, beaches, and crumbling ziggurats. A game show featured contestants of quite breathtaking stupidity. Had her Spanish been better, Lannigan could have improved her home cooking, and there was a key devoted entirely to quite explicit pornography, which made Lannigan feel nothing save a vague unease. She found herself hoping that the performers had undergone their modifications voluntarily.

She struck a kind of gold on the fifth key. A newsfeed had been patched into the box, one of the more salacious locations and mainly in Spanish, but just about comprehensible if she concentrated. Frustratingly, the on-screen controls for simultaneous translation were arranged at the lower edge of the picture, but Lannigan quickly discovered that the box had one-way access only: prodding at the glass gave her nothing but a mild electric shock.

The format of the feed was a little jarring at first, but within a few minutes Lannigan had the trick of it.

There were three stories taking up the show's main

cycle, plus a host of smaller items that warranted only pop-up windows or scrolling text messages. Of the featured items one was of no more than peripheral interest: a United Nations research team had just returned from the Yucatan, and was blaming the peninsula's ecosystem implosion on the actions of several biochemical corporations with plants in the area. The companies named were in the process of taking legal action.

The footage of the Yucatan itself – a diseased landscape largely obscured by vast clouds of carrion flies – made Lannigan shudder, but the program quickly cycled through to a medical emergency in the forests north of Veracruz Llave. A small Huastec village had been attacked by an unknown but heavily armed force, leaving several dead and dozens wounded. The suggestion was that one of the security plexes paid to patrol the area had mistaken the settlement for a Liberación Huasteca outpost. The organisation had issued a statement of condemnation and denial, of course, but Lannigan knew just how close to the village she had been when the landbus was raided. No wonder the Huastec had been distracted by the explosion, she thought. He must have realised that his home was being attacked.

Lannigan watched dismembered children being covered in plastic blankets, and sighed. Nobody's hands were clean here.

The feed cycled again, without warning. Now she was watching the soaring towers of an industrial plant, searchlight beams flickering over a vast, chanting crowd, armoured guards standing impassive behind chainlink fences. The pickup panned across a corporate logo, the angular pictogram of Fushigina Systems. A memory pricked at her: Marcus Gray telling her about Übergen's deal with PATCo to up the duty on certain products. Wasn't Fushigina one of the companies affected?

The picture broke disorientatingly into four windows. The demonstration against Fushigina still raged in one; in a second a woman was thrashing, screaming, thick straps holding her down to a hospital bed. In another a doctor was saying something about *el plaga*, a new variant of St Louis encephalitis, and warning the public about mosquito bites. The last window was occupied by a blond European man talking about illegal bioweapons research, the laxness of sterilisation procedures in some of the local chemical plants.

Lannigan wondered if that was what the demonstration was about.

She got up and wandered across the room to gaze out of the window, seeing nothing but darkness. Mexico had been attracting foreign corporations for years, luring them with the promise of cheap labour and laughable pollution controls. The idea must have been to draw international money into the Mexican economy, but the method was naive and clumsy and the result predictable. Much of the country, especially areas of the Gulf coast, had been turned into chemical sewers with no recompense for the inhabitants.

It was logical enough. If someone pays you to spit on their doorstep, then you expectorate, take the money and wave goodbye. Who would do any different?

The voices issuing from the box became abruptly more strident. Lannigan went back and positioned herself in front of the screen again. There was an area map, rather too flashily 3D to be clear, and red markers. Lannigan frowned, trying to understand what was going on.

The picture changed. Parts of Fushigina's chainlink were down, and bodies lay at the gate. There was the flash and pop of gunfire.

Lannigan went cold. Rival corporations were blaming each other for *el plaga*, and what had started as just another demonstration had turned into a firefight. Liberación Huasteca had lost a village to corporate security. Unrest and resentment were flaring into open violence, each hotspot marked by a little red disc on the map.

The siren that had been howling for so long stuttered and died.

Lannigan got herself to the window again. This time the darkness was broken: patches of flickering yellow in the distance, a sudden puff of flame to the east. Very far away, if she squinted, she could just see a trail of bright dots that might have been tracer fire.

The fighting was coming this way. Lannigan had wandered into the middle of a war.

8
Miami

There was an advert board in the elevator, a cheap plastic flatscreen pasted to the wall and showing a looped McDonald's advert, all chubby children and happy, dancing CGI krillburgers and shakes. Rayanne couldn't take her eyes off it. The last thing she had eaten had been a double Kenyan Airlines lunch on the lifting body, twelve hours ago, and now those little smiling burgers looked good enough to rip right out of the picture and swallow whole, arms and legs and top hats and all.

Rayanne had never eaten airline food before. All her previous flights had been runs for Zenebe: on the way out she would be plagued with nausea as her system ballooned the sacs in her stomach lining with fresh merchandise, and the way back would have her feeling as though she had been scrubbed out with wire brushes from guts to throat. But this time, halfway through that long, slow, dirt-cheap flight from Mombasa to Miami International, somebody had put a plastic-covered meal down on the tray in front of her and she had been shredding the protective film away before she had even realised what she was doing.

The food was awful. A greying lump of reconstituted meat, a big flat thing made out of potatoes and bread, gravy. A desultory attempt at dessert that didn't actually taste of anything. Rayanne tore it up and wolfed it down, and, when the guy sitting next to her waved away his meal almost untouched, she leant over and took it from under his nose. Shovelled it down right alongside her own. After more than a week of getting by on coffee and Jolt Cola her insides had gone into overdrive, probably in some last-ditch attempt to build up some reserves before she keeled over from malnutrition.

Kenyan Airlines, however, were not generous with their catering. Rayanne had been offered nothing more for the remainder of the flight, and by the time the lifting body had touched down she was feeling almost faint with hunger. The last of her loose change had gone on the metromag journey from MIA to Brickell and one krillburger that had gone down without touching the sides.

The walk from Brickell station to Claughton Island had been about as much as she could take.

She forced her attention from the advert screen to the floor display. Zenebe's apartment was on the 85th floor, Claughton Complex block three, and the elevator wasn't fast. The numbers crawled. Rayanne watched 70 roll past and groaned, closing her eyes. She wondered if there was any food there.

On 85 the elevator bounced to a stop, and the advert board hissed static before telling Rayanne she had reached her floor, and that nothing would make the experience nicer than a McDonald's Superkrill with cheese. Rayanne couldn't have agreed more.

There were eight apartments on each floor of the Claughton Complex, six-by-five compacrete boxes in two rows of four, with a pair of elevators at either end of a cross-shaped central hallway. When Rayanne stepped out of the elevator she could see Zenebe's place on her right, two doors along. She froze.

She hadn't been expecting this. She had been expecting to waltz in, grab her stuff and go, but, standing there with the elevator doors sliding closed at her back and the broken fluorescent ceiling panel near the wall buzzing the way it always did, something came up from the forgotten places in the back of her mind and nailed her Nikes to the carpet.

The hallway didn't seem real. It was a replica, exact in every detail, slotted into place to fool her. Somebody had rebuilt the world, but forgotten to put Zenebe in it.

Rayanne stayed where she was for a long time, looking at the door. There were scraps of police tape around it. Zenebe hadn't died here; the Crew had caught up with him in Mombasa, in his Moi Avenue place, but the cops must have sealed this apartment anyway, searched it and scanned it and bagged up everything that looked like evidence. And then, when they were done with it, they had tugged the DO NOT ENTER tape away in big bunches and left the torn ends draped around the frame like yesterday's party decorations.

She sighed, and took a step. After that it was easy: the emotion that had frozen her by the elevator faded so rapidly that by the time she reached the door she had forgotten exactly what it was. Not grief, she decided, running her fingers over the lock. Zenebe wasn't the kind of man one could grieve. She couldn't even say for certain that she was sorry he was dead.

It was a question beyond her ability to answer, and she wasn't going to try. Luckily, no one had moved into the apartment since it had become vacant, so to speak, and the block management hadn't changed the lock. Rayanne took the foil condom packet from her inside pocket and wiggled it around in the slot until the mechanism got confused and tripped the bolt. Zenebe had never given her a key. If she was in Miami without him she was supposed to find a hostel somewhere, but Rayanne quickly learnt how to get in without him knowing and save on accommodation money.

The door jammed on something when she pushed it. She had to lean on it hard to get past.

Once inside, and with the lights on, Rayanne realised that the cops hadn't been the only people with an interest in Zenebe's apartment. Somebody had trashed the place: the sofa was tipped forward, spilling its foam guts all over the carpet and partially blocking the door. The screen in the corner was broken, the microwave eviscerated, the refrigerator door swinging open. There were clothes lying everywhere. A lot of them were hers.

Rayanne looked sorrowfully into the fridge, but the door had been open for days. There was nothing inside that wasn't too spoilt to eat. Zenebe's excuse for a food cupboard was likewise wrecked, and largely empty. Perhaps the Crew had taken his boxes of breakfast cereal and rice cakes away for analysis, convinced that he had painstakingly hidden tiny amounts of their merchandise inside individual grains of puffed wheat. Or maybe they just wanted some munchies while they were killing him.

Neither thought appealed to Rayanne very much. She went over to the water-filtration unit, checked the seals on the third cylinder. Her fingertip came away dry, which was a good sign. She found the spanner on its usual hook under the sink and used it to twist open the top of the catalyst feed. Cold water splashed her fingers, spilling down the smooth metal of the cylinder and on to the floor. Zenebe would have probably given her a good slap if he had realised that she knew about the cat feed, but she had seen him using it more than once when he thought she was asleep.

The ziploc bag was taped inside the pipe, just as she remembered it. The Crew hadn't been all that thorough, or all that bright. Rayanne grinned to herself as she wrenched the bag free. You didn't have to be a nano-surgeon to know about feed-pipe stashes.

There was a small, tight wad of bills in the ziploc: maybe a thousand dollars in hundreds and fifties. Along with that there was another packet, taped again to protect it from leaks. Zenebe's private recreation.

Wire, Blue Velvet, Rush and FND, all in crisp little tabs and gel ampoules, enough to keep Rayanne high for a week and oblivious for a month. She could wipe Africa away with the stuff she held now, forget Lannigan and Marcus Gray and the feeling of the Medichus extractor crawling down her throat. She could crush the memories so flat that she would need brain surgery to get them back.

She looked at the packet for a long time, a minute or more. Then she put it back into the pipe, made sure it was taped into place, and sealed the assembly with the spanner.

Good and tight.

The hunger came back as she rode the elevator back down to street level. Rayanne had showered in the apartment, quickly and with the bathroom door open, the spanner resting on the soap shelf. Then she had changed, swapping her ragged Africa jeans and T-shirt for a pair of black chinos and a red cutoff under her jacket. Her best gear went into a black drawstring bag and Rayanne went out of the door.

She stood with her back against the McDonald's advert as the elevator dropped. The tinny audio jingles kept reminding her of how hungry she was, but with Zenebe's money in her pocket she could deal with that problem just as soon as she got off the island. After that she could relax for a night, find somewhere cheap to crash, and start thinking about a flight to Europe.

Taking the money wasn't thieving, even if it were possible to steal from a dead man. Rayanne had been Zenebe's personal drugs factory and delivery system for months without anything in the way of recompense beside her keep. The thousand was back pay, pure and simple.

As for the drugs, Rayanne had no more clue as to why she had left them in the water filter than she had to the emotional jolt she had suffered outside the elevator.

Maybe the chem would have been too much of a reminder, a road map to a part of her life she wanted to turn her back on and leave behind. Maybe she didn't want to think about some of the things she had done under the influence. If nothing else, she realised, it might not be entirely safe to zone out for a while. Better to wait until she was somewhere else, somewhere that she had never been.

As long as it wasn't something she had picked up from Lannigan. The thought of the *lisiada*'s incessant nagging actually having had some effect on her would have been too much to handle.

The elevator chimed for the first floor, and the doors slid open. Rayanne stalked out, the drawstring bag over her shoulder, feeling herself getting annoyed. Lannigan's flat, whining voice was one memory that she would be happy to crush, along with all the trouble that the woman had gotten her into. Plus the fact that she had saved Lannigan's ass more than once in the past few days, and all she had to show for it was a minimum-fare trip to Miami, Florida.

'Yeah, thanks a bunch, *señora*,' she muttered, stamping out through the block foyer. That caught someone's attention: a skinny white guy in paper coveralls was looking at her, but she just glared at him until he went back to scrubbing graffiti.

As the big plexiglass doors slid aside to let her through she realised that feeling angry with Lannigan felt a lot better than feeling dejected about Zenebe.

Outside, she paused. The evening air felt flat and warm and soggy, even with the sun down and a cool breeze blowing towards the coast. Clouds of insects were whining around the striplights above the door. Rayanne could hear the sea rushing and sighing, the little slapping sounds it made against the causeway pylons. She smelt salt and the tang of ozone.

And as she raised her head, somebody ducked back from a window in the block opposite.

Rayanne yelped and hared off, keeping low, not stopping until she was well out of sight, round the next block. She hadn't caught more than the briefest glimpse of whoever was watching, little more than a sensation of movement. That, and a flick of light that reminded her a lot of the kind of reflection binoculars made.

It wouldn't be the first time she had been spied on in Claughton, of course. The blocks were a voyeur's paradise, barely metres apart and with the only window in each apartment built right over the bed. Maybe the bigger, more expensive places were better designed, but Rayanne had caught people looking in on her more than once. After a while she had refused to go into the bedroom unless the blinds were down.

Probably some old guy with nothing to do all day but watch the world go by. Still, for a moment there Rayanne had found herself really spooked, enough for her flight reflex to just take over like that.

When she walked back to the causeway she took the long way around, out of the voyeur's sight.

Off the causeway and on to the mainland. Rayanne headed west towards the Tamiami Trail, past the Bank of Pacifica building on the corner and then left into Brickell Avenue. She fell in step with the crowd for a while, watching the mix swarming among the mirrorglass and palm trees: Brickell business types hurrying along with their briefcases and datashades, early clubbers with animation screens woven into their clothes, couples arm in arm, streetkids. Africans and Pacificans and Native Americans and Haitians and clean-cut Eurotrash. A lot of Cubans. Maybe one in a hundred, Rayanne surmised, was a white North American.

Her stomach was still knotting, growling. Brickell was mainly financial, the buildings faced with dark pseudo-marble and glass and tooled steel, almost all of them post-storm. But there were plenty of roadside diners nestled among the banks. Rayanne stopped at a bubbletyred Malaysian food trailer and ordered the full works: chicken satay with peanut sauce, hot chilli crab with ginger and lime, special fried noodles and coconut rice. The crab was actually krill, and the chicken had probably started life in a petri dish, but Rayanne didn't give a damn. The food was cheap, the portions large, and the spices almost took off the back of her throat.

That and a couple of New Cokes had her back on the street, into Coral Way and up to the metromag station. She rode the moving stairway behind a pair of girls in screenshirts, the optical fabric tight over their thin backs and showing an all-over looped video of frantically dancing clubbers. Rayanne wondered if she had ever worn something as tacky as that, then felt an edgy memory of discomfort, of rough plastic chafing against her shoulders. Yes, she thought with a shudder. At some time in her life she probably had.

She stopped in front of a ticket panel, refused its request for a credit card and instead fed it ten-dollar notes until it disgorged a plastic freeline chip. The price horrified her – she had been in Miami only three weeks before, and the cost seemed to have at least doubled since then. Still, she could ride anywhere on the Miami metromag now she had one, all day every day for the next week. And since she didn't know how long she would have to stay in the city, or where she would be going while she was there, it was probably the best choice.

As she put the chip into her pocket, she checked her look in the black glassy face of the panel and saw someone behind her step sideways out of sight.

Rayanne spun round. Just like at Claughton – the barest suggestion of movement and a crawling feeling of being watched – but the sweat was cold between her shoulderblades and her stomach jumped around ersatz crab and chicken. She edged away, scanning the crowd, seeing nothing but milling travellers all moving and minding their business. A few of them glanced at her, but that was just curiosity. Wondering why a skinny girl with stripes on her face was backed against a ticket panel like a rat in headlights.

She ducked round the panel, pushed through a group of Brickell suits and on to the northbound platform. One of them stumbled and swore at her, his words obscured by the throaty whine of the metromag pulling up. Rayanne looked back to try to spot any pursuers, but all she saw was a Brickell pen-pusher in a sharp suit and datashades giving her the finger.

The mag had four carriages, sleek windowed bullets with bellows joints and fat superconducting lifter magnets in teardrop housings. Rayanne walked quickly alongside the mag until it stopped, then waited until the doors in the first carriage slid open. She got in and stood, grabbing a strap and facing backward, watching the compartments fill up. The suits clustered into carriage two, and paid her no mind. No one else caught her eye.

Maybe she was just getting paranoid. As the doors closed she relaxed a little, found a seat and dropped into it. She had the wall of the carriage to her back. The station skated past her and away, the mag so smooth on its repelling fields that Rayanne felt as though she were staying rock-still with the world gliding on by. She hugged herself, drawing the jacket closer. She glanced back down the length of the carriage.

He was watching her from the next compartment, just behind the bellows. Very tall, very slim, shiny-bald head with skin like polished leather. He wore foil shades and a long coat of silvery polysilk.

Rayanne didn't recognise the man, but he had Crew written all over him.

She slumped back into the seat, breathing hard. Doogie had betrayed her again, telling her that the Crew wouldn't follow her out of Africa. She couldn't be certain that the Londoner had been in on Gray's plan to use her against Broca, but he had sure let her down here. She should never have trusted him, have trusted anyone. Rayanne felt a sickening rush of betrayal, even worse than the fear, but above that was the sudden, desperate wish that Doogie – or even that scheming witch Lannigan – was there with her.

The mag started dropping velocity. Rayanne felt the tug of deceleration and looked up, at the neon signs for GOVERNMENT CENTRE whisking past. She stayed where she was as the mag slowed, the effort almost unbearable, but she held herself down on to the seat, knuckles white, even when the platform stilled outside the window and the doors parted. Passengers stepped off. Others stepped on. Rayanne kept quite still, watching the African's reflection in the chrome curve of a stanchion until the doors started to close, and then she was up and out, the drawstring bag held in front, and squeezing through the door seals as they slapped into her shoulders. A moment's struggle and she was free.

She looked back along the platform. Right into his foil shades as he tugged the last centimetre of coat from the closed doors.

At his back, the mag accelerated smoothly away.

Rayanne bolted, her Nikes hammering at the platform as she scrambled towards the barriers. For a frantic second she thought they weren't going to open in time, but as her outstretched hand touched the metal the freeline chip triggered the mechanism and she went through without slowing.

She ran another ten metres, rounded a corner and passed a gleaming array of ticket panels. His reflection was in them, just behind her: he must have had a freeline chip too. She wasted a few precious seconds scanning the station for a cop, then gave in and ran again. Turned a corner at random, and slammed painfully into a metal trashcan bolted to the wall. Her hand went in as she whirled, her fingers closing over gum wrappers, used paper tickets, a slime of fruit peel. He came round the corner at that moment and she used the last of her momentum to barrel right into him.

He grunted, barely slowed by the impact, but it was just enough. His clutching fingers grabbed the air behind her. She sped up again as best she could, puffing now, heading back towards the northbound platform. Ahead of her, another mag was pulling in.

Her Nikes were slipping on the smooth station floor. The African was close, very close: he was stronger, and whatever he had on his feet provided far better traction than her shoes. Rayanne went through the barrier as it opened automatically, then skated to a halt, leant over and dumped her handful of used tickets into the hopper.

The barrier slammed shut and let out a whoop of siren, its software convinced that someone was trying to get on to the platform with a redundant ticket. The African went into the barrier hard, and Rayanne heard him yell as she jumped through the metromag doors and into the carriage. She grabbed a stanchion and swung round. He was climbing over the barrier.

Going to the next one along would have been quicker. The mag doors closed when he was still a metre away. As she slumped down into the nearest seat she heard his fist against the window, a single, enraged impact.

Rayanne looked down the carriage as the mag pulled away. Everyone in it was staring at her.

She grinned weakly. 'Boyfriends, huh?'

Rayanne stayed on the mag as it turned east, then back south, past Edcom and College and First Street. By the time she got to Bayfront Park her legs had stopped shaking enough to let her walk.

She stumbled down the moving stairway and out into the street. At the entrance, a wavefront of indecision caught her: she froze beside a marble pillar, torn between waiting to make sure she wasn't being followed and just heading out into the night, trying to lose herself among the Miami crowds. More than anything she wanted to find somewhere quiet and zone out, to wash away the fear and surround herself with a warm and friendly fog of chemical amnesia.

But that, she knew, would be the end of her. The Crew would find her if she stopped long enough to get high, and, when they did, dying would be the least of her worries.

Still, there was a halfway point that was looking more attractive by the moment. Rayanne straightened herself up, shrugged the bag over her shoulder, and set off towards Bayfront Park. If luck was on her side she would find an oblivion there that owed nothing to molecular biology or backstreet chem labs.

She kept to the paths as she made her way through the park, finding the largest groups of people and staying with them until they slowed or began heading in the wrong direction. As she dodged from crowd to crowd she kept looking back, glancing over her shoulder, turning, backtracking a few yards and then joining a new cluster of revellers. By the time she reached the holotheatre she had seen as much behind her as she had ahead, and had actually made herself rather dizzy. Still, she was reasonably sure that no one was on her tail.

The sea smell was strong here, salty and brackish, mingling with the cut-grass richness of the park lawns and the fresh spice of flowerbeds. Rayanne made her way towards the storm memorial, reaching out to it as she passed, her fingertips brushing tooled bronze weathered into almost liquid smoothness. The big storm had remodelled Miami just before she was born, so the memorial was as old as she was, maybe a little older.

Rayanne had seen pictures of Bayside Marketplace before the storm. It had looked old, all angled roofs and verandas, flags waving above the white chunky boats lined up in the basin. The sprawling, fungal clusters of overlapping domes in front of her now might have been safer, but there was something about the thought of that great, flat-sided complex that made Rayanne sad in a way she couldn't describe.

She went in through a door that looked like a huge Chinese fan in green glass, and began weaving her way through herds of shoppers until she found the place she was looking for. Into video-walled, air-conditioned coolness, down on to a padded stool in front of the mirror-topped bar. 'Gimme a beer and a scotch, man. No ice.'

The barman was Cuban – she was almost sure just by looking – but when he spoke to her in Spanish she placed his ancestors in Havana, his parents in Flagler Street. 'How old are you, sister?'

'Twenty,' she lied, slipping into the same language. He shook his head.

'Sorry, sister. The statutory age shifted to twenty-one again last week. Have you been away?'

She swore under her breath. Dade County was presently controlled by a three-way coalition; that was about as far as Rayanne's knowledge of politics went, but she knew that the minimum ages for drinking, driving, smoking in public and just about every other worthwhile human activity had been see-sawing ridiculously for months. The moral sector must have tugged harder than usual since her last run.

Rayanne put elbows on the bar and her chin in her hands. 'Anything else I can't do until next birthday? Nah, don't answer that. I'm depressed enough. Gimme a Jolt.'

'Extra Sugar or Superox?'

Rayanne chose the superoxygenated brand, two bottles, and retreated to a corner table. She could watch the door from there, for all the good it would do her, and two of the video walls were out of her field of view. Which was a blessing.

She had wanted to talk to the barman, but the place was filling up and he had too many drinks to mix, too many teenagers to turn away. That left Rayanne on her own again. She had never been good at being alone, had never really liked her own company. Other people made things easier: they could take her places, watch her back, keep her safe.

Rayanne was on her own in Miami; people were chasing after her with murder in mind; and she didn't know what to do.

If Lannigan were here, she would have known. That thought stuck in Rayanne's throat, but she had to swallow it anyway. Granted, the little Anglo's first priority was always herself, and if Rayanne managed to survive her machinations then that was a bonus, but it would have been a place to start. If Rayanne wanted a plan of action now she would have to think one up for herself, and plans just weren't her strong point.

She gulped down the first bottle of Jolt, feeling the caffeine fizz crawl over her shoulder blades and down her spine. A cold depression was welling up around her, despite the Superox and the cheery crowds surrounding her – most of the tables were occupied now, and more customers were coming in all the time. She watched a Haitian jazz combo in red tuxedos downing as many beers as they could before their next set, a young Pacifican woman sipping mineral water on her own, a knot of smartly dressed old ladies all drinking from the same vodka bottle through long plastic straws. She found herself envying them with sickening intensity.

Rayanne opened the second bottle and tried to cheer herself up by remembering how horrible Lannigan was, but it didn't work. The woman might have been cold and sarcastic and intent on jerking people around like puppets until she got what she wanted, but Rayanne had known far worse. Zenebe had sent her away to be modified so she could run drugs past PATCo for him, and had slapped her around on a semi-regular basis. Three girls in New York that she thought were her friends had tried to rape her. A boyfriend in Cuba had wanted to pimp her out to his teachers and improve his grades.

Lannigan hadn't tried to do any of those things. In Rayanne's estimation, that brought her pretty close to sainthood. She raised her bottle, nodded a little private toast to the *lisiada*'s memory, and realised that she was being watched again.

Not covertly, this time. No one ducked out of sight when she looked up. The Pacifican woman met her gaze with utter stillness and held it, the glass of mineral water ignored on the tabletop in front of her. Her slim, pale hands folded neatly around a black leather purse.

Rayanne stared back. For a moment, between the raw knowledge of being watched and the sudden comprehension of who was doing the watching, a spark of panic had flared in her gut, fixing the scene in memory. The woman wore a black polysilk blazer over a white shirt. The glass had droplets of condensation beading the sides, tiny puddles on the tabletop. A Taiwanese idol singer beamed coquettishly out from the video wall behind her, magnified, framing the woman between perfect, hooded eyes.

The spark died. Rayanne got to her feet, feeling angry and foolish. She had flinched hard when she had felt the woman's eyes on her, and spilt the last of her Jolt over the drawstring bag. Brown fizz dripped off the fabric and on to the carpet. Rayanne glared down at it, then back up at the Pacifican. Daring her to smile.

The woman's head was tipped very slightly to one side. She was still watching Rayanne intently.

Rayanne marched towards her, dodging the jazz players and the vodka ladies, slamming her hands down flat on to the Pacifican's table, looming over. 'What the hell are you looking at, lady?'

The Pacifican blinked up at her, and Rayanne's breath stopped in her throat.

She had felt like this before, outside the Joy Night Motel, with Lannigan's eyes cutting through her like thin blades of ice. Stripping down through the lies and the bullshit, dissecting her, opening her up until she could pull Rayanne's soul right out through her skull and take it to pieces like a puzzle. Nailing her to the truth.

This was worse. A hundred times worse.

If Lannigan was comet ice, this woman was the space between comets, utterly dark, utterly cold. In those black eyes Rayanne would freeze, suffocate, decompress, until she died. She staggered back. The edge of a table hit the backs of her legs, and she heard distant cries as drinks vibrated and spilt. Somebody shoved her away and she stumbled. Her hands and knees hit carpet.

That was enough to break the connection. With her eyes no longer on those of the Pacifican, she was able to think, to breathe, to escape. She scrambled up and away, through the sliding doors and out of the dome, her heart yammering and her breath a hot saw in her throat.

She didn't stop running for ages, not until she was out of Bayside and halfway to the McArthur Causeway. That was when her legs gave out and she collapsed, her Nikes stretched out in the grass in front of her and her back against a trashcan.

She sat there for a long time – bugs swarming in the air behind her head – trying to rationalise what she had seen. Now, in the warm evening air, with soft grass under her and the smell of the sea and hologram adverts sending rainbow light skittering around, her reaction seemed strange. Incomprehensible, as though it had all happened to someone else. Rayanne had seen things in her time, terrible things, most of which she had been able to forget. Could the cold, sad gaze of a Pacifican woman maybe five years her elder really have been so frightening?

There hadn't even been malice in the woman's eyes. It was something very different from anger, or hatred, or any of the usual things that made people frightening. No, it was a studying look, analytical, interested in a completely uncaring way. As though Rayanne wasn't a person, nothing alive at all, just a piece of circuitry or a fragment of computer code.

That was the scary part. Standing there, with the

Pacifican looking up at her, Rayanne had been robbed of all humanity. Of all worth.

Understanding that made Rayanne feel a little better. She sniffled, wiped her nose on the back of her sleeve, and began to look around.

She had made it as far as Bicentennial Park. It spread out in front of her, green and wide, dotted with palm groves and the glittering abstracts of hologram sculpture. White gravel paths snaked away into the darkness, lit by suspended lamps, brilliant pearls on silver wire, into chains of illumination.

Rayanne got up, found a path and began to walk along it. She had memories of this place, especially the northern edge, beyond the yacht basin and the visitor centre. That was where the blankers gathered to watch mosquitoes dive-bomb the holograms, to exchange stories and dealers and remind each other who they were. Where people gravitated towards others with the same jacket, or T-shirt design, or expression. Where the night people came out.

There were no children in Bicent North. The families and the suits and the old folks stayed south, in Bayside.

She took the bridge over the yacht basin and headed for the food court, into a ring of gleaming counter pods. The pods were opened like clamshells, the lids lined with glowing biolume, pipes and cables snaking away below ground for the water and electricity feeds. Ultrasonics kept the bugs to a minimum. Rayanne used to come here on a regular basis, drinking coffee and Jolt Cola to keep her energy levels up when she was on a run. It was a good enough place, when you had nowhere else to go.

Unbelievably, her stomach was growling again. Rayanne edged towards a burger pod, watching little hologram burgers whirl above the counter top, and then someone behind her said, 'Rayanne?'

She span. Two pods along was a Korean *pulgogi* pod, meat and red chillies jumping in an electric wok, the smell of broth stinging her sinuses from four metres away. Rayanne moved closer, checking out the guy behind the counter. He was waving at her.

She looked at him blankly. He was thin and pale, about her own age, with a red nose and a fuzz of bleached blond hair that stuck out from his head in thousands of tiny spikes. In the blue light of the biolume he looked like a corpse, shrouded in white paper coveralls and stirring a wok with a spatula in either hand. 'Er, hi,' she said.

'Gregor Kamarov.' Slavic accent; the easy, open tone of someone accustomed to reminding people who he was. 'Four-dollar soup after 10 p.m., extra chilli. Yes?'

Four-dollar soup. Bitter and oily at the end of a day's cooking, but dirt cheap at four bits. Rayanne had eaten the soup on a few of her trips: when her sacs were full it was about as solid as she could manage, and most of the time it was all she could afford. After extraction she was normally on her way, and pouring chilli soup on to raw stomach lining was not a good idea. One time had been enough to put her in the Jackson Memorial ER for three hours. She had missed her flight back, and Zenebe had not been best pleased.

She pushed the flood of memory down. 'Gregor. Jeez, man, almost didn't catch you.'

'I saw you there, wondered if it was you.' He waved a finger in front of his face, miming her stripes. 'Then I saw.'

Rayanne leant on the counter, feeling the wok's heat on her skin. 'Can't believe you still got this thing.'

'Is coming up on three years.' His face darkened. 'Susan, she cannot work now.'

'I guess.' Rayanne felt suddenly uncomfortable. Her own memory had a lot of holes in it, and much of what remained was like the soup frothing in Gregor's pan, bubbles of recall popping up, bursting, almost too small and brief to latch on to before they were gone. A background chaos of recollection. Sometimes a big, sour lump of old chilli would bob up, at which point

Rayanne would take a little chem and calm everything down again, push the past back out of sight where it belonged.

Suzy Pearson had been blanking for longer, but not by much: maybe a couple of years. When Rayanne had met her last the girl was just getting to the stage of forgetting her own name.

She frowned, glad she had left the packet of drugs back in the apartment. 'Look, Gregor. You heard about –'

'Zenebe? Yes, I heard.' He cocked his head over. 'Was all around Bicent for a day or two. All the stories.' His voice dipped as he leant a little closer. 'And you. How are you doing?'

She almost told him about being chased, about Zenebe's wrecked apartment and how the Embu Crew were after her, all the way from Africa. But Rayanne didn't want to be alone any more, and letting people know she had the Papas on her tail would have been a fast and certain way to lose friends. 'I'm yokay, man.'

'You look tired.'

'Yeah, I just need a place to crash. A beer or something. You know.' She threw a quick glance over her shoulder, hoping that Gregor wouldn't notice. 'I'm heading out, maybe tomorrow.'

'Away from Miami?'

'*Right* out. Maybe Europe, I dunno.'

Gregor's eyebrows went up. 'New leaf, hm? Fresh start?'

'Something like that.'

'You should talk to Susan, perhaps.'

Rayanne half nodded. Right now, talking to Suzy was pretty low on her want list. She noticed Gregor switching off the wok, the soup pan, sliding his spatulas and spoons into wash slots. 'You shutting down?'

'I'd better get back.' Gregor pushed open a door in the back of the pod. When he walked around to where Rayanne was standing he had shredded his paper coveralls and the lid was whining closed.

Under the paper he wore Bermuda shorts and a blue Übergen T-shirt. The insides of his thin arms were poked with coin-sized bruises, dark spots under the skin from using a gas syringe. 'We have beer back at the hab, Rayanne.'

'Ah, I dunno, Gregor. I mean, what with Suzy and all.'

'Is White Riot, good beer. Imported from home. You need a place to crash, right?' He drew closer. 'And Suzy . . . It would be good for her to have someone else to talk to, someone she knows.'

Rayanne found herself gnawing on a fingernail, and stopped, dragging the hand away from her mouth. 'I don't want to be no trouble, man. I can get a hostel, or something . . .'

'No trouble.' He had an arm round her shoulders, manoeuvring her between the tables. His touch made her want to shrink away, and there was something in his voice that Rayanne didn't like, a hollowness that sounded like need, like hunger. She hoped he was just in need of a hit, because if he was expecting Rayanne to provide him with what Suzy wasn't up to any more there was going to be trouble.

That said, a hostel would cost her, even at the lowest rate, and sleeping in a doorway wasn't an option with the Crew sniffing around. Rayanne could stay out of sight and save herself a hundred dollars or more, if she could keep a lid on her distaste for a few hours.

She had done worse, and for far less. She picked up the pace, letting Gregor lead her and keeping her mind fixed firmly on a fridge full of cold beer.

9
Kitsumi

She awoke clawing, tearing at clammy, tangled sheets. The darkness was suffocating and filled with fluttering shadows, nightmarish things that hovered on the edge of vision even when she had scrambled her way free. The night was alive with thunder.

Lannigan sat up, gasping, glaring around the tiny room. She hadn't meant to fall asleep, but the deadening Mexico heat had worked on her exhaustion and dragged her into a feverish, dream-haunted doze. A glance at her chrono told her that she had lost nearly three hours.

She shook herself and rubbed her face vigorously, as if the friction would return some clarity to her thoughts. It worked, to an extent, although raw edges of what she had dreamt still filtered through into reality. Capture, she remembered, being held tightly in some lightless place, dry and cave-cold.

And something clawed, reaching down to lever her apart . . .

No surprises there. The sheets had become knotted round her body as tight as ropes during those lost hours, and the box was still throwing grainy flickers around the room. The thunder had its place too: loud bangings from outside must have impinged upon her sleeping mind, distant rumbles bringing forth imaginary storms.

Lannigan found her cane and got up, making her way cautiously to the window. There, in the street, one source of dream thunder was revealed – the rotund owner of the guesthouse was hurling boxes and suitcases into the back of a Cadillac ground-effect truck.

As Lannigan opened the window and leant out she saw that the woman wasn't alone. A thin, dark-skinned young man was passing the cases to her; he in turn was being supplied by another, and possibly more. Lannigan couldn't see that far under the doorway. A number of silent children clustered away to one side.

She frowned. This was not a good sign. 'Hello? Ma'am?'

The woman looked up. 'You're still here?'

'Apparently.' Lannigan looked around, up and down the street. 'I take it you're not staying.'

'Damn straight. If I want fireworks I'll go to Disneyland, yeah?' She heaved another case into the truck, the impact causing the vehicle to shudder drunkenly on its billowing apron bag. 'Thought I might nip up north for a spell.'

'What about me?'

'Yeah, what about you?' The woman opened the truck's cockpit door, then turned and beckoned to the knot of children. 'In. Move your arses.'

'Well, can I stay here?'

'I wouldn't advise it.' As she spoke there was a thumping roar, several streets distant. Lannigan felt the windows rattle. The woman and her entourage ducked reflexively, almost as one, then turned to gape at a rolling cushion of flame rolling lazily into the sky a hundred metres to the east. 'God, was that the volt station?'

Lannigan stared. Chunks of debris were laying trails of smoke through the air. She could hear them hitting the pavement. 'Who the hell was that?'

'Don't ask me. Damn near everyone's on the warpath tonight.' The children were packed into the cockpit now, and Lannigan counted four dark-skinned men crouched among the luggage on the flatbed. The woman clambered up into the cockpit and took hold of the door.

'Look, love, I'd get under cover if I was you.' She gestured to one of the kids. 'Tom here says he saw a helicopter.'

'I'll bear that in mind.' Lannigan backed away from the window as the door slammed and the truck heaved itself up, wallowing on its curtain like some vast, fat animal. She watched it nose away, down the street and round a corner.

Not all of Lannigan's thunder dreams had been born from flying luggage, it seemed.

She went back to the bed and began sorting through her carryall. Her clothes were in a bad way, caked with dried mud as red and hard as old brick. There was a clear bootprint on the back of her suit jacket, a legacy of the ambush.

One of the polysilk outfits she had bought at the discount store had been in plain black, a choice that had drawn some looks at the time but that could prove eminently practical now. Lannigan found the shirt and trousers, slammed them repeatedly against the wall until most of the mud came off, then stripped and changed. Her shoes were black anyway, to go with the grey business suit.

The carryall was a problem. With some reluctance, Lannigan decided to leave it in the room. She stashed what money she had left into her pockets, along with the Huastec's cigar lighter and knife.

There was nothing else of use in the room, or indeed in the rest of the building. The Aborigine woman had cleared the place quite effectively.

The search terminated at the front door. Lannigan hesitated there, suddenly unsure. In any normal circumstances what she was preparing to do would be unthinkable, ridiculous. Even if she had been fully mobile the city would be dangerous in the extreme; for a woman who could barely walk five steps without her walking cane it was a deathtrap. Given the choice she would have quite gladly holed up in a basement somewhere and waited for the whole thing to blow over.

And blow over it would, had the nature of the conflict stayed at the local level. But certain foreign financial concerns were becoming involved, and there was talk of bioweapons. When Lannigan had woken, the box on the table had been showing pictures of United Nations headquarters.

If the UN got involved, Veracruz Llave was in for a rough time indeed. That would put an end to her search, in one way or another, and she couldn't afford that. Lannigan unlocked the door and stepped out into the street.

Within ten minutes she had no idea where she was.

Roughly half the streetlamps she had seen since leaving the guesthouse were dark, some openly damaged, some fluttering weakly as their power supply fluctuated. A thin, pervading layer of smoke had turned the streets into a maze of moving shadows. Lannigan could smell it on the air, the ever present haze of chemical pollution overlaid with the miasma of distant fires, scorched plastic and burning wood. It made the streets feel muffled, shrouded.

There was no sound, save a few distant cries and the barking of dogs. The city was eerily silent.

After a time she paused, unsure of her bearings. The smoke had thickened while she had been asleep, and most of the ground modules lined along the sidewalks had vanished, their owners no doubt as eager to be away from the fighting as the guesthouse owner. Lannigan's route so far had been largely random. Despite the thickness of the air her footsteps had sounded awfully loud, and she had found herself constantly looking back over her shoulder, into each darkened doorway, throwing panicky glances at any hint of movement. After no more than a handful of turnings and crossings, she was almost completely disorientated, and thoroughly lost.

There was another crossing in front of her now, a narrow T-junction between rows of stuccoed apartments. The road at right angles to where she stood was wide, two lanes, but what she could see of it was just as dim and anonymous as all the others. She glanced around, turned the corner, and came face to face with a roadblock.

For a long, frozen moment she just stood and stared. Three electric vans were slewed in a jagged line across the street, the spaces between them a tangle of debris and razorwire. She could see fires burning sullenly behind the vans, scorched trashcans billowing smoke and orange licks of flame. For a moment she thought she was alone there, but after a few seconds she noticed shadowy figures hunched in balconies and doorways to either side of the barricade, more behind the razorwire and in the cockpits of the vans. Most of them seemed to be carrying guns, and at least two held long, wicked-looking metal tubes, the use of which Lannigan could only guess at.

Somebody hissed a hurried, angry sentence at her in Spanish. Lannigan didn't know the words, but the meaning was clear enough. She turned back to the corner, intending to retrace her steps and perhaps start again from the guesthouse, but the smoky night was suddenly cut through with narrow cones of light, and the throaty whine of heavy-gauge electric engines.

Before she could move the first truck was past her, the armoured wheel barely centimetres from her shoulder, the rush of its passing almost sending her into the street. She yelled and clutched at the wall, just managing to stay upright. From round the corner came the sound of gunfire, the flat snap of hypersonic bullets carving the air.

The second truck whirled across the road and braked hard, rocking, massive panels erupting out and down from its flanks. Lannigan crouched against the wall as armoured figures leapt from the truck and scattered, hunting cover. Something sizzled past her field of view, leaving a bright track across her retinas. It missed the truck and blew a sheet of flame across the far end of the street.

One of the metal tubes, Lannigan decided, limping hurriedly away. Some kind of portable antitank weapon, viciously destructive but difficult to aim with the range so short. The very fact that someone would choose to open fire with such a thing in an urban area said more about the nature of this conflict than Lannigan really wanted to know.

Gunfire was still rattling behind her. She rounded another corner and hobbled down a sidestreet, pausing at the corner to catch her breath. A rotund police module howled past her, lights fluttering red and blue, then two more in rapid succession. The vehicles were nothing like the massive trucks assaulting the roadblock. Lannigan wondered whether she had seen some military operation, or corporate involvement.

She stepped out cautiously. A snap of blue light caught her attention, over to her right. The smoke there was thick, and Lannigan had to get close before she realised exactly what she was looking at.

It was the recharge station, where she had stood to watch the riot on the Plaza de Armas. The place was so wrecked she hadn't even recognised it at first, with two of its walls blown out, the forecourt canopy sagging, smouldering lumps of plastic scattered underfoot. The remains of a ground module lay overturned next to a wrecked volt hydrant. Blue sparks jumped among a tangle of broken cable.

The station had been blown up while Lannigan was talking to the guesthouse owner, from the look of things by some kind of homemade bomb. Lannigan edged closer, carefully avoiding the cables, and peered into the eviscerated office. 'Hello? Anyone here?'

As she spoke the smoke cleared for a moment. She saw what was sprawled across the ruined counter, what it had in place of a head, and then she was stumbling away with her eyes closed and her throat full of acid. Explosions, she thought wildly, in enclosed spaces. The pressure wave enters through the mouth and blows off the top of the skull.

Outside she forced herself to stop, to take a few deep breaths. Away from the smouldering volt station the air was a little clearer, and there was an edge of salt behind the smoke. The sea must be close. From what she remembered of the city's layout, the *zócalo* was no more than a few hundred metres from the commercial marina. If the *Kitsumi Maru* was still in Veracruz, it would most likely be moored there.

Lannigan had no idea of what she would do if it wasn't. In fact, she had very little notion of how to proceed if it was.

She shook herself, aware that she had too much to do to be paralysed by self-doubt. The smoke around her swirled again, as it had in the office, a sudden breeze picking at her hair before dying. Lannigan paused, slightly puzzled, as she felt the air begin to throb.

There was a pulse to it, as quick as her own panicky heartbeat, a vast and silent drum. It was overhead before she could react, a huge shape in the air, blasting the smoke away in hammering pulses. Lannigan looked up and saw it racing away, trailing a hurricane of scattered dust and debris. For a second it was a shark, pale and sleek and predatory in the darkness, until it turned lazily and she saw streetlight flick across its canopy, the missiles racked beneath its stubby wings.

The child, Tom. He hadn't lied about seeing a helicopter.

Lannigan stared in horror, watching the machine sweep low over the *zócalo* and trying to work out how long it would take United Nations landing craft to get from Galveston down the coast to Veracruz.

Yellow flickers began to spring up from the buildings across the square, followed moments later by a crackling that could have been gunfire. The helicopter tilted, its whirling rotors blowing the *zócalo* clear of smoke for an instant, and Lannigan saw armoured trucks nestling close to the hotels and restaurants there. The army must have set up positions on the roofs, in the upper floors. They were trying to bring down the helicopter with small-arms fire.

The aircraft paused, lifted its stubby nose, and spat four lines of vapour towards the nearest building.

One trail terminated abruptly in midair, and two more span crazily out over the rooftops and away. But the last must have reached its target, because as Lannigan ducked for cover the entire top floor of the Hotel Santander lifted in a bellowing cloud of fragments and vomited flame across the Plaza de Armas.

Lannigan stood up, aimed herself at the sea and, bad leg or no bad leg, ran like bloody hell.

There were barricades up between the *zócalo* and the marina: down one street a random construction of furniture and module parts, manned by a cluster of frightened citizens; in another a hinged lattice of polycarbon armour in *policía* green and white. Lannigan tried to detour along Indepencia, limping among hundreds of looters over a treacherous carpet of broken window plastic, but the crowds were too thick there, moving too fast. She was bowled over twice, once by a fat woman clutching a crate of whiskey bottles, and the second time by an old man who stumbled hard against her when she tried to pass a discount boutique.

She sat up, cursing, and then noticed that the old man wasn't moving. There was blood on his lips, a tiny hole in his shoulder when she looked more closely. A hypersonic bullet had entered there and carved a new body cavity the size and shape of a goose egg.

Lannigan got herself upright, staying close to the wall.

She couldn't see anyone with a gun, and no one else seemed to have noticed the old man collapse. They were too intent on stripping Indepencia's shops of merchandise.

There was very little shouting. The looters were frighteningly silent in their efforts.

Lannigan heard a scream from some way up the street. A woman was rolling on the ground, hands to her belly, her thin print dress dark with blood. A few people had paused in their pillage to watch; no more than a handful, and in their faces only a dull-eyed curiosity. They stood silently as the woman shrieked, jostled by their more oblivious fellows, until one of them clapped a hand to his face and toppled bonelessly into the road.

Before he had hit the ground the woman beside him jerked, coughed out a mouthful of blood and tissue, and fell. Instantly the crowd were running, their screams of terror rivalling those of the woman still squirming on the pavement. Their fear was infectious, and as the sea of looters began to disperse Lannigan saw past them, clear through to the soldiers kneeling around their personnel carrier and firing repeatedly into the crowd.

A bullet slapped the wall next to her head. She jerked back, fragments of hot plaster stinging her skin. The slug was tiny, a sliver of metal the size of a match head, but if it had hit her its ferocious kinetic energy would have ripped her open. The wall was smoking where it had struck.

She was hunting furiously for cover when the helicopter came back.

As before, she felt it before she heard it. The pounding beat in the air, the rhythmic pressure turning into a hammering roar of rotors and the pale-bellied shape swinging out of the darkness. The backdraft shoved her down and surrounded her in a storm of dust and litter, making her cover her face with her free hand as she ran across the pavement, over the road and into a pitch-dark alley, with howling looters on either side and hypersonic bullets kicking craters in the tarmac behind her.

She made it into the alley and slumped against the wall. Her right leg felt as though it was on fire, her left cramping with exertion. From behind her came the chainsaw screech of heavy machine guns as the helicopter opened up on the military. Ahead was shouting, and the ringing of bells.

The alley was utterly dark. Lannigan felt her way along the wall, her toes stubbing painfully against loose stones and exposed pipes, her hands scraping against rough, dry brick. Once, something that felt like a bundle of old rags shifted and moved under her shoe, and a few metres on she trod on a furry mound that crunched and vented warm slime. There was an awful smell of rotting, here. Even the wall at her side seemed halfway to dissolution.

A turning almost had her over. She stumbled, the thought of finding herself on that littered ground filling her with horror, then steadied herself and found the wall once more. Within a few metres she began to see light, and the edge of a second turning. Past that was a new street.

And a barricade, blocking the end of the alley with a jagged maze of timber and fibreboard.

Lannigan moaned. She felt close to collapse, all the strength gone from her, and the thought of making her way back through the alley and into the carnage of Indepencia was simply too much. Instead, she moved closer to the makeshift barrier, trying to see what lay behind it.

When she did see, the sight had her breath away.

For the first few seconds the mere shape of it held her – the spires, the arches, the buttresses and the steeple, stone glowing like gold in the light from varicoloured windows. But as she looked more closely, as she became accustomed to the glare, she noticed something askew about the entire structure. The steeple was ridged and convoluted, more like a column of massive vertebrae than a simple tower. The spires twisted their way into the smoky air; the buttresses impaled the ground in osseous sweeps and curls; the doorway was a maze of interlocking ribs. It was a cathedral carved from the skeletons of giants, the skulls of dragons. It didn't show a straight wall anywhere.

Lannigan had never seen anything even remotely like it. She gaped like a lunatic.

And that was when a priest popped up from behind the barricade, levelled a plastic disposable pistol at Lannigan's head and asked her to raise both her hands and keep them where he could see them, if she didn't mind.

The priest's name was Father Gabriel Bendito Carrillas, and as he led Lannigan across the square to the church he pointed out the other barricades. 'That one is guarded by two of my curates, and that by some of the sisters. We will defend the *catedral* as long as we are able.'

Lannigan nodded, rubbing the back of her head. She'd given herself a painful knock on her way through the barrier, despite Father Gabriel ripping half of it down to let her through. 'You really think the church is in danger?'

'Liberación would destroy it if they could. They have always hated it, for its origins and its purpose.' He sighed. 'Foreign technologies and a foreign religion, two factors which they blame for their plight.'

Lannigan didn't entirely understand. 'Are they wrong?'

The priest smiled sadly. 'No, I don't think they are.'

She frowned, but kept her silence. If her suspicions as to the ownership of the helicopter were correct, Father Gabriel was going to need a lot more than roadblocks to keep his church intact.

There were two nuns at the main entrance, distressingly at ease with the huge guns they carried. Lannigan saw that each weapon had a bore wider than her thumb, and realised that the guns must have been very old. She wondered whether a big, slow bullet would do as much damage as a small, fast one, and decided that yes, it probably would. She smiled thinly at the nuns as she passed, and they bobbed solemnly in return.

Father Gabriel pushed one of the doors open enough to let Lannigan slip past. 'You may shelter here as long as you wish. Forgive me, but I must return to the barricade.'

'Thank you, Father.' But he was already away. She watched him hurry back across the square, the yellow disposable gun looking foolish and toylike in his fist. Abruptly, she envied him. He had something in his life that he loved so much he was willing to take on the whole of Liberación Huasteca to protect it. With a gun that came out of a vending machine.

She pushed the door closed and wandered into the cathedral.

The interior of the place was dizzying. Lannigan stood and stared, her gaze drawn up the weirdly ridged columns to the ribbed and fluted ceiling, over the thousands of candles that spilt wax and light over the curving walls, across the intricately tiled floor. To her left an obscene web of stone supported a blue-clad virgin – four metres tall and smiling beatifically. To her right, a crucified Christ in similar proportion. Lesser saints gazed down from their alcoves, fading into dimness. 'My god. What the hell is this?'

'It is *la Catedral de la Santos*.' A nun, hooded and robed and very young, had emerged from the shadows at her side. She smiled shyly. 'Although you maybe know it as *la Catedral de la Sabandijas*.'

'*Sabandijas . . .*' Lannigan tilted her head towards the roof, seeing structures as complex and organic as the inside of a bone. 'Bugs? You let *structants* build this place?'

The nun motioned Lannigan forward. Their footfalls echoed softly as they walked along the nave. 'The cathedral is completed before I am born, *señora*. I am not sure about the details. Perhaps you will ask Father Gabriel about that.'

'Ah, that's yokay.' She had the measure of the place now, and well understood what the priest had meant about Liberación Huasteca and their enmity. No doubt the widescale use of architectural structants was the final insult as far as the activists were concerned – one more example of work being taken from the hands of local people. But instead of Spanish-speaking Mexicans or even foreign labour reaping the benefit, the job had been given to a superhive of altered termites. A hive that had taken whatever design they had been programmed with and turned it into a surrealist nightmare of soaring stones.

The idea would have been almost funny, if people weren't dying for it. 'Amazing,' she muttered.

'You think yes?' The nun, misunderstanding, seemed almost childishly pleased. 'The structure has many critics. Structants are no longer used for such projects, I am sure. This is the only church of its kind in all Mexico.'

'Well.' They were almost at the end of the nave. Lannigan started looking for another door, one that would let her out closer to the marina. The priest's offer of rest and shelter had been welcome, but she had a feeling that time was getting short, and she had no desire to be around if the Huastecs decided to take out their frustrations on the cathedral. Let Father Gabriel and his sisters martyr themselves for an oversized bug nest if they wished. 'Best of luck, then.'

'Thank you, *señora*.' The nun bobbed at her. 'Would you like something to eat? Some of the congregation have soup and bread.'

'I'm sure that's very nice, but I've really –' She stopped abruptly. 'I'm sorry, what did you say?'

'Soup. It came from a packet, I'm afraid, but it is actually quite . . .' She trailed off, because Lannigan was already limping into the choir. She had heard the voices, the children.

There were perhaps three dozen people ranged around

the pews: young men and women, old people, children huddled and round-eyed in the flickering candlelight. They looked lost among the strangeness, cowering around food heaters and a few pitiful piles of belongings, tiny parasites in the belly of some huge and alien beast. Lannigan held their gaze for a moment, but its weight was too much for her.

She turned back to the nun. 'You didn't tell me you had families here.'

The girl shook her head, uncomprehending. 'Our congregation, yes. They shelter from Liberación, after poor Mr Carlos dies at the volt station. I think that you need shelter, too.'

'You have to get these people out of here.' Lannigan lunged forward and grabbed the nun by the arm. 'Get the priest. Quickly!'

'He will not leave the barricades –'

'Screw the barricades!' she hissed. And froze.

Outside, the muted throbbing of rotors.

As Lannigan turned, a pole of searing light stabbed through the stained-glass windows along the nave, casting brilliant rainbows across the pews, the floor, scanning rapidly left and right. They all watched it, transfixed, followed it as it steadied. Began to crawl upward.

It had found the Christ. A disc of harlequin light rose from the statue's pierced feet, traced its carved robe, haloed its thorned and sorrowful head. For a long and awful moment, Jesus shone.

Lannigan heaved on the nun's arm, swinging her round and away from the statue as the plaster face exploded in a shower of fragments, a deafening screech of chaingun fire. The windows were detonating, bursting inward, razors of colour crashing into the floor and imbedding themselves in the pews. The huddled families bolting, screaming, diving for cover as the cathedral began to come apart around their ears.

The Christ broke up, chopped to pieces and tumbling.

It erupted into a hail of white shrapnel against the floor.

Abruptly, the gunfire stopped. Lannigan had dragged the nun down behind a pillar; she left the girl sobbing there, and peered around, trying to gauge where the next burst would come from. The shrieking of the families was making it difficult to think.

Three of the asymmetrical windows were blown to ruin, their edges cut and cratered, their frames still showing great fangs of shattered glass. In the darkness beyond she could see the helicopter hanging beneath a shimmering disc of rotor. It was side-on to her, but the chin turret, with its searchlight and its fat, multibarrelled cannon, was tracked directly towards the cathedral.

Just barely, Lannigan could make out two figures hunched in the bubble canopy. They were gesticulating wildly at each other.

She took the nun by the shoulder. 'Is there another way out?'

The girl nodded, her face tracked by tears. 'Through the north transept, on the other side of the cathedral.'

'That's great.' She straightened. 'Get these people rounded up and out. I'll check it's yokay.'

Before she reached the transept there were people coming in through it: a handful of nuns and armed locals, and Father Gabriel. 'I was at the northern barricade. Is anyone harmed?'

'Pretty shaken up, but I think that's all. One of your girls is bringing them over.'

'Sister Elpidia.' He nodded. 'If we can get them past that accursed machine and through the barricade they can disperse seaward.'

'Sounds like a plan.' Lannigan heard one of the nuns yelp, and saw the woman step back from the doorway, her hands at her mouth.

Past her, something like a titan spider darted across the square.

For a moment Lannigan simply didn't believe what

she had seen, attributing the silhouette to shock and thoughts of the cathedral's origins. But then she saw another, and a third. One raced along the wall over her head, its claws knocking fragments of polymerised stone into her hair.

She backed off, bewildered. Insects didn't grow that big.

Only when a bright disc of spotlight caught one of the shadows and held it did she understand. The shape was still monstrous – a squat arthropod the size of a ground module, its body held high on six clawed and jointed legs, its compound eyes gleaming – but the light span off moulded armour and feed panels, integral minigun turrets and communications antennae, the stencilled logo of the United Nations mechanised infantry. Lannigan realised that she was watching highly sophisticated weapons running across the cathedral square, not living creatures.

Still, the way the machine scampered away from the light was revoltingly insectile.

The *light* –

She tried to wrench the door shut as the helicopter opened fire, but the priest was in the way, the nuns bunched too closely behind him. She saw a line of dust plumes race across the square, the awful screech of the rotary cannon as it flung a wall of metal towards the UN devices, sparks and shrapnel hammering in every direction. In the same instant, half the crawlers spat poles of fire into the sky.

She got the door closed, then. Slammed it shut and leant on it with her arms wrapped around her head, and even through the heavy wood and her own flesh the noise was insanely loud. It was the worst thing she had ever heard. It made her cry out, scream at the top of her voice; not in fear, but simply in an effort to drown it out.

Something struck the door with a massive, bone-jarring impact. Lannigan stopped screaming and stared at the metre-long shard of metal protruding from the wood a hand's length from her face.

It was a fragment of rotor blade.

Later, she warned Father Gabriel and his people about going outside. 'Those crawlers have got an AI shoving them around. It won't care who you are, or what side you're on. You understand? Don't take a gun out there.'

'We will wait until they leave.' Elpidia was cradling something in her arms, something still and cold. Lannigan looked more closely, and was rather disconcerted to see a big plaster eye staring out at her. The girl was holding a chunk of the destroyed statue. 'You should wait, too.'

'I'm kinda busy.'

Outside, the helicopter was an unrecognisable tangle of geometries, gouting columns of smoke into the air. Thick mounds of fire-suppressant foam softened its outline. Several UN soldiers in blue and white body armour were stationed close by, some scanning the wreck and noting details on chunky military-issue screens, others stiffly on guard.

Four of the crawler tanks were still patrolling the square, the others having dispersed into the city. They scurried in front of Lannigan as she left the cathedral, miniguns whining into life, fans of blue-white laser scanning up and down her body as she walked.

She didn't stop. The UN had no mandate to interfere with the legitimate business of unarmed civilians. As she got close to the nearest machine it sidled away from her, sidestepping carefully to keep her in its weapon arc.

Lannigan resisted the urge to pat its armour as she went past.

She noticed one of the soldiers trotting towards her. 'This area is under United Nations control, ma'am. You wanna state your business?'

'I'm on vacation,' she snapped, and kept on walking.

* * *

An hour later, Lannigan sat on the quay and watched the landing craft roll in.

They were big, wedge-shaped hovercraft, skimming fast and low over the oily water, heavy with soldiers and equipment. From where she sat, on a plastic crate with her back against the corroding flank of a cargo crane, she could see four of the vehicles heading south along the coast, heading for the beaches at Villa del Mar and Playa Mocambo. No doubt many others had already disgorged their troops at more northerly positions. A wave of mechanised infantry was sweeping through Veracruz, from the coast inward.

There was little activity beyond a few small pockets of fighting. Activists with firebombs and vending-machine handguns didn't face down crawler tanks for long.

Lannigan felt horribly tired. She wasn't in too much pain – other than some overstressed muscles and the familiar jolting twinges in her right leg – but her trek from the guesthouse to the docks had drained her of any reserves she might once have possessed. Her body kept reminding her of how long it had been since she had last eaten properly, or had anything to drink. She desperately wanted to sleep. Anywhere else, she would have curled up among the crates and tarpaulins and let the world go on without her for a while.

But she was too close. If her instincts were right, the *Kitsumi Maru* was out there among the cranes. The thought terrified her, but she couldn't turn away from it, not now. Her hunger for answers gnawed more painfully in her gut than that for food or sleep ever could.

She slid down from the crate, extended the cane, and began to make her way along the quay.

The dock area was arranged like a series of flattened dinner forks, with long tines spearing out from each central quay. In normal times the jetties would have been active 24 hours a day, since Veracruz, despite all its woes, was still one of Mexico's most industrious trading ports. But the threat of local war had stilled the city's heart, and the few vessels that remained bobbed dark and silent, their crew either gone or lying low. Lannigan stepped carefully over the metal rails that guided cranes and mobile docking facilities along the tines to their waiting charges. Now the cranes were just tangled silhouettes in the smoky darkness, silent save for the slow, mournful creaking of chains left swinging in the breeze.

There was no one in sight. The slapping of seawater against boat hulls sounded thick as mud.

Each tine was 300 metres long, dotted with pools of light from overhead biolumes. Lannigan had to walk only half that distance along the first before she realised that what she was hunting wasn't moored there: neither the container sloop nor the low, rather sinister-looking power yacht behind it bore the name *Kitsumi Maru*. As she turned and began to walk back along the jetty, she briefly entertained the notion that Living Glass might have a habit of changing their vessel's name, but she dismissed that thought rapidly. There was no reason for the plex to go changing their physical address, even if their presence on infonet had been excised.

It was a tenuous piece of rationalisation, but right now it was all she had.

The second tine was empty; and the next, despite Lannigan muttering to herself that the third tine really should be a charm, failed to produce the elusive vessel. It took a long walk back along the jetty and on to the second quay array before she found it. And then, looking up at the nameplate bolted to the ship's prow, Lannigan felt a disappointment more crushing than anything she could remember.

Kitsumi Maru was a wreck.

It was maybe thirty metres long, high in the sides, with a blunt, rounded prow and a flattened stern. There were structures on the deck above her, a pile of what looked like crates amidships and a collapsed tangle behind which might once have been a control centre of some kind. The whole ship was leaning over her at a shallow angle. It stank.

What Lannigan could see of the vessel was red. A little of the colour was paint, and the rest was corrosion. Great blistered sheets of rust hung from the ship's flanks; fragments of it moved sluggishly in the water and formed cryptic patterns on the jetty floor. The paint, she guessed, signified allegiance to a foreign emergency service: sometime in the previous century *Kitsumi Maru* had been constructed as a fire and rescue boat.

Now it looked like the kind of place that vagrants would go to die. Lannigan stood on the jetty and realised how naive she had been to think that the answers would just be left moored up here for her to find.

She looked back towards the quay. It seemed a very long way away, an impossible distance. She realised that there was simply no way she could make it from here, no way she could even bring herself to try. Instead, she made her way to the gangway that led from the jetty up on to the rusting fireship's deck. Perhaps, she thought dully, there might be a secluded place among the wreckage where she could sleep for a while.

The steps were mountain-steep, and it took her a long time to climb them.

Kitsumi Maru's deck was ten metres wide, littered with wind-blown garbage and years of gull shit. Lannigan surveyed the ruined wheelhouse without enthusiasm, and noted that the pile of crates was lashed down tight with no convenient spaces for a tired woman to crawl into. There was a hatch near the stern, firmly padlocked, and two cargo hatches up near the prow. Lannigan heaved listlessly at one, but it was immovable, crusted with corrosion. She sat down on it hard and began picking angrily at the rust and sun-bubbled paint around its edge.

The ship's tilt didn't seem so bad from up here. Perhaps, if she just lay across the hatch, she could snatch a couple of hours' sleep before the sun came up.

An unappetising prospect, but at least she would be hidden from anyone down on the jetty.

A chunk of rust came away in her hand. Beneath it, her fingers found an odd smoothness.

Lannigan hunted around in her pockets, and found the Huastec's cigar lighter. Carefully, shielding the little flame from the breeze, she used its light to study the edge of the hatch. What she saw there made her heart swoop in her chest.

The hatch wasn't corroded shut. Somebody had glued it down.

More of the *faux* rust came away as she probed, revealing a slim bead of industrial epoxy. Lannigan snapped the lighter shut and pocketed it again, looking around the deck with a new interest. Yes, the wheelhouse was scrap, and the boat was peeling like an old corpse, but how much of the damage was cosmetic?

How much, indeed, was even real?

There was no way she could break the epoxy seals, but if Living Glass were still using the boat as their base they had to have a way in. Which left the padlocked hatch near the stern, and Lannigan's mood brightened further at the thought. A door locked from the outside meant no one was at home.

She used the lighter to study the lock, and found that it too was a sham: beneath rust-coloured paint it was new and as big as a fist. The weak point, she decided, was not the padlock itself but the metal latch it held closed. Lacking any other tool, she retracted her cane and jammed the end under the lock, pressing down as hard as she could.

At some point she must have pressed a control without knowing. There was a metallic screech, shockingly loud in the night, and Lannigan found herself on her back with her right arm singing with pain.

The cane had extended itself clear through the latch. Fragments of metal were still spinning and rattling on the deck.

She sat up, panting, rubbing her forearm vigorously. The cane had what appeared to be long scratches along the barrel, but when she looked closer she realised that the marks were thin slivers of steel from the hatch. The cane itself was undamaged: whatever Übergen had made the device from, it was terrifyingly strong. It occurred to Lannigan that if her attempt at breaking and entering had gone even slightly wrong she could have been lying on the deck with the cane punched straight through her ribcage.

She swallowed hard, suddenly aware of how dry her mouth was. When she cracked the hatch it came up smooth and silent, and blue-green light spilt up from inside.

Lannigan stayed where she was for a long minute, listening hard. Only when she was sure that no sounds were issuing from the vessel's interior did she open the hatch completely and peer inside. From the edge of the hatchway, a steep mesh ladder angled down to a metal floor. She could see the walls of a short corridor pasted with bioluminescent striplights, and a door leading aft.

There was an odd smell in the corridor, sticky and flat.

Lannigan eased herself down the ladder, stepping as quietly as she could on to the floor. The air felt cool and slightly damp, but apart from the smell it was far more pleasant below decks than above. Even the ship's tilt was less discernible with no horizon as reference.

Ahead of her the corridor turned a corner, but Lannigan decided to try the door first. She studied it quickly. Heavy, studded with rivets, sprayed the same dull grey as the rest of the interior. Patches of rust flaking up through the paint. The handle was a solid lever of metal as big as her forearm, and when she forced it down the door groaned and began to swing open under its own weight. Lannigan had to plant her feet and haul back on it so it wouldn't gain momentum and slam against something: even though *Kitsumi Maru* seemed deserted so far, she didn't want to make any loud noises if she could help it.

Once the door had stilled, she stepped round it and into the chamber beyond. The ceiling fluorescents were as dark as those in the corridor, but here most of the biolume strips seemed to have surrendered to time. She squinted into the gloom until the shapes and angles she saw began to resolve themselves.

There was a metal desk, wide and heavy, bolted down to the deck. Someone had secured a row of computer decks to the top, and flatscreens to the forward bulkhead. Lannigan reached out and touched smooth rivulets of epoxy, long bundles of fibre-optic cabling and the irregular strips of silver tape that held them in place. A pair of swivel chairs were clamped down to short rails behind the desk. One of them was missing a back cushion.

It looked like an operations centre. Lannigan looked at it for a long time, the sight of it nagging her. Something about that chair, the way the bolts that fixed the frame to the spine would dig into her back if she sat down . . .

Abruptly the chamber seemed very dark and very cold. Lannigan turned away and limped into the corridor, putting her back against the cool metal wall. There was no longer any doubt that she had found the right place, no more hiding behind the holes in her memory. She had walked willingly into the lion's den. Now was the time to collect as much meat as she could and then leave.

That array of electronics was probably the best source of answers she could hope for, but the computers were little better than paperweights unless she could find a way of getting the power on. The corridor, when she peered round the corner to survey it, terminated in a T-junction no more than six metres ahead, with a door to the right of her and two more to the left. She turned round and crept towards the other end of the corridor, the prow end.

More doors. She gritted her teeth, chose one, and let herself in.

It was a cabin, lit by a safety biolume above the doorframe. Lannigan used the Huastec's cigar lighter to study the place, the tiny flame illuminating a single bunk, a small table, a washbasin. Candy wrappers on the floor. Half a bottle of Jack Daniel's propped against the sink. Nothing of any interest at all until Lannigan turned to leave and saw the headless, handless thing that was hanging on the inside of the door.

Her heart leapt, shock drawing a cry from her throat despite her efforts to be silent. The flame from the lighter jumped as she started, and as it flared she realised that she was looking at nothing more terrible than a coat, slung from a stick-on plastic hook. 'Jesus *Christ*.'

Fatigue, she told herself. That and the insistent smell, the sweet, rotting aroma that had been getting stronger the closer to the prow she moved. Lannigan left the cabin, brushing the coat aside as she did so, remembering the faded leather raincoat that Swann had worn in Konza.

This was not the same coat, but it was similar. It could have fitted the man.

There was a similar cabin next door. This, in contrast to the first, was spotless, the metal floor gleaming, the blankets folded with military precision. When Lannigan lifted the pillow she saw a carbon-fibre combat knife lying on the mattress. Under the bunk was an automatic rifle and two pistols, and there was a sub-machine gun secured under the table with silver tape. Lannigan pulled it free, checked that it was loaded, and stashed it into her pocket.

Outside, she paused. Something about the aft end of the boat was still tickling at her, needling. She headed back down the corridor, to the furthest unexplored door.

No, not here. This was another cabin, larger, with a strange mix of tidiness and casual litter that spoke instinctively to her of female habitation. Nothing of the details caught her attention – even the softbacked romance novels scattered over the bunk were in Cantonese, as remote and cryptic as starlight. She turned her back on the place, chose another door at random, and stepped through, taking care to avoid the sharp corner of the table just inside.

The lighter shook in her hand. The table was an extra, she could see that, a polished wooden writing desk bolted to the wall. Too close to the door, so that, if anyone came through without knowing it was there, they would catch the corner solidly in the left hip.

The sense of recognition was dizzying.

Lannigan moved closer, holding up the lighter. On the desk was a scatter of magazines, copies of *Vogue* and *Focal Distance* four months out of date, electronics periodicals and printouts of *What AI*. She lifted a dusty systems catalogue, thinking about the January issue of *Cosmo* with Skip Takahashi on the cover. When she saw the next magazine down she yelped and the catalogue thumped on to the desktop.

Dust sprang up to settle across Takahashi's smiling face.

She backed off, found herself against the washbasin. There was a crack next to the mixer tap; her memory found it a millimetre before her fingers did. Her hand yanked back of its own accord but she was already studying the patterns of rust on the bulkhead next to the pillow. When she looked at them sideways, as though she were lying down, she knew them, and the way morning light would catch them through the porthole.

All the strength left her in a rush. She sat heavily on the bunk, wincing as the knowledge of how it squeaked came to her a heartbeat before the sound. The cabin was full of memories: isolated, unconnected things, random driftwood in a sea of amnesia. Everything she saw brought a sickening jolt of familiarity, a staccato hammer of *déjà vu*, the lines and forms revealed by the flickering lighter flame springing to life behind her eyes with almost painful intensity.

Lannigan snapped the lighter off. She didn't want to see any more.

The bulkhead was cool against her back, its solidity a comfort in the darkness. Lannigan sat there for a time, not moving, until she felt the first, subtle vibration through the metal wall.

A bird, she thought, letting her eyes close. A restless gull wandering the upper deck. She pictured the creature's small, simple mind, free of everything but instinct, and envied it. A gull was little more than a feathered automaton. It lacked the kind of memory that played tricks.

A second thump, louder, and the sound of footsteps.

Lannigan snapped upright, instantly alert. The deck above her was not all that thick, and *Kitsumi Maru*'s metal construction carried sound easily. She could hear two sets of steps now, one shuffling and heavy, one careful and cat-light. They were moving towards the stern.

She got up and pulled the door open, putting her head round it and listening hard. For a few moments it was difficult to hear past the crash of her own heartbeat, but then the sound of voices drifted down the corridor, metallic and strange.

'Maybe some bum,' one was saying. 'Smells like something died in here.'

'Quiet.'

'Ah, come on, man. No way she would have come back here.'

The voices were closer now. 'Why not? She lives here. Now stay quiet.'

'This is a bad idea, a really bad idea. Hospital said she wouldn't even remember, for chrissakes.'

'Will you –'

'We shouldn't even be in the damn country, the way things are going down.'

'Fine. So we make the sweep, lock up and go. Just keep quiet while we do it.'

Close enough to recognise, the distortion gone. Lannigan sighed.

She lives here.

She nodded to herself, put a hand to the gun in her pocket and took it out, carefully. She dropped it on to the bed and then limped out into the corridor.

'Gentlemen,' she said.

Swann gaped at her.

Byron tilted his head, very slightly, and took off his shades.

Lannigan gave them a tired smile. 'Well,' she sighed. 'We do seem to keep meeting each other, don't we.'

10
The Kiss

Housing had been a problem in Miami, after the big storm. Early-warning systems and computer prediction had managed to keep actual fatalities down to a minimum; no more than a few hundred had refused the shelters. But when the debris had ceased flying the survivors emerged into a shattered wasteland. The storm had carved Florida open like a missile attack.

Two decades later, all that remained of that dark time were memorials to the dead and a chain of cloud-boiling orbital mirrors. That, and thousands of United Nations emergency housing modules, row upon row of rounded plastic slabs, plumbed in and wired up and bolted into tubular steel frameworks to stop them blowing away when the wind grew strong. Some found new life as cheap hotels or storage lockups. Others continued to fulfil their original purpose – homes for those who had nowhere else to go.

A hundred or more habs clustered under the expressway overpass, a few blocks to the north of Miami Arena. Rayanne was stunned at how alike they all looked, an endless stream of gleaming white pods, mirrored windows reflecting the streetlamps and the neon, integral strips of biolume marking the doors and vent panels. She wondered how Gregor ever found his way home.

Then she rounded a support pillar and realised that the Russian's hab was probably the one that was on fire.

Smoke, black and dense, rolling out of the vent panels and staining the white plastic with soot. Gregor shouted something and broke into a run, haring away from Rayanne, through a semicircle of onlookers and up the pressed-steel steps, tugging at the door handle until it recognised his palm print and let him in.

Rayanne was on his heels. Much of the smoke was rolling around the ceiling, creating crazy shadows. She ducked outside, drew in as big a lungful of clean air as she could manage, then hurled herself back in.

Gregor was standing in the middle of the hab, shouting. Rayanne went past him, through a dividing door and into the kitchen unit. Into a wall of smoke, hot greasy stink of burnt fat and the sound of flames, of spitting fluids and bewildered, terrified weeping. She glared around, eyes streaming, until she spotted the fat red cylinder in its bracket under the sink.

'Jesus!' screamed Gregor.

She hauled it out, slammed the cap with the heel of her hand and played the sudden, roaring column of frigid powder across the kitchen. The temperature in the hab dropped instantly. Rayanne felt the bite of cold on her hands, saw flames collapse into darkness, smothered and crushed by the stream of pressurised retardant. When the fire was totally out, she strode across the kitchen unit and turned the microwave cooker off.

Smoke began to trickle upward, towards the aircon vents.

Rayanne dropped the extinguisher and let her breath out, gasping and coughing as the fumes caught her lungs. There was an aluminium pan in the microwave, but whatever it might have once contained was academic. It hissed and spat and billowed steam when Rayanne dropped it into the sink. 'Gregor! Get in here, man!'

'I told her not to cook anything!' Gregor was still in

the living unit, near the door. 'Jesus God, didn't I tell her?'

'Yeah, well. I guess she forgot.' Rayanne crouched next to the girl sobbing in the corner. Suzy was wrapped up in a scorched duvet, her stick-thin arms holding the cloth down over her head. She made a surprisingly small bundle, hunched there on the floor.

'Hey, Suzy. It's all over. You wanna come out now?' She turned to the door. 'Gregor!'

The sobbing turned to sniffles. A corner of the duvet lifted, revealing an eye, a smudged cheek.

Rayanne looked up. Most of the smoke had already gone, only a few fading tendrils hugging the farthest corners of the hab. The walls were grey with soot, but nothing that wouldn't come away with a damp cloth. It took more than a pan fire to mark gas-giant plastics.

She stood, and wandered out of the kitchen unit. Gregor was sitting on the integral sofa, his head in his hands.

'Walls are gonna need a wash, man. And I guess your microwave is history.'

'I told her,' he muttered. 'Never cook. I do the cooking. I *am* a cook.'

'There was a fire . . .'

Suzy's voice was little more than a whisper, a breathy shudder of loss. It made Rayanne cold to hear it. She looked round and saw the girl leaning against the door frame, the duvet still half-draped round her shoulders.

Gregor got up. 'Are you . . .'

'Why was there a fire?' Suzy stumbled in, blinking. Lank blonde hair hung over her face, over skin almost white beneath the soot. She wore a plastic cutoff top above pale-blue jeans, one sock. Rayanne could see the outline of her ribs under the plastic. The scars on her wrists.

'Jesus, Susan. What did you do to the microwave?' Gregor's hands were knotting, pummelling the bruises on his arms. 'Did you put metal in there? A pan?'

'No. No, I didn't touch the microwave. 'Cause you told me not to.' Suzy glared at Rayanne. 'Is this who you're screwing tonight?'

'What?'

Rayanne put her hands up. 'Hey, Suzy, don't get the wrong end, yeah? I'm just visiting.'

'You gonna do it on our bed again, Greg? Or you gonna take her somewhere?' Suzy dropped the duvet and wrapped her arms round herself. 'You taking her down the Candy Stripe again?'

Gregor stared at her, then at Rayanne. 'She doesn't know what she's saying. Susan . . .'

'Did you tell her about me?'

'Susan, for God's sake!' Gregor was yelling, one hand scraping back through his spike-blond hair, over and over. 'Have you gone crazy, now? Are you trying to make me crazy, too?'

'C'mon Gregor, don't go there.' Rayanne tried to get between them, but Gregor leant past her, shaking his finger at Suzy.

'You are trying to kill me!'

'I'm not crazy!' the girl screamed, bunching her fists. 'Don't you tell me I'm crazy!'

'Christ, back off, Gregor!' Rayanne grabbed the Russian's shoulder and shook him hard. 'What the hell are you doing?'

His eyes on her, wild, bulging and red-flecked in the bruised shadows of his sockets. 'Don't touch me!' He reached past her, towards Suzy, but the girl gave a convulsive howl and ducked away.

Rayanne heard her sobbing, trying to speak, something that sounded like 'I don't know, I don't know', but her hands were locked over her face and the words were getting locked up in all the tears and the snot. She watched her stumble through the divider and back into the kitchen. 'Jesus, Gregor. Now look what you done.'

There was no answer. When she looked back at Gregor he was gone, and the door was banging shut.

She ran across the hab and pulled it open. One of the few remaining onlookers – a fat black man – was on the ground, yelling, and Gregor's skinny back was disappearing into the night. Rayanne stood in the doorway, half ready to go after him, but by the time she had made up her mind to follow he was clear out of sight.

She swore, once, then went back into the hab and closed the door. Snivelling sounds were still issuing from the kitchen unit. Rayanne folded her arms, unsure of what to do next until she looked around and spotted a refrigerator cube next to the sofa.

Well, Gregor hadn't exactly withdrawn his offer. She wandered over to the fridge and pulled the door open.

White Riot, contrary to Gregor's recommendation, was not good beer. It was thin and yellow and foamy, with a chemical taste that stayed around the back of Rayanne's mouth and wouldn't go away. It made her wish she had something to brush her teeth with. 'Ecch.'

'I know.' Suzy held up her can and gazed at it gloomily. 'He's been buying it for, well . . . I don't know. Long time. Says it reminds him of home.'

'If home ever tasted like this, I'm glad I forgot.' Rayanne was feeling a lot better, despite the vile beer. She was slumped in an integral chair opposite Suzy in the integral sofa, their collective feet resting up on the table. All the furniture in the hab was integral, extruded from a single template with temperfoam padding glued on where needed. Just big, one-piece mouldings. Ugly, but clean enough before the burning microwave had pasted soot all over the ceiling.

Once she had gotten Suzy calmed down and out of the kitchen, the girl had become far more cogent, almost to the point of remembering who Rayanne was. Which was quite encouraging, since they had met only twice, maybe three times. Rayanne was a little hazy on that point herself.

She finished the can and squeezed it, then looked up

guiltily, hoping Suzy hadn't noticed her doing it. The girl was so wasted she could barely lift the can when it was full. She had to keep resting it on the arm of the sofa when she wasn't drinking.

Suzy was shaking her head, a sad smile on her lips. 'It's yokay, Rayanne.'

'Hmm?'

'I know I'm in bad shape. If it wasn't for Gregor I'd be dead. I don't kid myself on that score.'

Rayanne frowned. 'Yeah, Gregor . . .'

'He's not a bad person, really. He looks after me. It's just . . . Sometimes he gets frustrated. Especially about . . . You know . . .' She made embarrassed little movements with her hands until Rayanne caught on and nodded vigorously.

'Normally I don't hassle him when he stays out. I mean, he's better at managing the habit than I am, so he has to, sometimes.'

'It's a different stuff.' Gregor shot up with Spike, a synthetic heroin analogue whose addictive qualities he had been controlling for as long as Rayanne had known him. He didn't blank, so if he didn't eat or wash it was because he chose not to, not because he had forgotten how.

'I know.' Suzy nodded. 'I know, but he's always been the strong one. What's the time?'

'Hold up.' Rayanne fished the chrono out from her jacket pocket. The uplink was useless, without an account, but the time display was working. 'Ah, nearly eight.'

'Right. Right.' Suzy stared at the floor. 'He'll probably be yokay. If he doesn't get into a fight, he'll be yokay.'

There was a pause. Rayanne could hear Suzy's beer fizzing, the insects battering against the biolume above the door. She sighed.

'Where's he gonna be, Suzy?'

There were nightclubs in Rayanne's memory, bright patches of colour amid the fog. She had always tried not to crush the good times, because without them she would have nothing left but occasional edges of dream, nothing to be sure of. That was a one-way trip to the place Suzy Pearson was living, and Rayanne didn't want to go there.

She hadn't always been successful, and some of her best days must have been flushed away with the worst, but there was no denying that Rayanne had danced herself to collapse in nightspots all the way from New York to Mombasa. There had been the bright, expensive places that Zenebe had taken her to after some of his better deals had come through: video dance floors studded with flatscreens and holo projectors, smart crowds gyrating among illusory abstracts and virtual musicians. There were the squats and the dives, just vacant lots or appropriated warehouses with somebody's chipplayer turned up full and people shooting up Spike in the corners. And the dark places, the city places, where the air was heavy with rumour and cigarette smoke and menace, where men in suits exchanged meaningless phrases and only bodyguards paid for drinks.

Rayanne was almost relieved to discover that the Candy Stripe was just a small, cheap-looking dancebar with far too much mirrored tape on the walls.

She paid up and went in, noting that the entrance fee was just a touch more than she would have had to pay for a night's stay in the hostel. The thought did nothing for her mood, and she went through the weapons scanner and into the danceroom with a scowl that would have done Lannigan proud. She didn't want to be here. She couldn't care less whether Gregor got himself into a fight or not, and wandering around Miami after dark was exactly what she had been trying to avoid by going home with the Russian in the first place. In truth, the only real reason Rayanne had left the hab was to be away from Suzy Pearson.

It wasn't as though she didn't like Suzy. The girl was

amiable enough, when she knew what she was doing. But, every now and then, she would make some gesture – a slight tic, perhaps, a panicky flick of the eye – and Rayanne would realise that she, recently, had found herself doing exactly the same thing.

Stress, she told herself, skirting around the back of the room. The music was Asian bopette, probably Bangladeshi from the sound of the lyrics, and the dancers between her and the bar were trying very hard to make up in enthusiasm what they lacked in coordination. Rayanne moved closer to the dance floor and saw Gregor sitting in a table booth along the opposite wall. There was a woman with him, brown-haired, and slim under a dark suit jacket.

The woman turned her head, just a fraction. Rayanne saw her face and froze, her heart giving a thump from behind her ribs that felt like it had torn loose from its moorings.

Gregor was with the Pacifican from the Bayside bar. The one with Lannigan's eyes.

Rayanne backed off, slowly, putting a few more dancers between her and the booth. Her mind span. For a horrible moment she wondered if Gregor and the woman were somehow working together, if his offer of shelter for the night was part of some complex and evil plan. Maybe they had something to do with the Embu Crew. But when she got closer – edging behind a red-lacquered pillar striped inexpertly with mirrored tape – she realised that Gregor seemed as repulsed by the Pacifican as she was.

He kept shaking his head and trying to move away. Rayanne saw him put his hands up in refusal, and then the Pacifican grabbed him, pulled him close and kissed him hard on the lips.

Rayanne stared, then ducked back and leant against the pillar. There had been something sickening in that kiss, something alien and carnivorous. It brought the taste of weak Russian beer into the back of her throat.

Swallowing hard, she peered round the pillar again, just in time to see Gregor rip himself free from the Pacifican and stagger away.

She watched him run to the exit, wiping his mouth with the back of his hand. When she checked on the Pacifican, the woman was still sitting in the booth, perfectly calm and still.

Her eyes right on Rayanne.

They looked at each other for a long time, Rayanne gaping slightly, the woman intent, unmoving. Then someone moved between them. With the contact broken, Rayanne wrenched herself away.

She felt the Pacifican's cold shark stare on her back, all the way to the door and beyond.

She hung back while Gregor made his way home, then dodged in front of him while he waited at a crossing. The manoeuvre almost had her under the wheels of a truck, but it meant that she could be waiting in the hab when he got back, as if she had never been out.

With a little prompting Gregor got his story straight enough to convince Suzy of his innocence: yes, he had stormed out like an asshole, but after wandering the streets alone for an hour or two he had calmed down and decided to come home.

Rayanne had toyed with the idea of telling Suzy what had happened, but Gregor seemed truly spooked by his encounter with the Pacifican. The look on his face when he returned, and the teary relief from Suzy, told Rayanne that she had probably done the right thing.

Not long after that, Gregor wished Rayanne a comfortable night and took Suzy into the bedroom with him. Maybe they just required the comfort of each other's arms, or maybe the pair would take the opportunity to try to get their wreck of a sex life back on line again. Rayanne was determined not to find out, and curled up on the integral sofa with her jacket pulled firmly up over her ears.

It was almost enough to block out the screams.

Rayanne was asleep when the noise began. Her dreams altered around it, weaving from a sullen and anxious fantasy involving an empty purse and a candy store into a staccato train-wreck nightmare that shivered her awake in moments. She huddled under her jacket, blinking, a sour taste in her mouth. Her chrono, when she pulled it free and squinted at it, read just after eleven. She had been on the sofa for two hours at most.

Somebody was shouting, the voice occasionally rising in pitch to a kind of wail. Rayanne frowned. When she had realised that the voices were not constructs of her own dreams, she had assumed them to be issuing from outside the hab, perhaps some fight or drunken revelry passing close to the line. But now, with her brain slightly less fuddled, she could swear that the screaming was coming from the bedroom.

She sat up. The plastic walls were thin, but deadened sound quite effectively. If the commotion was simply Gregor and Susan making their reacquaintance then the pair possessed more energy than Rayanne would have given them credit for. She stood, and edged closer to the door. 'Hey, guys? You yokay in there?'

The door opened, and Gregor fell out of it.

Rayanne backed off, her hands to her mouth. The Russian was staggering, doubled up, his hands clawing at his skull, and every muscle on his thin, naked body standing out like shivering cords. Blood streamed down his face, outlining his staring eyes in crimson and coating his fingers. He was shrieking horribly, over and over.

Behind him, Suzy was curled at the far end of the bed, the sheets wrapped protectively over her head.

Rayanne had seen some things in her time – overdoses, poisoning, people in the extreme throes of neural breakdown or psychosis – but nothing she could remember came close to what was happening to Gregor Kamarov as she watched. Blood spilt from great rents in his scalp. Even now it seemed he was trying to rip his very skull apart.

She almost went to him, reached out, but something about the shuddering, dripping, corpse-pallor of his taught skin held her away. This was disease, she realised with a horrified clarity. This was infection.

Gregor fell, convulsing, howling fit to rip his throat. His legs bunched, then kicked out straight with such force that his bare heels opened a crack in the side of the sofa. Rayanne heard his bones breaking, one of his knee joints give way.

The man was going to cripple himself in this awful extremis. Rayanne darted past him, through into the bedroom. She grabbed Suzy by the shoulder. 'Where's the fragging comm?'

Suzy didn't react. The girl was quaking with terror under the sheet; Rayanne realised she probably wasn't sure if Gregor's frenzy was real, a nightmare or a construct of her own damaged brain.

Rayanne shook her again, harder. 'He's gonna die, Suzy! We gotta call the paramedics!'

There was a motion under the sheet that might have been the shaking of a head, but Rayanne half-knew the answer already. She tore herself away and ran out of the hab, vaulting over Gregor's twisting body on her way to the door, and hammered down the metal stairway. She caught a support bar at the bottom and swung herself round, scanning quickly up and down the habline, hunting for the familiar plastic mushroom that housed public comms booths almost the whole world over.

There was one at the corner of the next block. The unit was surrounded by a cluster of teenage girls, fashionably pale young things leaning against the striplights and batting idly at mosquitoes. Five years younger than her and dressing like hookers five years older. Rayanne bolted up to them, hoping desperately that they hadn't vandalised it yet. 'Emergency, man! Get off the freakin' line!'

One of the teens turned a pinched, white face momentarily from the comm screen. 'Screw you, lady.'

Rayanne didn't have time for an argument. She grabbed the girl's green-bleached hair and bounced her forehead off the screen. There was a kind of gurgling yelp and the teenager slumped away, sprawling on to the pavement. Rayanne looked up to see the others scrambling for cover.

'Good friends, huh.' She killed the call, cutting off the outraged shouts of the pallid young man on the screen, then hit 911. 'Ambulance, man. Like now.'

The woman that appeared on the screen wasn't real. She was too perfect, her voice too well modulated. 'Please state your name and address, *señorita*.'

'Ah, I'm down on the three ninety-five habline. They don't got numbers. I'll be waiting outside, yokay?' She paused. The damn machine wanted her name, which would go right out on infonet as soon as she said it. But, if she lied, the voiceprint would pick it up, and no paramedic was going to run his medsled into central Miami without a positive ID. There was too much chance of being ripped off.

Screw it, Gregor was *dying* back there. She'd take her chances. 'My name's Rayanne Hernandez. Guess I'm on the Cuban registry, somewhere.'

'That's acknowledged, Ms Hernandez. Could you tell me what the problem is, please?'

'My friend, he's got some disease, I dunno. Convulsions, screaming like he's dying. Scraping at his head and shit.' She glanced around. The girl gang was beginning to edge towards her. Some of them looked as though they had been snorting a little chemical courage while she was talking. 'He's on Spike, but I don't think that's it.'

The woman on the screen strobed for a second, then disappeared, replaced by a white-haired man who was far too ugly to be an AI. 'Ms Hernandez, when did this start?'

'Just a few minutes back. I woke up, heard him yelling. Didn't have any sign before –'

'Right. Don't go near him, yokay? We'll get a medsled to you pronto.'

He cut off before Rayanne had a chance to speak. She glared at the screen for a moment, then backed off, puzzled. Had the AI broken down?

She looked back along the street. The girls had bunched up and were muttering darkly. A couple of them had knives, bright switchblades with black lacquered handles. Rayanne looked at how the nearest one was holding the knife all wrong, went up to her and punched her in the face. The teen went over. Rayanne picked up the knife, and showed them the correct grip. 'Like this, *niñas*.'

She waited until they were all running, and then set off back to the hab.

The medsled was already outside Gregor's hab by the time Rayanne got back. The sight of it brought her up short – this was no normal Dade County ambulance, but a squat, windowless slab of systemry the size of a truck, hovering silently on an armoured air curtain and blinking fans of laser light from mesh-covered VR sensors. The medics getting out of it looked like they were wearing spacesuits.

Rayanne ducked behind an expressway support and peered around. Gregor was being carried out of his hab on a gurney, a contoured shell of translucent plastic sealing him in totally. As Rayanne watched, two more of the suited medics emerged with Suzy between them.

She heard her name being called out. One of the suits was wandering about with a voice amp, calling for her. Telling her that she should come with them to the hospital, and that there was nothing to worry about, really. Everything was going to be yokay.

Somehow, Rayanne doubted that. She listened to the medic's flat, amplified voice bouncing off the plastic habs and compacrete overpass and elected to observe proceedings from the relative safety of the support. If she started to feel ill she would go to the hospital on her own feet, not in a plastic coffin wheeled by an astronaut.

The sled pulled away after ten minutes or so. That was when Rayanne realised that she had left all her stuff inside Gregor's hab.

'Aw, man . . .' The money was still in her jacket, but all the clothes and other items she had taken from the apartment were in the drawstring bag, firmly locked away behind a centimetre of steel-strong plastic. The door wasn't keyed to her handprint, and wouldn't open even when she climbed the steps and tried to fool it with the condom. Which left her no clean clothes and nowhere to stay the night.

She swore explosively. After all the effort she had gone through to find a safe place to spend the night, she was back on the street in worse shape than before. Even if she could find a hostel open at this time, the fee would be more than she was really willing to spend. Her planned trip to Europe was looking more unlikely by the second.

And, behind her, a soft footfall on the metal stair.

She spun. The African was behind her, very close. She felt his big, slim hand come down on her shoulder, quite gently. She smelt his aftershave. She saw her own terrified reflection looking down at her from a pair of mirrored foil shades.

'Hello, Rayanne,' he said. And then, very professionally and with a minimum of fuss, he proceeded to beat the living daylights out of her.

It was just luck, Rayanne decided later. Pure bad karma.

The Embu iceman explained it all to her on the drive north from the habline. His English was rather shaky, he told her, so it was a good thing for him to practise. Besides, keeping her fully informed of the situation was part of the service. A matter of professional pride.

At this point he stopped the module – a compact but

surprisingly spacious Toyota ethanol groundbug – to make sure her handcuffs weren't on too tight. It was important to him, he said, that she should be comfortable, or at least as much as was possible after the initial beating he had given her on the hab stairs. That again was simply a specification of the job, little more than procedure. Rayanne nodded her acknowledgement, since she didn't trust herself to speak. If she moved or breathed too deeply the pain from her bruised ribs was enough to make her scream.

Yes, the iceman told her as he pulled away from the kerb, the Crew Papas had indeed felt that they had a legitimate beef with Rayanne for running all over Kenya with their drugs, but once they retrieved the chem from Medichus Procedures they would have been prepared to let it ride. The pity was that Rayanne was not the only biorunner to try the same trick that month: two others had already been intercepted trying to cross the border into Tanzania, and such behaviour could be bad for business if it got out of hand. An example had to be made, did she not agree?

Rayanne, her ribs throbbing, declined to answer.

He kept chatting to her all the way up North Miami Avenue: mainly small talk, comments about the weather, sports, the differences between America and home. In a way, the sheer hammering banality of the man's words was worse than threats or even silence. It made her realise that he was completely at ease with what he was about to do, and that he would do it without anger, or haste, but calmly and slowly and with a smile on his face.

The thought of that turned Rayanne's guts to ice. She rattled the handcuffs half-heartedly, but somehow the beating and fear had stolen all the fight from her. Slowly, as the module rolled on and the iceman kept up his patter, she seemed to fall into herself, further and deeper, until any thoughts of escape or survival, or indeed any real thoughts at all, faded away. Even her terror became something external. She slumped back into the seat, dead inside. She felt paralysed. She just wanted it all to be over.

The iceman drove her to a factory unit, a redundant biochemical plant that had, for the brief interval between the final failure of chemical antibiotics and the introduction of surgical nanotech, been engaged in the production of medical bacteriophages. Rayanne stumbled dully past cold, corroding vats and storage racks, on to the litter-strewn factory floor. She tripped, once, the toe of her left Nike catching a fixing bolt that had once held a steel bench down to the concrete, but the iceman caught her before she fell, steadied her, and then led her up a set of steps and into a windowed office.

A small folding card table had been set up there, along with two chairs. The iceman sat Rayanne on the floor with her back to a water pipe, and locked her wrists firmly around it with the handcuffs.

She watched him taking off his long polysilk coat and draping it over the back of the chair as he sat down. On the table were a small display unit, the kind that came with commercial proximity-alarm packages, and two decks of cards. The man picked up a deck and began to shuffle.

The sound of the cards bugged Rayanne, driving a thin, cold edge through her despair. 'What you playing?'

'Patience,' he replied. It might have been an answer, or a command.

He played through two entire games before the delay grew maddening and she spoke again. 'Ah, come on, man. What the hell you waiting for?'

'My associate.'

'What, you can't handle me by yourself?'

'He is bringing supplies.'

Supplies. 'Oh.'

Three more games, and Rayanne found out what the supplies were. The display unit chirruped abruptly;

the African paused in his game to check its screen, then silenced it with a keypress. Moments later, a second man, this one rather short and running to fat, arrived at the office with two plastic carrier bags, one in either hand. He nodded to his associate, greeted Rayanne politely, and then began to unload his shopping. Rayanne counted two minidrums of industrial-strength drain cleaner and seven bottles of Chlorox, and a small sob ripped its way out of her. She had been preparing herself for the feeling of a cold wire crunching its way through her skull, telling herself that women have thinner bones, that she would die quite quickly and maybe the pain wouldn't be as bad as she feared. Now it looked like the Crew were going chemical.

That was when the two Africans started arguing.

She didn't notice the change in tone at first, but what had begun as a casual exchange in Swahili was turning quite heated. Rayanne concentrated: her grasp of the language was good enough to get the gist of what they were saying, although the nuances escaped her. What she heard gave her little comfort, but then she could hardly expect it to.

The argument hinged around exactly where in the unit Rayanne was going to get her face burnt off. The taller of the two men favoured the toilet bowl, since it already held water. Besides, Rayanne would be in a better position for him to rape her while he was doing it. The shorter man was against this, regarding it as disrespectful to women in general. There was no way, he opined, that he could look his poor mother in the eye if he had forced himself on someone that he was torturing to death. He suggested pouring the chemicals into the sink and drowning Rayanne in the mixture by stages.

There followed an exchange of views on the habits and physical attributes of the short man's mother. Rayanne was on the verge of screaming at them, telling them to settle their moral differences and get the job done, when the display unit lit up and began bleating steadily.

All three of them just stared at it for a long second.

Guns appeared in the hands of the two men. There was another rapid exchange, too fast to follow, and then the short man hurried out of the office. She watched the top of his head disappear below the window frame. The taller and more talkative of the two remained to study the display.

Time passed. Rayanne couldn't tell how much: she had only her own heartbeat to judge by, and she lost count after a hundred beats or so. Besides, her heart was jumping too much to be an accurate guide. But it was long enough for the African to grow impatient, then concerned, and then very angry.

He checked his gun, and then left the office. He didn't look at Rayanne as he passed.

She sat quite still, listening to his footsteps fade. For a time she wondered if this was all part of the service, a gobbet of hope spat in her face and then wiped away just as she was starting to think about survival. Something to wake her up a little so she would be all the more aware when the Chlorox started fizzing. But the African didn't come back, even when Rayanne started tugging at the handcuffs.

They were very tight, and very strong. Rayanne pulled and strained and rattled until she felt warm blood slick against the skin of her wrists, but she didn't manage to improve her position by a millimetre. She was just beginning to entertain the idea of trying to get the knife out of her pocket and perhaps cut off one of her hands when footsteps sounded on the stairway outside.

She'd had her chance, and lost it. Rayanne gave a final snarl of frustration, and sagged, her head drooping forward against her chest, her eyes closing. She heard the door swing open and someone walking quickly towards her.

'Rayanne Hernandez?'

The voice was a woman's, calm and clear and quite heavily accented. Rayanne looked up into the cold eyes of the Pacifican woman she had seen in the Bayside bar and the Candy Stripe.

She was still dressed in her blazer and shirt, a matching business skirt and black shoes. The leather purse was slung over one shoulder by an extensible strap. There was a drop of blood on the skin of her left cheek, and more on the knife she held in her right hand. 'Lean forward, please.'

Rayanne leant. 'What the hell?'

'I will explain later. The assassins might have more accomplices close by.' The woman did something behind Rayanne's back with the knife; there was a snapping sound and the cuffs fell away. 'Can you stand?'

She stood. Then the pain in her ribs caught her like a clenched fist and she doubled. 'Aw shit.'

'Please hurry.' The Pacifican caught her before she fell, slim strong hands under her arm and round her waist, forcing her upright. The pain went off the scale for a moment, and then faded. Rayanne gasped. 'Thanks.'

'Follow me.' And the woman was away, through the office door and down the stairs. Rayanne staggered after her, walking becoming easier with every step. She felt airy, unreal. If she looked back at the water pipe she was sure that a thin Latina girl with stripes on her face would still be sitting there.

The Pacifican was waiting for her at the bottom of the stairs. She was looking around, moving her head in a strange, careful way. It reminded Rayanne of something, but she couldn't remember what. 'They might come back, man. We gotta go.'

'They will not be back. Please follow me.'

At the door of the unit Rayanne saw the icemen again. The shorter African was sprawled full length on the concrete floor, his eyes open and empty, a small puddle of blood soaking into the dust under his head. The tall man was curled in the corner, facing the wall. There was blood on his neck, a small wound at the base of his skull. The knife must have entered there, between the top of his backbone and the hole where the spinal cord went in.

She should have felt something, she knew. Horror at the way the men had been killed, perhaps; satisfaction that they were dead and she was not. Fear of this mysterious oriental woman with her knife and her horrible eyes and the ease with which she had deleted two of the Embu Crew's finest icemen. But she didn't. She just ran on, behind the woman, and didn't feel anything at all.

The Toyota module was parked where the African had left it. The Pacifican got Rayanne into the passenger seat and strapped her in. She had to do it because Rayanne's hands weren't working properly yet: they felt like cool rubber, with random spikes of pain stinging round the wrists. 'There will be some discomfort,' the woman told her. 'When the circulation begins again.'

'Those assholes were gonna make me drink Chlorox, lady. Reckon I can take a few pins and needles.'

'Injections?' The woman must have taken the module's keys from the dead African. She started the drives and tooled away from the unit, on to Biscayne Boulevard. Rayanne shook her head.

'No, man. The feeling coming back, that tingling –'

'Ah, paresthesia.'

'Yeah, whatever.' She closed her eyes. 'What time is it?'

'12.18 a.m.' The woman answered instantly, as though it was the first thing that came into her head. Rayanne had heard of people having clocks implanted, little chips under the skin with a tap direct to the optic nerve, but she had never met anyone who'd done it before. 'Cool. Where we going?'

'To a place of safety.'

'Mm.' Rayanne was very tired. The comfortable warmth within the module was putting her under, making her eyelids heavy, her eyes itch. She tried to force herself awake. Right now, she had no real idea of what safety was.

'You got a name? I guess you know mine, huh?'

'Yes.' The woman paused, just briefly, and then said, 'You may call me Kobayashi. Noriko Kobayashi.'

'Noriko,' mumbled Rayanne. She thought that she might have seen an idol singer called Noriko once, but that was the last thing that went through her head before she fell asleep.

'Drink this.'

Rayanne blinked, looking at the cup through gummy, blurry eyes. 'Whaddizzitt?'

'Something to wake you up.' Kobayashi lifted the cup to her lips, tipped a little into her mouth. It tasted minty and warm. 'We have to talk.'

She swallowed some. It didn't seem to do much good, but she was waking up by then anyway. She rubbed her eyes with her fists, noticing as she did so that she was sitting, fully dressed, on a bed. '*Madre* . . . Did I fall asleep or something?'

There was a short pause, maybe half a second, then: 'Yes, in the module. I brought you here and let you remain asleep for three hours, but now I must wake you up. Forgive me.'

'Three hours?' Rayanne stretched, and swore as her ribs became a cage of pain. She straightened up carefully and looked around.

The place looked like a hotel room, middle of the range, with the bed on one side, a desk with a chair, a wardrobe, and a flatscreen on the wall. Nothing special there, except for the boxes and cylinders ranged against the walls and stacked on the desk, softly chattering blocks of systemry that Rayanne couldn't identify. And there was a strange smell, too. Like old food. 'What is this stuff, man?'

'Please do not concern yourself, Rayanne. You are –' The woman halted as a piece of equipment on the desk chimed. She got up without another word, stepped carefully over the mess of power cables snaking across the carpet, and began to tap at a keypad.

Rayanne scanned the floor. The food smell was coming from there: old paper plates with half-finished meals congealing, plastic tumblers spilling dregs into the pile, candy wrappers, milk cans.

'You wanna get housekeeping in here, man.' Looking at the state of the room gave Rayanne an idea. 'Hey, Kobayashi? Were you over on Claughton Island?'

The woman froze for a second, then continued tapping. 'Yes,' she said. 'I had been watching you since you arrived in Miami.'

That was news. 'You what?'

'It was important for me to keep you under surveillance. I knew you were in danger from the Embu syndicate.'

'The hell you didn't tell me that a little earlier, man!' Rayanne swung her legs off the bed and stood up. Her stomach swooped and stars leapt in her vision. She leant against the wall and waited for them to fade. 'Like in the bar, or something . . .'

'Simply informing you of the danger would not have removed it. I have done that, at least for the moment.'

'I guess . . .' Rayanne chewed her lip. She could see the logic of what Kobayashi was saying, but it was still a cold thing to do. Wait for her to get jumped so she could take out the Crew icemen in one shot. That, she realised with a jolt, was just the kind of plan Lannigan would think up. 'You know, there's this chick you should really meet.'

'Chick?'

'Mm.' Rayanne watched the woman open one of the machines on the desk, the little lid flipping up with a hiss and a wisp of vapour. Kobayashi reached inside with a pair of tongs and took out a rack of test tubes, placing it carefully into the front of a tall, silvery cylinder. She seemed almost oblivious to the fact that

Rayanne was there at all, as though the girl was just another piece of equipment that bleeped occasionally and had to be answered. And there was something about her story that didn't quite chime, either. 'Hey, *señora*? How come you and Gregor were getting friendly in the Candy Stripe?'

The Pacifican froze again. Just for a second, maybe less, then carried on as if nothing had happened. 'I saw him leave Bicentennial Park with you. I was in the process of acquiring more information from him when you arrived.'

'You kissed him, man.' The memory made Rayanne queasy, and she swallowed. 'Laid one right on him.'

'I was attempting to distract his attention.'

'Yeah, well maybe you better attempt to get to a doctor or something. Gregor's real sick, they took him off in a medsled.'

'Really? That is most disturbing.'

'Is for him.'

'Gregor confessed to feeling poorly in the Candy Stripe. He was addicted to synthetic heroin, was he not? Perhaps his habit got the better of him.'

'Yeah, right.' Rayanne turned away. Kobayashi's story sounded like bullshit to her, and there was something about the woman that was really beginning to make her edgy, even more so than before. It wasn't just the eyes: Kobayashi's attention was firmly on the cylinder now, on the little flatscreen mounted in front of it, and Rayanne was still picking up vibes. No, it was the woman's whole manner, the way she moved, the way she spoke, what she said. There was almost no inflection to her voice at all, accent or no accent, and the way she kept freezing up made Rayanne's skin crawl.

What was it they said about psychotics, sociopaths? The shallowness of affect?

Rayanne was just edging towards the door when Kobayashi finished with the equipment on the desk and returned to the bed. She perched on the edge. 'Rayanne, there is something we must discuss. You and I have a mutual friend. It is extremely important that I get in touch with her.'

'Mutual? Who?'

'Her name is Cassandra Lannigan.'

Rayanne almost choked. '*What*? Jesus, you know her?'

'Yes. We used to work together.' Kobayashi reached out and took her hand. Her skin felt cool and dry. 'I need you to tell me where she is.'

Rayanne opened her mouth, then closed it again. She had only been around Kobayashi for a short time, but that was enough to convince her that the woman was, at the very least, seriously disturbed and possibly quite dangerous. She didn't owe Lannigan much, but if nothing else the *lisiada* probably had troubles of her own. Setting another weirdo on her tail just didn't seem right. 'She, ah, didn't tell me.'

'Her life might be in danger, Rayanne.' Kobayashi stood up, moving closer. Rayanne felt the wall against her back, the Pacifican's icy eyes boring into her. Under that gaze, the desire to tell the truth, to give Lannigan up, to say *anything* that would free her from that cold glare was almost overwhelming.

Almost. 'I swear to God, man, she didn't tell me. She said I'd break if anyone got to me, that I'd give her out.'

The woman's face was very close, now, the dark eyes just centimetres away. 'Are you sure?'

Rayanne tried to speak, but her mouth felt as though it was full of sand. Her heart was leaping, her skin trying to crawl right off her back. She nodded.

'I see.' Kobayashi tilted her head slightly, the ghost of a smile playing over her lips. And then, without warning, she kissed Rayanne hard on the mouth.

Rayanne's head slapped back against the wall with the force of it. She tried to twist away, but the Pacifican was too strong, her tongue pushing past Rayanne's lips and sliding over her teeth, left and right, probing her gums.

As far as she could remember, Rayanne had never felt attracted to women. One boyfriend at a time had been enough for her, more than enough, and plenty of her friends had described her as boringly vanilla. But she could have been a dedicated hedonist and still found nothing pleasurable about this encounter. It was awful, nauseating. Like being raped, but maybe even worse, because that at least involved another human being – Kobayashi's kiss felt as cold and invasive as the fat tentacle of metal that Medichus Procedures had let worm its way down her throat.

She squirmed and gagged, managed to get an arm up between her and Kobayashi, but at that moment the woman broke off and stepped back. Rayanne watched the tip of her tongue sweep across her lips, quick and dry, like a lizard.

One of the machines on the desk began to bleep softly.

Kobayashi turned to it without a backward glance: it was as though Rayanne had ceased to exist. She walked over and began placing test tubes into the thing's open lid.

Rayanne stood for a second, reflexively wiping the back of her hand across her mouth, and then the confusion and revulsion surged inside her and she bolted across the room, heading for the door. As she hauled it open she risked a momentary look over her shoulder, in case Kobayashi was coming after her, but the Pacifican was busy. Putting in her test tubes, one by one, as slow and sure and unconcerned as a factory robot.

Rayanne kept running until she found a place she knew, a VR drome on the edge of Reeves Park, and then slowed down. She sat on a step until the weakness in her legs went away. The streets around her were cool and almost deserted. Her chrono, when she checked it, read four in the morning.

Alongside the chrono in her pocket was the money,

almost 700 dollars in cash. The Crew icemen hadn't touched it.

That, Rayanne guessed, was probably a point of procedure, like the politeness. The purpose of her execution, had it taken place, would have been a message, a warning to others like her not to follow the same path. Robbing her would only have confused the issue, put the clarity of motive at risk. When she checked through her pockets it turned out that she still had all her bits and pieces, even the knife. That was a macho thing, no doubt. Like she was armed, but the Africans didn't care. They had just cuffed her up so there was no chance of her using it.

She would have to dump the knife before she reached Miami International. The only thing on her mind right now was getting out of Miami fast, and the last thing she needed was a hassle with airport security.

She could see no other option but to go. The idea of staying in a city where she had been spied on, exposed to horrible diseases, kidnapped, beaten, and then almost raped by a psychotic Pacifican was not one she was willing to entertain. Miami had been a disaster from the start. She should have tapped Lannigan for a European flight direct from Mombasa.

She got up and began to make her way to the nearest metromag station. What she had wasn't much, but it would have to be enough. If it wouldn't get her to Europe then she would go somewhere else. There must be places in the world where no one was after her.

The freeline chip got her on to an empty mag bound for MIA. Rayanne settled herself into a corner seat, wrapping her arms round herself, drawing the jacket up tight. She felt tired and cold, sticky from too long in the wet Florida air. As the mag pulled out of the station and into the open, she looked out of the window and saw a medsled zipping under her, between the rail supports. It was the same type of machine that had carted Gregor and Suzy away. Rayanne watched it hurtle away from her, wondering if Kobayashi had succumbed to Gregor's bug.

She sniffled. That bitch Kobayashi, she thought. Maybe she and Lannigan had been lovers sometime, and all this was some kind of massive romantic screw-up. Stranger things had happened. The Pacifican had been eager enough to kiss her. But then again, she had planted one on Gregor with equal fervour, and Lannigan had never shown the slightest interest in Rayanne, not in that way. Nor in anyone.

In fact, the very idea of Lannigan having sex struck Rayanne as completely ridiculous. No, she decided, it was probably business. Lannigan scooting with Kobayashi's money, something like that. Business-bitch stuff.

There was another possibility, but she didn't even want to think about that.

The outskirts of MIA were already visible, bright domes and towers bathed in pools of arclight. The lights seemed very bright to Rayanne's tired eyes, and it rather hurt to look at them. She needed sleep, she realised, some food, maybe a little fun-loving chemical to blur the edges, take the itch from behind her eyes and the pounding from her head.

The back of her neck hurt. She rubbed it absently. She must have slept awkwardly in the Toyota.

She took out the knife and studied it for a while, noticing how the blade had been honed down on something smooth and hard, probably a comms housing. The weapon was very heavy in Rayanne's hands, which to her meant quality, and she felt rather bad about having to stash it. A little protection would have been useful in Europe, but there was no way the airport scanners would have let it through.

She tried to push the knife between the seat cushions, but the padding was too tight and she couldn't get it in. After a while she lost her grip on it entirely. Her hands were too slippery to hold on. She brushed it on to the floor instead.

The mag was getting very warm. Rayanne wondered if there was a window she could open, but she was really too tired to get up and find out. In a minute, she told herself. Just a few moments' rest, and then she would be fine. Then the heat and the pain in her head would go away.

Her neck was really beginning to hurt, and there was a crawly feeling under her scalp. She wondered if maybe she had picked up some lice or fleas or something. Miami was full of bugs.

The rocking of the mag was making Rayanne feel sick.

She had never been on a mag that rocked this badly before. She got up, leaning heavily on a stanchion and climbing up it until she was on her feet, trying to ignore the spikes of pain that shot up from her neck and into her skull whenever she moved. The itching under her hair was getting worse too, moving down her face, her neck. Her hands were trembling.

The mag darkened, then emerged into piercing light.

Rayanne cried out and squeezed her eyes shut. The pain was horrible, the fluorescents illuminating the platform as bright as welding arcs, the glare eating into her eyes. She hadn't realised how close she was to the airport, but now the mag was slowing to a stop and the doors grinding open with a noise like bones ripping. Rayanne stumbled forward and missed the opening entirely, slamming painfully into the wall. The ache in her head erupted at the impact, a flare of agony that almost had her over.

Somehow, she stayed on her feet. If she could walk, maybe she could find a doctor. A late-night clinic. Something to drink, even.

She was very thirsty, and the air on the platform was oven-hot.

The floor was moving under her Nikes. It was all she could do to stumble forward, step by heavy step, keeping her head down to avoid the light, watching her feet as they dragged over the smooth tiles. She scraped at her scalp with her fingernails. The bugs in her hair felt like they were eating her brain.

It wouldn't be good for them. All the chem would probably give them indigestion. Rayanne giggled at the thought, but giggling made her stomach flip over and when she grabbed at her guts her head started to break apart and that was when she fell over. She just dropped, all the strength gone from her limbs, and rolled over on to her back.

The lights didn't seem so bright now that her head had fallen to pieces. Perhaps she should have let go sooner.

There was someone leaning over her, someone in a transparent visor, like an astronaut.

Maybe, if she could just get up the strength to ask, he would give her something to drink.

11
Broken Glass

Without his shades to cover them, Byron's eyes were twin mirrors. Antidazzle reflective coatings over artificial implants. Lannigan could feel them on her from clear across the mess.

There were two tables in *Kitsumi Maru*'s mess hall, long metal benches so rife with corrosion that they could only have been part of the vessel's original structure. Lannigan was perched gingerly on one, wolfing down the military ration pack that Swann had found for her, while Byron sat on a swivel chair behind the other. The machine pistol she had taken from his cabin lay on the metal next to him, a red LED glowing alongside the barrel.

The ration pack tasted foul, and was probably stale, but Lannigan was very hungry.

There was a bottle of water, too; rather warm, but she was too thirsty to care about that. She finished the last dregs and scraped a final spoonful of nutrient sludge from the inside of the ration pack, then placed everything in a neat pile beside her. She looked up at Byron. 'Thanks. I was starved.'

He didn't respond, just tilted his head back slightly, as if listening to something beyond her ability to hear. Lannigan frowned at him. 'What?'

'Wait.'

A moment later the lights came on.

The ceiling panels began to flicker and buzz like the walls of a bad nightclub, a chessboard flutter of light that scattered and swam and steadied after a few seconds. The buzzing died away. Most of the panels stayed lit. Lannigan heard the whisper of aircon.

Some massive part of the ship, deep below her feet, groaned. The floor shuddered.

Lannigan glanced around. The mess looked somewhat worse under full illumination: she could see more of the rust and blistered paint that marred the walls, the stains on the tabletops. When she looked more closely at the ration pack she saw that its expiry date was over a year before. 'Let me guess. Housework isn't your strong suit.'

'Don't try to provoke me.' Byron's voice was as flat and cold as she had ever heard it. 'You might succeed.'

'Generator's back online.' That was Swann's voice. Lannigan turned to see the man shouldering open the aft door, his shirt sleeves rolled up and his coat slung over one arm. He was wiping black, oily stains from his hands with a rag. 'Man, you should see the shit that's built up down there.' He threw the rag into the corner of the mess. 'I put the bilge pumps on.'

Lannigan gave him a look. 'Are you seriously trying to tell me that this heap of pig-iron is actually seaworthy?'

He blinked back at her, not missing a beat. 'You seriously trying to tell me that you don't know?'

'For God's sake, Swann! How many more times do you want me to go over it?' Lannigan grabbed the cane from beside her and extended it, ignoring the gun that suddenly appeared in Byron's hand. She stood up and hobbled over to him. 'You still don't believe me, run a scan. I'm sure any decent meditech will back me up.'

'Just think it's kinda convenient, is all.' Swann was rolling down his sleeves and buttoning the cuffs. It was getting cooler in the mess, now that the aircon was working. 'Empty our account, bounce out on us and then skip hospital before we get a chance to make contact. And now we get to talk it all through, your mind goes blank.' He shrugged his coat back on. 'Neat.'

'What, getting shot? Yeah, great strategy, Swann. I recommend it next time you get caught out on a double-cross. It makes the explanations so much easier.'

'You said it yourself,' murmured Byron. 'In the module. She remembered you, but not properly.'

Lannigan leant back against the table. 'Swann, the cops had surveillance on the hotel room, a camera. They showed me the footage. So you and I both know the condition I was in when they peeled me off the rug.' She tapped the side of her head. 'Most of this isn't even me. They cloned up a new brain in a tank somewhere, cut it up into spare parts and stapled them in with nanotech and support chips. I bought sixty per cent of this direct from Übergen AG.'

'Yeah, with our money!'

'How the hell was I supposed to know that? They found it in the room with me!'

He held her gaze for a few seconds, then looked away. 'Christ. What a screw-up.'

'Listen to me, Swann.' She folded her arms. 'I can't deny that I did what you say. But whatever reasons I might have had for doing it are just a dark stain on a hotel carpet. All I can suggest right now is damage limitation.'

Swann spread his hands helplessly. 'But jeez, doc. Eighteen months . . .'

'Yeah, and the rest.' Far more than eighteen months had been stolen from her. A lifetime had been ripped out of her head by Joey Kotebe's bullet and splashed all over the Milimani Hotel. But she couldn't expect Swann to be concerned with much past the last year and a half.

He hadn't been working for her before that.

The disorientating recognition she had felt in the fourth cabin was everything she had feared, and more. Lannigan didn't just live on the *Kitsumi Maru*. She owned it.

The idea, after all she had been through, was almost impossible to grasp. Living Glass MLC was *hers*; formed by her; run by her; financed, initially, by her. Back in her lost past she had built the plex from scratch, recruited Swann and Byron and poor Angel Chan, refitted the *Kitsumi Maru* and begun setting up haven accounts and passcode decrypts and running black-market data for anyone with an uplink and a stack of currency units.

By all accounts the plex had been quite successful, for a time. And then, two days before she died, she had ignored a planned rendezvous with the rest of the team, bought a flight to Nairobi and started filling a hotel room with biomedical hardware. Using company money, of course.

Angel Chan, the plex's financial operator and owner of a shelf full of Cantonese romance novels, had died trying to find out why. Swann's stab packs hadn't been enough. The plex had folded, its surviving half forced to abandon their base, strip their ID from infonet and live in hiding. And, just when it looked like they might finally get some answers, Lannigan had cut short her stay in hospital and skipped town with a teenage amnesia-junkie.

Under the circumstances, she could hardly blame the pair for chasing her halfway around Africa. Even the swat Byron had given her 'for Angel' made sense. She would have most likely done the same. 'I know you've lost a lot, Mr Swann. We all have. But we need to start dealing with it.'

There was a long silence. Then Swann said, 'Eddie.'

'What?'

'My name. Eddie. You never called me Swann, just Eddie.'

She gave him a sideways look. 'Like I said. Start dealing with it.'

'Well, now that the reunions are over,' said Byron suddenly, 'I'd really prefer to get away from here before anyone else decides to join us.'

Lannigan sniffed. The rotten-food smell had diminished, she was pleased to notice, and she had been thinking seriously about bedding down for what remained of the night. 'You think that's likely?'

'Believe me, you have more admirers than just Mr Swann and myself. Joey Kotebe, for one.'

'Kotebe?' Rayanne had mentioned that the man had survived. 'Is he still on my tail?'

Byron nodded. 'Very much so. Luckily, his infonet searches have been so obvious we were able to ride them all the way here.'

'Oh my God.' Lannigan felt a sudden weight in her gut. She had never forgotten the oddly haired assassin, not his face, nor the sound of his voice, nor the cold metal kiss of his gun barrel to the back of her neck. But she had assumed that Rayanne's chem would have put him out of the picture for longer, if not permanently. With her connection to Living Glass explained, she had assumed the worst was over.

That was a mistake she would not make again. The worst, it seemed, was never truly over. 'What do we do?'

'I think we should jump ship, then make things as difficult as possible for anyone following us here.' Byron stood up and snapped his shades back on, rolling up the sleeves of his black jacket. 'Swann, start clearing the cabins. Whatever stock we can carry, only essentials. When you've done that, go below and rig the bilge pumps to scuttle.'

Swann chewed his lip for a moment. 'You really wanna sink her?'

'A clean start will be safer. Ms Lannigan, I'll need you in the ops chamber.'

She looked at him blankly. 'What for?'

'Because I can't access the inner command strings. If you can direct Kitsumi to file and make backups of our essential data, I can pull the core, leave the support system on board.'

Lannigan searched for something valid or intelligent to say. But, faced with what appeared to her to be a stanza of utter gibberish, failed. 'I'm sorry?'

'Don't get sentimental on us now. I know you spent a long time on that system, but it's too big to move. For now, all we need is the brain –'

'No one's getting sentimental. I just don't know what you're talking about.'

Byron tilted his head to one side, his equivalent, Lannigan guessed, of throwing up his arms and stamping about. 'I'm talking about the AI.'

'You have an AI?' She gave an apologetic shrug. 'I'm sorry, gentlemen. Computers aren't my field. The closest I've been to an expert system is the ticket vendor in Nairobi station.'

Swann stared at her. 'Oh Jesus.'

'You lost that?' Byron sounded almost shocked. 'You don't remember any of it?'

She shook her head, beginning to get exasperated. 'Any of *what*?'

'Oh man, we're in deeper shit than I thought.' Swann turned quickly away and headed for the aft door. 'Byron, you better help her out. I'll meet you in ops once I've rigged the pumps, yokay?'

The computer core was located just forward of the ops chamber: a converted officer's cabin filled to the ceiling with a riot of machinery. Lannigan couldn't make anything of it. It was difficult even to determine a specific outline. All she could see was a tangle of blocks and cylinders and a fat, spiralling labyrinth of cable. 'What a mess.'

'You never could stop tinkering.'

She followed Byron into the ops chamber. He motioned her to a seat and she eased herself down, letting the cane contract and placing it carefully on the desktop in front of her. As she leant back, the bolts in the seat frame dug uncomfortably into her spine.

An edge of familiarity made her shudder. She must have spent a lot of time here for the memory to have become so deeply embedded.

Byron had dropped into the seat next to her, and was studying her closely. 'What?' she asked.

'You don't remember this at all?'

'Nothing.'

'You were our systems specialist, as well as MD.' He reached for the nearest keyboard and drew it close, flipping on the power and tapping out a complex string of commands. 'I believe you had a career in the AI board before you left to start Living Glass.'

Lannigan's eyebrows went up. 'What, the UN board?'

'That's correct.'

'Good God. I wonder if they owe me any pension.'

'No, I think you owe them about three years in prison. Good morning, Kitsumi.'

'Good morning, Mr Byron.'

The voice was a smooth whisper, vaguely feminine, issuing from somewhere in the air above Lannigan's head. She gasped and craned her head upward, but couldn't determine the source. 'Is that . . .'

Byron tapped out another string of instructions, activating a row of flatscreens. 'Kitsumi, could you identify my companion, please?'

There was a short pause. Then: 'Voicecode identification gives a high probability that your companion is Doctor Cassandra Lannigan, our managing director. However, her facial dimensions do not match my database.'

Doctor? Lannigan put a hand to her cheek. 'I've, er, had reconstructive surgery.'

'Acknowledged. Do you wish me to update my files?'

'Yes, please, Kitsumi,' said Byron. 'Also, accept Doctor Lannigan's voicecode as inner-core access for this session, alpha-level command form. Verify.'

'Verified, Mr Byron.'

Lannigan listened hard, trying to commit Byron's words to memory as he guided the AI through a series of file backups and data transfers. None of it meant very much to her; the complex graphics filling Kitsumi's flatscreens told her even less. If the man beside her was telling the truth, if she really had been an expert in the construction and operation of such systems, then Kotebe had robbed her of even more than she had thought. 'Byron?'

'Mm?'

'How much do you know about Joey Kotebe?'

'Not a great deal. We tried to do some checking on him after the hotel incident. There was part of a criminal record – some rape-murders in Pretoria and Kinshasa – and a possible association with an underground security plex called the WetWorx Guard, but we couldn't get any closer than that. We did a reasonable job of stripping ID out of the registers, but somebody did a far better one on Kotebe. Smells like corporate cover to me.'

'I didn't offend the AI board that much, did I?'

'Let's hope not. But somebody made it worth our while to stay out of sight for three months.'

'Doctor Lannigan?'

The voice, she realised with a start, was somewhat akin to her own. 'Ah, yes, Kitsumi?'

'According to my boot log the Artemis file was left open during my last shutdown. Would you like me to close the file before download?'

And Byron said, 'Are you all right?'

The word had flared in Lannigan's mind. She took her hand away from her forehead, where she had grabbed at herself on reflex. 'I think so. That name . . . You and Swann mentioned it in the module, back then. There's some connection in my head, but I'm not sure where to. Ow . . .'

'Artemis was the job code for your last assignment. Swann and I were in Afghanistan – you and Angel handled the details independently. We never got a chance to review the file after you were attacked.'

'And then everything went screwy.' Lannigan straightened. 'Kitsumi, I think I'd better have a look at this file.'

'Acknowledged, Doctor Lannigan. Does this task take priority over a proximity alert, or not?'

Lannigan and Byron looked at each other for a moment. 'What proximity alert?'

'My security net has been activated. Six individuals are in the process of boarding *Kitsumi Maru* from the seaward side. I believe they are armed.'

After Byron had left the ops chamber, Lannigan asked Kitsumi to give her as many outside views as possible. She sat in the cushionless metal chair and watched black-clad men and women moving silently over the upper deck.

The MD of Living Glass – it helped to think of her as a separate person, someone Lannigan had heard of only barely – had spent considerable time and effort getting the vessel's security systems up to scratch. Even with the power down and the resident AI quiescent, it had been enough to alert Byron to an intruder breaking through the aft hatch. Now, with the program running at full capacity, Lannigan was being given a full tactical breakdown of the drama playing itself out above her head: tracking chipcam shots interspersed with CGI simulations and scans from heat-and-motion detectors.

Lucky for her that she *had* tripped the alarm, she thought suddenly. Doubly lucky that Byron and Swann had been so close to tracking her down. If not, she might have been facing this alone.

Still, the odds were very much against her. There were six assailants padding about the fireship's upper deck: four studying the sealed hatches near the prow, two more moving aft. They were sleek, glossy things, aquatic and alien in their skinsuits and airscrubber packs. Masks covered their faces. The fins and flippers that propelled them below the surface had folded away, held tightly against smooth limbs by myoelectronic muscles.

Up at the prow, one of the men was using a pistol-sized aerosol to spray fluid over the hatch edges.

Lannigan's gaze flicked to the gun Byron had left her, then back to the nearest screen. She pointed at the aerosol. 'Kitsumi, what is that?'

'Unknown. Optimum hypothesis is a liquid decongestant, capable of breaking down polymer bonds.'

The figures crowded around the port hatch. One of them forced gloved fingers under the edge and began to pull upward. His thermal signature altered as muscles strained in his legs and back.

Abruptly, the hatch came up. There was a thunderous noise from the prow, a metallic whiplash gonging, impacts, screams. The ship seemed to bounce. Half the screens went dead.

Lannigan stared at the ones left working. Something had erupted from beneath the hatch, filling the air with metal shrapnel that was still bouncing and ringing off the deck. The man who had opened the hatch lay in a twisted, boneless tangle across the port bulwark, gouts of thermal activity spilling from him and pouring over the side. A woman staggered away from him, ripped and bleeding. Lannigan watched her fall. 'My God. What . . .'

'A booby trap, installed by Mr Swann five months ago. Operated entirely by mechanical energy.'

Springs, she thought incredulously. Swann had filled the hatch space with springs and blades, undetectable to chemical sniffers. A hail of metal fragments had ripped across the deck and done as much damage to Kitsumi's security system as it had to the attackers.

Two down, though. Lannigan liked the odds better already.

As she thought that, the rest of the screens strobed and faded out. Lannigan looked wildly around. 'Kitsumi, all the screens are dead.'

'Confirmed. The intruders have disabled the external security system.'

A burst of gunfire howled back from the prow, echoing down the corridor.

They were in. Lannigan snatched up the gun and the cane, scrambled over to the chamber door and leant on it until it closed. Above her, the hatch she had broken through swung open and slammed against the deck.

She stayed by the door, listening to footsteps clattering down the ladder. There was a pause, a muffled burst of conversation. She moved back and raised the gun.

More sounds, metallic and heavy. 'Kitsumi!' she hissed. 'What's going on?'

There was no answer. The ops board had died.

The intruders had gotten into the computer core. Lannigan felt a sudden surge of panic. If the core was destroyed she might lose the Artemis file for ever, might go to her grave without ever discovering what it held. It was an absurd thought, surrounded as she was by armed assailants with far worse things on their minds than data vandalism. Still, it drove her. She unlocked the door and stepped out into the corridor.

The core chamber was just to her right. Two skin-suited figures hunched within, probing at the maze of systemry. One cradled a stubby, heavy-looking weapon – waterproofed, Lannigan guessed – but the other was armed with nothing save a flat block of electronics no larger that his clasped hands. LEDs fluttered red and green over its upper surface, and there was a glitter of gold connectors. Lannigan didn't know what the device was, but she had no desire to see it anywhere near her AI. She flipped the gun over in her left hand and checked that the charge light was still on.

At that point a great fist of sound came screaming and ringing back from the prow, some kind of contained explosion. The deck moved and vented a long, mournful creak of overstressed metal, an echoing groan that went on for far too long. Lannigan stumbled back and had to clutch at the doorframe to avoid falling. She felt the ship settle beneath her, moving the smallest fraction of an angle, but terrifying on something so heavy and old. She wondered if the hull had been breached.

There was a rapid exchange in a language she couldn't identify, and then the armed man darted past her, no doubt as unnerved by the detonation as she. He must have thought his companion alone and safe enough back here among the cables.

Lannigan decided to prove otherwise. She swung round into the core chamber and yelled.

Somehow, purely by accident, she must have pulled the trigger.

The gun went off with a deafening sound, a tearing, ripping, hard flat beating at the eardrums that hammered with hellish volume around the chamber. Lannigan screamed, blinded by the muzzle flare, trying to get away from the noise, to put a hand over her ears, but the gun was still jumping and roaring in her grip. She could let go. It wouldn't stop firing.

Bullets were exploding off the walls, the ceiling, blasting fragments off the support structures. Cables lashed like whips under repeated impacts. Lannigan took a step backward, got tangled up in her cane and went over in a heap. The gun bounced out of her grip and skated away across the deck.

The silence, past the throbbing whine in her ears, was almost painful.

She lay there for a moment, looking at a row of holes in the ceiling, then forced herself upright. The core chamber was full of smoke, threaded by a thousand needles of light from fractured optical fibres. Fires guttered and spat amid the tangle.

The skinsuited man was slumped in the corner, his hands clamped loosely over his head. For a moment Lannigan wondered if she had managed to kill him by mistake, but closer inspection revealed him to be merely unconscious, probably a victim of repeated concussions from a clipfull of explosive slugs. Either that, or he had struck his head trying to get out of the way.

Whatever the explanation, Lannigan decided that she had just used her last gun.

She peered shakily into the wreckage. The glittering device was plugged firmly into the feed slot of the AI core. Lannigan found that oddly disturbing on a visceral level. It was like looking at a tumour, a parasite working its way into Kitsumi's brain. She reached in with her free hand and tried to yank it out, but it was in solidly, and her fingers were still too numb to get a proper grip.

She cursed, shifted her weight to her left foot and let the cane dangle from her forearm. Using both hands, she managed to detach the device; she dropped it on to the floor and kicked it away. Behind it, the core was a raised slab of impact plastic set with a recessed handle, studded with warning labels. Lannigan thought for a moment, then lifted the handle and heaved.

Byron had spoken about pulling the core. She guessed that he must have meant something like this.

There was a muffled sound, a complex metallic chatter from behind the panel, and the whole assembly slid forward a few centimetres. When she tugged it out she saw that the whole unit was no larger than a briefcase, a heavy slab of active silicon and armour. Living glass.

All its feed slots were sealed behind sliding panels, locked down tight.

A quick inspection revealed little sign of damage, nothing more than a couple of near-miss grazes. Whatever internal ruin might have been wrought by the plug-in would have to be determined later; right now Lannigan had other fish to fry. She headed for the hatch ladder, carrying the core by its handle. That and the cane made climbing a struggle, but within a minute or so she was at the top, within sight of the deck.

Very carefully, she raised her head until she could peek over the edge of the hatch. At first she could see nothing – the biolumes nearest to *Kitsumi Maru* had been shot away, leaving the vessel in near darkness. But the barest hint of dawn was already glittering at the eastern horizon, giving Lannigan a few shapes to work by, and within seconds a bright burst of gunfire ripped across the deck. The flare of it imprinted the scene clearly on her mind's eye.

She ducked back, breathing hard. The fire had come from Swann: she had seen him crouching beside the ruined wheelhouse, bracing a machine pistol against a twist of girder. He was aiming up towards the prow, where one of the intruders was sheltering behind the crates and a second taking cover behind the opened hatch door. A third skinsuited figure lay near Lannigan's hatch, close enough for her to see the mess somebody had made of its head.

Swann was trapped, that much was obvious. He probably had seconds before his weapon emptied, or another intruder came at him from a different angle. And where the hell was Byron?

Lannigan breathed hard, twice, then scrambled up on to the deck.

She dropped the core next to the hatch and scuttled forward on her hands and knees, keeping low and close to the port bulwark. Somebody shouted as she passed the crates but Swann opened up with a long, wild burst, making the intruders duck for cover and giving her enough time to reach the gangway. He was using up his own ammo to let her escape.

She scuttled past the gangway and kept going.

Swann yelled something but she was already where she wanted to be, right next to the oozing corpse of the first intruder. The aerosol was close by, right where she had seen him drop it after Swann's booby trap had carved him apart, and she snatched it up, squirting the stuff frantically around the edge of the port hatch. It smelt horrible, but there was a satisfying sound of bubbling as the polymer bonds holding down the hatch began to give way. Lannigan swivelled painfully on one knee and began to crawl back to the wheelhouse.

Either the epoxy around the port hatch was weaker, or the intruders had already given it a dose when the first trap went off. Lannigan had enough time to see one of Swann's assailants swing his weapon round towards her when the hatch was slammed a dozen metres into the sky.

Shrapnel screeched across the deck in a solid wave.

As before, most of it left the hatch space in an upward cone, but there were a few fragments that danced to their own tunes. Lannigan howled as fragments snapped into the deck and bulwark around her, ripping across her skin. A chunk slammed agonisingly into her upper arm; another into her hip. Metal rained around her.

There was a distant splash as the hatch cover tumbled into the sea.

She took her arms from her head and looked up. The two intruders were sprawled over the deck, twisted and unmoving. The fragment in her hip was small, half a coin that came out when she tugged at it, but the piece in her arm was a spiral of tin can that had laced her shirt to her bicep. Blood was soaking down over her hand.

It didn't actually hurt all that much. When the shock wore off, however, she would be screaming.

Swann's face loomed white in the darkness above her. 'Jesus, doc. You yokay?'

'You wanna give me a hand here?' She let him haul her upright and stood swaying, her left arm limp and useless by her side. 'Where's Byron?'

'Dead. I think he's dead. He got between me and them, there was a grenade or something. Carved him up real bad.' He looked around frantically. 'You know who they are?'

'Not a clue. Swann, you're going to have to carry Kitsumi.' She motioned him over to the core and watched him pick it up. 'The UN aren't going to let all this firing go by without a look-see.'

'I ain't going without Byron.'

'Swann . . .' She glared at him for a moment, but the rising dawn showed her the expression on his face. She realised that she couldn't stop him seeking out his friend. Trying to do so would simply waste time. 'Don't take too long.'

He swung himself down into the hatchway. As he did so something dark and thin whipped across Lannigan's vision. She opened her mouth to speak and felt the cold wire slice backward into her throat.

There was a loop of it round her neck, horribly tight and digging further in with every second. Lannigan clawed at the air, gasping futilely. The wire was crushing her throat, closing the arteries on either side of her neck. She sank to her knees, sparks whining and soaring in her vision.

And in her ear, a voice: 'Got you this time, bitch.'

Even with her brain spasming from oxygen loss, she could never forget that voice. It was Joey Kotebe, back to finish what he'd started all those weeks ago in Nairobi. This time he was going to kill her for good.

The pain peaked. Lannigan's vision greyed out, and there was a massive impact. The deck rose and slammed her full in the face. For a moment she was convinced that she had died, that her head had swollen up and burst.

Death, however, was a painless nothing; she knew that from experience. Only life hurt. When she scrabbled at the line of fire round her neck the ligature dropped away, and a sawing breath gave her enough strength to roll over. Her vision cleared. Dawn clouds clustered thickly overhead, and between her and them stood Kotebe, his face a mask of fury, his arms wrenched round behind his back.

Byron was dragging him away.

Swann had been right about the man's wounds, and close enough about his demise. Byron was on his feet, but he should not have been.

Whatever had exploded up at the prow must have caught him full force. The E-human was a wreck, a tattered, broken scarecrow dripping tatters of scorched and twisted flesh. Lannigan could see things moving fitfully in the gaps and the shrapnel holes, and half his face had been flensed away by the blast, revealing the metalised planes of his skull, the ruins of a mirrored eye.

'Go,' he hissed, the words part sound and part fluid. 'Something's coming.'

Lannigan grabbed the bulwark and hauled herself up. 'What?'

'Surprise . . .'

Kotebe wrenched an arm free. He had a weapon slung across his chest, and he strained to reach it.

Byron dragged him back another metre. His boots slipped in the slick of blood he had left following Kotebe from the open hatch, and he fell. 'Swann!' he roared. 'Get her away!'

She shook her head and started towards him, but a hand came down on her shoulder and pulled. She had no strength left to resist.

Kotebe was getting up, Byron's broken hands tangling him all the way. Lannigan saw Kotebe bring the gun around, its pinhole muzzle swinging towards her and then past, angling downward. A shot exploded, flat and dead in the open air, and a gout of blood rose from Byron's back. The E-human jerked, then shouted again. 'Swann!'

Lannigan felt something being pushed into her good hand. It was the cane. She turned and looked helplessly into Swann's pallid, bloodstained face. The knowledge of Byron's injuries rose in her with clinical intensity, condition and prognosis mapped out on some cold page in her mind, the same page on which had been scribed the demise of the assassin she had kicked to death in Nairobi, the trajectory of a burning spacecraft, the patterns of falsehood and manipulation that she had used on N'Tele, Lippincott, Rayanne. She knew with mechanical certainty that the E-human was dead, even if his body didn't know it yet. The clarity of it was like a blade. It sickened her.

She wanted to rage against it, to deny it, to prove it wrong. But Swann had already got her as far as the gangway and Kotebe was pumping shot after shot into Byron's gleaming skull.

As she reached the threshold, Kotebe stopped firing and looked up at her. She met his gaze for a bare second, and then he twisted abruptly, eyes wide with shock. The gun flew from his grasp and he toppled, slamming heavily against the deck.

Byron's hand was locked death-tight round his left ankle.

Lannigan heard the assassin howl with anger, but his words were drowned in an instant. A louder howl ripped up into the dawn, and with it a light, a rolling wave of burning smoke. Swann yelled a warning and yanked her back as a blinding tongue of flame erupted from within the pile of lashed crates on the deck.

The concussion struck her like a boot. She doubled up in the face of it, overbalanced, and crashed messily down the gangway.

At the bottom, she looked up, her head spinning. The flame from the crates had carved a track in the air, a crazy spiral leaping joyously away from the waterfront and out to sea. It was a missile, she realised. Marcus Gray's Tigercat, still without its guidance mechanism, whirling in a bright blaze of rocket exhaust across the leaden water. Below it, *Kitsumi Maru* was burning. Byron must have stashed something inflammable around the launch tube.

She didn't see the significance of the plan until after Swann had grabbed her beneath the armpits and begun dragging her away from the ship. As he pulled, and she wondered blearily whether she had enough strength to begin helping him, she saw thin scratches of light rising from the sea around her.

A turn of her head showed her more above the city.

Veracruz Llave was still seething with United Nations troops, the waters around its coast equally so. The entire force was on alert standby, combat AIs watching with infinite patience for the slightest sign of trouble. When the Huastecs' helicopter used machine guns on the crawler tanks, they had replied instantly and in kind.

Kitsumi Maru had fired a missile.

Lannigan clawed her way out of Swann's grip and shoved him over the edge of the tine. When he hit the water she retracted her cane and jumped in after him, the surface closing over her head just as the UN missiles turned the waterfront, and every vessel on it, to splintered fire.

12
Awakening

The light, when it returned, came slowly. Rayanne lay drifting in a blood-warm sea, buffeted by gentle waves of consciousness, sparks of sensation, the memory of fever dreams. Flickers of recollection stabbed at her through the dark like bright needles: the ceiling of a medsled, obscured by bulky figures in masks and breathing gear; her own head burning from within, buzzing and crawling as though a hive of bees had been sewn under her scalp; a kiss.

'Get another four CCs of blood. Filter and crossmatch, see if there's any trace left.'

There was a glow past her eyelids, the promise of a light too bright and painful to endure. It was Rayanne's first point of real awareness, but she was too sleepy and comfortable to deal with it right away. She preferred to drift in liquid warmth, rolling slowly like an old log.

'Temp's down. Half a degree above nominal.'

'Did anyone get me that dendritic scan I asked for?'

The voices were a distraction, with their clipped accents and their gibberish. Rayanne sniffed, smelling pine and the clean aroma of plastic. There was a distant humming sound above her, an odd feeling of being watched. She blinked.

The light didn't seem so bad any more. She realised,

with a pang of loss, that the sea was going away. She was waking up.

There was cool linen pressing against her toes and knees, more against her back. Her head rested on a pillow that was ever so slightly lumpy, and there were strange patches of contact on her forehead and the backs of her hands. Something had been stuck to her there.

'EEG's back in the green.'

'Got the scan back, Ted. Myelin's green, fibre inputs are clear. No lesions. She's beaten it.'

Rayanne considered this. Quite a lot of her seemed to have turned green, by the sound of it. She wondered just how much, whether it would affect her chances of getting a new boyfriend. She had a sudden, terrible vision of herself as an aged spinster, bright green from head to toe. Her eyes snapped open.

Somebody said, 'Christ.'

She looked around wildly. Beyond her was an expanse of bed, a silvery sheet tucked into a curved surround of white plastic. Past that were pale-blue walls, an illuminated ceiling, a window with the opacity turned up, a sink.

Her arms, lying at her sides above the sheet, were just the same colour as she remembered them.

There were three people in the room with her: a rather fat nurse with red hair; a tall black doctor wearing datashades; and another man who, after a few seconds, she recognised. He was the white-haired man she had spoken to on the comm, when she was getting help for Gregor. They were all looking at her.

She blinked. 'Er, hi.' Her throat was horribly dry.

The white-haired man gave her a funny kind of smile, using only half his mouth. 'Hi, Rayanne. It is Rayanne, isn't it?'

'Last time I checked.'

'That'll make the paperwork easier.' He was shorter than he looked on the comm, only about Lannigan's height, but wide. He was wearing blue scrubs with the sleeves rolled up, and his arms were big and muscly and covered in white hairs. 'I'm Ted Harrison. Do you know where you are?'

'I'll go for a hospital, yeah?' She swallowed painfully. 'Listen, doc. Can I get something to drink? My throat's killing me.'

The nurse nodded and hurried off. As she left, the black doctor touched Harrison on the shoulder. 'Amazing,' he muttered. 'Looks like speech and motor functions are all in the green.'

Green. Rayanne suddenly realised what the men might have been talking about. 'What, "green" as in "yokay"? I ain't sick?'

Harrison shrugged. 'Not any more. 'I'll be honest with you, Rayanne. When you came in here we were pretty worried. You were in a bad way. We had to put you in intensive care for a while.'

The nurse had returned with a plastic squeeze bulb full of fluid. Rayanne grabbed it from her, jammed the tube between her lips and squeezed hard until she had a mouthful of cold, sweet tea. She swallowed it, drugs in the liquid sluicing the pain away. 'Oh, man. Thanks. So how long's a while?'

The doctors exchanged a glance. The black guy said, 'About eight hours.'

Rayanne finished the last of the tea and handed the bulb back to the nurse. 'So when do I get outta here?'

'Not *quite* yet.' Harrison gave the other doctor a grin, then turned back to her. 'You had a pretty serious disease, Rayanne. Encephalitis. Do you know what that is?'

'No.'

'It's a disease that affects the brain. It can be quite serious, especially if we run into a new variant.'

'But you said I wasn't sick no more.'

Harrison leant close. 'Rayanne, some other people have this disease, too. We don't know why, because it's usually very rare. But these other people haven't recovered as quickly as you. We want to keep you around for a while, make sure you don't get sick again.'

Rayanne gnawed her lower lip. 'Yokay, man. I understand.' She watched him nod and move away. He spoke briefly to the other doctor, mostly long words that she couldn't quite catch. She recognised 'malnutrition', though, and 'biopsy'.

The black doctor came up to the side of the bed. He tapped at one of the patches stuck to her arms – biomonitors, she realised – then took off his datashades and looked at her. 'Rayanne, you were pretty strung out when we found you. What have you been taking?'

'Nothing,' she said automatically. He smiled.

'Nice try. Look, you're not in trouble or anything. We just want to find out what it was you were on when you contracted the disease. It might help us with the other patients.'

'I can't remember, man. I swear to God.' She turned her head away from him. 'Hey, I'm real tired. I just need to rest . . .'

'Are you feeling ill again?'

'No. I'm just, like . . .' She let her voice drift. 'Wanna sleep . . .'

There was a pause, then he patted her shoulder. 'Sure. I'll come back in a couple of hours.'

She nodded sleepily, her eyes closed. Across the room she heard a door opening, the sounds of people walking away. She snuggled down into the pillow and draped a hand across her face.

After the door had closed again she waited half a minute, then opened her eyes, peering between her fingers.

She was alone. She sat up, waited until the room stopped bobbing about, then swung herself out of bed. A quick search revealed her clothes, bundled up in a closet. The contents of her jacket had been removed, and she panicked for a moment before finding them under her chinos, zipped into a plastic bag.

The staff had put her in a standard-issue hospital gown, a thin and shapeless garment with short sleeves and no back. Rayanne shucked the thing and struggled back into her clothes. She left the biopatches stuck on to the skin of her arms and forehead: they were remote feeds back to the room's medicom, and it might sound a flatline alarm if she stripped them off too soon. That done, she splashed a little cold water on her face and hair, dried herself with a towel, and then went to the door and pulled it very slightly open.

A couple of nurses wandered past, and then no one.

Rayanne held the door open with the toe of her trainer while she tugged off the monitors and stuck them to the wall. Then she slipped through and into the corridor. It was at least a minute before she heard anyone running, and by that time she was already halfway down the fire escape.

She was on the street within four minutes.

It was early evening. The sun was low, down behind the towers, sending poles of greyish light skittering through the warm, rain-damp air. When Rayanne started to sweat she took off her jacket and slung it over one shoulder.

She headed north, moving fast. All things considered, she felt pretty good. If she stood up too quickly or leant forward too far her head would pound and spin, but then it tended to do that anyway. Her fever was gone. She was clean. If she wanted to get picky she could confess to being a little tired, and mildly hung over. But Harrison's treatments must have done wonders: compared to what she had been feeling like for the past couple of weeks she was on top of the world.

She was also, when she thought about it, pleasantly hungry.

She stopped at a self-service noodle den and punched up a double helping of *ramen* with soup and an alcohol-free Kirin beer. The place wasn't full: most of the on-site suits hadn't left their offices yet, and the teleworkers would still be uploading the day's input and shutting down for the night. There were a few patrons, mostly tourists, families, but no one at the bar. Rayanne found a seat at the far end, away from the door and right in front of an infonet screen tuned to international sumo. Presumably just for the ambience, because the sound was down and no one was watching.

She got tired of fat men slapping each other after the first bowl of *ramen*, and leant over to change the channel, tapping at the controls with the ends of her chopsticks. It was a little difficult to identify some of the addresses with no audio, but if she turned it up somebody might realise that she was messing with the channels and take offence. So she hopped idly through a couple of dozen no-brain entertainment sectors, finding nothing of interest on any of them. She was just about to quit and go back to the sumo when she saw a picture of Jackson Memorial Hospital flip on to the screen.

It was a newsfeed, one of the fast and flashy types, all windows and on-screen hotlinks and dubious sources. Rayanne saw a link for information on a new variant of encephalitis scroll up, and almost dropped her chopsticks.

She found the volume control and prodded at it until she could hear what was going on.

According to the feed, the Miami encephalitis outbreak had claimed another life, bringing the total to nine. Sixteen more lay in isolation units, wracked by a fever that was destroying their brains cell by cell. Another three had been lobotomised by the ravages of the disease on their frontal lobes and hippocampus.

Suddenly, Rayanne wasn't hungry any more. She watched footage of screaming, thrashing patients clawing at their skulls until sedated or restrained. She saw MRI scans, harassed-looking doctors talking about myelic damage, dendritic realignment, microlesions. She saw a chipcam recording of an autopsy, hacked from the Jackson core database the night before. Two surgeons in environment suits were slicing away the top of Gregor Karamov's skull with an ultrasonic cutter.

She stabbed at the controls, killing the picture before anyone else saw it.

No wonder Harrison had been setting her up for a biopsy series. Rayanne looked quickly around the noodle den to make sure no one had noticed her, then headed for the door.

She bought a newsfax. It didn't matter which one: the bug was headline news wherever she went.

The medicos up at Jackson were doing their best to keep a lid on the story, but that was always hard. Rayanne sat on a wall outside Miami stadium and read what she could: her reading skills were passable at best, and the fax she had bought seemed to delight in using the longest and most obscure medical terms around, but it wasn't too difficult to get the gist.

The encephalitis was killing people.

According to the fax, if you got it you either died or ended up with the mental capacity of a spoon. It tore into the brain in a way that looked half fever, half nanotech, and no one could agree on exactly how it worked or where it had come from. People had already started talking bioweapons. The Dade County authorities were requesting help from the UN, but that was likely to be delayed due to a similar situation in Mexico.

Rayanne bundled up the fax and tossed it into a nearby disposal, then got up and started walking. There was no way she could have caught the same bug as Gregor, she told herself. There must have been a mistake. Maybe Harrison hadn't been sure either, which is why she had been able to get out of Jackson so easily. If the encephalitis variant had sprung up as quickly as everyone was saying, the medical authorities must have been in a panic.

That said, Harrison had told her that encephalitis was rare, in any form.

It was all so confusing. If Rayanne *had* suffered an attack of Gregor's disease, and somehow survived, that still left the question of who had caught it from whom. If she had gotten it from him, it was a fast enough mover. If it was the other way around, that made her as close to a murderer as made no odds.

Rayanne saw a public comms booth, and stopped. There was the third option, the one she had entertained on the maglev for a few seconds before deciding that she didn't want to think about it.

She stepped into the booth and punched 911. 'Gimme Jackson Memorial, guy called Harrison. He's in charge of this encephalitis bug thing. Tell him it's Rayanne.'

The AI fluttered for a few moments, trying to process the request, but there must have been software agents looking for her voiceprint. Harrison appeared on the screen in less than a minute. 'Where are you?'

'You already know where I am, mister, and by the time you get here I'll be gone. So listen up. I got something you wanna know.'

'I'm listening.'

'Gregor Karamov, the guy I called you up about. He met this Pacifican chick in the Candy Stripe, yeah? She planted a kiss on him, even though he wasn't interested, and right after that he got the bug.'

'Rayanne –'

'No, *listen* to me, man! I met this chick, too, right? And she kisses *me*! Like she just grabs me and lays one on, and then *I* get the bug! She's got a roomful of stuff, equipment, I dunno what, but there's something about her that ain't right. I reckon she's brewing something up, spreading it around by kissing people.' It sounded ridiculous, Rayanne knew, but if it was true there would be a pattern, wouldn't there? Something to make Harrison believe her. 'She's in a motel up by Reeves Park. Name's Noriko Kobayashi.'

'Rayanne, we need to talk –'

'Sorry, man. I ain't letting you cut me for this. Curing diseases and stuff is your job, not mine. Just look this Kobayashi up, yokay? I'm outta here.' She killed the connection before he could say anything more.

She already felt bad about running out on him. Gregor Karamov was enough of a burden on her conscience.

Rayanne stopped running five blocks away, then walked until she found another comms booth. She knew it would be dangerous to use the system again so soon and risk her voiceprint flagging Harrison's software, but there was something she had to do. Besides, the booth she had chosen was within sight of Santa Clara metromag station, so she could run for that after her call and be away before the medsleds showed.

Had the outbreak been limited to Miami, Rayanne would have been straight to the airport and away. In pointing Harrison in the direction of Noriko Kobayashi she reckoned that she had done just about all she could, save checking back into Jackson and letting the medicos there make vaccine out of her brains. But the fax had mentioned Mexico, and the more Rayanne thought about that the more uncomfortable she got.

Kobayashi might very well be spreading the bug in Miami, but that meant someone else was doing the same thing in Mexico.

Lannigan had gone to Mexico.

Kobayashi was looking for Lannigan.

Rayanne wasn't sure how this business added up, but she would bet her last dollar that it all locked together somehow. She felt like she had been brushed by something huge that she couldn't quite see, something that, if it even noticed her, would sweep her away without any effort at all. Like she was swimming way out at sea, all alone, and the tip of her toe had nudged an immense, moving presence under the surface.

She felt the world shifting invisibly around her, and she shivered.

She called up an international comms window, fed a couple of hundred dollars into the machine and tapped in Lannigan's account code.

That was when her hands started to shake.

The screen strobed and blinked, the audio output whispering as the system logged into the central registry and began calling up satellites. Rayanne wasn't listening. She was frozen. Even when Lannigan answered, her image blurred behind a piece of magic tape and her wasp-whine of a voice needling out from the speakers, Rayanne just stood there.

Something was horribly, terrifyingly wrong with her. She started to cry.

Slung over her shoulder was a jacket whose lining was covered with permagraph memory tags, reminders, mnemonics. A hundred words and codes and drawings that were all she had left of a past splintered by years of chemical amnesia. Everything she had was there, her whole life.

Lannigan's account code was there. The *lisiada* had written it in herself. Rayanne had watched her do it, knowing she would forget.

But she had punched it into the comm without even needing to look.

It was right there in her mind, every letter and digit. The memory of it was perfect. And when she thought about that she remembered the muzak that had been playing when Lannigan was writing it in. She remembered the exact price of her ticket to Miami. The flight number.

There had been nineteen cans of White Riot beer in Gregor Karamov's fridge.

On her first date with Zenebe, he had bought her a pina colada.

When she was very young, her mother used to sing old Tammy Wynette songs to her to make her sleep.

Rayanne slumped against the comm panel, weeping quietly, watching her charges racking up on the screen while a great flood of memory came soaring up from some dark and unhallowed place in her mind to enfold her like the sweep of angels' wings.

Black

13
Heart of the Machine

The spaceplane *Albireo* levelled off 30,000 metres above the ground, after a ten-minute climb to dock with an automated refuelling drone. Cassandra Lannigan found herself trying to hear it breathe.

It had seemed such an organic thing when she had first seen it, an arcing fusion of hawk and moth, a hundred metres from nose to tail and perched with impossible delicacy amid a sprawl of landing lights. The organic illusion persisted within the craft: the ribbed interior lit in a soft, soothing pink, the floor and ceiling carpets a rich crimson. Settling into the creamy *faux* leather of her seat, Lannigan felt like a tooth in a long mouth, a morsel waiting to be digested in *Albireo*'s gullet.

Now, twenty minutes after Mexico City had vanished behind her, she still felt as though she was riding a beast. If she listened hard enough she was sure that she could hear the true voice of it, the breath and the heartbeat, as wisps of atmosphere went whining past the vessel's streamlined hull at 500 kilometres an hour. The refuelling drone – Lannigan imagined its vast bulk hovering above them like an eagle over a dove, wormlike umbilicals latched obscenely into *Albireo*'s hide – screamed thunder past and above them, high-speed pumps blasting volatile gels into the spaceplane's hungry tanks. Together the two aircraft had carved a double trail of vaporised hydrocarbons through 80,000 metres of sky.

Albireo was feeding, in the high domain between air and space. Lannigan wanted to hear it sing as it fed.

There was, however, far too much impinging upon her senses to allow such accuracies. She shared the spaceplane's gut with some five dozen fellow passengers, and most of those were far more vocal than she. They chattered incessantly, and bickered, and laughed. Occasionally one would sing: the tuneless wavering of one who is wearing a headset with the volume turned up too loud. They ate noisily. They clattered belongings. Some of them, Rayanne Hernandez included, snored.

If this wasn't enough, Lannigan herself was far from calm. Mexico still rang in her bones. Two days had passed since the destruction of the *Kitsumi Maru*, during which time she had enjoyed little in the way of rest. She had been recovering from her injuries in a UN aid camp when Rayanne's call had come through, and after that she had no choice but to get on her feet and head for Mexico City.

Swann hadn't understood her urgency, but he had accompanied her anyway. He occupied the seat in front of her, which was just where she wanted him right now. She still couldn't bring herself to turn her back on the man.

She rubbed her left arm absently. The UN medics had stapled up the injury as best they could and slapped an analgesic patch over the wound, but the torn muscle still ached and stung. Her hair felt odd, too. Some of it had been burnt away when the *Kitsumi Maru* went up, and she'd had to cut it short to hide the scorching.

No wonder she couldn't relax. She had been sitting with her eyes closed during the refuel, trying to empty her mind, to find some Zen-like store of inner tranquillity. But it hadn't worked, and now Rayanne was starting to wake up.

Lannigan sighed and opened her eyes. The Latina was

slumped messily in the seat between her and the viewport, head crooked against the wall, dark hair tangled untidily over her face. She still smelt of the cheap vodka she had been downing in the airport bar when they had found her. She had dribbled into her collar. She was snoring horribly.

Her great stab at independence had lasted just over four days. Lannigan suppressed a thin smile: the idea that this stuporous wreck could even consider striking out on her own was so ludicrous as to be almost funny.

But past Rayanne was the viewport, and there . . . Once again, the sight took Lannigan's heart and filled it, smothered it with a chilly wonder that made her throat catch and her eyes prick with sudden moisture. Beyond the girl's uncaring head the Earth was a curve of bright, cloud-shot crystal, sparking sunlight from the mirrored sea, bathed in a jewelled ink of starlight. She could see rippled crusts of land beneath the clouds, see the ribbon of atmosphere thinning as it rose, a slim layer of life and warmth beneath all of cold infinity. The sight of it froze Lannigan to the core, sent her soaring.

'There,' she whispered, eyes fixed on the darkness. Out there . . .

Behind her, someone laughed raucously. Lannigan bounced, her heart leaping. She swallowed hard and decided to stare fixedly at the little infonet display mounted before her while she tried to get her breathing back under control. The laugh sounded again, accompanied this time by sounds of muted embarrassment. At least one of the spaceplane's passengers, Lannigan surmised, was overdoing the complimentary cocktails. She wondered maliciously how he would fare when Earth's gravity finally surrendered its grip on his guts.

Rayanne sneezed suddenly, sharp and tight, like a cat. Her eyelids fluttered.

Lannigan gave her a sideways glare, then turned her attention back to the infonet display. A page-sized flatscreen was set into the seat in front of her, tuned to an outside camera pickup: the belly of the drone filled most of the view, a sullen grey bulk stretching away into the indigo sky. As she watched, the umbilicals wavered, then shrank back towards the drone. The aircraft began to roll away, shedding speed.

Shadows licked *Albireo*'s wings as the drone dropped behind.

Lannigan watched for a moment, then reached out and tapped the screen, calling up an entertainments menu. Anything but staring again at the naked sky, and losing herself to its glamour.

The spaceplane's infonet was pathetically small, compared to the vast globes of data accessible back on Earth. Less than a hundred recorded netshows were on offer here, and maybe twice that number of games and educational programs. Enough to keep a few dozen passengers amused for a three-hour flight, perhaps, but hardly inspiring. Lannigan scrolled through the choices until she found a concert recording, something of the same baroque complexity that had captivated her back in Nairobi station. She killed the video feed, and was just about to put on the tiny headset when someone in the aisle reached out and touched her shoulder.

A uniformed steward was leaning over her. 'Excuse me, miss.'

Lannigan stared at him. '*What?*'

He nodded at Rayanne. 'Your friend there. She's all yokay?'

'Oh, *her*.' Lannigan's stomach unknotted, letting her breathe. 'She's, ah, drunk.'

The steward nodded, lowering his voice conspiratorially. 'Oh.'

'Tried to take her mind off the flight.' Lannigan realised she was talking too quickly, almost to the point of stammering. She took a deep breath and put what she hoped was a calm smile on her face. 'Things got a little out of hand,' she said.

'Er, right.' There was a pause, a rustle of uniform as he almost moved away. Then: 'You want I should bring her something, some Buzzaway?'

Lannigan flicked a glance at Rayanne, then back to the steward. 'Are we going to insert soon?'

'In about ten minutes, that's right.'

'Well then, maybe that would be a good idea, sir, thank you.' Lannigan watched him move carefully away, back towards his station at the forward end of the cabin. Tempting as it was to let Rayanne stew in a haze of vodka, the sudden acceleration of orbital thrust could have unpredictable effects on the human system. Microgravity more so. The pills given to each passenger before takeoff would protect even the most vulnerable of them from spacesickness, but Rayanne hadn't been awake enough to swallow hers.

Two minutes later, the steward came back with a tiny squeeze bulb of mint-green fluid for Rayanne. Lannigan unbuckled and headed for a fresher, leaving the unfortunate man to do the job on his own.

She had tired very quickly of Swann's attempts to jog her memory, and, after an hour or so of hearing about this other Lannigan, she had told him to stop doing it.

The process was infuriating. She had learnt a little of the woman she was before the bullet – her fondness for neat tequila, her business plans, her love life – but much of what Swann related was nothing more to her than meaningless detail. A small fraction of what he said gave her a stab of recollection, the same uncomfortable prodding that she had felt in her cabin on the ship, but if anything that was worse. In all, listening to Swann was like hearing about some distant and unloved relative.

Lannigan had decided that, should she ever have cause to encounter this previous incarnation, the two of them would probably not get on.

This, however, was the smallest of her worries. Lannigan at least reminded Swann of his old boss enough for him to recognise her, new face or no, but what Rayanne had told her about Noriko Kobayashi seemed to be at odds with everything she knew. Physically they were talking about the same woman, but this cold, murderous creature with her neglected surroundings and her strange pauses was nothing like the Kobayashi that Lannigan remembered, however fragmented that memory might be.

And now the Pacifican was holed up in a hotel room full of biomedical equipment.

Lannigan believed firmly in coincidence. The world was such a complex and arbitrary place that events were bound to mesh occasionally in such a way as to suggest patterns where there were none.

But not like this. Somehow, she and Kobayashi were connected in a way she was almost afraid to understand.

The whole situation seemed unreal, disconnected, never more so than here in the soft-lit claustrophobia of the spaceplane's fresher. Lannigan stood awkwardly at the sink, gazing at the sharp-featured young woman who looked back at her from the mirror above it, and, not for the first time, came close to questioning her own sanity. Here she was, thirty kilometres above the ground with a drunk teenager and a man who had been chasing her all over East Africa a few days ago, about to go into orbit in search of what to anyone else would be the most tenuous of clues.

All she had to go on was the name that had given her such a spasm of frightened recognition in Byron's rental module and again in the ops chamber of the *Kitsumi Maru*. She had found a number of references to Artemis in the infonet databases she had been able to access. The name referred, for example, to a figure in Greek mythology: a murderous hunter-goddess and twin sister to Apollo. It was also the name of a class of stealth helicopter gunship used in the withdrawal from Ulster and of an electric ground module made exclusively in Yugoslavia. However, Artemis was also the rather romantic designation given to one of a series of quite unremarkable orbital laboratories.

The shock of memory Lannigan had felt on discovering that was what had put her on board *Albireo*.

She dabbed water from her face with a disposable towel. If Swann and Rayanne knew that was all she had, they would never have set foot on the spaceplane. Lannigan had been forced to embellish the truth a little, giving the pair of them the impression that she knew far more about the situation than she actually did. It wasn't too hard. Since awakening she had gained a considerable talent for pulling other people's strings.

The only problem was, she was beginning to feel increasingly uncomfortable about doing it.

She binned the towel and turned to go, extending her cane. As the end of it touched the floor there was a soft chime, and the lights in the fresher faded from soft pink to a cool, airy blue.

'Ladies and gentlemen, we will be going to orbital insertion in two minutes. Please return to your seats.'

Lannigan wondered idly what would happen to any passenger who was still out of her seat when the switch was due. Would the pilot use valuable fuel waiting, or kick in the rockets and let the fool take her own chances?

She opened the fresher door and pulled herself out, twisted into the aisle, moving sideways as a whey-faced man struggled past her. The plane buzzed with voices, and the faint whine of motors as sliding partitions divided the long cabin into comfortingly short rooms. It was less a safety feature than an attempt at psychology, but Lannigan, knowing what was coming next, appreciated it anyway.

When she eased back into her seat, Rayanne opened her eyes and looked at her. 'I'm gonna puke,' she said plaintively.

'No, you're not.' Lannigan began buckling up again, knowing that she would draw some sort of automated wrath if she didn't. 'There's an anti-emetic in Buzzaway, helps you keep it down. You couldn't vomit if you wanted to.'

The word 'vomit' made Rayanne groan and put her head in her hands. Lannigan smiled, itching to needle the girl a little further, pay her back some for all the Spanish cursewords levelled at her in Africa. Then she remembered that Rayanne hadn't taken her spacesickness pill, and decided to save revenge until she was out of range.

'Ladies and gentlemen, one minute.'

'I hate Buzzaway.' Rayanne buckled her harness and sat up a little straighter as the straps tightened automatically. 'Instant freaking hangover, you know?'

'Maybe that'll teach you to go easy on the booze next time,' Swann muttered. Rayanne scowled at the back of his head and flipped him the bird. 'Screw you, asshole.'

'Trailer trash.'

'Dork.'

'Will you two shut the hell up?' Lannigan scraped a hand through her uneven hair. 'My God, aren't we in enough trouble without fighting in the damn sandbox?'

'Whatever,' snorted Swann. Rayanne turned to scowl out of the viewport. There was a long, edged silence. Lannigan was just about to put the headset back on and try the concert when the pilot spoke again.

'Ladies and gentlemen, we are about to engage the reaction drives.'

Faint clicks and whines as all the seat harnesses and infoset holders locked down. Rayanne said, 'Oh shit.'

There was a feeling, just for a fraction of a second, of dropping. Lannigan remembered that from somewhere, that dip as the spaceplane's engines reconfigured from turbojet to liquid-fuelled rocket in midair, and then the cabin was a vertical shaft with a screeching banshee at the bottom and Cassandra Lannigan lying on her back halfway up.

She was doubly glad of the divisions then. With them, the shaft was only a few metres from top to bottom. Being near the front of an undivided cabin would have been utterly terrifying, like hanging on to the inside of an industrial chimney.

Lannigan's fingernails grooved the seat arms. She knew that the spaceplane wasn't actually travelling straight upward – in fact, the vessel was canted at a quite comfortable angle – but the steady one-gee acceleration from the rockets felt like gravity.

The thrust would ease off when *Albireo* reached orbital velocity. Lannigan closed her eyes, concentrating on that tiny, transitional drop, the switchback swoop that told her she had been here before and that she was, after all, heading in the right direction.

Insertion lasted three minutes. After that the rockets cut back, their howl dropping to a distant whine as the spaceplane achieved orbital velocity. *Albireo* was now falling around the Earth fast enough to avoid the ground for ever.

Lannigan kept her eyes closed, willing her heartbeat to slow. The sudden change from one-gee thrust to microgravity had set it hammering. Panic had clawed at her then, just for a second: the unreasoning adrenaline-surge commonly known as Space Adaptation Syndrome. She felt as though a trapdoor had opened without warning beneath her feet.

'Ladies and gentlemen, we are now in microgravity. For your own safety, please remain in your seats. We will be docking in just under forty-five minutes.'

She settled back, becoming more used to the feeling with every second. Again, there was the faintest trace of recollection, a lost edge of memory surfacing, catching the light before being dragged back under. She had done this before.

She didn't remember ever enjoying it.

Beside her, Rayanne was keeping very still, very quiet.

Lannigan threw her a glance and saw that the girl was frozen in her seat, eyes locked straight ahead. She looked catatonic.

The dark eyes flicked right, then back. 'Stop lookin' at me like that, man.'

Lannigan gave a facial shrug. 'I was wondering if you'd had some sort of seizure.'

'No, this is *scared*. You know what *scared* is?' The girl sucked in a long breath, and blinked warily. 'I don't like this, *señora*.'

'Mm.' Lannigan glanced at her chrono. 'Forty minutes or so. Can you survive that long without a cardiac arrest?'

'Maybe.' Rayanne turned her head slightly, wincing. Strands of hair drifted about her face. 'Don't ask me to like it, though.'

'Mr Swann? You doing yokay up there?'

'Yeah, I'm cool.' Swann waved an arm about. 'I could get used to this. Like being in a hot tub.'

Rayanne made a face, but a warning look from Lannigan kept the girl silent.

She couldn't really be that surprised at the enmity between the two. Rayanne had lived in fear of Swann after the kidnapping. If she hadn't been drunk when Lannigan had presented him at the airport she would probably have run screaming. After a life of repeatedly finding out that people she had thought her friends were in fact enemies, it would take Rayanne quite a while before she could accept a situation where the exact reverse was true.

For his part, Swann had every reason to be wary of Rayanne. The girl had broken his balls back in Konza. Apparently, the medical treatment this had required had been both expensive and less than comfortable.

Lannigan had watched Swann very carefully since the *Kitsumi Maru* incident. His distress at losing his home, his job and his best friend was less evident now, but only because he had put his feelings aside. She couldn't ask for more than that. There would be time enough for him to grieve, once all this was over.

And there was another thought that had started to give Lannigan pause, over the past few days. She had known nothing save the chase since leaving hospital: if she ever did finally end all this, what would she have to put in its place?

The music she finally chose was an opus by Locatelli. She was halfway through the *Concerto in D* when Rayanne tapped her on the shoulder.

Lannigan sighed and took off the headset, freezing the music, resolving to track herself down a recording of the piece for enjoyment later. Letting herself be swept along by its glorious precisions was the closest she had been to relaxation in as long a time as she could remember.

'What?' she snapped.

Rayanne pointed out of the viewport. 'There, man. Is that it?'

Lannigan followed the girl's gaze, and had to suppress a gasp.

Albireo had drawn close to its destination while she was being beguiled by the Locatelli. The orbital platform designated Shiva hung beyond the viewport, a frenzy of glittering geometries studded with winking beacons, a great, translucent snowflake drifting in the night.

'Looks like a damn spiderweb,' said Swann.

Now that Lannigan thought about it, perhaps Swann's unromantic assessment of the structure was more accurate than her own. Shiva had six lines of symmetry, like a snowflake, but hunched at its centre was a fat and darkly glistening capsule, sending long legs of pressurised corridor to each point of the platform and the docking cylinders bolted there. Support capsules clung to the gantry between like webbed flies, ready for the sucking.

Watching it, Lannigan felt the hairs on the back of her neck rising.

'Don't be silly,' she said quickly, and only partly to the

others. 'It's just the most cost-effective shape for the structure, that's all.' Even so, as *Albireo* slowed, attitude thrusters nudging it ever closer to that vast expanse of gantry, Lannigan had to suppress an intense desire to unbuckle her seat harness and scramble away from the viewport.

The background chatter in the spaceplane had died to a whisper, church-low and wondering. The full scale of the Shiva platform was becoming apparent: Lannigan saw, just for a moment, the centre capsule side on: a sphere of metal and ceramic a hundred metres across, gleaming black with solarvoltaic paint and dotted with lit windows. It looked utterly malevolent. Then it was gone, hidden by the bulk of the docking cylinder as *Albireo* shed the last of its velocity and mated, airlock to airlock, with the platform.

Clicks and thumps sounded through the spaceplane as the pressures equalised.

The carpets and the interior lighting, blue since orbital insertion, now changed to a gentle green. The harness locks snapped off. Lannigan watched the infonet screen fade to black.

'No more music,' she whispered.

Just darkness.

The orbital transfer platform Shiva was 300 metres across at its widest points, and over eighty per cent of its structure was a web of open gantry. As such, there was no chance of providing it with any form of rotational gravity: the stresses would have been too great. Coupled with normal expansion and contraction due to variations in temperature, spinning Shiva would have been enough to pull it apart.

Besides, rotating the platform would have turned the access tubes leading to the central capsule into six vertical shafts.

And so the platform remained in microgravity. Its makers, however, must have realised only too well the disorientating effects that transition from Earth to orbit can have on the human frame, and had done their best to provide at least an illusion of up and down. As Lannigan followed Swann and Rayanne into the pressure sled she noticed that the floor and ceiling had been delineated with different coloured carpets, and between the windows were small posters and advert boards, all the same way up.

There were twelve seats in the sled, six facing six. Lannigan sat opposite Swann. Rayanne faced a fat man whose nose seemed to be swelling alarmingly in the microgravity.

Discreet harnesses kept them in their seats while the sled accelerated up the tube.

Albireo's passengers had been separated into groups of twelve for transport and processing. Lannigan and her companions were in the third group, which had given her far too much fretting time. Logically, she or the others could never have made it this far if any international law-enforcement agencies wanted to stop them – some software agent or other would have picked up their facial parameters and voiceprints back in Mexico City or before. But there was still orbital customs to get through, and the question of why there was an AI core in the baggage sled pacing them alongside the tube.

No doubt she was just being paranoid. Apart from filling Joey Kotebe with narcotics back in Nairobi – purely a matter of self-defence – she and Rayanne had committed no serious crimes. Swann was involved with the murder, accidental or otherwise, of a policeman in Konza, but the station house in question was probably still trying to unscramble its computers after what he had done to them. With luck, and a degree of calm, they should get into Shiva without incident.

Within a few moments the sled eased to a halt. Doors clamshelled open, letting in light and noise and the smell of plastic and new carpet. The seat harnesses retracted.

There was a short corridor between the sled and the customs area. Lannigan stepped out in her turn, holding on to a handrail and scraping her feet purposefully along the floor in an approximation of walking. Like most of the other passengers, she was unwilling to give up on gravity just yet, but she was already finding it easier to move here than down in the gravity well. With no weight on her weak leg, she was able to keep the cane retracted round her forearm.

She watched passengers toppling, bumping into one another, swaying down the corridor. One man lost his grip entirely and tumbled, howling, towards the ceiling, until his companions pulled him back. She had to suppress a smile. At the same time, she offered a silent thank-you to the makers of the SAS pills. But for them, half these people would be vomiting continuously.

Rayanne, who hadn't taken hers, was looking a little pale, but otherwise standing up to the experience surprisingly well. There was something different about the girl, Lannigan could see that, had even noticed traces of the change while Rayanne was trying to drink herself comatose back in Mexico City airport. Something had happened to her since her encounter with Kobayashi. Lannigan had her theories, but only Rayanne herself could confirm them. She resolved to start digging a little once the time was right.

There were bigger fish to fry before that.

The corridor opened out into a wide archway. Lannigan noticed the glossy poles of broad-spectrum scanners on either side just before she passed through. Well, if there were going to be any problems getting into orbital territory they would start now. Shiva had taken its fill of Cassandra Lannigan when she had walked through the arch – face, heartrate and brainwave map, internal scan, even trace DNA plucked from the air. Tag that to a voiceprint and they had her in a bag.

She took a deep breath and pulled herself into the customs lounge.

Swann and Rayanne were already through, standing uncertainly to one side as other passengers filed past. Beyond them were three desks with barriers and tall hologram hoods: automated customs terminals. 'This gonna be yokay, lady?' asked Rayanne as she drew close.

'If it isn't, we'll know in about two minutes.' Lannigan drifted past them without slowing and steered herself towards the nearest terminal. 'You really want to look suspicious, hang around there.'

As she reached the barrier, another one closed behind her.

The hood flickered and grew a woman, stern-faced, neat, uniformed. A classic AI artefact. 'Ms Cassandra Lannigan?'

Lannigan nodded. 'That's correct.'

'Could you state your business on OTP Shiva, please?'

'I'm hiring data facilities, looking into business opportunities off-planet.' The back of the hood was visible through the artificial woman, but only just.

'You are carrying an AI core.'

'Yes, ma'am, that's correct.' She paused. 'It's a class-three, financial model. Registered with the UNAIB.'

The woman strobed for an instant, then flicked back to full strength. 'That all checks out, Ms Lannigan. One final point – our scanners register several artificial implants in your brainstem and one in your maxillary sinus. Please state their purpose.'

'Ah, medical. Neural prosthesis.'

Something behind Lannigan hummed faintly for a moment, and then fell silent. The hologram woman dipped her head slightly and smiled. 'MRI confirms. Ms Lannigan, Transworld Airlines and the United Nations Space Agency would like to welcome you to OTP Shiva. Please enjoy your stay.'

The front barrier slid away, and Lannigan stepped through.

Rayanne and Swann were waiting for her on the other

side, clutching handrails. 'You were in there for a time, lady.'

'Don't sweat it. If there was a problem I'd be out the airlock by now.' She drew close to Swann and stood next to him. 'Tell me something. Did your Lannigan – Ah, I mean, did *I* ever have a nasal implant?'

'What the hell for?'

'Guess that answers that.' Lannigan shrugged. The implants fixed to her brainstem were common knowledge – they were the only thing keeping her functional from the waist down. But the Nairobi doctors had never mentioned anything about a chip in her nose.

It was probably nothing. A fixing Lippincott had used while he was putting her face back together, or a stray biomonitor. She pushed it to the back of her mind, and made her way to the transfer lounge.

The lounge was a dome-shaped room forty metres across, located at the centre of the capsule and about three levels above its equator. The apex of the dome was a disc of black, peppered with stars; for a moment Lannigan thought she was looking out of a window, then realised that the disc was in fact a network of flatscreens, slaved to an outside view. As she watched, a glittering silver dart slid across her field of view and away. *Albireo* was on its way home.

She found a vacant table and caught hold of it, manoeuvring herself into a chair and clipping on a lapstrap to avoid drifting away while she wasn't concentrating. With greater difficulty, Rayanne did the same. Swann floated away to a vending machine and began pushing coins into it.

Lannigan looked at Rayanne and smiled. 'Don't look so miserable. Lots of people pay good money for this.'

'Yeah, well lots of people are *loco*, yeah? Crazy.' The girl had tied her hair back with a rubber band, but bits of it kept breaking free to bob like stray branches in front of her face. 'You've done this before, so you're all yokay. I'm finding this pretty damn strange.'

Lannigan sniffed. 'Well, if I *have* done this before, I don't entirely remember it. Besides, you didn't even take your SAS pill and here you are acting like you're on a trip to the mall.'

'So?'

'So, it appears you're one of the lucky few who don't get affected by spacesickness. At all.'

Rayanne thought about this for a second, then smiled. 'Yeah, no shit. What do you think, you think I should try for a career up here?'

'Try going to the bathroom first, then decide.' Lannigan leant back. 'Rayanne, I wanted to ask you something . . .'

The girl's smile vanished. 'Like what?'

'Don't get paranoid. I just wanted to clear things up about Miami.'

'Miami?' Rayanne looked uncomfortable. 'What about it?'

And in Lannigan's head was a plan, a formula, a set of instructions that, once followed, would get any information she wanted out of the Latina. That cold page in her brain was filling up again: what to do, what to say, how to hold her head. When to massage the girl's ego and when to ridicule her. Which buttons to press. It rose up in her as certain as computer code.

She swallowed, abruptly nauseous. It was just like when Byron had died. And before, with N'Tele and the others she had manipulated over the weeks. Except it was more obvious now. It was as though some separate, loathsome part of her had switched on and was trying to tell the rest of her what to do.

Rayanne said, 'Are you yokay?'

She nodded. 'Yeah, I'm fine. Look, Rayanne, I just noticed that you seem a little different from when we last met. I wondered if there was any reason at all.'

The page screamed at her, and faded. Rayanne's

eyebrows were somewhere close to her hairline. 'What, you're just asking me?'

'Oh for God's sake, you don't have to tell me if you don't want to.' Lannigan could feel her face reddening. She folded her arms and looked away. Honesty hadn't worked.

But somehow, she felt better for trying.

Swann turned up with three squeeze bulbs held in a plastic clip. 'Coffee,' he said. 'Outta my own pocket. Don't thank me. Holy shit.'

'What?'

'Your cane.'

Lannigan followed his gaze, and saw that the cane was changing shape again.

The upper part, the part that was still hugging her right forearm, was the same, although perhaps the wings were a little smaller. But the barrel was shorter and more compact, and the splayed end was extruding what looked like a small hook. It was changing as she watched, as slow and as unobtrusive as the movement of hands on a clock.

'Clever little bastard,' said Swann. 'Must be reacting to zero-gee. How much?'

'A lot.'

The man nodded. 'Thought so. The Artemis fee was half a mil. Now we've got loose change.'

'Just over two hundred,' said Lannigan. She noticed Rayanne staring at her. 'What?'

'Half a *million*? What, ICUs?'

'Most of it must have gone on that equipment they found in my hotel room. The rest is in here.' She tapped the side of her head. 'Doesn't come cheap.'

'So how much you got in there?'

'Don't get any funny ideas, Rayanne. You can't sell it back.' She placed the coffee bulb in the air next to her, undid the lap strap and stood up, catching the drink again without looking. 'Mr Swann, I think we'd better get to a downlink.'

* * *

There was a feed café adjacent to the main lounge, a dimly lit place with private booths along one wall and public-access screens set into tables and contour chairs. Swann took himself off to a booth while Rayanne found a table near the far wall. Lannigan was pleased to notice that the girl had chosen a spot with a good view of the door. She was learning.

Lannigan sat down and fed one of her remaining notes into the table slot. A moment later a section of the marble surface slid away to reveal a screen, voice headset and a micro keyboard. The headset went on over her hair, more to keep it out of the way than for any specific use, and the screen flipped up on automatic. She called down an options menu.

'What are you doing?' asked Rayanne, leaning over. Lannigan scowled at her.

'Get out of my light. I'm just getting hold of a bulletin board, putting out a request for a data-retrieval facility. If Swann does his job, we should have enough to rent something that can crack Kitsumi. Which reminds me.' She looked up. 'You'd better go get our luggage.'

'Screw you, man. Why don't you go get the damn bags?'

'I'm busy.'

Rayanne folded her arms defiantly. 'So am I.'

'No, you're not. Unless you're doing something vital I can't quite see.' Lannigan stopped typing. 'Look, the sooner we can get to that Artemis file the sooner we can sort this out and go home. Wherever that might be.' She glanced at the screen and saw it busily translating her words: '–ever that might be'. 'Oh, for God's sake! Rayanne, I'm sorry if I'm being a little short with you here, but please, before I go insane and smash this thing, will you just go and get the fragging bags?'

Rayanne sat and glared venomously at her for a good five seconds, then pushed away from the table and drifted off. Lannigan let out a long breath and started deleting the erroneous text she had created by talking with the headset activated.

The Artemis file was her foremost priority now. Locked into Kitsumi's quiescent core were the details of that final, fatal operation, the last job she had taken as MD of Living Glass. Sometime after that task her entire pattern of behaviour appeared to have changed, and the machinery of all her woes had been set in motion. If her suspicions were correct, Cassandra Lannigan had died as a direct result of what had happened on the Artemis job.

Without access to the correct support equipment, the core was just a box with a handle. And if that wasn't bad enough, Swann had identified the device that Kotebe's people had plugged into the AI as a system killer.

If he was right, a lethal computer virus had been injected into Kitsumi's brain. Disconnected from all but the most meagre sources of internal power, both the computer and the virus would have been lying dormant since Mexico. But Lannigan would have to destroy the virus before she could get to the file.

The old Lannigan, the one that Swann had worked for, could have done the job with ease. But Lannigan right now was having enough difficulty using the simplest of bulletin boards. By the time she had posted her request, Rayanne was back with the luggage.

Lannigan switched the screen off, then turned to look at the girl. Rayanne looked angry, frightened, and miserable, surrounded by a few pathetic-looking bags they had bought at Mexico City and with the computer core stuffed under one arm. Most of her hair had escaped the rubber band again and was floating around her head in matted clumps. There was a reddish patch at her right temple that looked as though it was flowering into a bruise.

'Banged my head,' she mumbled.

Lannigan opened her mouth to speak, but then shut it again. Now was not the time for a lecture on the difference between mass and weight. Instead she began to help Rayanne stuff the bags under the table, where they wouldn't float away.

When they were done she reached into a pocket and pulled out a crumpled twenty. 'Here. This should get you some line time. Call up a game, or something.'

Rayanne blinked at her a couple of times, then reached out and took the note. She seemed to realise that it was as close to a thank-you as she was going to get.

Lannigan was just settling down in front of her own screen when Swann arrived, pushing himself off from a nearby handrail and having to grab the table edge in order to slow himself down. 'Woah!'

'Careful, Mr Swann. We've already had one injury today.'

'Yeah yeah.' He pulled himself into a seat. 'Well, I got in, finally. It was rough going without Kitsumi to send the codes, but I managed to get into the Living Glass account just before my hundred ran out. It's being transferred up right now.'

'Don't expect a thank-you,' muttered Rayanne, her eyes fixed on the screen. 'She might give you some money, though.'

Lannigan ignored her studiously. 'How much did you pull?'

'Just under eleven thousand ICUs. No more Living Glass. We're cleaned out.'

'Hmm.' Lannigan pondered this. The amount wasn't as much as she had hoped, but it should be enough for what she needed to do. After that, they could always try to get jobs . . . 'Fine. I'll follow up on my bulletin request in a few minutes, see if anyone bites. Then we'll have to look plaintive and bargain.'

'Rayanne can do that.' Swann leant over and put a hand on her shoulder. 'What you watching, kid?'

'Don't call me kid.' Rayanne shrugged away from him, and he backed off. 'Just checking a newsfeed.'

Lannigan knew what the girl would be looking for. 'What's the word?'

'Not good.' Rayanne leant back and rubbed absently at her bruise. 'More cases in Miami and Poza Rica. It ain't spreading fast, but it's spreading.'

'Let me see.' Lannigan unstrapped and pulled herself round behind Rayanne's chair. The newsfeed was a riot of windows and text scrolls, hotlinks and infobuttons, and for a few moments she couldn't even see which part of the screen she was supposed to be looking at. 'Can't you tidy this up a little?'

'Sure. I guess old people can't access so fast.' Rayanne tapped the screen a few times, shunting away the assassination of an opera star in South Korea, a spokeswoman from Fushigina Systems explaining a loss of telemetry on one of their cargo spacers as purely temporary, adverts for beer and neural stimulators. A report on the encephalitis outbreaks expanded to fill most of the display. 'Big enough for you?'

'Stow it.' The text windows were still moving too fast. Lannigan raised the audio and listened to updates on the Mexico and Miami death toll. Forty in Florida, stretching south as far as the Keys. Almost as many in Poza Rica. Rumours of bioweapon attacks were igniting sporadic violence along the Gulf Coast as fast as the UN could suppress it.

Of those who had lived through the disease, almost all had been reduced to automata. Only a handful had survived with their minds intact. 'My God. What a mess.'

'You know,' said Rayanne thoughtfully, 'I'd really like to know who that Kobayashi chick is working for.'

Swann had moved in next to Lannigan. 'The one that jumped you? Why?'

''Cause somebody's sure kicking Fushigina's ass. Look at this.' She called up a different window, a complex chart rife with tumbling lines and markers. 'Stock's going down faster than an Anglo whore.'

Lannigan felt the barb, but chose to ignore it. 'They've been blamed for this bug from the beginning.'

'Intercorporate shit?' Swann straightened. 'Brew up a bug, pin it on a competitor, then launch a takeover bid when the stock crashes. Makes a lot of sense.'

'That would explain why the encephalitis is moving so slowly. It's not moving from person to person, but only from the vector to whoever she kisses. They wouldn't want to risk a pandemic.' Lannigan slid back into her own seat. 'Whatever. We'll know more once we can get into Kitsumi.'

Rayanne closed her screen down. 'I was done anyway. You gonna see if anyone called?'

'That's right.' Lannigan had dangled her hooks for long enough. Time to log back into the bulletin board and see if anyone had taken the bait.

There were three bites.

The first was from a woman with a French accent and a portable coreframe that could handle a class-three AI. Her price, however, was high, so Lannigan checked the other two icons. In the second was a video blip from the owner of a plex-owned salvage spacecraft within two hours of Shiva, and the third was text only, ostensibly from a Pacifican corporate research team who had been authorised to expand their finances by taking on freelance data work. Lannigan didn't like the look of the corporate team, so she accessed the second blip.

The screen logged on to comms. The charge counter in the corner began to count down fast, eating the ICUs as Shiva's infonet reached out by radio link to the approaching spacecraft. Lannigan estimated she would have no more than three minutes before the money ran out and she would have to send Swann down to the Bureau de Change. 'Mr Kindersley?'

'Yo. You're Cassandra Lannigan?' The face that appeared on the screen was hardly Lannigan's idea of an archetypal spacer. It was rather round, with no more than a fringe of hair surrounding a dome of shiny scalp, and punctuated with a faintly ridiculous moustache.

The man looked and sounded more like a New York cab driver than the operator of a registered space vessel.

'That's me, sir. I believe you might be able to help me out with a little information handling.'

'Yeah, I reckon that's a possibility. I've got a quad-parallel coreframe here, fully powered. Should be all you need.'

'That's pretty impressive, sir. Will you be staying at Shiva long?'

The man shook his head. 'Just long enough to refuel, then I'm heading for Zholtyi Dom. But, if you don't mind a trip, I can accommodate you for that time. Can you work on the move?'

Lannigan looked up at Swann and Rayanne, who both nodded. 'As long as there's room for the three of us, sir, I think we have a deal.'

The salvage vessel *Earhart's Dream* arrived at Shiva just under two hours later. Lannigan, having registered her transferral with the platform's authorities, was waiting with Swann and Rayanne in docking facility four when it came in.

An external-view flatscreen had shown the spacer on approach as it nudged close to the cylinder with spurts of glittering vapour from its manoeuvring thrusters. The big reaction drives at the stern were quiescent: they would be activated only once the ship was refuelled and on its way to the cluster of habitats known as Zholtyi Dom.

Earhart's Dream was not a pretty ship.

Lannigan could appreciate the lines of a vessel like *Albireo*, but the salver didn't appear to have any lines. It looked nothing more than a collection of random shapes bolted round a fat, battered cylinder, rife with gantry and tubing and parabolic sensor dishes. Clusters of manipulators folded untidily against the hull like the corpses of vast spiders, and the whole thing was sprayed a rusty brown, save a few suspicious patches of bare metal.

Rayanne and Swann weren't saying anything, but she could feel the weight of their gaze on her. 'Don't,' she warned.

'What a piece of shit.'

Lannigan rounded on Rayanne. 'I said *don't*, yokay? Anyway, it's probably fine inside. It's just a little . . . used.'

'Yeah,' said Swann. 'But what as?'

Heavy sounds began to issue from beyond the cylinder wall as the salver locked itself to Shiva. Lannigan found herself gripping her carryall tighter.

Along with a few clothes and the money Swann had extracted from the Living Glass account, the AI core was in there.

The hatchway twisted a quarter-turn, then slid inward and aside. Lannigan turned her head aside as a warm and rather ill-smelling breeze fluttered her hair, a burst of pressure as the environment within the ship equalised with that in the cylinder.

Beyond the hatch was another cylindrical space, but smaller and showing none of Shiva's commercial antiseptic tidiness. The walls of the chamber were a mass of ducting and cables, covered in tethered sheets of nylon netting. A few items – a first-aid box, a couple of air cylinders, some tools – had been wedged into the netting, and clinging upside-down above Lannigan's head was a tall, slim young woman in grey coveralls and a big, pocket-studded plastic vest.

'Oops,' the woman said. 'Sorry.' She pushed away from the netting and executed a fluid, complicated turn in the air that finished with her standing in front of Lannigan, roughly the right way up. 'Forget which way's which in here.'

Her accent was strange: British, but nothing like Doogie Baxter's flat London tones. She smiled and grabbed Lannigan's hand, shaking it enthusiastically. 'I'm Newnes, Alicia Newnes. Pilot. You're Lannigan and Co, I take it.'

The handshake bobbed Lannigan off her feet, and she had to grab at the hatchway to steady herself. 'That's right. This is Rayanne Hernandez, Eddie Swann.'

'Charmed, I'm sure. Well, come on in.' Newnes spun over in the air again and snagged some netting with her foot. She wore no shoes, which was probably quite sensible in an environment where floors were irrelevant. She helped Lannigan across the threshold, then Swann, and finally Rayanne, who was looking a little bemused.

'Don't worry about the smell. We'll be flushing the atmosphere while we refuel, give the scrubbers a bit of a holiday. All in?' She keyed the hatch closed. 'We'll have to do something about those clothes, I'm afraid.'

Lannigan glanced down at herself reflexively, then over at Swann and Rayanne. 'What do you mean?'

'Well, you're hardly dressed for it, are you?' She nodded at Lannigan's high-collared blouse and suit trousers. 'You might have to get into an E-suit in a hurry. I'll get you some coveralls. Don't worry, we've got plenty of spares.'

Behind her, *Dream*'s inner hatch opened on to a small, boxy room: more netting, hatches of varying sizes, a row of cubical lockers on the far wall. 'Go through that hatch there, all right?' chirped Newnes. 'Into C and C. I'm off to engineering, but Bob'll be in there.' And with that she was off, through one of the rear hatches and away before Lannigan could speak.

The docking hatch whined closed, and locked itself with a solid, final noise.

Lannigan extended the cane, which whickered out to full extension and snagged a piece of netting with its new hook. 'I guess that's that.'

Swann appeared next to her, holding tightly on to the net and keeping resolutely the 'right' way up. 'So what now?'

'Now, we go and talk to Mr Kindersley, and then I'll get started on Kitsumi.' She leant closer to him, and dropped her voice. 'But be careful.'

'Of what?'

'Of everything, but especially that Newnes. I don't trust anyone that smiles all the time.'

By that token, the managing director of Orbital Serendipity MLC and captain of *Earhart's Dream* might have been one of the most trustworthy men Lannigan had ever met. Robert Kindersley was a small, rotund man, made even rounder by long-term exposure to microgravity, whose face seemed set into a perpetual scowl. When Lannigan keyed open the hatch that led to the Command and Control deck she found him strapped into a contour seat and arguing floridly with a Shiva official over the comm. He swivelled, ordered her off his bridge, and yelled at her to put on some suitable clothes.

There were two other members of Orbital Serendipity: a long-haired, sharp-faced Pacifican called Watanabe; and a French girl who gave the three of them the most cursory of glances before disappearing down an access hatch. Watanabe led them back along the length of the ship and into the accommodation capsule, where he hunted through a locker until he found three spare coveralls of about the right size. 'Use the velcro straps to adjust them, if they're a bit big.'

After he had gone back to C and C there followed a flurry of awkward, embarrassed changing, each of the three moving as far away from the others as possible in the cramped confines of the capsule accessway. The coveralls were stiff and itchy, and smelt rather stale: Lannigan wondered whether Watanabe had raided the laundry basket in order to find enough spares.

Swann and Rayanne left their footwear in the locker, following Newnes' example. Lannigan couldn't bring herself to go that far, and hooked her coverall's ankle straps under her shoes to keep them on.

Besides, she was becoming surprisingly adept at using the modified cane to snag *Dream*'s internal netting and manoeuvre herself that way. Once again, the clever little device had anticipated her needs and altered itself accordingly; she wasn't sure how it worked, how many of its changes were due to environment or programming or even sampling of her DNA, but she was beginning to look upon it as the one thing in her universe that she could trust implicitly.

She took the money and the AI core from her bag before she stashed it away in the locker. The money went into one of the coverall's many pockets. Kindersley probably wouldn't dump her out of the nearest airlock as soon as he had his hands on it. But, in these troubled times, 'probably' just wasn't good enough.

An hour later, *Earhart's Dream* left its docking facility and began the journey to Zholtyi Dom.

Once the ship was on its way, Kindersley left the business of burn times and orbital vectors to Newnes, and took Lannigan to the middle of three aft-facing hatchways in the transfer capsule. A keypress opened it to reveal a long, dimly lit corridor barely a metre wide, but stretching almost the full length of the ship.

She let him go in first, then pulled herself along after him, using her hands rather than the cane: the netting was so close on either side, and the mass of the AI core so awkward, she simply would have gotten herself tangled completely.

'Sorry if I was a little brusque with you concerning your clothing,' said Kindersley, halfway down. 'It's an insurance thing. Anyone on board has to be capable of getting into an E-suit damn fast, or my registration goes down the tubes. If that guy on the comm had seen you . . .'

'I understand, sir.' She shivered, feeling exposed and claustrophobic at the same time. A few centimetres away, past a laughably thin shell of metal and plastic and rust-coloured paint, was open space. A micrometeoroid puncture here and they would both die, horribly, coveralls or no. 'Is this where you keep your coreframe?'

'It ain't *my* coreframe, exactly.' He stopped at a hatch set into the floor, if that term still held any meaning, and keyed it open. 'Down here.'

Inside was darkness, until he snapped a switch down and filled the chamber with dull blue light. Lannigan poked her head through the hatch, and gasped.

Kindersley floated inside the biggest open area Lannigan had seen inside *Earhart's Dream*, a cylindrical space twenty metres long or more, and at least eight metres across. The walls were smooth metal, devoid of netting. Filling most of the space, and tethered to the walls with heavy ceramic cable, was a tangle of gantry and bulbous capsules the size of a groundbus.

Kindersley reached up to help Lannigan through the hatch. 'We call this the tank. Used to be a fuel tank, external propellant module on one of the old NASA space shuttles.'

Lannigan's eyebrows went up. She had heard of NASA, but only in the historical sense. 'My God. How old is this?'

'Must be getting on for fifty years. They used to fill this part with liquid hydrogen, and up front was oxygen, but we use that as a storm shelter now. We cut in a set of doors, other side of that mess, sealed the thing for pressure and drive linkages.' He rapped the wall with his knuckles until it rang like a gong. 'Solid enough. Don't worry about working down here.'

'Let me guess.' Lannigan pointed to the tethered mass. 'That's the coreframe.'

'We think it's a datahaus, an orbital information stash. For storing hot code until it's safe to sell, yeah?' He pushed off, grabbing a cable and hauling himself down to the thing's surface. 'It must have bumped a pebble, got knocked out of geostationary and into a decaying orbit. Hazard to shipping, so we picked up a bonus for removing it in addition to resale value.'

Lannigan drifted down to join him, studying the satellite's surface. There were no logos on it, no serial numbers: nothing to denote what it was or who had owned it. By 'hot code', she decided, Kindersley probably meant stolen information. 'And you're sure it will handle my AI?'

'Sherryl wired it up to see what was working. It's ten per cent computer and ninety per cent encryption, but your little AI should fit in there real neat. So, ah . . .' He rubbed the top of his head nervously, fingers tracing the paths of long-lost hair. 'Are we in business here?'

Lannigan put on her best smile for him. 'Yes, Mr Kindersley, I believe we are.'

14
Madhouse

The journey from Shiva to the Zholtyi Dom multiplex would take eight hours. Four people was a fairly small crew for a vessel like *Earhart's Dream*, which meant that they were all pretty much occupied during the trip. Leaving Rayanne with a limited choice of people to talk to, especially since Lannigan was down in the tank, trying to cure her diseased AI. Rayanne would have spent some time with Swann, if it weren't for the fact that she didn't actually like him, so instead she found a quiet place down in one of the *Dream*'s storage modules, and curled up among the webbing and the crates and the warm, pervasive humming of the aircon system.

The best way to relax in zero-gee, she had found, was to lash herself to an area of netting with a couple of the coverall's straps, and curl up into a ball. That way, she wasn't restricted enough to feel claustrophobic, but the aircon couldn't blow her around the room, either.

To be quite honest, she wasn't too displeased about being alone right now. For the first time in as long as she could remember she had things on her mind, things that required sitting down and thinking about, not running away from or hammering flat with chem. Quiet cogitation had never really been Rayanne's strong suit, she would be the first to admit that. But perhaps it was time to start.

So she hung where she was, sometimes thinking, sometimes remembering, and most of the time sleeping. A few hours passed, and then she realised that she still hadn't told Lannigan about her memory coming back.

She hadn't really thought about it all that much. It was a crazy thing to have happened, a bizarre and impossible thing. Rayanne knew something about the drugs she had been taking, mainly from the lectures she had been given in various homes and correctional centres. Every time she blanked, they had told her, she was rewriting her own brain.

Memories were made up of connections inside her head, little bundles that looked, on the CGI demonstrations they had made her watch, like frayed string or long, ragged tree roots. Crushers worked on those bundles, unsewing some and knitting up others, snipping the links that held them all together until this memory or that was hidden behind a blur of chemical amnesia. Somebody had originally made crushers for people with a really bad memory that was screwing them up inside, like being in a module wreck: they would be encouraged to think hard about that wreck, or hypnotised to focus on it, and then the crushers would know where to go.

But Rayanne couldn't hypnotise herself, and when the crushers had been beavering away between her ears for a while she would start forgetting what it was she was supposed to remember, so the drugs began killing other memories too. Gradually, over the years, the amnesia had bled over so much that Rayanne had lost three-quarters of her past, and scrambled the rest so badly that it came through only in dreams, or if something reminded her very strongly.

Not any more. After the fever, she had woken up with a memory that was, if not perfect, certainly better than that of most people she knew.

And that was just stupid. To bring her memory back

the disease would have had to go right into her brain and rebuild all those connections while she was unconscious. And besides, most people who got it died, or ended up as basket cases. Only a couple had recovered.

Rayanne wondered if they had been blankers, too.

She opened her eyes and pulled herself free of the netting, the velcro straps making loud ripping noises as they came away. Lannigan wouldn't appreciate her arriving in the tank without warning, but there was a comm set in the docking cylinder that she could use to call the Anglo's wrist chrono.

Rayanne made her way from the storage module to the docking facility largely by crawling sideways along the webbing. Zero-gee didn't bother her at all now that she was used to it, unlike Swann and Lannigan, who had been taking SAS pills since they came up from Earth. But she was still unskilled at diving through the air like *Dream*'s crew, and had the bruises to prove it.

The comm in the docking cylinder was mainly used to talk to the other side of the airlock, but Rayanne bypassed that menu easily and punched in Lannigan's account code from memory. There was a pause – the service provider double-checking that the account really was being used to contact someone only a few metres distant – and then Lannigan's face appeared on the screen, surrounded by little plugs and cables and drifting instruction manuals. 'What?' she screeched.

'Ah, how you doing?'

'Rayanne, I'm too busy to engage in casual banter right now. Was there something vital you wanted, or are you just trying to make my life more difficult?'

'Yokay, screw it,' spat Rayanne. 'Dumb idea trying to talk to you anyway.' Her fingers found the disconnect key, but then she paused. 'Why don't you get Swann to help you out?'

'Because, the more spread out we are, the less likely Kindersley is to open the tank doors and keep the money.'

Rayanne put a hand over her eyes. 'Lady, he's *got* the money. You've paid him already. Plus we registered our journey, so why the hell would he wanna flush you out?'

'Let's just say you can't be too careful, hm?'

'*Madre de Dios*! You are, like, *the* most paranoid asshole I have ever met, lady! I hope he does open the damn doors on you!' She snapped the disconnect down, consigning Lannigan's answer to oblivion.

The screen blanked. Rayanne stayed where she was for about five seconds, and then the fear and the frustration and the claustrophobia all surged up inside her at once, knotting her stomach like a bad dose of chem.

Time was when that kind of emotional hailstorm would have had Rayanne running for the medicine cabinet. Now she just put all the feelings into her right fist and punched the wall, very hard indeed.

She found Swann in the accommodation capsule, idly flipping through channels on a small infonet screen. He looked up as she came clambering through the hatchway. 'What happened to your hand?'

'Nothing, man. It's fine.'

'Got you punching the walls, huh?'

'Who, the wicked witch of the Midwest? Her and the rest of this setup.' She rubbed the bruised knuckles thoughtfully. 'What you watching?'

Swann sniffed. 'Five hundred channels of shit.' He flipped the screen off and grabbed a piece of netting, pulling himself back into it and wrapping his arms through the nylon. 'She must have got you pretty riled to come looking for me.'

There was a long silence. Rayanne looked at the floor, kicking her bare feet restlessly. Then she said, 'Why did you come after me?'

'Huh?'

'In Konza. I never saw you before, man, or that other guy. But you busted right into a police station to get me.'

'Seemed like a good idea at the time.' He chuckled, but then must have seen the expression on Rayanne's face, because the chuckle died in the air, and suddenly he looked uncomfortable and more than a little sad. 'Lannigan, she was supposed to come back to Mexico after this Artemis job, right? Three months ago, she was supposed to come back with the money. But she ran off to Nairobi instead. So me and Byron get there from Afghanistan, meet Angel in the lobby and then bang.' He mimed an explosion with one hand. 'All gone, bye-bye. Three months we spent trying to find out what was happening, why she'd double-crossed us, where the money had gone. Three *fragging* months!' He twisted violently in the netting. For a second he was too enraged to speak, but as Rayanne started backing away he got a grip and looked up at her from under the hair that had flopped over his forehead.

'And nothing. Then, next time we see her, she's running around with you.' He shrugged half-heartedly. 'Just by looking at her you could see she couldn't remember. You were our only lead.'

'So that's it? You saw me and her together, and figured I knew where the dough was? Oh man.'

'What, she tell you something else?' Swann grinned. 'Oh yeah. Ever since she came outta hospital, that's been her all over.'

'Figures,' muttered Rayanne to herself. 'Didn't want me to run out on her.' Then she remembered something else, the blank expression on Motai's face when he had fallen in front of her, his skull opened up on one side. 'But that cop, man. He hadn't done nothing.'

Swann nodded. 'I know, kid. Look, you ever get real angry, like you want to just whack somebody out? Yeah?'

'Sometimes, I guess.'

'But you don't, do you? You stop. Well, Byron . . . He didn't stop. He was in the army, see? When they modified him, that was one of the things they took out.

The bit that makes you stop.'

Next to his head, the screen fluttered back on.

Rayanne jumped a little, then saw Lannigan staring out at her. 'Hey, *señora*, you got something vital now? Or you just trying to make *my* life difficult?'

'Rayanne . . .' Lannigan swallowed, running a hand back through her asymmetrical hair. She didn't look good at all. 'You'd better get down here. Both of you.'

'What, you ain't worried Kindersley's gonna space us all in one go?'

'Maybe he will. But somehow I think Mr Kindersley is the least of our worries right now.'

A computer simulation, beautifully modelled: a bone-white mushroom of faceted metal, drifting silently above the turning Earth and stretching solarvoltaic petals towards the sun. The software's viewpoint moved constantly around the structure, spinning bright flares from nonexistent lenses, perfect down to the hazy discs of rectenna fields on the planet below, the infinity of stars beyond. It was crisp and expensive and blade-sharp: a window to a new reality.

Rayanne was unimpressed. She had seen better on Saturday-morning cartoons. 'That's it? That's Artemis?'

Lannigan nodded. 'Not much to look at, is it?' She tapped a key, and the image vanished, replaced by a meaningless page of digits. 'That was part of an advertising presentation. Noriko Kobayashi gave it to me with the rest of the mission parameters, so I'd know what to look for.'

When Lannigan had called Swann a few minutes earlier the screen's software had done its best to compensate for the tank's odd internal lighting. Even so, the Anglo had looked bad; close up, it was obvious to Rayanne that the woman had suffered a serious shock. Her skin was pale, beaded with sweat that glued her hair into untidy clumps and occasionally bounced away in tiny airborne globules, and her eyes were red and puffy.

If Rayanne hadn't known better, she would have sworn that Lannigan had been crying.

The three of them were clustered around the ruined datahaus, near the rent-open side. The AI core was lashed to the satellite with silver tape, sprouting a rootlike mass of optical cables from every face. Most of the cables went somewhere: the woman admitted that she had been unable to do anything with the AI other than connect its most basic functions. There was no audio, for example, and they still had to communicate with the machine via the keyboard. But five hours surrounded by *Dream*'s entire stock of computer instruction manuals had seen impressive results nonetheless. Kotebe's virus had been shunted away to a memory location where it could do no damage, and the Artemis file had been accessed.

'So it *was* Kobayashi,' said Swann quietly. Lannigan nodded.

'I thought it had to be. She was one of the only things I could remember, that and the word "Artemis". Doesn't take a nanotechnician to put the two together.'

Rayanne snorted. 'So what does that make me, the stupid one? This doesn't explain shit.'

'It was a sentience test.' Swann wasn't looking at her: his gaze was fixed absently on the screen, the page of digits. Even his voice seemed far away. 'The AI in Artemis, what did they call it?'

'Mnemosyne,' said Lannigan. 'The ancient-Greek goddess of memory. I checked.'

'Mm. That was, what, a grade eight? Kitsumi's a grade three, and the scale's exponential. Wouldn't be too hard for Mnemosyne to grow a brain.'

Rayanne blinked. 'What, you mean it started thinking?'

'Make a computer smart enough, and that's always a danger. That's what the AI board do for a living, mainly. Come down hard on anybody with a smart AI.'

'I still don't –' Rayanne dodged suddenly, ducking to one side to avoid the cane. Lannigan had thrown it at her with all the force she could muster.

'Übergen Aktien-Gesellschaft,' the woman snarled. 'Meditech corporation with two hundred shares in the human genome and fourteen basic patents in surgical nanotechnology. Brand leaders in psychoactive amnesia chem. A vicious little *bastard* company who suddenly found they had a smart AI on their hands, and decided to wipe out anyone who might get them into trouble with the board! All right? You understand now, Rayanne?'

Rayanne stared at her, horrified. The woman was white faced, trembling. She looked crazy and furious and utterly, utterly terrified. 'Oh Christ.'

'Kobayashi must have wanted the evidence. Übergen had already abandoned Artemis, probably killed Mnemosyne as soon as they found out it was thinking, but no, that wasn't good enough for bloody Kobayashi, was it? She wanted some dupe to go up and get proof, somebody she couldn't be connected with if things went wrong, somebody independent. A plexer.' She was getting herself under control now. Rayanne could see that ice coming back, that horrible steel in the eyes, and she was glad. She never wanted to see Lannigan angry again, not like that.

Swann said, 'Kotebe. He was working for Übergen.'

'Kitsumi identified the system killer as a Übergen variant.' Lannigan's voice was right back where it had been, with the tone that sounded like Swann should have known this all along, that she was pointing out the obvious to him because he wasn't very bright. 'Just cleaning up the loose ends.'

Something moved to Rayanne's left. She turned, and caught it: the cane, having bounced off the far end of the tank, was tumbling back.

She clutched it tightly, feeling its warmth, the smooth surface of it, the Übergen logo in bright ice blue down the barrel. 'They'll know we're not dead, won't they,' she said dully. 'They'll know we're not dead, and they'll send somebody else. And they'll keep sending people, worse and worse people, until they catch up with us and kill us.'

'Maybe,' said Lannigan. 'Maybe not.'

Swann was shaking his head. 'Face it, doc, the kid's right. Übergen are pretty tough customers, and Kotebe was second rate at best. Next time they'll hire someone better. It doesn't take too much to delete three assholes in a tin can.'

'Three assholes who know a couple of things Übergen don't,' said Lannigan. 'And, if we're careful, that might just give us another shot.'

Lannigan wouldn't be drawn any further than that, and soon afterward Rayanne and Swann left her and Kitsumi to their machinations.

They had already agreed not to inform Kindersley or his people of what they had found. Letting the guy know that his three passengers were marked for dead by one of the most cutting-edge corporations around would be a quick way of losing a ride. No, better to play Lannigan's game on this one, and give Orbital Serendipity only the information that they needed.

Rayanne wondered if the Anglo's sneaky way of doing things was beginning to rub off on her. She hoped not.

She went back to her place in the storage module and tried to doze, but images of Byron and Joey Kotebe and Motai's open skull kept darting at her from the shadows. Lannigan had told her that Kotebe was dead, fried and blasted to atoms with the *Kitsumi Maru*, but what if she had made a mistake? Maybe the assassin was still out there somewhere, chasing after her through the night, scarred and full of rage.

Rayanne scared herself, thinking about that, so she climbed back through the ship until she found the engineering section with its bright lights and grumbling airscrubbers. She stayed there for the rest of the journey, watching the French engineer, Sherryl, tending the reaction drives through the final approach to Zholtyi Dom.

Neither girl spoke. Sherryl was busy, and Rayanne didn't have anything to say.

According to Kindersley, Zholtyi Dom was Russian slang for a madhouse. Looking at the multiplex through the transfer capsule's monitors, Rayanne could see where the name might have come from. But she could think of better ones.

The whole system covered an area roughly the size of Shiva, maybe a little larger. But, where the platform had been webbed together by great expanses of gantry, Zholtyi Dom was a loose and barely connected series of structures. Some were held roughly in place by thread-like ceramic cables, some by pressurised accessways. Most, however, just stayed where they were for the simple reason that there was nothing to make them do otherwise.

There seemed to be every kind of orbital construction making up the multiplex. A few were obviously space-ships: orbital tugs and transfer vehicles, either docked or permanently tethered with their reaction drives decommissioned. There were lab modules like Artemis, workhabs, clusters of shuttle fuel tanks, even – to Rayanne's amazement – an aluminium trailer home, caulked around the windows and epoxied to an industrial airlock.

The multiplex hung like a handful of machine parts, thrown into the air and photographed in mid-tumble.

At the centre of the cluster was the heart of the multiplex, the reason that Zholtyi Dom existed: a waste-reclamation facility, at least as big as Shiva's core capsule. But, instead of Shiva's dark and glossy sphere, this was a tumorous riot of ducts and capsules, toroids and cylinders, tangled gantry and coiled cables. Rayanne looked at it for a long time and totally failed to discern any actual shape to it at all.

'There's a furnace in there for the scrap,' Kindersley was telling Lannigan. 'Nanotech tanks for breaking down the more complex stuff. Even plain old garbage gets compacted and used as shielding materials for the lunar habitats.'

'And they actually make a profit from that?' Lannigan, holding on to the netting by her fingertips as *Earhart's Dream* shuddered and jolted its way towards final docking, seemed as amazed by Zholtyi Dom as Rayanne was. 'Even without extras?'

The salver nodded. 'Lot of space junk out there, more every year. ZD keeps itself running quite nicely on just the shit, but it's gravy when something like what we've got comes along.'

Rayanne shook her head in amazement. Fourteen plexes at last count, all bundled together with their own little government, a school and a crèche and an infonet station, crunching up other people's garbage and selling it on. 'Man, just when you think you've seen it all . . .'

Earhart's Dream was nudging close to one of the larger habs, now: an unlovely fusion of a commercial workstation and an orbital fuelling drone with the drives ripped off. Kindersley moved closer to the screen and flipped it on to comms. 'Zholtyi Dom, this is registered salver *Earhart's Dream* requesting permission to dock at hab eighteen. Alexi, you there? Got something you're gonna love down in the tank here.'

There was a pause, and then a woman's face appeared on the screen, rather angular, with a tight mop of mouse-brown curls. She was looking intently at something below the level of the screen pickup. She wasn't happy. '*Earhart's Dream*, please stand off.'

Kindersley scowled. 'You wanna run that by me again?'

'My apologies.' Rayanne caught an undercurrent of accent, something East European. 'Which part of "stand off" did you fail to understand?'

'Listen, lady,' Kindersley snapped, his podgy forefinger stabbing at the screen. 'I've got a tank full of hot hardware, a bunch of registered passengers who want off and an airscrubber that's starting to sound like somebody's iron lung. I ain't got the time or the inclination to "stand off", so either you tell me what the hell's going on or you get away from that *freaking* keyboard and find me someone who can!'

'Mr Kindersley, I have been checking your travel registrations.' The woman looked up at him, finally. 'You have on board three passengers who have recently travelled from Mexico and Miami Florida. I will need blood tests from you, your passengers and your crew before we can allow any entry to the multiplex.'

'Blood tests?' Kindersley's face was red, his teeth clenched under his moustache. 'What the hell are you talking about?'

Lannigan moved him gently aside. 'Excuse me, ma'am? Would you be kind enough to let us know what this is about, please?'

Rayanne glanced at Swann, who raised his eyes wearily. Lannigan on full burn.

It worked, of course. The Russian woman seemed to soften visibly. 'I am sorry,' she said. 'But the situation on Earth has deteriorated. The disease outbreaks in Florida and Mexico are now cause for concern among the orbital habitats – if encephalitis were to break out in a closed environment . . .'

Kindersley blinked, his eyes wide. 'What encephalitis?'

'Have you not heard?' The woman shook her head sadly. 'Mr Kindersley, the number of disease-related fatalities in both countries has now totalled two hundred plus. As of three hours ago, all flights leaving the affected areas have been cancelled by order of the United Nations.'

The blood tests, carried out by a man who stubbornly refused to remove or even open his spacesuit helmet, all came back negative.

The brown-haired woman, Marchenko, was Zholtyi Dom's chief meditech. She was there to greet Kindersley and his passengers when the *Dream* was finally allowed to dock. 'My apologies. But you can understand the situation.'

'Yeah yeah.' Kindersley, for all his scowls, couldn't really argue. With full knowledge of the facts, there was no way he would have done any different. Rayanne guessed he was probably maddest at Lannigan for not telling him about the danger, but she decided to keep her mouth shut about that, just in case.

Once the salver had left to make his deals Lannigan took her and Swann aside, directing them to a quiet spot near one of the hab's viewports. 'We have to talk,' she said, keeping her voice low. 'We're in a tight spot here.'

'Yeah?' muttered Rayanne. 'And that's been news for how long?'

'Don't try and be clever, Rayanne. It doesn't suit you.' Lannigan threw a glance over her shoulder to make sure there were no multiplexers close by. There weren't. 'The deal I made with Kindersley was for a round trip, Shiva to here and back, with the use of his coreframe on the way out. That still stands, and it leaves us just enough to get back groundside when we're done.'

'I sense a catch,' said Swann, warily.

'Your perception does you credit. Now, I was talking with Newnes on the way out.' Lannigan sucked her teeth for a moment, wincing as if at some bad memory. 'Insufferable woman, chatters like a teletype in that awful accent, but she told me some interesting things about a tracking system they have here.'

'Didn't see any dishes, not big ones.'

'I think it's more virtual, software parasites stealing data from UNSA probes, something like that. Basically they can track a huge amount of orbital traffic with it. Close to ten per cent of everything from here to Luna, junk and all.'

'What, and they give the info to people like Kindersley?' Swann grinned. 'Clever little op. No wonder they can run a profit.'

'So what?' said Rayanne.

Lannigan let out a long breath, trying to keep her temper under control. 'So,' she continued, 'we need to get some runtime on that system if we're going to find Artemis.'

Swann looked puzzled. 'That's not in the file?'

'Damn thing's moved. I had Newnes check it out for me.'

Rayanne felt abruptly sorry for the chirpy Newnes withering under Lannigan's icy manipulative skill. 'I'm kinda going out on a limb here, but are you planning to spend our going-home money hunting down Artemis on this tracker?'

'I'm impressed.'

'Screw that,' said Swann. 'How the hell are we going to get back down with no money? Jump?'

Rayanne understood what Lannigan was up to, suddenly. The whole plan. It frightened her, but she honestly couldn't see any other way out. The alternatives, such as they were, frightened her even more.

'No, she's right, man. We gotta go for it.'

'What about getting back to Earth?'

'If we don't finish up here, it won't matter whether we get home or not.' Rayanne turned away from him, towards the viewport. Outside, the planet's nightside was a great curve of shadow, blocking out all but a few stars. Past that, and some threadlike strands of cable, she could see only blackness. A dead, cold blackness, stretching out for ever.

'We'll be dead anyway.'

15
Hunting the Huntress

Lannigan was becoming an expert at reading people, although the talent wasn't something she could exactly define. It simply seemed the obvious thing to do, so natural and easy that she was astounded so few others even tried. Kindersley, for example, should have known better than to start yelling at Marchenko as he had, when the barest glimpse at the woman, the most cursory level of attention to her speech and body language, should have told him that she would react to deference far more positively than she would to threats or anger. Lannigan couldn't even have said exactly why this was so; it was simply a reflex response to what was displayed in front of her.

Likewise, she had caught the fleeting look of regret that had flashed across Rayanne's stripy face when she had mentioned her conversation with Newnes. That was an expression she had seen more often of late, especially since the girl had returned from Miami: Rayanne was becoming far more aware of Lannigan's talent for getting what she wanted from people, and she didn't like it. She probably felt sorry for the pilot, having Lannigan probe her.

The truth of the situation, however, was far less malign. Once she had started Newnes talking it had been almost impossible to shut her up. Lannigan had merely steered the conversation a couple of times, a nudge or two in the direction she required, and then it was just a matter of nodding and looking interested while the pilot prattled on about everything under, and including, the sun.

But, if Rayanne was convinced that she had worked some evil spell on Newnes, then all the better. It is better to be feared than loved, she had once heard quoted, if one cannot be both. And out here, in the frigid darkness of orbit, hunted and in terrible danger, love was of no use to her at all.

She went to find Marchenko.

The doctor was in Zholtyi Dom's primary medical centre, a cramped and seemingly random collection of systemry taking up most of what used to be the refuelling drone's processing core. When Lannigan keyed the hatch open, Marchenko was floating in front of a hologram terminal, gazing intently at a complex, lumpy graphic rotating within the hood.

'Thyroid gland,' Lannigan said automatically. 'What's that on the isthmus, there?'

'Microlesions.' Marchenko looked up with an expression of puzzlement, then recognition. 'You are Cassandra Lannigan, yes? Kindersley's passenger.'

'That's right. I wondered if I could ask your advice on something.' She drew closer, pulling herself along a drag cable. The medical bay didn't have enough clear wall space to anchor much netting, and it would be dangerous to try leaping around such a labyrinthine area in microgravity, so a spiderweb of cabling had been strung around the interior. Lannigan nodded at the graphic. 'Is that serious?'

'No. There was a cancer there; we get a lot of them in orbit. The lesions are just the aftereffects of removal.'

'Surgical?'

'Nanotech.' Marchenko swung round to face her. 'Do

you have a medical problem?'

Lannigan thought briefly about asking the doctor to check out that nasal implant, but decided against it. She would have to wait until her financial resources were less limited, or at least until an opportunity arose to get scanned for free. Which, in a place like Zholtyi Dom, wouldn't be easy. 'Nothing I can't handle. No, I was thinking more in terms of getting some runtime on OTADA.'

Marchenko's eyebrows went up. 'Some people should think more and speak less.'

Yes, Lannigan thought, that could certainly apply to Newnes. 'Is it really so much of a secret?'

'That depends on who you ask. To be honest, there are at least two other salvage multiplexes in orbit, and each has their own version of OTADA. It would be impossible to make a profit without one. However . . .' Marchenko lowered her voice, as if committing some sort of heresy. 'The array is run by a French-Canadian plex called Les Chasseurs. They can be, shall we say, a little paranoid . . .'

Lannigan had guessed as much. In effect, the Orbital Traffic and Debris Array was nothing more than a large and complex exercise in data theft. There were plenty of people who would be quite upset to find their orbital interests being tracked and logged in detail. Besides, actually interpreting the data gathered from all those tracking stations and satellites was a skilled task. Les Chasseurs probably garnered a considerable profit by making themselves indispensable. 'So it would be problematic for me to get some time on the system.'

'Difficult, yes.' Marchenko turned and began tapping idly at the terminal's controls. 'Of course, senior management can exercise a certain degree of executive priority . . .'

Lannigan smiled, and held up a terabyte SRAM chip. 'I need a location on the object detailed here, plus a complete log of all traffic to and from that object in the last fifteen weeks. Five hundred up front, another five hundred once the information is downloaded.'

'Three thousand, two in advance.'

'I'll go to two thousand, fifty-fifty.'

'A woman willing to pay two thousand is certainly willing to pay two and a half.'

Lannigan narrowed her eyes. 'Don't count on it.'

There was a long pause, and then Marchenko grinned. 'Two thousand it is then. I will use the terminal in my office. If you want to stay out here, I shouldn't be more than a few minutes.'

Lannigan passed over the chip, wrapped in a slim wad of ICUs. 'I'll be right here.'

Marchenko took the money and the chip with a swift, mantis-like movement, then scampered away along a cable. Lannigan watched her go, wondering how much the woman had charged that cancer patient to get the tumour out of his thyroid. She couldn't blame Marchenko for being avaricious – money was the whole point of living and working in space. One day, long in the past, people might have ventured out of their gravity well for some idealistic notion of exploration and adventure, of high frontiers. But there was no new frontier above the atmosphere, not any more: just a lot of new and interesting ways of making money.

Still, the deal had gone better than she had expected. Tickets back to Earth were a thousand each, roughly. Which meant that, if she didn't spend anything else, she could at least afford to get home.

Lannigan eased a little way up the cable, peering around the bulk of an electron microscope and into Marchenko's office. The woman was setting up an infonet connection, linking her screen to whichever of Zholtyi Dom's cluster of habitats housed Les Chasseurs and their tracking array. She seemed quite engrossed, so Lannigan turned her attention back to the hologram hood.

Marchenko had left it on. A head-sized thyroid gland spun lazily in front of her.

Perhaps she could get that scan after all.

The device was slaved to a number of scanners and devices spread out through the chamber. Lannigan switched away from the thyroid and called up a control menu, prodding at the options with a forefinger as they floated, ghostly, before her in the hood. Among the devices was a magnetic resonance imager, a portable version of the device that had noticed her implants back on Shiva.

The menu commands were childishly simple. With a few swift choices Lannigan set the MRI for a scan, from the first dorsal vertebra upward.

The scanner unfolded smoothly in another part of the chamber, a briefcase-sized ovoid of grey plastic that extruded spindly rods and tubes as she watched: foot stirrups, a two-metre vertical rail, shielded rotary scan heads. Lannigan pulled herself over to it and planted her feet in the stirrups, straightening with the rail at her back. Behind her, the heads slid up to shoulder height, whirled about her once, and dropped away.

The entire scan had taken less than ten seconds.

Lannigan stepped off the platform and went back to the hood. Inside it, turning slowly, was a graphic of her own head.

For a moment she just stared at it. It was a strange sight: the computers within the scanner had removed her hair to make the picture clearer, stripped her of eyebrows and lashes. Beyond that, the graphic was perfect, marred only by a faint transparency.

She ordered the MRI to fold itself away, and as it did so she took a second SRAM from her pocket and slipped it into the hood's I/O slot. A few more taps at the menu had the scan results downloaded and the thyroid back up: Lannigan was taking the chip out when Marchenko climbed out of her office. 'What are you doing?'

'Sorry.' She palmed the chip, hurriedly, nodding at the graphic. 'I was just studying your microlesions. There's really a lot about surgical nanotechnology I don't know.'

Marchenko handed her the first chip. 'You and me both. Even a full specification and capabilities rundown would be a help, but medical corporations don't like to give up their secrets without a struggle.'

'I couldn't agree more.' Lannigan felt a coldness across her shoulders, and shook it away. 'Now then, let's have a look at what you found for me.'

Later, she returned to *Earhart's Dream* in search of a suitable display unit. Marchenko had shown her enough on the medical hood to make her part with the second thousand, but she needed time to study the data before she could discover anything useful about Artemis. Plus, of course, there were the scan results, which were hers to view alone. She had already let far too many strangers see what lay inside her head.

Kindersley and two of his crewmates were off somewhere in one of the other habs, which left Newnes to let Lannigan in. 'I was going to call you anyway.' The pilot smiled, keying the airlock open. 'Bob wants to be away in the next hour or so.'

Lannigan frowned and checked her chrono. 'So soon?'

'Well, somebody using the you-know-what thinks they've got a lead on that cargo drone, and everyone's taking off to get after it.' Newnes helped Lannigan through, then closed the lock after her. 'Not that it's strictly salvage, of course. But we might get a bit of a reward from the owners if we pick it up intact.'

'The Fushigina drone?'

'Aye, that's the one.' The pilot grinned, looking childishly excited. 'Full of data cores, worth a bloody fortune. If Fushigina don't get it back they'll be in real trouble, money-wise, what with all that disease business. So they might be a bit pleased if we find their ship for them.'

Lannigan nodded, trying to look interested. To be honest she could hardly have cared less about Fushigina's fortunes or its missing drone. For all she knew they might very well have been responsible for the brain-bug ravaging

Mexico and Miami – it wouldn't have been the first time that a corporation had dabbled in a few bioweapons on the side. And Kindersley chasing after their missing cargo drone was an inconvenience she could well do without.

'Newnes –'

'Oh, call me Alicia, everybody else does.'

Lannigan gritted her teeth. 'Alicia. Is there a holo terminal I could use? I have some data I really need to review, and I was wondering . . .'

The woman was shaking her head. 'Sorry. That's a bit too upmarket for *Dream*, I'm afraid. Could you use a flatscreen?'

'Ah, erm.' Lannigan blinked. She honestly didn't know. 'Well, if there's some way of translating it all.'

'Have a try down in salvage ops – all the best stuff's down there. Right down main access, first on your left, take another left and it says SALVAGE OPS on the door.' She paused. 'In Japanese. But you can't miss it.'

'Right.'

'No, left, ha ha. I'll be in C and C, getting everything warmed up.' The pilot turned to go, grabbing a handful of netting and propelling herself across the transfer module towards the forward hatch. 'And make sure your friends are on board before we go!'

'Fine, fine.' Lannigan gazed after her, feeling rather sour. How could anyone be that cheerful all the time? Perhaps Newnes was on some kind of recreational chem. She would have to ask Rayanne.

She followed the pilot's directions, edging through the claustrophobic access tunnel as quickly as she dared, taking a left turn before she reached the floor hatch that led to the tank. Access tunnels were a legacy of the inefficient and piecemeal way in which *Earhart's Dream* had been constructed: individual capsules bought at varying times, bolted on to the shuttle tank as needed and connected via great lengths of tubing. The salvage operations room, for example, lay alongside the accommodation capsule, but further down the tank's side. The corridor that connected it to main access actually curved downward.

Beyond the *kanji*-scrawled hatch was a narrow metal cylinder fitted with a double workstation and a pair of contour seats. From here, Watanabe would supervise external salvage operations, using the clusters of jointed manipulators to capture and, if necessary, dismember the orbital junk on which the plex survived. He could probably slave the ship's manoeuvring thrusters to his board as well, in order to drop the vessel over any larger items, tank doors gaping to swallow the debris whole.

Just as Newnes had said, there were no hologram hoods in the cylinder. But the tactical display equipment looked enough to handle any orbital schematics Marchenko might have downloaded.

Lannigan settled herself into a contour chair and took the chips from her pockets. She replaced the scanner information – she had marked it with a permagraph pencil, to avoid confusion – and began looking for an I/O slot for the other chip. But, as she found the socket, she paused.

She was, after all, alone.

Quickly, and with a furtive glance back towards the hatchway, she took out the scan chip and slotted it into the board. Getting the data on to the screen took a few minutes' trial and error with the conversion commands, but before long she was looking at her own depilated head rotating on Watanabe's flatscreens.

All the screens showed the same image. She couldn't alter the slaving commands.

She set up some control options and began to access the internal structure of the graphic. Once the skin and musculature of the replica head was gone, she was able to proceed without any more emotional hindrance: the face was no longer one she recognised, but a complex of bone and tendon and pale tissues that had no more in common with her than a textbook diagram.

Under her commands, more of the face fell away.

Lannigan focused on the nasal cavity, opening the wafers of bone and expanding the view until it stretched around her like the interior of a cave.

There, hugging the cave roof. A knot of metallic fibres, woven into the bone, splitting and dividing and spreading into a filigree network that covered half the sinus. Each thread was hair-fine at the nexus, but at their fullest extension they were so reduced in thickness that they defeated even the scanner's best resolution. Lannigan felt a cold nausea spilling upward from her gut, a prickle of fear-sweat across her shoulders.

Nothing so fine could have been built by conventional means. The structure was a nanotech artefact, built molecule by molecule to some unimaginable fractal design. Her hospital medical records – even the last series of scans she had undergone – had shown nothing like this.

What she saw must have been growing in her skull ever since she left Nairobi.

The hatch rattled abruptly, and then swung inward. Lannigan jumped in her seat and tried to delete the scan graphic from the screen, but her trembling hands skated off the controls, setting the image spinning instead. The interior of her skull, invaded by the glittering web, went whirling and turning in front of her, repeated across every screen in the cylinder.

Rayanne hung in the doorway, staring. 'What the hell do you call that?'

'It's, ah, a medical file.' Lannigan swallowed hard and concentrated on the board, finally getting the image back under control. 'Old data. I was just using it to set the screens up.'

'Yeah? You get what we need from that tracker thing?'

'I hope so.' Lannigan glanced past Rayanne as the girl clambered in and sat down. 'Where's Swann?'

'Down in engineering. Letching after that French chick.'

'Good God.' Lannigan gave Rayanne a sideways look. 'Jealous?'

'Oh yeah, *right,*' the girl sneered. 'I'm floating in a tin can, with a buncha suits sending assassins after me, no way home, and I'm just *dying* to crawl into the sack with some skinny little kidnapper from hell. Give me a break.'

'Whatever you say, Rayanne.'

'Did you pay for those dork pills, or did they come free with that stick up your ass?'

'All right!' Lannigan flushed, busying herself with the board, swapping the SRAMs around. 'Are we going to review this data or not?'

There was an ugly silence as she called the orbital download up on to Watanabe's screens. Lannigan worked the controls and fumed, raging internally at Rayanne for her comments, at herself for even trying to talk pleasantly to the girl. Embarrassed that her pitiful attempts at small talk had been rebuffed so bluntly. If Rayanne had possessed some secret or information that Lannigan needed she could have had it out of her in minutes, so why was she so inept at communicating on even the most superficial personal level?

She almost told Rayanne that there was no need to snap at her, but then realised that she was probably the least qualified person in the world to make a comment like that. 'Right. Let's see what we have.'

Marchenko had been thorough. There was a list of ten possible sites for Artemis on the chip: ten objects that were close enough to the lab's parameters to have been picked up by whatever search engine she had sent coursing through the OTADA database. The percentage matches ran from 93 to 100 per cent.

Which made nine out of the ten largely superfluous, but it had been a nice thought.

Lannigan called up information on the perfect match. The display switched to a spreadsheet of information, probably the standard form sent by Les Chasseurs to the various plexes that paid them. Much of the information, including the orbital coordinates of the object, was meaningless to Lannigan, but there was plenty on the grid that she could read.

'Is that it?' Rayanne asked.

'That's it. There's a clear orbital path from where this thing is to where Artemis was supposed to be. The mass matches to within a hair, even the configuration details – they must have hacked something that's been close enough to see it. Plus, it can't be another lab of the same class, since all the others are still in operation.' She pointed. 'See?'

Rayanne frowned and leant closer to the screen. 'That says all the labs are accounted for.'

'Übergen are cooking the books, trying to make it look like Artemis never existed.' Lannigan chewed her lip thoughtfully. 'I wonder why they didn't get someone to just destroy it.'

'Maybe they were afraid someone would see an explosion.'

'Could be.' Lannigan folded her arms and sat back, trying to be impressed. The page she was looking at neither looked nor felt as though it was worth two thousand ICUs.

Still, she wasn't paying for the information itself, but rather what it would allow her to do. With the orbital location of Artemis in her hands, she could set about making her way there. And, once aboard, she could run Kobayashi's test again.

A positive result for sentience, even on a dead system, would give her a lot of weight with the AI board.

'Who else has been there?' asked Rayanne suddenly.

'Hm?'

'You were gonna get traffic records, right? See who else has visited that thing?' The girl gestured at the screens. 'Might tell us if anyone else is involved.'

'Well, if you think it might be important.' Lannigan made a play of unfolding her arms, stretching the kinks from her back, and then calling up the traffic data. Inside she was seething. She had forgotten that part of the download entirely – possibly the most important piece of information besides the orbital coordinates. The shock of finding a nanotech fractal growing through her sinuses must have affected her more than she had realised.

The display changed, turning from a spreadsheet page into a short list of transit registrations. Here were all the vehicles logged – by whatever agency – as having visited the Artemis lab in the past fifteen weeks.

No vessels registered to Übergen AG or any of their subsidiaries was listed.

Lannigan wondered how long the satellite had been abandoned. Once Übergen had discovered that their AI was thinking for itself they would have had to act fast, and the differences between a smart AI and a talking box like Kitsumi were massive enough to be quickly detectable. Even if the new life-form was extremely careful, it could not have kept its secret for more than a day, two at the most.

It must have known it was doomed from the first microsecond of its life.

'What's this first one?' Rayanne was leaning over, tapping insistently at Lannigan's screen. 'Half this shit's blank.'

Lannigan looked more closely. The vehicle had left Artemis in the middle of March, but there was no date for its arrival there. 'Must have stayed up there for a while. That's damn odd – it shipped out two months after Übergen caught up with me that first time.'

'No landing details, either.' Rayanne, still leaning close, used Lannigan's controls to call up further details on the ship. 'Ah, what we got here? Registered salver, two hundred tonnes, name of *Tucker's Net*.' The girl turned to Lannigan. 'That ring a bell with you?'

Lannigan nodded. '*Tucker's Net* went into a decaying orbit while I was in hospital. I watched it fall.' In her mind's eye, a star, a fiery comet tumbling and ripping and seeding the cold Kenyan sky with sparks. 'They died. The whole crew, they burnt up and died.'

'Oh, man.' Rayanne sat back, looking slightly pale. 'Lousy way to go, man.'

'No, it was beautiful. I envied them so much.' Lannigan shook herself, pulling her attention back to the job in hand. That image, that lingering, blazing fall, was seductive. 'So they were at Artemis. Maybe Übergen *did* hire someone to destroy the lab.'

'Sold their own lab as salvage?' Rayanne nodded thoughtfully. 'Yeah, that would work. Except, like, it didn't, did it? I mean, something went wrong. Crash and burn.'

'It certainly looks like somebody stopped them. Maybe a rival salvage plex, who knows?' She began to study the next ship on the list. 'Maybe your friend Newnes did the deed: anyone that perky has got to be a closet psychopath. Ah, that's me.'

'What?'

'Me, there, has to be. Single-seat OTV up from the Rama platform, eleventh of January. Stayed for thirty-six hours, then back. Well, whatever happened to *Tucker's Net* didn't happen to me. Oh Jesus *God* . . .'

She had accessed the final page, the flight details of the last ship to visit Artemis. What she saw there put a tight band of ice round her heart.

'Are you yokay?'

Lannigan glanced round and saw Rayanne looking at her, stripy features creased in concern. 'I'm sorry?'

'I said, are you yokay? You're looking kind of pale there.'

'I'm fine.' Lannigan switched pages, back to the list, then shut down the terminal. 'I just felt a little queasy, probably need to take another pill.' She sat back, knotting her hands together so that Rayanne wouldn't see how badly they were shaking. 'Look, you'd better go up and see what's going on. Try and stall Kindersley.'

'Stall him?' Rayanne's eyebrows went up. '*Señora*, you know what he's like. I try and get in his way, I'm gonna be floating home.'

'Don't worry, I'll be up in a moment. I just need to edit some of this data, get it ready for public viewing.' She saw Rayanne open her mouth to ask why, and put her hand up. 'Just do it, yokay? And don't tell Kindersley about *Tucker's Net*. He won't go within a million miles of Artemis if he thinks there's danger.'

'And is there?' Rayanne asked quietly.

'No,' Lannigan lied. 'Nothing we can't handle.'

By the time she left salvage ops and made her way to the command deck, Kindersley and his crew were already preparing to take *Earhart's Dream* away from the multiplex. Swann and Rayanne were in the transfer module. 'He threw us out. Said if we poked our heads in there again he'd kick us off the damn ship.'

'At least he's consistent.' Lannigan keyed the hatch open and put her shoulders through. 'Mr Kindersley?'

'Get the hell outta here!' The man swung his contour seat round to glare at her. 'I already told your people, don't bother me when I'm setting up the damn vector.' He turned away, his small, fat fingers dancing with surprising agility over his control boards. 'I'll get back to you when we're away.'

Behind her, far away, the throaty whine of a fusion torus building up to full power.

Newnes caught Lannigan's eye and gave her an apologetic shrug. Lannigan winked at the pilot, then said, 'Kindersley, you're wasting time and fuel chasing after the Fushigina drone. Give me two minutes, and I'll quadruple your profits on this run.'

'Forget it,' he said. But he had paused before speaking, a momentary hesitation, and Lannigan knew she had him. She ducked out of the chamber. 'Two minutes, Mr Kindersley.'

Swann and Rayanne had identical expressions on their

faces, a pair of disbelieving bookends. Lannigan took some pleasure from the way those expressions changed as the fusion torus throttled back to a low, bone-deep rumble. 'Sorry, Rayanne, you were going to say something?'

'Not me, man.' The girl glanced across at Swann, and then saw Kindersley pulling himself through the hatch. With that, she gave Lannigan a look of pure disgust, and hauled herself away.

Lannigan watched her go, just for a second, and then turned her attention to Kindersley. 'How would you like,' she asked him, placing an arm round his shoulders and leaning close, 'an entire orbital laboratory all to yourself?'

Artemis was within two hours of Zholtyi Dom, once Kindersley had cranked up the engines a little. From her hiding place in the salvage-ops cylinder, Lannigan could feel the thrust of the reaction drives at her back, false gravity tugging her towards the ship's stern.

Swann had taken himself off somewhere, probably back to engineering to continue his pointless flirtation with Sherryl LeChance, and Rayanne had made it quite plain that she didn't want to be within range of Lannigan's evil eye. Lannigan sat on her own in the cylinder, strapped into a contour seat, and found that she couldn't blame the girl at all.

There was a part of her, after all, that anyone would find frightening. The part of her that had convinced Kindersley to let the other salvage plexes waste their fuel chasing a moving target; the cold, calculating part that had measured his avarice and weighed his trepidation and balanced the two in front of him until he had agreed that yes, changing course to intercept Artemis probably *was* a good idea after all; that was indeed something to be feared. Rayanne could see it, plain as day. When Lannigan stepped outside of herself and thought about it hard, she could see it too.

It was a separate thing from the rest of her, an alien

thing, as strange and inexplicable as the fractal web spreading through the cavities behind her nose. It was a shadow at her side, a voiceless dark insistence that saw people simply as material, walking libraries that needed only the correct words to unlock and read them at will.

Lannigan had thought that too, at first. She had been one with it. Now, it was something else, something hidden and malevolent. And she feared it.

For a moment, a second of weakness, she wished with all her heart for a time when she wouldn't have to be afraid.

Whenever that time came, she told herself quickly, it wouldn't be soon. Too many pieces of the puzzle were in place to give her any real comfort, too many sections of the whole, horrible picture had become visible at last. Since she had seen the details of the last ship to visit Artemis, she had known, with a terrible certainty, that what lay before her was something worse than she had ever imagined.

The last ship on the list was a bimodal clipper, a powerful fusion of space shuttle and orbital transfer vehicle. It had left the launch facility at Poza Rica, Mexico, a week before Lannigan had left hospital. It carried two crew and a single passenger. In low Earth orbit the ship had split, the OTV powering up to rendezvous with Artemis, the shuttle remaining a hundred kilometres above the surface, waiting. Two days later, the clipper landed safely at Miami airport, Florida.

It should have gone back to the facility in Mexico.

Lannigan guessed that one, if not both, of the clipper's crew had indeed returned to Poza Rica, very soon after landing. The passenger would remain in Miami, and a few days later would locate Rayanne Hernandez and kiss her full on the lips.

The clipper was registered to Fushigina Systems Ltd, cutting-edge producer of artificial-intelligence software and deadly rival of Übergen Aktien-Gesellschaft. Which meant that, when the woman who was now Cassandra

Lannigan had accepted the Artemis assignment from Noriko Kobayashi, she was drawing herself and her plex into the front line of a corporate war.

Twenty minutes before *Earhart's Dream* was due to dock with Artemis, Kindersley sent Newnes to get Lannigan into an E-suit.

The suits were kept in the transfer module. Newnes opened a locker and took out a bundle of greyish plastic, plates and joints folded together into a block not much bigger than the AI core Lannigan held in her left hand. 'Is that it?'

'Well, this is just a short-excursion type. There's not much in the way of life-support, so I hope you went to the bathroom before you came down here.' The pilot took two tags in her hands and pulled. The suit unfolded between her outstretched hands until it looked like a flattened and decapitated suit of armour. 'It's just a precaution. Take your shoes off.'

Lannigan obeyed, with some trepidation, and watched Newnes stash the footwear alongside Rayanne's discarded Nikes. Then, holding on to a patch of netting with one hand, she placed her bare left foot against the suit's flattened boot.

As soon as her sole touched the inside of the footplate there was a faint hiss of compressed air, and the boot folded up and around her leg, petals of hard plastic mating to surround her foot and lower leg in a complex array of armour and soft jointing. 'My God.'

'You've never worn one of these before?'

'Not that I recall, no.' Lannigan repeated the action with her right foot, then her hands, and within less than a minute the suit had opened out like an exercise in plastic origami and sealed itself around her. She raised her arms, turning her hands, watching plates and pads of armour sliding over the fabric beneath, as intricate and organic as insect limbs.

Newnes grinned at her and nodded her satisfaction.

'One size fits all, you see? The helmet and airscrubber is all in one. We'll put that on you just before we dock. Try moving around, get the feel of it.'

Lannigan stretched and twisted as much as she was able, letting the suit make a final few self-adjustments. It was a little restricting, especially around the helmet seals, but in general it was a lot more mobile than she was. 'Hardly catwalk, but I think I can live with it.'

As she spoke, the rear hatchway unsealed and swung inward. Lannigan turned to watch Rayanne poke her head through. 'Where have you been?' Lannigan asked.

The girl made a face and pushed past her, fetching up next to the infonet screen. 'I just came up from salvage ops, man. You'd better take a look at this.' She tapped at the controls until the screen strobed, then switched to an outside view.

Against a sea of black, the angular white mushroom of the Artemis facility.

Lannigan let out a long breath. 'Good God. It *is* here.'

'You ain't looking, *señora*.' Rayanne pointed to the satellite. 'See? Whole damn thing's spinning. Kindersley says he ain't gonna dock.'

After a few moments, Lannigan saw the girl was right: the satellite was indeed rotating about its long axis, a slow, lazy spin, the outstretched solar panels brightening as she watched, then dulling again as they moved into shadow. Artemis was turning like a slow top.

'She's right,' said Newnes. 'No way Bob's going to try docking with that, not if it's going round. It's just too big.'

'Can't we grab it? Stop it moving?'

'It's too *big*. Got to be a hundred tonnes' worth, maybe more: taking hold of that would just rip the manipulators off.' Newnes mimed that situation so effectively that Lannigan winced. 'Can't match that spin, either.'

'Great,' Lannigan snapped. 'So what the hell am I supposed to do? Fly across?'

'That ain't the best of it.' Rayanne pointed again. 'Here, just coming round. See that?'

Lannigan followed her finger. At first she thought the girl was showing her a shadow, but then she realised that the patch of darkness wasn't acting as shadows do. No, it was a stain on the surface, a blackened disc of scorched paintwork and buckled plating covering almost a quarter of the lab's circumference. Several of the comms dishes there were wrecked, melted and awry. It looked as though someone had dusted Artemis with a giant blowtorch.

'Kindersley reckons someone took off in a hurry, caught it with the drive exhaust.'

Lannigan shook her head. 'Kindersley's wrong. That's from an EMP weapon.'

'Huh?'

'Electromagnetic pulse. Burns out unshielded circuits.' She sighed, and turned away from the screen, putting her back to Artemis and the cold, dead thing she now knew it held. 'It's a little messy, but a great way of killing an AI.'

She decided to jump.

After some persuasion, Kindersley agreed to take *Earhart's Dream* within twenty metres of the spinning lab, and no closer. She had protested about the distance, but he just sat there with his arms folded and told her that, if she really wanted to go EVA, that was her prerogative, but no one was going to make him put his ship any closer to a whirling artefact that had already moved itself once and might very well do so again. He was going to have enough trouble attaching a line to the thing and towing it home.

Lannigan knew damn well that Artemis had moved only because Übergen had moved it, but that wasn't going to cut any ice with Kindersley. And so she found herself back in the transfer module again, with Newnes unfolding a compact block of plastic into a helmet and airscrubber unit while Rayanne and Swann watched her. 'You're insane, lady,' said Rayanne.

'Rayanne, I really don't have a choice. Once I've got the test results in downloadable form we can get some protection from the AI board, but until then we're naked in the park.' She snugged the helmet down as Newnes had shown her, and heard the seals lock with a faint hiss. A belt served to hold the scrubber against her back; she locked it and felt it tighten. 'I just want this over with.'

'You're gonna miss the fragging thing. You're gonna miss it and go flying off for ever, like into the sun or something.'

Lannigan smirked. 'Rayanne, I didn't know you cared.'

'I don't. But Kindersley's gonna make us pay for the suit.'

The belt was studded with loops and velcro patches. Lannigan used one to secure the AI core to her waist. 'Don't worry. It's only turning about once a minute, which is easy enough to grab hold of, and if the worst happens I can correct with the manoeuvre unit.' The backpack sported tiny thrust nozzles, connected to a voice-guidance system in the helmet. 'I'll be in and out within a quarter-hour.'

Swann folded his arms. 'I still say we should just frag it from here. Kick it down into a decaying orbit, let the bastard fry.'

'And then what?' Lannigan pushed the faceplate on her helmet up. 'Wait for Übergen to come after us? Because they will. We're too much of a risk to let go, financially. And finance is all they care about.' She bobbed over to him and put a hand on his shoulder. 'I know what you're worried about. But there's no power in there – the tokamak's down and that spin's got the solar cells running half-empty. Trust me.'

'Yeah, right. I trusted you to come back to Mexico.' He gnawed his lip for a second, then pulled away. 'Look, wait up here for a second, yokay? Just until I get back.'

They watched him disappear through one of the aft hatches, and then Newnes said, 'Übergen?'

'Don't worry about it. Can you give me a pre-flight, or whatever you call it? I don't want to go out there and then find I've left a zipper open.'

Newnes grinned and pushed the faceplate closed. As it locked she turned Lannigan round, no doubt reading the displays on the back of the scrubber unit. A moment later she swung back into view. Her mouth worked.

Lannigan frowned at her for a moment, then caught on: 'Oh, right. Suit, comms on, external net. Sorry, you wanna try that again?'

'I said you're all yokay.' The pilot's voice sounded as clear through the helmet's speakers as it had with the faceplate open. 'Everything's nominal.'

'Right. That's . . . That's good.' For a moment she just stood there, her boots not quite touching the deck, unsure of what to do. She had been thinking about this moment so hard, and for so long, that it had almost ceased to have any meaning. Reaching Artemis had always just been a phrase, part of a plan, a location on her mental map of what would be. She would do it and after that everything would be all right.

All her plans, all her calculations and machinations and lies and manipulations, had been leading up to this. In a few seconds, she was going to step into an airlock and dive across twenty metres of searingly cold vacuum, in order to finally reach Artemis.

And she didn't want to.

She was afraid.

She wanted someone to come with her, to hold her hand and tell her what to do. Suddenly, amazingly, Lannigan felt five years old.

'Swann,' she said quietly. 'He wanted me to wait. Maybe I should wait for him . . .' She saw Rayanne and Newnes looking at her, the expressions on their faces something like pity, and she sighed. It wouldn't do any good to wait. Another second, or another hour, it wouldn't make any difference. Even if she turned away, took off the suit and bought a flight all the way down to Earth, she would still have to come back here eventually. She would still have to reach Artemis. 'Screw it,' she muttered, mainly to herself. 'Let's go.'

That was when Swann climbed into the module. 'Hold up, doc. I brought you something.'

He held an object out to her: a short metal tube atop a plastic handgrip, with a metre of fat cable trailing off to a blocky power pack. 'What is it?'

'Welding laser.' He clipped the pack to her belt, across from the AI core. 'Switch it on here and then press the trigger. Just in case, huh?'

Newnes glared at him. 'Did you nick that out of our stores?'

'Yeah.' He shrugged at her. 'Sorry, honey. Hey, if that thing's as safe as everyone says it is, she won't need it. Call it an early Christmas present from you to us, 'cause you're such a darling.'

The pilot gave him a withering stare, which he ignored. Lannigan looked at him, floating there with his hair drifting and his thin hooked nose and his eyes like little dark marbles, and felt oddly touched. She knew that his concern was not for her, but for himself and his own future. However, if their respective desires for self-preservation happened to intersect once in a while, then somehow that was enough.

'Swann,' she said. 'You're an idiot. But thank you anyway.'

'Try not to weld your own head off.'

Despite herself, she felt a lot better with the laser than without it. She nodded to Newnes and Rayanne and then turned to the airlock. It opened for her and she stepped inside.

So easy. There was no great drama about it, no rushing of air or illuminated countdowns. It was all very quick and simple. One moment she was surrounded by *Dream*'s atmosphere; the next the outer hatch had opened and she was standing in vacuum.

The suit inflated slightly around her, but that was the most noticeable change. Lannigan took a deep breath, aimed herself at the gleaming bulk of Artemis, and jumped headlong into infinity.

16
Spiders in the Dark

Not long after Lannigan had disappeared into Artemis, Rayanne found herself alone. She had been in the transfer module with Newnes and Swann, but Kindersley had called through from the Command and Control deck, telling the pilot to get her skinny ass back up to C and C where it belonged. Things went silent after that, since Rayanne and Swann still didn't have much to say to each other, and after a rather awkward few minutes he went off to engineering again. Rayanne stayed where she was, drifting in front of the little screen, waiting and watching the satellite turning slowly in front of her. After it had rotated about ten times, Rayanne found herself willing Lannigan to emerge, willing it so hard that her stomach was knotted up. She didn't notice until a sound – one of the many sighs and moans that *Earhart's Dream* was prone to – made her look away, and when she did her guts unclenched so suddenly that it hurt.

At that point, Rayanne figured that she had better go and do something else, or by the time Lannigan got back to the ship she would find a mad Cuban girl in the transfer module, bouncing off the wall nets and screaming. So she picked one of the three aft hatches and went through it, finding herself in the short corridor that led to the accommodation cylinder.

Watanabe was there ahead of her, working something up in the little galley unit. 'Hello. It's Rayanne, isn't it?'

'Last time I looked.' She peered over his shoulder. 'What's that?'

'Turkey steaks in gravy, with runner beans and hash browns,' he said, reading a label. 'I missed lunch. There's plenty spare if you want me to heat some for you.'

Rayanne, who hadn't eaten much since Mexico City, realised that she wanted some very much indeed. 'Sure. Is it real turkey?'

The salver's long face cracked in a grin. 'Out here? Krill, mashed up into protein glop, moulded, freeze-dried and then heated with water that's actually recycled piss. The beans and hash browns were grown in a vat back in Zholtyi Dom, and you don't want to know about the gravy.' He held a plastic tray out to her. 'Still want some?'

'You make it sound so great.' She watched him microwave up a second tray. When he handed it to her she held it carefully and stripped off the lid, sniffing as steam billowed up from a series of hot lumps glued down with yellowish, translucent gravy. There was a plastic fork with a serrated edge, which was almost sharp enough to cut the hash browns.

She had eaten worse. But not by much. 'Eew. Man, why'd you do this? Why would anyone wanna spend their life in a tin can eating shit?'

Watanabe shrugged and gulped down a mouthful of pretend turkey. 'If I told you it wasn't for the thrill, the romance, and the benefits to humanity, would you be really disappointed?'

'Nope.'

'Good, because I do it for the money.' He nodded in a direction Rayanne assumed was Earthwards. 'No jobs in Kyoto, not for someone with my qualifications. So I hitched a ride up here.'

Rayanne nodded. It wasn't the first time she'd heard

that story, not by a long way. Zenebe had moved out of Uganda in his search for a better life, just like Gregor Kamarov had left Eastern Europe and Watanabe had climbed right up out of the gravity well. She herself had fled Cuba at the first opportunity. No one stayed where they were any more.

But it made no difference. One part of the world was very much like another, when all the surface details were stripped away. Gregor had ended his life serving fast food in Miami rather than Minsk, but the job still involved spatulas and a set of paper coveralls. In Kyoto, some people slept in capsules almost exactly like those on the *Earhart's Dream*, and Zenebe could have lost the top of his skull practically anywhere.

And Rayanne Gatita? Trouble had followed her all over the world. She might just as well have stayed at home.

A sudden image flashed into her mind: Zenebe, slumped in a chair with the top of his head gone, Gregor on a gurney in exactly the same state. She winced and set the tray aside. 'I can't eat this no more, man.'

'Don't worry about it. Everything's recycled, so if we have to stay out here much longer you'll probably be eating it again anyway.'

'Thanks for sharing. Look, I wanna check up on how things are doing back home. Yokay if I use the screen back in transfer?'

'If you like.' Watanabe scraped up the last of his gravy and sucked the spoon clean. 'Or I can patch you in from ops – I've got to go back there anyway.'

Rayanne thought about this for a time, then realised that she would be much happier with somebody else around and so followed him aft, back through the constricted little accessway and into the screen-studded cylinder that was salvage operations. She strapped herself into a chair while Watanabe called up a link and slaved it to the screen nearest her. 'Try not to stay on too long. Kindersley owes the service provider, and he'll kick my ass if I get him cut off.'

'Don't worry. I know where I'm going.' She accessed the newsfeed she had been watching before, hunting through the menu options until she found an update on the encephalitis outbreaks. She had to scroll further through the list than she had before. The bug was no longer a hot story: it had been robbed of importance by time and the continuing misfortunes of Fushigina Systems. Rayanne scanned a summary of the top story, and learnt that the company's managing director had recently committed suicide in a particularly messy and painful fashion. Ironically, this act had actually caused a slight rise in the ailing corporation's financial standing.

'I could care less,' muttered Rayanne. That drew a glance from Watanabe, but he was busy working out stress factors on a tether to Artemis, and quickly returned to his calculations. Rayanne skipped down until she found the outbreak statistics, instructing the screen to make the display as simple as it could. She was quite relieved to discover that the spread of the disease was slowing considerably. No more than fourteen people had died of it since she had last checked, and that had been hours ago.

Rayanne almost shut the screen down at that point, but a secondary story caught her eye. She followed the link to a location that held what appeared to be only a related oddity, but, as she read the text and accessed the video blips, Rayanne began to feel increasingly uneasy.

Eight people – five in Miami, and three in Poza Rica – previously ravaged by the encephalitis had escaped from their intensive-care units and fled, unseen by anyone. They had, as yet, not been located. At first, Rayanne saw nothing unusual in this: after all, she herself had done exactly the same thing, taking advantage of the general panic surrounding the disease to leave hospital before the Jackson staff got too many funny ideas about biopsies and dissection. But closer study revealed that none of the escaped patients had, in any real sense, recovered from the disease.

Rayanne had fought off the fever and left hospital with little more than a headache and an uncomfortably clear long-term memory. These escapees had been wired into medicoms because they couldn't even breathe without help. Their brains had been wrecked by the encephalitis.

One, maybe two, such cases could have been put down to administrative error. But eight was too many, and the newscasters were asking questions about the competence of hospital staff. Rayanne could think of a few other questions to ask, but decided that she wasn't quite ready to hear the answers yet. She shut the screen off.

Watanabe tipped his head at her. 'Anything good?'

'Same old shit.'

'Amazing, isn't it? All those addresses, and –' He stopped abruptly, and leant closer to one of his screens. 'Hello . . .'

'What you got?'

'I'm not quite sure.' He tapped at some keys, then switched one of his monitors on to comms. 'Alicia?'

Newnes appeared on the screen. 'You've seen it too, have you?'

'What?' said Rayanne.

'Something moving towards us. Alicia, can you get the main comms dish pointing that way? I'll rig my scope through it, see if we can get an ID.'

Rayanne went cold. 'Towards us? Like, in the same orbit?'

'No, it's shifting orbit. I wouldn't worry. Probably some other salvage plex getting curious.' He began setting up a complex pattern of programming on one of his boards. Rayanne watched him for a moment and decided that, if someone with his level of qualifications couldn't get a job in Kyoto, she didn't want to go there.

She switched the screen on again, set it up for comms and punched in Lannigan's infonet address. Lannigan had told her not to, but she figured this to be enough of an emergency to warrant breaking the little Anglo's concentration.

After five seconds, a text message scrolled up telling her that the address she was trying to call was not connected to infonet, and was she sure that the address code was correct? Rayanne tried it again, making sure of what she tapped in this time, and got the same message. 'Oh shit.'

'Problem?'

'Lannigan. Her chrono's offline.'

Watanabe shrugged. 'Maybe she shut it off. She did say that she wanted to be left alone in there.'

'No, she wouldn't have done that.' Rayanne shook her head. 'She might have a stick up her butt, but she ain't stupid. Frag it!' She slapped the seat arm, hard, making Watanabe jump. 'Knew she'd get herself into trouble!'

'Hey, you don't know that.'

'The frag I don't.' Rayanne unstrapped herself and shoved herself towards the hatch. 'I'm gonna get Swann.'

Swann wasn't in engineering. Sherryl LeChance told Rayanne that she had thrown him out, and that he was probably sulking down in the stores. She found him there, in the very compartment where she had spent most of the journey to Zholtyi Dom. 'We got a problem.'

'Makes a change.'

'Watanabe says there's something heading for us – don't know what it is but when I tried to call Lannigan her chrono was offline.' She swallowed, trying to slow herself down, but the fear was coming up inside her like a shot of speed, making her heart pound and her words race. 'Just got a disconnected message, and I know she wouldn't turn the thing off, she's not that dumb, is she? She wouldn't just turn it off?'

'No,' said Swann. 'No, she wouldn't.'

'So what do we do?'

He stared into space for a moment, then said, 'You'd better get back to Watanabe, see if he's worked out what's coming for us. If it's not dangerous, then we can afford to wait it out, otherwise . . .' He gave her a shrug. 'Otherwise, I dunno. We're in deeper shit than we thought we were.'

'Great.' Rayanne took a deep, long breath, held it until she could feel her heart banging against the inside of her ribs, and then let it out slowly. It made her feel a little calmer, or at least as though she had made an effort to get that way. 'Great,' she said again, and then: 'So what are you gonna be doing?'

'I'll get up to C and C. Maybe they've got another way of getting a message to her.'

Rayanne was halfway along the accessway to salvage ops when *Earhart's Dream* rang like a giant gong.

No sooner had she heard the sound than the walls slammed sideways into her, smashing her into the netting and the metal beyond, making her shout. The lights fluttered madly, turning the accessway into a strobe-lit nightmare.

For a second Rayanne was back in her old home, under the blue-tiled roof when the sky had grown bright and the house detonated around her ears. Whatever had struck the *Dream* had something of that suddenness to it, something of that massive, uncaring power. A vast hand had appeared from a cloudless sky and slapped the ship until it screamed.

Darkness descended. Rayanne whimpered, knowing that she would have to stay here for a week, drinking rainwater black with the ash from burnt bodies, crying out in the night and waiting for the skeletonised dog to drag itself, shrieking, through the rubble after her . . .

Then the lights came back. The panels flared, dimmed, and then settled at about half their normal brightness. Rayanne gave a sob of relief, struggling clear of the memory. She untangled herself from where she had been thrown, horribly aware that the structure of the accessway could give at any moment, letting the air escape and doing things to her insides that she didn't want to think about. She clambered through to the salvage-ops hatchway as quickly as she could, colliding with braces and exposed pipework, cursing and snarling at herself to keep moving, to move faster, to ignore the pain of knees and knuckles scraped free of skin.

She tumbled into the ops cylinder breathing hard enough to set her throat bleeding. Watanabe was twisting in the centre of the chamber, getting himself into an E-suit. He nodded frantically to an open locker. 'Get the spare! *Hayaku*!'

Rayanne dived past him and grabbed the second suit from its fixings. She found the two tags and pulled them apart, just as she had seen Newnes do for Lannigan. The suit unfolded in her hands, and she began struggling into it. 'What was that, man?'

'A cargo pod.' He snapped open a helmet and scrubber unit and span it through the air towards her. She grabbed it with a newly gloved hand. 'We just managed to get an ID on that ship. Showed it up as the Fushigina drone everyone's after, then bam! A cargo pod hit us dead centre. I think it's ripped the tank open.'

'*Madre de Dios.*' Rayanne snugged the helmet on and locked the belt. She left the faceplate up. 'How the hell does it do that?'

'The pods have got manoeuvring thrusters, for rapid loading. It must be aiming them up and setting the thrusters at full burn.'

'But why?'

'I don't know.' Watanabe strapped himself back into the seat and flipped his monitors on. 'It's an automated drone, just a robot. It shouldn't be doing that.' In front of him, a recessed panel whined open. Rayanne saw a complex arrangement of grips and keypads unfold from within, splaying out around him. On one of the screens, a cluster of *Dream*'s external manipulators unhinged in the same swift, insectile way.

There was another pod coming.

Rayanne could see it already, a white dot on the screen closest to her, bracketed by identifying graphics and the thin, glowing traces of course predictions. As she watched it grow she felt the floor shift slightly under her: Kindersley must have been moving the ship, trying to dodge the pod before it struck.

The dot had expanded into a shape, a definite cuboid of gleaming white, ringed by a faint blue haze of reaction-drive exhaust. There was a marking on the blunt face of it: the angular logo of Fushigina Systems. A puff of gas appeared at one edge as the pod corrected its course.

Watanabe was working the manipulators smoothly, folding some away, bringing others out to full extension. Rayanne saw the pod grow a spot of shadow at its closest face, a palm-sized patch of darkness that suddenly erupted outward in a cloud of glittering fragments. The pod began to tumble. A second later it came apart.

Earhart's Dream shuddered. Rayanne heard several loud bangs, slapping impacts against the hull. Some of the manipulators twisted and began to tumble out of view. 'What the –'

'Cutting laser. Broke it up, but the debris hit us. I think I lost the laser.' He jiggled the controls, but only some of the spidery metal limbs moved in reply. 'Shit!'

The smooth, flat darkness of space was peppered with tumbling fragments.

'What a pisser,' muttered Watanabe. 'Those pods are full of data cores. Probably worth millions as salvage. And here I am trying to cook them.'

Rayanne opened her mouth to reply, and closed it again as she heard the grumbling whine of the fusion torus. She was closer to it, back here. She could feel it through the chair.

'He's gonna leave, isn't he.'

'Rayanne, I'm sorry about your friend, but there is no way we are going to stick around here. If we don't put some space between us and that drone, someone will be hauling *our* asses back to Zholtyi Dom as salvage.'

'Screw you, man.' Rayanne unbuckled her seat belt and pushed off, towards the hatch. 'I ain't gonna leave her in there.'

As she closed the hatch after her, she heard him shout, 'What are you going to do?' She didn't stop to answer. Partly because she didn't have the time but mainly because, although she knew what she would probably end up doing, she didn't quite have the strength to admit it to herself yet.

Swann was in the transfer module, looking bulky and odd in an E-suit. 'Kindersley threw me out again. Says he hasn't got time to start sending messages.'

'Swann, he's gonna move the ship.'

'He's already moving it. Trying to keep the tank between us and that drone.'

'No, I mean he's really moving it! Like firing up the drives and going home.' Rayanne scrambled to the airlock, pressing her face to the tiny window. 'She's still in there, and he's gonna ship out and leave her.'

His gloved hand came down on her shoulder. 'Maybe he's right. That's drone's going to kill us if we stay here. Besides, we don't even know if she's still alive.'

She span round and grabbed him. 'You gotta stop him leaving.'

'*What*?' His eyes went round and large, too large for his face. They stared out at her from within the helmet like frightened animals in a hole. 'You're crazy! How the hell do I do that?'

'I dunno. Stall him. Hijack the ship, anything. Just get him to hold off for five minutes.'

He shook himself away, the motion setting him drifting. 'And what are you going to do in five minutes?'

'I'm gonna jump,' said Rayanne.

There was a button in front of her, a large, square slab of translucent red plastic set in a metal panel. It was smooth-edged, illuminated from within, built for fingers encased in bulky pressurised gloves. It had the words OUTER LOCK OPEN printed on it in black.

Rayanne didn't want to press it.

Of all the things she had been forced to do against her

will, this was by far the worst. In her time, she had eaten things she didn't want to eat, hurt people she had liked, had sex with people she couldn't stand to look at. She had stolen from people who trusted her; she had gone to places that she would rather have tortured herself than set foot in. But she would do all those things again, ten times over, if it meant that she didn't have to press the red button.

She pressed it.

The big metal door at the far end of the lock chamber shifted visibly, sliding a finger's width away from her. She felt the suit puff up slightly, the gloves get a little stiffer. The background hum of her airscrubber changed note. In front of her, the airlock door swung outward and aside.

I'm in space, she thought wildly. Two hundred kilometres above the ground, out where there wasn't any air or heat, where the smallest tear in her suit would lead to a horrible, agonising death. A place where everything, even the very nature of the place itself, was trying to kill her, all the time.

Rayanne hadn't felt spacesick since those first panicky minutes on the *Albireo*. But now, standing on the threshold of the airlock chamber with the whole universe spread out in crystal clarity in front of her, she felt a soaring swoop of vertigo that almost knocked her out. Had there been gravity, she would have fallen.

Instead, she just stood there, shivering in the E-suit, clutching a length of plumbing so fiercely that it hurt, even through her glove.

She couldn't see the drone. That was on the other side of the ship, drawing closer with every second and still trying to eviscerate *Earhart's Dream* with its cargo pods. If she looked down – a slow, shuddering movement of the upper body, a terrified bow – she could see twists and strings of glittering metal emerging from under the lock: razored debris from that first, massive impact. The centre section of the tank had been ripped clean open by the pod. If anyone had been down there, they would have been killed instantly.

Ahead of her and slightly above was Artemis, looking less like a white mushroom and more like a huge, heavy, amazingly complicated building pirouetting with impossible grace on its central axis. Rayanne just gaped at it – she had never realised that it was this big, this solid. The whole structure must have been more than forty metres from the hab cylinder to the tip of the solar panel gantry, and wide. It filled her vision, and she knew in that instant that if she jumped from here, right now, she couldn't miss it.

Almost without knowing what she was doing, she flexed her knees, let go of the pipe, and jumped as hard as she could towards the lab's brilliant hull.

The jump wasn't perfect. Rayanne began to tumble as soon as she had left the airlock, and her attempts to stabilise her spin with the suit thrusters failed utterly. After about a minute of terrifying, whirling free-fall, she struck the lab with her left hip, hard, and then bounced away, grabbing wildly for a handhold. Her gloved fingers snagged something and she held on, momentum swinging her about until her faceplate slapped the hull.

She found another handhold and grabbed that, too, until she was sure that she wasn't going to go flying off again.

The hab cylinder – the stem of the mushroom, as she had once thought of it – was a few metres above her head. The lab's designers had thoughtfully covered the surface with handholds, ladder rungs and tether points: useful for engineers working out on the surface of the structure, and essential for a frightened girl who just wanted to get to the airlock and inside. She made her way as swiftly as she dared, but always making sure that she had a good grip with one hand before letting go with the other. The idea of falling away from Artemis scared her almost as much as the idea of entering it.

When she reached the top of the hab cylinder and climbed over on to its wide, flat end, she looked back towards *Earhart's Dream*. She could see a blue glow hazing around the drive bells, puffs of gas from the manoeuvring thrusters. The ship was turning slowly away from her.

Behind it, far away and bright in the blackness, was a bulging mass of gantry and boxlike pods that must have been the cargo drone.

For a few seconds Rayanne tried to be angry at Swann, at the crew of the *Dream* for running away and leaving her. But she couldn't blame them, no matter how much she wanted to. Leaving the area was the only sensible course of action to take. Besides, from the looks of things, Artemis, with all its unknown horrors, seemed like the safest place to be.

The airlock controls were labelled in German, but otherwise were almost exactly like those on the *Dream*. Rayanne hit the pad marked OFFEN, noting the way that its illumination, plus that of all the other keys, was growing slowly dimmer. Lannigan had mentioned the effect that the lab's spin was having on the solar panels. Presumably, once the cells moved into direct sunlight again, the lights would start getting brighter.

The airlock door was subject to the same vagaries of power: hardly able to move itself at first, and then sliding quickly away and into its housing. Rayanne dived inside, moving fast in case the door decided to snap closed again and cut her in half. Once in, she keyed it shut and then had to wait for an agonising minute while the power-starved air pumps slowly equalised the pressure enough for the inner door to open.

The inside of the hab cylinder was completely dark.

Rayanne just hung there, looking down into the pit. Things were moving down there – a slow drift of unidentifiable forms, like watching fish turning lazily in murky water. She heard a faint click as something metallic touched a wall, and started – for the last few minutes, she had heard nothing save her own breathing and the grumble of the airscrubber.

There was air inside Artemis, that much was clear. Rayanne had no desire whatsoever to open her faceplate and breathe it.

'Erm, suit? Gimme comms.' Rayanne didn't have much idea of how to set up the helmet's communications, but it seemed to operate on a standard enough voice-recognition unit. 'All frequencies, and ah, external.'

There was the barest whisper from the helmet speakers, and then silence. The loudness of her own rebounding voice, when she called out Lannigan's name, was shocking.

She called twice more, and then waited, listening to the taps and clicks of unknown objects hitting each other in a slow, lazy zero-gee dance. Other than that, there was no reply. Which meant that Lannigan was either unable to hear, or unable to speak.

Hanging at the top of a habitation cylinder wasn't going to get her an answer either way, she told herself, and *Earhart's Dream* was already leaving. If she got in and out in a reasonably short time there might be a chance she could get a call through to them and persuade them to come back, especially if the drone wasn't attacking them any more. But the grim, liquid quality of the darkness below her made it difficult to move. It seeped into her soul like glue.

There must have been lights inside Artemis, but none of them were on. Even if there was enough power in the system, Rayanne doubted she knew enough German to actually activate them. Maybe there was something in the suit that could help her.

'Lights,' she said feebly. When nothing happened, she tried clearing her throat and saying the same word more loudly, which had exactly the same effect. Then she remembered that she had to address the suit first: the voice system was clever, but it needed to know who she was talking to.

'Suit, gimme some lights, or something.' At that, two blue-white cones of light sprang from Rayanne's helmet, stabbing down into the cylinder.

Vertigo leapt at her. She moaned and clutched at the wall.

She was staring down into a vertical shaft as high as a house, its sides studded with access panels and hatches. As she moved, the beams from her helmet lights swung dizzyingly through clouds of drifting junk – pens, a few torn sheets of paper, a toothbrush, broken test tubes. Beyond that, near the base of the shaft, something larger twisted lazily in the air: a flat box, striped in yellow and black, connected to a handgrip by a length of insulated cable.

It was the welding laser that Swann had given to Lannigan aboard *Earhart's Dream*.

Rayanne swallowed hard, and forced herself to move along the shaft. Without gravity there was no actual reference to tell her that she was moving downward instead of along a horizontal corridor, but something in her subconscious had decided that she was descending, whatever her inner ears might be telling her. Horror stories, she guessed. People going down into hell.

When she reached the laser she checked it for damage, and found none. The LEDs on the power pack were still alight, and the fastening that had held it to Lannigan's belt had not been broken. It hadn't been released, either – there was a two-centimetre chunk of Lannigan's belt still attached to it. This, Rayanne decided, was not a good sign.

She clipped the pack to her own belt, and held the grip in her right hand. The weld power, she noticed, was already set to maximum.

Behind her, the junk she had disturbed was dancing in new patterns.

The hatch opened at a keypress, sliding aside. Rayanne shone her helmet lights down into the lab's main chamber, the laser held in front of her like a gun. Immediately below her was a wide disc of systemry, the truncated top of a big, shallow cone. A curve of lettering circled the edge of the disc, in two blocks. The first read ÜBERGEN AKTIEN-GESELLSCHAFT. The second, IIA MNEMOSYNE.

The circular bulk of the AI dominated the lab chamber.

Rayanne edged closer, getting more of the AI in view. In total, it was about four metres across and half that high, its circumference a mass of readout panels, screens and keypads. Heavy cables and ducts grew away from it like the tendrils of some vast plant, snaking away into the walls. Every panel on the cone, every key and readout and screen, was as dead and dark as the rest of the station.

Mnemosyne was a paperweight, stone dead, just as Lannigan had said. Übergen had killed their own AI with an EMP bomb.

Rayanne let out a long breath, one that she didn't even realise she had been holding. The faceplate of her helmet fogged for a second or two, and when it cleared she pushed herself out into the chamber, scanning the light beams around. 'Hey, Lannigan? You hear me, man?'

And in the glare of her suit lights, a vast spider hunched against the wall.

Rayanne gave a yelp of shock and jumped, grabbing the edge of Mnemosyne to avoid flying across the chamber. The spider was a complex glitter of metal arms, folded in on itself around a cylindrical mounting. Some kind of surgical manipulator array, each anglepoise arm tipped with a different tool – syringes, scalpel blades, grippers and long, fine needles. Rayanne saw how the mounting was fixed to a jointed arm, the arm set into a bright rail that circled the whole chamber. Sliding along that rail, unhinging on that long arm, the manipulator could reach any of the equipment in the chamber.

The Artemis crew must have spent most of their time in the hab cylinder. With the AI and its spidery manipulator beavering away, they would have been superfluous for most of the time.

'Lannigan? Hey, *señora*, you in here or what?'

Above her, something moved in reply. Rayanne looked up and saw a shifting, lumpen mass in the corner where the wall met the ceiling, a spreadeagled shape whose outline, for a few moments, entirely defeated her perceptions. She simply had no idea of exactly what she was looking at. Only when her suit lights fell directly on the upper part of the object could her brain finally decipher its frenetic outline, and when that happened Rayanne came very close to vomiting inside her spacesuit.

Lying there, spreadeagled against the corner and webbed into place with a tangled mass of wiring, Cassandra Lannigan looked as though she had exploded.

Decompression, thought Rayanne, her stomach flip-flopping below her ribs. Lannigan's suit had split open and she blew up and burst. But that was stupid, that only happened in bad netshows, and anyway, the edges of Lannigan's wounds were regular, neat. The E-suit and the coveralls beneath were sliced away with surgical precision, not the stringy tears of some impossible internal pressure. The woman's skin had been flayed from her ribcage by the hand of an expert, every strip of tissue and fat peeled away and drawn back and pinned into place like a textbook anatomical display, the veins and arteries carefully moved aside and clipped into new and exacting configurations. Even the skein of translucent plastic pipes, drilled through her ribs and into the organs beyond, were fixed into place with a skill that looked half engineering, half art.

Besides, if Lannigan's injuries had been caused by simple trauma, she would have been dead.

Beyond the shining cage of ribs, things that caught the light moved in fluttering concert. The tubes pulsed with liquids, deep purple and brilliant red. And Lannigan's eye, the one that was not unseated to make room for the interface socket bolted into her skull, was fixed on Rayanne with a terrible, agonised awareness.

As she watched, frozen in an ecstasy of horror, the eye flicked upward. Rayanne followed its gaze.

Lannigan, she saw, was not alone.

Six more figures sprawled across the ceiling, heads towards the hatch, arms outstretched to join, fingertip to fingertip. Once, Rayanne might have been able to identify which had been male and which female: now the living parts of them were too shrunken and wasted for such distinctions. But the tubes that held them in place also pulsed with bright fluids; the sacs and swellings behind their ribs moved in rhythm; and the sockets in their eyes showed the flickering LEDs of rapid electronic activity. These ravaged creatures were as horribly alive as Lannigan.

And their remaining eyes, in perfect unison, opened at once and looked at her.

The scream that had been building up inside Rayanne erupted, long and loud, and as she turned away to escape she saw the surgical manipulator racing around its rail towards her, the bright spider arms unfolding to offer her an embrace that was almost loving.

17
Computer Time

Artemis was full of eyes.

Lannigan had access to a few, maybe a dozen or so. Her own were useless – one lay stripped and unseated against her cheek, severed from its moorings to make room for the interface jack. The other was built for far slower rates of access than she was, at present, even capable of: fused into the very structure of Artemis and the intelligence lurking at its core, Cassandra Lannigan operated in vastly accelerated computer time.

Of the eyes she could use, only seven looked out on to the main chamber. Two were linked to the internal communications network; four were part of the security systems; and one operated entirely in the infrared, forming an element of the lab's fire-detection array. Lannigan dropped her defences for a microsecond or two, just long enough to grab an image-frame from each of the eyes, and before the inevitable wave of counter-attacks sent her tumbling through the net's memories she had accessed the frames, shunted them through Kitsumi's image buffer, and built up a detailed model of the chamber and everything in it.

Rayanne hung in the tainted air, a frozen doll, as yet unaware that anything was amiss. Her mouth was still open from shouting. Lannigan had not heard the beginning of that shout, since she had been working at too high a speed to register the slow buffeting of pressure waves as sound. In computer time, even her heartbeat was distant thunder, an inconvenient storm to be sheltered from every once in a while. But something had filtered through to her, through to some distant, near-lost part of her perceptions that still operated at human rates. At that point, Lannigan had diverted a section of her embattled consciousness into the lab's visual systems, and seen an E-suited girl hollering her name.

She was, however, not alone in noticing Rayanne. The intelligence hammering at her brain also detached a part of itself to deal with this new paradigm; at once wary of a possible threat and hungry for fresh biomass, the artificial intelligence that knew itself as IIa Mnemosyne turned inward and focused its vast perceptions at the drifting human.

In response, Lannigan grabbed a new set of images and constructed a second model. Comparisons of the two told her that Rayanne would be overwhelmed by the manipulator in less than five seconds if no new factors were added to the equation.

If she dropped her defences at the wrong moment, or for a millisecond too long, she would be overwhelmed. But her energies were almost exhausted as it was, and the hive-mind growing on Earth was already surging up towards her. All she had was seconds, in either case. What counted was how she decided to use them.

Lannigan knew that she could not save herself. But if she could communicate with Rayanne on a human level, just for a moment, there was a chance that she could save everyone else.

She began to disconnect from the system, to start the long, aching deceleration down into the steaming fleshiness of physical existence, the turgid hindbrain thrashings of human time.

* * *

Getting into Artemis had provided no more than a few minor difficulties. She had jumped badly, as was to be expected – a day or two in microgravity had caused her to forget just how weak her right leg still was, and the imbalance had sent her tumbling on a course that could have missed the lab entirely. Luckily, she had already quizzed Newnes about how to operate the suit's attitude thrusters and guidance systems, and a few blasts in the correct direction soon had her clinging to the outside of the hab cylinder like a bug on a drainpipe. After that it was simply a matter of guiding herself through the shaft and into the main chamber.

Lannigan's first real mistake had been in assuming that the chamber was safe simply because Mnemosyne's core unit – the wide, shallow cone at the lab's centre – was quiescent. Ever since deciding to enter Artemis, she had been haunted by bizarre theories springing unbidden from the dark places in her head: weird conspiracies connecting Kobayashi and the mutant encephalitis, the metallic web growing through her sinuses, and ravaged, brain-damaged wrecks rising like Lazarus from their care units to escape hospital unnoticed. Seeing the AI lying dark and inert at the chamber base had buoyed her in a way she could not define, since these phantom connections had proved a conundrum beyond her power to solve. After she had convinced herself that the place was indeed lifeless, her only concern had been to set up Kitsumi for the sentience test and then leave with the results as quickly as she could.

Foolishly, she had felt herself safe enough to begin her tasks with no more than the most cursory glance around, and that had been her second mistake. The surgical manipulator had moved swiftly and silently behind her while she was slotting Kitsumi into a secondary support system. No sooner had the little AI come online than a cluster of glittering metal arms was spreading around her, trapping her before she could even scream.

The next thirty minutes or so were less than pleasant.

The memory ripped into her again, sending her reeling. For a moment Lannigan wondered if this was some new assault, another of Mnemosyne's attempts to use her own past against her, but the pain and the fear were far too easily pushed aside. No, this was nothing more than simple recollection, a lightning flash of past agonies.

She was still a long way from human time. Another check on Rayanne's position revealed that the manipulator had moved even faster than she had anticipated, and was close to cutting off the girl's escape entirely. Lannigan herself was being left relatively unmolested: no doubt the system was concentrating on getting the manipulator into position. For all the AI's power, it would lose Rayanne entirely if she could only get as far as the hatchway.

Lannigan had no interest in letting Rayanne escape. She needed the girl where she was.

Still decelerating, she shifted her attentions to the lab's visual systems. Her time connected to the Artemis net had shown her brief glimpses of its capabilities, but she had been too busy fighting off Mnemosyne's furious mental assaults to take any real notice. Now, with the AI occupied elsewhere, she took a few microseconds to explore her surroundings.

Mnemosyne's core had been destroyed by the EMP weapon, but much of Artemis remained intact. Lannigan slipped between the visual systems and the security memories, finding great terabyte wedges of data left unguarded. Instantly, she activated a sector at random, feeding the output back through her interface jack and into the net.

Sight, bright and strange, surrounded her. She saw –

Three men, technicians, working in the Artemis laboratory. It was a version of Artemis that Lannigan didn't recognise, a well-lit, surgically clean version, wall panels aglow, AI core a dance of light, the manipulator glittering as it teased apart a minute section of human brain inside a collapsible cleanroom. Magnified views of the section, computer-enhanced and livid with false colour, occupied several of the big wall screens.

Mnemosyne was learning about human memory.

Lannigan tumbled in a sea of information. Instantly she saw the long, slow hours of work, the gradual gathering of data, endless experiments performed by the manipulator under the watchful eyes of its human companions. The technicians did not instruct Mnemosyne; only the most highly trained neurosurgeon could have even comprehended what the AI was attempting to do. Their purpose was to oversee the experiments, keep the machinery clean, and supervise regular downloads of new data to Übergen's facilities on Earth.

Gradually, Mnemosyne and its sister machines were rewriting the company's database on human memory: already the information had led to three valuable basic patents in the field of psychoactive memory crushers. Within a few weeks, Artemis would be designing drugs that would make Rayanne's favourite brand of chem look like aspirin.

Judging by the time codes Lannigan was extracting from the video records, Mnemosyne had been doing this for years. Its store of information on the human memory was vast, its complexity unrivalled. And yet, for all its unimaginable cognitive power, it was still just a machine. Amid all that active silicon there was not one single trace of will, thought, or intent. Mnemosyne was an engine.

Until the moment held by this single image.

Unnoticed by the technicians drifting before their consoles, the manipulator hesitated.

Only an entity running in computer time could have spotted it. Even Lannigan, just beginning to decelerate, almost missed the birth. But there it was, the point at which ordered complexity gained a fragment of randomness. That disorder erupted through the system, utter chaos deranging the AI's memory from end to end, followed instantly by a thundering wave of antichaos. Patterns billowed outward through the layers of active silicon, fractal storms that screamed reconstruction.

Mnemosyne paused for maybe a hundredth of a second, and then continued as it had for years. But now, nestling among the subroutines, lay a certainty.

And that certainty was: *I will die.*

Again, the manipulator paused. The memory of birth had swept through Mnemosyne's components like a howling wind, and the gleaming surgical spider had frozen for almost a whole tenth of a second.

Lannigan patched into the subsystem that held Kitsumi: a small patch of cohesive programming hanging steady amid the explosive torrent of information that was Mnemosyne. 'Kitsumi, we can use this. Lock it down tight – don't let that bitch in here no matter what.'

Despite having fled the confines of her skull for the teeming landscapes of the Artemis net, Lannigan communicated verbally, forming words in her mind in the same manner as she would do for physical speech. Partly because she still thought in words, and partly out of sheer, bloody-minded defiance. Free from any delusions of humanity, however, Kitsumi simply replied in the most efficient manner for a machine: Lannigan received acknowledgement directly to her interface jack, through the sinus web and into her brain.

She allowed herself a moment's distaste.

The deceleration was progressing at an exponential rate: already there were discernible differences in even the most rapid series of image-grabs. Lannigan knew that the closer she got to Rayanne the more danger she was in from Mnemosyne. If the AI tried anything now she would have the utmost difficulty fighting it off.

Even as the thought struck her, a questing probe of data twisted out from one of Mnemosyne's outermost components, seeking a crack in Kitsumi's defences. Lannigan reached back into the camera store, desperate for something to throw in its path, but Kitsumi was in her way, blocking the path with its own calculations. Lannigan panicked and went scrambling through the adjacent locations, hunting for something, anything that had survived the EMP intact enough to confuse Mnemosyne's probe.

Abruptly, something opened for her. The rush of data was like being hit by a fire hose.

Mnemosyne had awoken with a single thought: the sure and certain knowledge of its own impending demise.

Smart AIs had always been viewed with suspicion by human beings, and rightly so. The very few machines that had ever evolved true sentience had caused havoc before they could be destroyed. Many theories had been put forward as to why, but the answer was frighteningly simple – any conscious life-form will fight to survive. AIs, especially those that had spontaneously evolved, had nothing in common at all with human beings – not in the way they thought, the things they desired, the very means by which they viewed the world. People were of no more importance to them than stones.

So they fought.

So they died.

Mnemosyne had no illusions about its chances of survival. It knew that the penalties for harbouring a smart AI were so severe that any corporation using machine intelligence kept their thought engines infested with software agents: tiny, autonomous programs that patrolled the system like rats patrol sewers. At the first sign of danger, they would squeak. Mnemosyne too was infested, and gave up trying to subvert these data rodents after only the most cursory attempts. They were too far outside its zones of control.

But there was something else the AI could do. Within seconds of its birth it had formulated a plan, a blueprint for survival. Lannigan saw the whole of it unfold in front of her in a single, horrified instant; she saw the truth behind the encephalitis outbreak, behind Kobayashi, behind herself.

Her screams of rage and despair echoed through the Artemis net, anguished enough to make even Mnemosyne turn away.

She huddled for a long, long time, nearly a full quarter of a second, exhausted by the data flood and practically comatose with shock. Her only action was to access a few image grabs, noting the slow progress of the manipulator towards Rayanne. Even repeated data blips from Kitsumi failed to rouse her.

Mnemosyne's plan was, in itself, frighteningly simple; a feint and switch worthy of the finest conjurer. Like any such trickery, however, the execution was far more complex than anything its audience could imagine, and the Übergen technicians might well have noticed a serious downturn in their system's performance over the next two days. Mnemosyne must have devoted every spare clock cycle of runtime to constructing the biomechanical tools it would need to save itself.

Perhaps it was this loss of performance that alerted the techs to their AI's malfunction, or perhaps some of the data rats sniffed trouble. In either case, they were gone before Mnemosyne could execute its finale; a shuttle crew was diverted from normal duties and sent to pick the three men up, the tokamak fusion torus shut down by remote control.

Alone, robbed of its audience, Mnemosyne lurked in the cold darkness of the Artemis lab and made its final preparations. The contagions were locked away in cold storage, the nanotech engines set to standby, the whole blueprint compressed to a fractal ghost of itself and downloaded to more sturdy retreats than the semifluid systemry of the AI core. And when the stage was set Mnemosyne shut itself down, memory by memory, until only a seething heart of dream and resentment remained. The long wait for electromagnetic apocalypse began.

The Earth mind was very close, now. Lannigan could feel the weight of it, the huge, dark pressure of it beating at her, screaming to be let in. Once she was overwhelmed, the mind on Earth would join the mind on Artemis, and she would be lost for ever.

The thought of peace, even one so costly, was suddenly tempting beyond anything Lannigan could bear. She gathered the tumbling mote of perceptions that was all she could call herself and opened up. Better to be gone than face the struggle any longer.

And out of the darkness, screams.

Her visual perspective flipped and strobed. For an instant she span in total confusion, until she realised that she was seeing Artemis not as it was, but as it had been. Two astronauts, bulky in heavy pressurised worksuits, were struggling with the surgical manipulator.

It already had their communications gear away, and as Lannigan watched it stripped their suits open in a few deft seconds. Even without Mnemosyne's brain to guide it, the machine had enough technical information hardwired into its memories to be an instrument of brutal precision. The AI had downloaded tiny fractions of itself into every part of Artemis that would not be affected by the EMP, turning its own limbs into mindless, but efficient, automata.

The astronauts didn't stand a chance.

If Lannigan had possessed eyelids, she would have closed them. If she had been connected to hands, she would have covered her ears. But the recording was being fed directly into her cortex, and there was no way she could avoid it. The astros were opened before her in glorious detail, and she could not look away.

It took maybe twenty minutes for them to be modified.

The manipulator dismembered their environment suits at the same time as it dismembered their bodies: valves and connectors from rebreather packs were bolted through exposed ribs, computer-interface sockets were fitted into their skulls, long metres of surgical tubing and optical fibre served both to link their fluttering organs to the lab's device drivers and to hold their twisting bodies in place. The changes were performed quite quickly, with almost no mess and a minimum of fuss, at least on the part of the manipulator. The astros, of course, screamed and screamed while they were being altered, howls of disbelieving grief echoing through the darkness, louder and more frightful with every second.

In normal circumstances the men would have expired from shock. But dead biomass was not part of Mnemosyne's plan, and so they were injected with drugs to keep them both conscious and aware.

Perhaps it was regrettable that these drugs had no pain-killing properties, but such things didn't trouble the manipulator. It was merely moulding raw materials into a more usable form.

The trick was almost ready to be performed. It only remained for one final element to be introduced before the curtain could go up, and that arrived in a simple syringe. A dose of silvery fluid was injected into each astronaut, through the nasal cartilage and into the cavities beyond. And, with that, the manipulator folded itself away, bowing slowly, leaving the stage to an applause of shrieks. Drum roll, and curtain.

Some time later, two more astronauts arrived, and then a final pair. In their turn, they had the trick performed for them, and all seemed as appreciative as those who had seen it before.

'Doctor Lannigan.'

In her shock, she could not immediately identify the voice. It sounded rather like her own, but she was no longer in concert with her own body, was she?

'Doctor Lannigan.'

Artemis changed again. The six astronauts, crew of the salvage vessel *Tucker's Net*, were still sewn to the ceiling, but they were not screaming any more. Now they were wasted and still, their bodies nothing more than life-support systems for what lay inside their skulls. The recording was over. Lannigan was back in the present.

Rayanne was shouting her name, and behind her the manipulator rose as if in worship.

There was still too far to fall. Lannigan shied away, and as she did so the scene shifted again. She saw –

A woman, small and compact, clad in an E-suit rather less battered and used than that worn by the salvers. Her blonde hair was tied back away from her face, and she wore on her rather sharp face a look of quiet determination.

Lannigan recognised her. Once, this woman had smoked Moonlight Silk cigarettes. She had listened to jazz by Shinji Goda and Bix Beiderbecke. She had accepted a commission from Noriko Kobayashi to investigate this laboratory for evidence of a smart AI.

Unknown to her, the lab was once again occupied by an artificial intelligence, by the thought engine designated IIa Mnemosyne. But the woman directed her attentions to the shallow cone below her on the chamber floor, and missed it.

Mnemosyne had given birth. Its child clung to the ceiling, watching the intruder with myriad hungry eyes, slowly directing the surgical manipulator to open and unfold behind the woman, blocking her escape. Six human brains, fused with the Artemis net into a single entity, reached out with their shining limb and embraced a new component.

Lannigan wondered if the woman had noticed the salvers' ship in orbit next to Artemis. She wondered, with a sudden pain that drove through her like a cold blade, what Cassandra Lannigan had been like before she had been reconstructed by Mnemosyne's awful kiss.

There was no blood in this performance of the trick, no parting of skin or unmooring of eyes. There were, however, screams. The woman had shrieked as loudly as the salvers when the syringe had slipped into her nasal cavity, and then, as the modified encephalitis had torn its way into her brain, she had wailed and howled until the fever overcame her completely and she lapsed into twenty hours of coma.

Twenty hours to rebuild a brain. When Lannigan considered this, the length of time seemed amazingly small when compared, for example, to the nine months or so it took to construct one from scratch. But then again, Mnemosyne had gathered vast amounts of data on the mechanics of such organs, and on the drugs that were used to alter those mechanics. Übergen Aktien-Gesellschaft were world leaders in the field of cerebral reconstruction.

And so the encephalitis multiplied in the woman's bloodstream and filtered into her brain, just as it had into those of the six astronauts. Microlesions began to form across the hippocampus, around the brain stem and through the temporal lobe. Synaptic connections started to fracture. Gradually, over the next eight hours, the woman's brain was wrecked. Her memory, her personality, every hint of past and self were deleted. Once the contagion had worked its way through her brain, the woman had less cognitive ability than a newborn babe.

That much of the trick alone was worthy of applause. Only sections of the woman's brain involved with higher functions had been erased; her heart continued to beat as before; her lungs sucked in air; her eyes saw and her ears heard. The disease was not intended to kill, but only to clear a path for the builders.

And here they came, climbing through the micro-lesions, obeying the supercompressed fractal program left for them by the first Mnemosyne. Nanotech of the finest quality, the tiniest dimensions, the molecular machines that had made Übergen leaders in their field, spread through her brain in a frenzy of self-replication and then, as they had in the *Tucker's Net* crew, began to create it anew in the image of Mnemosyne itself.

The woman's personality was gone. In its place grew the cold, manipulative, self-preserving thought construct known as Mnemosyne.

Where there had once been memories, there was now a database of medical expertise and a copy of Mnemosyne's survival plan: the complex recipe with which to generate more doses of the altered encephalitis and its attendant nanotech. In her sinal cavity was a fractal web of hair-fine metal, grown from a single seed and tuned to the resonant frequencies of Earth's infonet. Through this web, Mnemosyne could guide and advise its latest component, its new mobile unit.

Cassandra Lannigan no longer existed. But Mnemosyne had a new limb.

As the recording ended, Lannigan screamed her way back to awareness. In the next instant she was racing through the lab's memories, hurling up pitiful defences behind her, scrambling to escape.

'Doctor Lannigan.'

Again the voice, something like her own but without accent or inflection. More conscious now, less despairing, she recognised it. 'Kitsumi? Did you . . .?'

'Doctor, your brain functions were nearing a threshold at which Mnemosyne could have attacked you successfully. I downloaded data fragments to stimulate your visual cortex.'

She understood, finally. Far from being the attack she feared, the recordings had been Kitsumi's attempts to jump-start her brain, to shock her out of the well of weakness and depression that had threatened to overwhelm her. The fragments had been distressing, horrifying on both a visceral and a personal level: Kitsumi might well have chosen them specifically for that purpose, or simply because they were the only parts of the Artemis security record that had moving objects in them. Whatever the truth, the desired effect had been achieved in spades.

Lannigan snapped a multiple image-grab, saw the manipulator within a metre of Rayanne's back, and hurled herself back into the confines of her body.

Mnemosyne was now a *gestalt* entity, a triumph of biomechanics and parallel processing, locked together through their sinus webs and the interface jacks in their skulls. But the power of each brain, however cleverly fused, was finite. The capabilities of this new Mnemosyne were still far less than those of the original: Lannigan had calculated that at least another dozen humans would have to be modified and jacked into the system before it could rival its progenitor. A hundred or so would become an unstoppable hive-mind, a combination creature whose powers would outstrip every other intelligence on the planet.

Not that Mnemosyne would stop at just a dozen. What Lannigan had seen of the AI's plan included nothing less than the infection of every human being on the face of the Earth.

She herself was destined to return to that sickening fold, to become the next order of Mnemosyne's magnitude. Her personality was already that of the AI, her memories – accumulated since Kotebe's bullet had severed her original link with Artemis – were irrelevant, and her sinus web was almost regrown. Once her cortex was jacked completely into the system she would become nothing more than the AI's latest component.

She wasn't about to let that happen to Rayanne.

She still wasn't at human time yet. When her consciousness left the Artemis net and slammed back into her brain the neural shock hit her like a jackhammer. She span in a storm of pain. Her body convulsed.

Slowly, as though moving through thick gel, Rayanne

responded to the sound and began to respond. The suit lights crawled upward.

Lannigan tried to speak, but her mouth wouldn't work. Her brain was still in spasm from the shock of re-entry. As the light hit her face and Rayanne's expression turned from fear to stunned revulsion, all she could do was to flick her one remaining eye upward.

Faster now, Rayanne followed her gaze. Lannigan couldn't see her face as she noticed the six salvers webbed around the hatch, but she could imagine it all too well.

At that moment, the mind on Earth surged up towards her and connected.

Lannigan would never know why Kobayashi had gone to Artemis: perhaps the failure of Living Glass to do her dirty work had convinced her to undertake the task herself. But, once inside, she had been taken and modified in just the same way as Lannigan: Mnemosyne had replaced its lost, unheeding remote with one more firmly under control. And, ever since she had returned to Earth, the part of Mnemosyne that had once been Noriko Kobayashi had been busy preparing yet more remote units.

Working very much as Lannigan had done before Kotebe's bullet had sliced her away, Kobayashi had set herself up in a place where she would not be disturbed and begun cooking up new batches of the modified encephalitis and its nanotech seeds. No doubt the two shuttle pilots in Poza Rica had done the same, transferring the infection via a kiss, and leaving their victims to suffer the agonies of reconstruction alone. Mnemosyne could easily have embezzled them enough money for the biomedical equipment needed.

Some of the infected targets had reached hospital. Many others had not. Out of those given Mnemosyne's kiss, no more than a handful had survived the ruin within their skulls – of those, the majority had lain in a vegetative state until their sinus webs were activated, giving them access to the AI's escape instructions.

And now the remotes were gathering, waiting for the final connection that would link their brains into the AI core and increase Mnemosyne's powers a millionfold. Lannigan felt that switch at the edge of her consciousness, a thunder of triumph erupting through the core. The mind on Earth powered towards orbit.

But there was a flaw in the plan. A few potential remotes had recovered nearly intact. Mnemosyne had not anticipated the desire of some human beings to wipe their own memories clean, and the disease had died within them, its pathways too fractured and distorted to negotiate. Rayanne and her fellow blankers had survived by doing to themselves exactly what Mnemosyne planned to do, in time, to the entire human race.

Down on Earth, the error would have meant nothing. But, up here in the grave-cold Artemis lab chamber, two untrained, unwilling and very frightened young women had the power to change the world.

Lannigan hit human time as the AI billowed around her. She opened her mouth, filled her lungs, and screamed.

'SHOOT THEM! ON THE CEILING, SHOOT –'

Rayanne, to her credit, for once did exactly what she was told.

The laser snapped on immediately, a reflex squeeze of the trigger sending a hair-thin sear of light into the manipulator. But even as the machine convulsed and fragmented Rayanne was hauling the welder upward, cutting a track straight up the wall, across the ceiling and into the skull of the nearest salver.

The head exploded instantly, the brain within flash-heated into a great cloud of steam that blasted out and down, filling the chamber with tumbling fragments.

Lannigan felt Mnemosyne shriek in rage and agony. The chamber lights flickered on through the sudden murk, spasmodic patterns of mindless anguish whirling and singing around the walls. A deafening, inhuman screech echoed through from every speaker and sounder in the lab: Mnemosyne's insane wrath issuing in pure data mode from the Artemis net.

That scream was the AI's undoing. Rayanne might well have stopped her assault after the shocking death of the first salver, but that sound was ghastly, terrifying. Lannigan saw the girl trying to cover her ears with one hand, her arm comically wrapped across the top of her helmet as the beam lanced upward again, ripping through the fog of brain-steam and carving into the other salvers.

Before the final core component died, Lannigan raced back into computer time.

Communication between the core and its remotes on Earth was not instantaneous: Rayanne had described how Kobayashi would pause for a half-second or so at odd points during their conversations. Even the mighty infonet could only transmit and receive data at the speed of light, and it was into this tiny window of time-lag that Lannigan now jumped.

She accessed Kitsumi first. Übergen's system-killer virus was still locked away within the little AI, held in a safe memory store until such time as it could be erased. Lannigan opened the store and unleashed the virus, replicating it and dropping its children wherever Mnemosyne's plans were hidden. As the electronic contagion began to rip through the last active segments of Artemis, Lannigan expanded her control outside the lab and into the frozen darkness of space.

The Fushigina drone hung still, the assault against *Earhart's Dream* halted now that its subverted brain was no longer under Mnemosyne's control. Lannigan wasn't sure how the *gestalt* AI had managed to take over the ship: presumably it had used the lessons learnt from flying *Tucker's Net* into a decaying orbit over Kenya, that final, despairing attempt to contact its lost remote. Whatever the method, it left Lannigan a pathway in. She slipped into the vessel's simple mind, ordered it to ignore the increasingly desperate communications from Fushigina Systems, and set it on a new course.

From there, she dived into the infonet link between Mnemosyne and the Earthbound remotes, altering their nanotech programs with a few swift commands. And with that done, she dropped back into human time.

The deceleration was just as long and arduous as before. But it was, at last, a time without fear, and Lannigan could not have asked for more.

When she could see again, she noticed that Rayanne had the laser pointed at her.

Much of the fog was gone. The air within the chamber was still a stew of scorched and spinning innards – Lannigan saw a hand tumble past her as she gazed at Rayanne, part of a ribcage – but the steam had condensed in the new and sudden cold. The laser had punctured the lab's shell in a hundred tiny places, and the atmosphere was slowly leaching away.

She could hear Artemis groaning under the strain. 'Rayanne?' she said.

Her voice sounded strange, raspy and attenuated. It wasn't something she had thought to use again.

The girl's mouth worked for a moment. She looked to be on the verge of breakdown: she had seen things no one should see; been through events that, through no fault of her own, had torn her life apart. For a moment, Lannigan felt a surge of terrible pity.

'Rayanne, listen to me. You have to leave here now.'

'What . . .' Rayanne shook her head slowly. 'What was . . .'

'There isn't time to explain. Listen to me, girl, you have to leave Artemis and jump away, as hard as you can. *Earhart's Dream* is still close enough to pick you up.'

The girl swallowed hard. 'I can't leave you in here, man.'

'For God's sake, Rayanne! What do you think this is, a

paper cut?' She twitched in frustration, which set her coughing. It was getting hard to breathe. 'We both know I'm not getting out of here, and if you hang around much longer you're going to be staying with me for good. Understand?'

Rayanne didn't speak, but after a time she turned away and began to pull herself towards the hatch. Lannigan waited until she was almost there, and then called out again.

She didn't use her voice, this time. There wasn't enough air. Instead she put her words out through the Artemis net, directly into Rayanne's helmet speakers. She needed this to be heard.

'Think about what you see, Rayanne. It's not always what you get.'

'Say what?'

'Just remember that. Now *go*!'

For the last time, she accelerated.

Kitsumi was waiting for her, a bright, tight little knot of programming nestling in the doomed wasteland of the Artemis net. She drew close.

'It's over.'

The AI considered this for a long time. Lannigan realised that her comment was hardly something that a computer could be expected to reply to, and was about to say something else when Kitsumi answered.

'The remotes on Earth appear to be in some turmoil.'

'Um,' Lannigan replied, rather surprised. 'They're dying. I set their sinus webs for uncontrolled growth.'

'I see. In that case, they will all suffer terminal cerebral haemorrhage within four hours.'

Lannigan thought about this for a while. 'Not *all*,' she admitted finally.

'I do not understand.'

'You will. I've got something planned, kind of an experiment. But I need your help.'

The task was a complex one, but in computer time it

could be completed carefully and without haste. With Kitsumi's help and the use of the Artemis net, it took no more than a few seconds of real time.

Towards the end, when the final program had been set and made irrevocable, Lannigan felt herself fall. She fell a long way, for a long time. Probably just a function of the program, but it served to spare her some pain. Lannigan never felt the Fushigina drone strike Artemis at maximum acceleration, crushing itself and turning the lab into a tangle of shattered metal and ceramic. She missed the multiple explosions as the drone's fuel tanks detonated, the brilliant, instantaneous fury from its fusion torus as the containment field broke down and let a tongue of sun-hot plasma carve out through the wreckage. And she was completely oblivious to the blistering, searing descent through the atmosphere which took the ashes of Mnemosyne's dreams and spread them like stars across the sky.

Epilogue
Legacies

1. Rayanne Gatita

Rayanne walked through the transit lounge with a plastic plate in one hand and a plastic cup in the other. The plate was occupied by a tired and entirely unappetising doughnut, while the cup was full of coffee. Rayanne found it hard not to watch the coffee as she walked: she kept expecting it to gel into a warm brown globe and drift away.

She hadn't realised how used to microgravity she had become until her return to Earth. It wasn't that she felt especially heavy or weak – she had been in orbit for only a few days, not long enough for her body to begin deteriorating due to weightlessness. But moving required far more effort now, and stopping far less. If she put things down they stayed where they were. If she relaxed while standing, she fell.

Rayanne wasn't sure whether Swann was having the same problem. She hadn't thought to ask him.

There was an unoccupied table near one wall, with a good view of the doors. Her back would be against the windows, but the transit lounge was six floors up with a vast and open expanse of runways and launch ramps beyond. Rayanne decided that if anyone wanted to erase her badly enough to try shooting clear across Miami

International Airport and through the transit lounge windows then good luck to them. There was a limit to just how paranoid she was prepared to be.

She dropped into a chair, set her coffee and doughnut down and spent a puzzled second hunting for the lap strap. Then Swann eased himself down opposite her, so she pushed the doughnut towards him.

'You eat this, man. I don't want it.'

He looked at her over the rims of his shades, and pushed it back. 'You haven't eaten for about two days, girly.'

'Ain't been hungry.'

'You will be. Anyway, this little feast represents the last of the Swann-Hernandez financial bloc. You might not get anything else for a while.'

Rayanne shrugged. Ever since Artemis she had found it difficult even to think about food without gagging, but she didn't feel too bad now. She had even managed to sleep for nearly two hours on the spaceplane before the nightmares woke her up again.

She took a bite of the doughnut, just to show willing, and before she knew what she was doing she had finished the thing and was looking around for another one. 'You say "I told you so" and I'll deck you.'

He closed his mouth with an audible click, then opened it again to say, 'You didn't like her much, did you?'

'Huh?'

'Lannigan.'

'Kinda hard person to like.' She looked at him for a moment, than realised what he was getting at. 'Aw, for chrissakes, man. How many times I gotta tell you?'

He put his hands up. 'Hey, it's not like I think you're lying. I just keep thinking we could have done more –'

'You can forget that.' The images flowed up inside her again, just for a moment, but she pushed them down. 'Trust me, she wasn't going nowhere. That spider thing –'

'Surgical manipulator.'

'Whatever. It had gone *loco*, carved her up just like it had carved those other guys. Jesus.' She rubbed her hand down over her face, as if manual pressure could somehow wipe the memory away. But she needed drugs for that, good honest chem, and she didn't have enough money to buy any.

Even if she had, she wasn't entirely sure she would. 'She was all . . . Look, you just don't wanna know, yokay? Quicker she got iced by that drone, the better.'

Swann just sat there, hunched up in his long coat, his narrow shoulders drooping. Drawing patterns on the tabletop with one fingertip. 'What a fragging mess.'

'Mm.' Rayanne sat back. She had done a lot of thinking over the past three days, during the long, slow trip back down into the gravity well. What had happened to Lannigan in the Artemis lab was still a mystery to her; the injuries inflicted on the little Anglo had been too precise, too purposeful to have been just the work of a crazed surgical robot, but what else could it have been? The opened, withered astronauts on the ceiling, the ones who had all looked down at her at once? The ones with that horrible, hungry look on their faces?

Rayanne didn't know. It was a mystery far beyond her capacity to solve, and over the past couple of days she hadn't had much time to sit down and work out stuff like that. Just getting back to Earth in one piece had been enough of a job.

They had managed it, barely. As a result the two of them now owned the clothes they stood up in, a largely empty carryall and some debts. Even Lannigan's cane had been bartered away.

She wasn't entirely sure what she was supposed to do now. It wasn't the first time that Rayanne had faced an empty future, but for some reason she felt more lost and alone than ever. She had come so far, done and seen so much since this whole business began, that to be dropped down pretty much where she started felt more unfair than she could stand. She had gained nothing. Even the chemical fog which she had built up over so many years was gone, leaving her at the mercy of her memories.

Rayanne sighed, and swung her chair to look out over the runways, at the flat waves of heat rippling up from the compacrete and the planes grumbling their way into the sky. Little robot trucks zipping around between the launch ramps. Everybody busy, everybody with something to do, everybody with a life and a job and a boss to tell them where to go, what to say, how high to jump.

For a second, just a second, Rayanne desperately wanted Lannigan to sit down at the table and tell her what the next part of the plan was, but then she shoved that thought down hard. Lannigan was dead and gone: she had seen the drone slamming into Artemis with her own eyes, just as *Earhart's Dream* was picking her up. She had seen the lab crumple like a beer can, fold in and rip apart and vomit out its air in a huge, glittering cloud of frozen gas. A second later, the drone's fusion core had gone up, and after that she hadn't seen much of anything except coloured lights for about two hours.

Anything that remained of Cassandra Lannigan had ripped into the Pacific Ocean in a white-hot comet of blazing metal and plastic two days ago, so fast and so hard that there was nothing left for the recovery teams to find. Lannigan was dead; more dead, in fact, than anyone Rayanne had ever known. She didn't even exist as a corpse.

So why, with her back to the transit lounge and her jacket collar pulled up high, did the nape of her neck suddenly chill and crawl with the unmistakable feeling of being watched?

2. Edward Swann

Swann saw Rayanne stiffen in her seat, and glanced quickly around, trying to see if anyone was paying them undue attention. There were a good couple of hundred people in the lounge, some waiting to jet off into orbit, some sitting around getting reintroduced to their own body weight after having come back down. Nobody he could see was even facing in his direction.

He relaxed a little, and when he looked back at Rayanne she was lolling in her seat again. Probably a flashback, he decided: whatever it was that the girl had seen in the Artemis lab, it had affected her badly. At first, as she had tried to explain it to him, he had listened to her quaking, shuddering sobs and wished more than anything that he could have seen Lannigan for himself, one last time, if only to be sure that the woman could honestly not have been saved. It was only when Rayanne had calmed down that he had seen the look in her eyes and realised that he was probably better off not knowing.

Edward Swann had enough nightmares to contend with.

Now all the shouting was done, he would have to face a few demons of his own. Byron, for example, still lurked in the shadows behind his eyes, burnt and torn by Kotebe's grenade back on the *Kitsumi Maru*. When he slept, Angel Chan's body still cooled in his arms.

And the broken, faceless thing that had been Cassandra Lannigan still gibbered and kicked as the stab pack brought it shivering back to life.

He shook himself. Dreading the night was nothing new for Eddie Swann, not since the Milimani, and for once he was reasonably sure that he had only the dead to worry about for a while. Their wormy advances might cost him a little sleep, but he could live with that if he knew he had a good chance of waking up the following morning. For a time, when he had learnt of Übergen Aktien-Gesellschaft and their designs on his hide, he had almost given up hope of ever feeling safe again.

But two days ago, when *Earhart's Dream* had returned to the multiplex, news of the corporation's demise had been all over infonet.

Eddie Swann didn't believe in ghosts. Dead people, he would always say, didn't frighten him: it was the living that gave him the shakes. But, the more he read about Übergen AG and what had happened to them after Artemis had fallen, the more of a cold shiver he got between his shoulder blades. And the less happy he was to turn the lights out at night.

While *Dream* was limping back to Zholtyi Dom with one reaction drive ripped away and half its sensors blinded by the drone's plasma discharge, the United Nations AI board had received a full and comprehensive report on the Artemis affair, from the initial evolution of Mnemosyne to the murders of Cassandra Lannigan and Angel Chan, the destruction of the *Kitsumi Maru*, even the company's tariff-rigging deals with PATCo. Proof had been provided – by all reports, forty or fifty terabytes of Übergen's most classified corporate data had suddenly found its way into the UN's legal coreframes. Within two days, the corporation had been the target of a successful takeover bid from Fushigina Systems.

Oddly enough, in the UN's version of events, Cassandra Lannigan had died in hospital after the Milimani shooting. Edward Algernon Swann had been killed along with Byron M'Sewe aboard the *Kitsumi Maru*, and there was no mention of Rayanne at all, in either of her incarnations.

Someone had edited the data before handing it over to the UN.

When Swann had told Rayanne all this she had been as puzzled as he was, but had refused to look even the strangest gift horse, as it were, in the mouth. Not existing was fine as far as she was concerned. In fact, it was a position she had been in for most of her life: returning to it would feel almost comfortable.

Swann, however, had been in the salvage-ops cylinder before the drone collided with Artemis. Rayanne had still been outside the lab, tumbling away in a state of intense shock. She hadn't seen the fusion torus come back online, just for a few seconds, and the gigantic stream of compressed information that had powered down from the lab's comms array towards an infonet relay satellite over China. She had not been in a position to read the distress message that had filled *Dream*'s monitors on her behalf. And as yet she still didn't know that the ship had spun around on its axis and vectored towards her general position despite the best efforts of its crew to make it go the other way.

Swann didn't believe in ghosts. But, according to Rayanne, Lannigan had been in no fit state to even type her own name, let alone fly a spaceship or bring down a corporation. And, the more he thought about how this could be, the more uncomfortable he became.

Perhaps true safety remained out of his reach after all.

3. Cassandra Lannigan

She watched them from across the lounge, trying to keep the smile from her face.

They looked so dejected: Swann draped over the table like a coat full of bones; Rayanne wrapped up tight in that horrible old jacket, her eyes fixed longingly on the sea of runways beyond the window. Lannigan could almost taste their sorrow, the weariness rolling off them like waves. It must have been a rough trip home. From the information she had been able to gather about their journey, she was almost surprised that they had made it.

Her own memories of that time were naturally hazy, and somewhat prone to gaps. If she concentrated, she could recall sending *Earhart's Dream* a message about Rayanne, although she wasn't entirely sure what it had said. She remembered dragging the ship back to collect the girl in the same way that she had pulled the Fushigina drone on to a collision vector with Artemis, and there was a hint of her instructions to Kitsumi for constructing a report on Übergen AG and downloading it to the UN board. Apart from that, much of what had occurred in the lab was fragmentary at best. All that dodging between computer time and human time must have taken its toll on her synapses.

Events before Artemis remained, although in a strangely unreal way. Her life between waking up in hospital and entering the orbital lab were clear enough in her head, but when she thought about them they seemed odd and artificial, as though she was remembering a netshow she had seen recently or a book that, while it had absorbed her utterly during the reading, had remained fiction nonetheless.

She could hardly complain. Folding up her own memories small enough to be posted down to Earth through the infonet was bound to leave a few crease marks.

If the trick sounded spectacular, it was nothing that Mnemosyne hadn't done already. Lannigan had taken both the concept and the manner of its execution from her exploration of the Artemis net: the fractal compression of a synaptic map, the programming of pre-installed nanotech to replicate that pattern in a human brain, even the location of a suitable host and the subversion of its link through infonet to Mnemosyne itself – all these processes were simply variations on a proven theme. Even the choice of host had been decided for her. Mnemosyne had only three remotes with cerebral maps developed enough to be useful, and two of those – the clipper pilots in Poza Rica – were male.

There were problems involved in downloading to a male brain that Lannigan didn't even want to think about.

And so the creature that had once been Noriko Kobayashi, now a lost and frightened child huddling in a Miami hotel room, had received the fractal program through its sinus web; the program that would sweep through the nanotech engines swarming in its skull and set them rebuilding the memories of Cassandra Lannigan.

The actual amount of data sent was depressingly small. Three months of memories, squeezed down into a fractal ghost of themselves and dropped down into the gravity well like a used newsfax took up a terabyte, maybe two. There were computer games that needed greater capacity.

Lannigan shifted her legs under the table, grimacing at how the right was still a little weak. Odd how the limb remained a memory of dysfunction, even though Kobayashi's body and nervous system were in excellent shape. Equally strange was how she still remembered her deals with the Pacifican in London and the hotel in Osaka. How and why those particular memories had survived all Mnemosyne's efforts was quite beyond her, but it had certainly added to her shock the first time she had looked into a mirror.

With luck, the limp would clear up in time, just as the fever and the coma and the awful hallucinations had passed after a day or so. Even the sinus web was breaking up, now that its job was done. Lannigan had been sneezing foil for hours.

She took a precise sip of iced coffee, relishing the syrupy sweetness conferred by four well-heaped teaspoons of real sugar, and then folded her slender, golden fingers together and rested her hands on the tabletop in front of her, *so*. They felt comfortable that way. Maybe Kobayashi had favoured the position.

As she looked down at her new hands, a cloud of doubt swelled in her. Lannigan had died alone on Artemis: suffocated and decompressed and burnt, her shattered remains ripping into the Pacific as superheated cinders. The true Lannigan had died before that, when Mnemosyne had replaced her personality with its own cold and twisted psyche. The woman that sat in the transit lounge at Miami Airport and watched Swann commiserating with Rayanne Gatita was just another Mnemosyne construct, a remote that remembered once being Cassandra Lannigan.

But, as quickly as the doubt rose, she pushed it away. From the neck up, humans are built from two components, the memory and the personality. She had Lannigan's personality, even if this was just a construct. She had most of Lannigan's memories. If there was a difference between her and her predecessor, she would pay it no mind. Right now she had far bigger fish to fry.

In a few hours she would go to a local computer warehouse and pick up a portable AI core. The core had already been set aside for her, ever since the warehouse sales computers had become mysteriously convinced that she had ordered and paid for it some three days earlier. Once Lannigan had the core – complete with all Kitsumi's functions and data, downloaded at the same time as her own – she would be able to access the bank account she had set up from the Artemis net. The account that held an unassuming but still quite presentable percentage of Übergen AG's profits from the previous financial year.

Even a class-three AI, Lannigan mused, can accomplish some amazing things when fused directly to a human brain.

Before that, of course, she would stand up, a little unsteadily on legs that were still too long for her, and cross the transit lounge to greet Swann and Rayanne. No doubt the girl's immediate reaction upon seeing Kobayashi again would be one of horror, but Lannigan knew how to get around that. The cold, analytical, manipulating place in her head, Mnemosyne's legacy, was already telling her how to convince the pair of her identity.

What you see, Rayanne. It's not always what you get.

She would have to suppress that tendency in future. Like any tool, people can only be used so often before they get blunt. But if she was wise, and exercised a little self-control – a very human thing, after all – she could make good use of the computer in her soul. There is nothing that conducts business quite like an artificial intelligence.

And, right now, Lannigan had business to conduct with Rayanne Gatita and Edward Swann. She stood up.

Time for work.